THANK GOD IT'S FRIDAY

# THANK GOD IT'S FRIDAY

by
Robert Gardner

Metropolitan Press

2536 S.E. Eleventh • Portland, Oregon 97202

# DEDICATION

"Them who can, do; those who can't, teach."

*Old Western Proverb*

For Charlie, Jerry, and Stanley who kept the faith; and particularly for Elizabeth who made it all possible.

# CHAPTER ONE

Monday morning comes to Timbertop, Washington as it does to most parts of our industrialized Western World—an ugly abortion torn from the weekend vacation's cozy womb. To a blessed few (an endangered species) the same morning births the love child that promises another unfolding week of adventures. One of these fortunate few, Arthur Theodore Cromwell (Timbertop School District's Head Custodian—sixteen years of tenure) continues such a romance with his "position." Truly an enigma in this age of computerized hang-overs, A.T., like any person in love, lacks words to explain the why of it.

"Gosh," he'd say, with his half-hushed whiskey tenor, "it just feels good to be here."

Then he gives you the smile—a constant thin lipped smile that gives his round face salt and pepper crew cut head the look of a nut brown jack-o-lantern—and you feel good, too, just to pass the time of day with old Crommie (Crummy, if you're one of those smart-ass kids who needs something off key to be noticed).

So, despite the light snow and slightly sub-freezing of this late in January Monday morning, A.T. happily stomped those eight long blocks that lay between his modest home and Timbertop High School, arriving there, as he usually did, at five a.m. (one hour before his designated time—an act that infuriated the union representative who, after being told to "fuck off" by A.T., both privately and publicly, now assuaged his impotence by back biting, fruitlessly, a man defended by everyone.)

1

A short, stocky man with his salt gradually pushing out the pepper in his GI haircut, A.T. looked ten years younger than his fifty-five years (a condition generally accorded people happy with their way of life.) Timbertop's old timers, though, remember A.T. as "that wild Cromwell kid" who went off to World War II's Marine Corps with an unsigned high school diploma, two fists feared in every tavern in the county, and the joyful blessings of our sheriff and his deputies who had too many times endangered cars and life trying to trap A.T.'s '36 souped up Ford on the county's back roads. Oh, they called him half-cougar and half whirlicane in those days, but he came back home a month or two after V-J Day talking quiet, not hunting fights and driving the old '36 like it was paper mache'. He looked skinny, then, kinda jaundiced in the face and bony underneath his corporal stripes. In thirty days he went off again, back to the Corps, later to Korea, then to other places we only heard rumors about.

His folks moved on to some other place, and we kinda forgot the Cromwells 'cept once in awhile some other whirlicane kid would come out of the high school and down at the Pastime we'd talk about how much that kid was like "that wild Cromwell kid." Then all of the sudden it turned '61 and A.T. came back to town, bought a house, and worked at the mill a few months for he hired on with the school district. This time he came home with a GED diploma, an honorable discharge, a regular monthly pension, some khaki shirts with sergeant strips, a soft, round faced sweet little wife, Barbara, and two boys then aged twelve and fourteen who both turned into damn fine Timbertop jocks. For a month or so the old Pastime crowd waited for A.T. to put in an appearance, but though he gave us a big smile and a quick friendly handshake at the supermarket or down on the bank corner, he never came to the tavern and gradually he left the gossip.

Today, people around Timbertop who know only A.T., Our Custodian, are quick to tell newcomers:

"Our A.T. never met a stranger nor made himself an enemy."

Us old-timers shake our heads at that one, and we got our own point of view among ourselves (no sense arguing with strangers who've only been around ten or fifteen years.)

"They's got to be some of that whirlicane still twistin' inside that Cromwell boy," one of us generally remarks. "Just gonna take the right heat to set her rolling."

Nothing seemed to bother A.T. this morning, though, and after eating his usual breakfast of wheaties and fruit he softly kissed his round faced wife goodbye so as not to waken her, got his last-night-prepared lunch box from the frig, poured a thermos full of well sugared coffee, and, bundled up in a great grey wool parka, he followed his quick bursts of frosty exhalations through the morning's semi-darkness to the high school's furnace room.

Now, A.T. could never put it into words for you—he is long on listening and cryptic on talking—but each time he let himself into the high school's high ceilinged dimly lit hollowness he experienced that kind of transcendence that many feel on entering a big cathedral. No nostalgic memory thing for him—the Timbertop H.S. he struggled through in his youth we demolished for this present one over twenty years ago. No, his feeling came from some inner source he found unexplainable, even to himself; it seemed he loved the silence, the safety, and the oneness he felt with this tall brick structure. Especially he relished these two hours before the troops charged in and changed each silent room into a human zoo cage.

In his careful, meticulous, manner (as he did everything), A.T. draped his parka from a coat hook lag bolted to the furnace room's concrete wall. Above the hook a copper plaque (presented at a special assembly from the "Class of '72") designated this spot for "A.T. Cromwell—Head Custodian" (on each end of the plaque a Marine Corps Eagle perched on top of its world). Other trophies from ball teams, shop classes, home ec classes, A.S.B. Officers, other graduating classes, and even a thankful faculty found places on a white sheet of peg board fastened to one wall or in an old wooden book case that came to the furnace room as a reject from the library. But it was the Head Custodian plaque that A.T. saw first every morning, and it gave him a warm shot of joy—the pride-emotion he knew each time his grandchildren came to visit. This morning, as always, he gave the bronzed treasure his ritual wink of greeting, then he moved off to check a maze of

3

gauges, dials, and valves that assured him all rooms around and above him got their proper share of heat.

In the district's two elementary school buildings the weekend's heating situation got left to chance, but A.T. dropped by here, casually, on Saturday afternoons and Sunday evenings—his building never suffered the crisis of a cold Monday morning for teachers and students. Ensconced, at last, at his old chipped and scarred discarded wooden teacher's desk that owned one corner of the furnace room, he savored his first cup of coffee for the day. At this time, brown eyes half hooded like a drowsy cat, he projected his work day and drifted in and out of the past and present.

Before classes started today he needed to replace a couple of shower heads in the girl's locker room. As usual, he noted to himself, several ground floor windows got broken over the weekend. Well, a couple of sophomore boys may or may not have been responsible (he spotted them loitering around the school Sunday afternoon), but regardless they'd get an opportunity to freeze their little asses helping him clean up and repair the panes. Mr. L. could arrange their release from class. No use to bother Mr. W. (the principal) with a little deal like that. He'd better salt all the walkways before the school buses came in—he'd get plenty of volunteer help on that one, once he started. Funny how kids loved to work if it wasn't something they had to do. His own two boys had been conned that way. Now, grown, their favorite reminiscence eulogized times that A.T. had Tom Sawyered them into work.

Good boys, he thought, now. Got a lot of their mother in them. Thank God they didn't turn wild ass like me. They don't even know I never got no diploma when I graduated here back in '40. By God if it hadn't been for the Corps Christ knows what I might have ended up. End of a rope, probably, or bottom of the Ennis Creek Canyon. Well, them years is gone except for a little sweat remembering now and then. Still and all, I wouldn't trade them 'cause they sure make my living now just that much better.

He glanced up at the ancient Bendix system clock face in its unglassed wooden frame—almost a quarter to six.

4

"Piss on that rubber-assed union bastard," said A.T., to the thermos jug now getting back its plastic cup top. "He ain't gonna be alive at this time of a morning, it cold and all, so I'll just do my own thing and let her go at that."

Despite his ire at the union reps pickiness, A.T. paid his dues regularly and never missed a meeting. It wasn't the union, *per se*, he opposed. He felt the union should only tell him what he could do—not what he couldn't do.

Hitching his bibbers up on broad, muscular shoulders, he let himself through the inside door into a long, poorly lit hall that extended left and right to the building's full length. Each morning A.T. first inspected all the rooms, a small notebook and stub pencil in his hands. Any omissions or sloppiness by the six night sweepers he carefully noted and placed on that person's time card. A gentle reminder that Head Custodian, A.T. Cromwell, expected things to be done right.

Several miles from the high school, in a three year old split level ranch style house that boasted 2,800 square feet of floor space where it sat on its quarter acre plot, Mr. W. (Wellington) High School Principal responded to his electronically buzzing alarm clock with guttural curses as he fumbled for its always elusive off-alarm switch. His threshing about awoke his wife (as, subconsciously he knew it would), and she punched two sharp nail tipped fingers into the fat roll just above his hip line.

"Shut that damn thing off!" she hissed at him.

"Whyn't we get rid of the bastard and get a sensible alarm clock?" he grumbled, helplessly switching one knob then another.

"For Christ's sake unplug the damn thing if you have to!" snarled his wife. "A radio alarm was your idea, remember? Wake to soft music, you said!"

"Good God, Emily! Do you have to start the day nagging just because you ended yesterday that way?" he snarled back at her. "There, that did it! Now, how do I get the music back?"

"Forget it. You've got a faculty meeting this morning, remember? Put the coffee on and wake me when it's done. I don't know why you go on with this silly damn job, anyway."

5

"Look, Emily, we settled that bit last night, remember?" growled Mr. W. (also known more intimately as Roger). "I'm not going in with Bud, and that's final."

"Okay! Okay! Let's go on being second rate citizens so you can present to the world the gentility of your position as a school administrator," she said, caustically. "Don't say shit in public if you've got a mouthful—don't travel with people just because you like them—and, above all, don't stand up for what you believe in if it happens to conflict with a school director. Right, old Rog! The hell with money—who needs it—after all you got respect in the community—God and the High School Principal."

"No more!" he threatened, from his swaying position at bedside.

A false snore answered his outburst, and he stumbled, in the near blackness, along the bed rail until his searching hands found the robe on their door. With a super effort he managed to struggle into its form before he slipped out the door into murky light that filled a long hall to their kitchen. Shuffling along shag carpet in his bare, starting to chill, feet, he made the cold inlaid linoleum of the kitchen where his toes turned up like Oriental slippers. After a major engagement with a three pound can of Folgers and the coffee pot, he lurched back down the hallway to his bathroom sanctuary. Here, painfully, he studied the ravaged reflection of Roger Wellington in the dark, crystalline depth of the room wide mirror.

Our High School Principal came to us at Timbertop as a football coach the same year A.T. Cromwell joined the district as a custodian. He looked a lot different then, Roger did, two hundred and ten pounds of muscle fresh from three football letter years as a center for West Pacific College and four successful years as football coach and P.E. teacher for the Rapid City Wildcats (smaller school district about eighty miles from here). 'Course most all of us that follow football around Timbertop remembered Rog from his high school play at Castleview (our bigger neighbor down the road). Rog played a helluva middle line backer in high school, and most of us thought Pinky Hamblin up at WPC made a hell of a mistake when he moved Rog Wellington into offense.

6

Well, who knows better how to coach a ball team than a guy who don't have to prove it.

Anyway, Mr. W. came here with a lot going for him, and he turned out some pretty good ball teams using gutty young kids like A.T. Cromwell's two boys. He got a lot of space for his boys in the *Castleview Daily News*, even the Portland *Oregonian*, and the football team took up better than half the Timbertop *Weekly Advocate's* front page from the middle of August until the middle of November. Lots of pictures then, too, of Coach Wellington and his kids. Ain't been another coach, ever, at Timbertop able to get that kind of newspace for our teams, and a lot of us guys at the Pastime wish the district could find another promoter like Rog.

Well, Roger, Mr. W., Mr. Wellington, he's almost bald as a basketball, now, but he had a fine head of yellow curls when he came here from Rapid City, and the girls in school and the young faculty wives made them female moves at him like they do most young coaches. He didn't finish that first year out, though, before he got married to Emily Boogard (she taught third grade), and she made just about the prettiest bride picture (and the biggest) I ever saw in the *Castleview Daily News*. Some of us got to worrying, then, that Coach might try to get a berth over at Castleview (his folks are old there and his brother is big), but he came back that fall and gave us a winning team.

If you've only known Mr. W. since he got to be principal, you wouldn't recognize the guy he was when he first came here. He smiled a lot, then, "one of the guys" in the faculty room, at the bowling alley, and once in awhile, even, at the Pastime Saloon. His laugh kinda washed over you like a sonic boom, and his talk carried a big load of excitement, especially when he talked about sports. Now, you know, he lays it on you with that hard, kinda flat feel nothing voice, and, though I hear he still booms a laugh now and then at a private party or a principal's meeting, no one around the high school or the Pastime remembers hearing it since he got the vice-principalship back in '65.

That same year he picked up the title of Athletic Director (a new title here in our district), and the first of several new football coaches got hired in under his needle. Old Rog, Coach, rarely

7

made the faculty lounge, quit showing up at the bowling alley, and never came back to the Pastime, that I know about. Maybe it took a year, maybe a part of a second, but pretty soon he became Mr. W.—like a new person instead of a remake of the old.

Things started changing then, too, between him and Mrs. W., Emily. They argued a lot on things they once agreed upon—mostly doing with the school business—and Emily quit teaching elementary at the end of that year to take a job as office girl in a Castleview Real Estate office owned by Roger's brother, Fred Jr. (called Bud). Seems like Bud parlayed a small piece of his folk's Lakeside Resort property into the start of a small fortune while Roger was up at Western shoving a football back between his thighs. As the years passed things got less cozy between Roger and Bud, and it gave Mr. W. a new set of stomach cramps when Emily went to work for his younger brother.

As a school administrator Mr. W. felt pressure from a dozen or more directions everyday, but the pressure from his brother's offers to make money caused him more ulcer potential than superintendents, school directors, students, faculty, or disgruntled parents put together. In '71 he got the high school principalship, but that promotion turned to ashes in his mouth instead of ambrosia when his brother put together a million dollar deal—took his family on a round the world cruise—gave their parents a new Mark IV for Christmas, and gave Emily a five thousand dollar Christmas bonus while Mr. W. struggled to pick her out a forty dollar bathrobe.

Last year the school directors passed him over for the vacated superintendent's position (a split decision he lost three to two), and this year, Bud, himself, started pressing his older brother into joining him in another deal that offered a near million potential. It was that offer he and Emily had argued the night before through a full fifth of scotch. Now, Monday morning, the worst of all days of the week, he faced the worst of all mornings of the month—a faculty meeting.

Gradually his blurred, burning eyes focused the ravaged specter in the mirror into a thing of doubtful substance. With a groan he realized that no amount of Visine could cleanse the network of bloodlines from his eyeballs by seven thirty faculty time. Once again his damn teachers would share a buzz about the dark glasses needed to hide his drinking indiscretions. A dull throb at the base of his skull made shaving an impossibility of the moment. In desperation he finally shed his robe and sidled into the always dripping shower stall. As he got past the first jolt of cold water and into the soothing charge of warm water pellets, he heard Emily pad into their bathroom and clang down the toilet bowl ringseat.

"Don't slip and break your ass," she called through milk colored plastic panels that separated them.

No sarcastic retort popped immediately into mind, so he used the klout of silence as a rebuff. His inflamed eyes stared downward as the hot water caressed his nape. Beneath his chin he studied his flabbing breasts, his sagging paunch, and some gray hairs starting to show in his crotch. God! Not yet forty and falling apart. The toilet flushed and he heard Emily pad out of the bathroom. Reluctantly he turned off the water and slid one milk colored panel open for his exit. A brisk towel rub helped his headache, but the eyes still looked like a couple of fish eggs.

"Teachin' I'd call in sick," he snarled at his image. "I must a been insane to take on administration. Ahhh, shit. Another fucking faculty meeting."

Dressed, at last, he choked his way through toast and coffee. The kitchen clock showed a few minutes until seven. Lucky God damn kids of mine, he thought, they can sleep another half hour.

"Better wear mukluks this morning," said Emily, sweeping into the kitchen in her forty dollar Christmas robe. "What time you want dinner? I'll write out instructions for Betty."

"Five—five thirty—I've got P.T.A. tonight," he mumbled. "How come Betty's got to make dinner? Where'n hell you plan to be?"

"Bud's getting some investors together tonight and he wants me to keep notes," she explained, as she had once explained things to her third graders. "I see no reason for me to drive thirty miles home on slick highway then turn around and drive thirty miles back again."

"Who'll be here with the kids?" he asked, aimlessly.

"Roger. Betty is fourteen years old! Bobby is twelve. They're not babies anymore. You didn't want to hire a housekeeper. Too much money, remember?"

"Okay. Yeah, okay," he mumbled rapidly, helplessly. "Well, I'd better get going."

"Your mukluks?"

"Yeah. Oh, yeah," he said, vaguely, seeing her there in front of him still small, still trim, not showing the spinoff of sixteen years like he did.

"What do I tell Bud about his offer?" her voice made icecycles form in the room, and its coldness touched a raw nerve in him.

"Tell him to go fuck himself," snarled Roger, animated, again, for the first time since their initial alarm clock scene.

"Look asshole," cold steel in her voice, now, "I'm putting my money into this project. You play your silly game, if you must, but I'm going to start looking out for me, number one."

Struggling into his overcoat from the back kitchen closet, he slammed through a door into their two car garage. His own car, a three year old Pinto, puffed black smoke as it overchoked in starting. Her car, a new issue Cougar, seemed to leer at him as he punched the button for the automatic garage door and backed through its lifted opening out through a crunch of snow onto the cul-de-sac. Not until his feet got wet as he left his car in the faculty lot where A.T. had salted the icy crust did he realize that he had left home without putting on his mukluks.

As Mr. W. unlocked his office door (precisely at seven a.m.), George Anderson, our basketball coach, finished his routine fifty pushups in a small alotted place on his small frontroom rug. All six foot seven of his lean, muscular body made an impressive sight as muscles flexed and straightened, and his adoring wife, Madge, experienced sensual shivers up and down her back as his tight, narrow asscheeks made its plunges down toward the floor.

"Breakfast ready, baby," she called from the doorway. "Better hump a bit. Don't wanna be late."

"Yeah!" he grunted, springing upright like a big black cat. "Got one checkmark in old W's little green book, already."

George provided quite a novelty for us when he joined our staff at Timbertop three years ago. The first black, ever, to teach in our classrooms, and the second black family ever to live in our town. Oh, his hiring caused some mean talk and angry growls, at first; old Miles Pettigrew knew he was damn lucky to have his two year's superintendent contract before he hired Anderson, but the gripes slowly faded away when George played a hell of a winning forward on our town team and his high school team started winning ballgames that got us as far as the district tournament. Last year most everybody said how great it was when George came back again—we finished second in the district (a new high for our Axemen basketeers). This year the boys really moved out right from the beginning. So far we got only one loss and that to Castleview (a triple A team); we're double A so it don't count in our league standings. Now most everybody tells how lucky we were to get George from his coaching job at Pigeon Rock (a small B school) where he had a great record, and we all know about the great showing he made for three years at West Pacific (Mr. W.'s old alma mater).

Some of the hoity-toity folk still grumble that George runs a sloppy P.E. program (especially Board Member Ray Cosgrove and Girl's PE teacher, Marsha Kemper), but I guess as long as our boys keep winning ball games nobodies gonna make big enough waves to wash George out of his spot. Besides, the kids dig Big George, especially the jocks and the girls who try to put the make on him. Those girls really bother Coach, at times, but he better learn that's the way it is with coaches.

Girls don't bother Madge none; she knows her George never thinks much about sex. What does bother her is the scraping along on seven fifty clear each month George manages to bring home after income tax, social security, teacher's retirement, and medical insurance deductions. She doesn't push him, or needle him, often (she knows how much her George loves basketball), but she does remind him (after painful battles with their budget) that should George decide to go into his old man's plumbing business his income would pretty much double.

11

"Think I'll bundle the girls up warmlike and let them play out in the snow today," she said, for conversation, as George moodily stirred his coffee after only toying with the two eggs in a plate in front of him.

"It'll be a help when they get old enough for school," said George. "Never knew how much we'd miss that paycheck you used to get."

"Could put them in nursery school," suggested Madge, safe with past experience in this area.

"Not by a damn site," George said, grumpily.

It touched a sore nerve when Madge talked about farming the kids out while she worked. His own mother went through a series of live-in high school girls while George and his sister were little; she complained about it (where George's old man couldn't hear), and the children never knew their mother much preferred manning a desk at the plumbing shop to cleaning a house and dirty hands and faces.

"Anyway, no summer school for you this year, at last," Madge said, cheerily, "you can get in three whole months working for your dad."

"Don't know about that—Eph wants to take in a summer football clinic," dogged George.

"Come on, honey," said Madge, keeping her voice sugared to hide the bitterness there, "you don't even like that assistant football job they saddled you with."

"It's an extra six hundred bucks," he said, absently.

"Hey, what is it with you this morning?" said Madge, moving in behind him and draping slim arms around his neck. "You got more than a faculty meeting on your mind—more than money, even, I think."

"Nothing, babe, nothing," he mumbled, catching one of her slim fingered hands in his giant paw then pulling it to his lips for a soft kiss. "Just this damn stomach of mine. Not only sour now, but it gets pains in it, too."

"It's just the tension from wanting to win the championship so bad," she lied glibly. "Part of the price of being a winning coach."

12

Madge knew much better than that. She knew the nights when he twisted and turned in some sleeping nightmare of his own making. Many times she heard him mutter in his sleep: "I'm black. My God, I'm black." She knew about the psychiatrist he saw several times before their marriage. George never told her, but a teammate from Western mentioned it to her casually (out of George's hearing) when he visited them at Pigeon Rock. She let on to him that she knew all along, but she never mentioned the incident to George. Something terrible knawed away at the inside of her wonderful big husband, and it seemed to get worse with each passing year. This, as much as the money, made her keep on pushing for the plumbing business back in George's hometown of Cicero, Washington.

George never realized, really, that his blackness made him any different from anyone else until he left Cicero for college just outside of Seattle. An honor student in high school, a super jock in basketball, and the most popular boy in his class, his few dates at home were with white girls and white boys (the Andersons were the only black family in town.) President of the student body in his senior year, class speaker at commencement, he had been best man for Charley Granger who married George's sister, Louisa, as he might have married any other young girl from the area around Cicero.

"God, I never thought about my being black," George confided to Superintendent Pettigrew, when he applied for the job at Timbertop. "I never realized it until I got to Western and the black students there started filling me full of it."

"I understand that," said Miles Pettigrew, with all the secure graciousness of his sixty-one years and retiring at the end of this two year contract. "I went to high school right up the road from here at Elk Valley. Several of my best friends in school turned out to be Indians. But they never realized it until a few years ago when Indians started getting organized and going after benefits."

"Let's be frank, Mr. Pettigrew," George said to him, "Is my being black going to be a problem if I get the job here?"

"Being different is always a problem, George," said Pettigrew, waxing philosophical "doesn't make any difference if its brains,

13

money, religion, color or what have you. If you're different from the mainstream, you're going to have problems. The real problem is, if you get the job can you handle being different?"

"You darn rights," George answered, sitting up very tall and straight. "You just give me the chance."

Well, he got the chance, all right, and he moved Madge (pregnant with Patti) and two year old Stephanie into the little two bedroom house where they still lived. He came prepared to be called "nigger" and to be isolated by at least some members of our town. Trouble is, nothing ever came up to confront him, and he started living on a time bomb that seemed to have an endless fuse. Once he even brought it out with Ephriam Suder (our varsity football coach who played guard on the townteam basketball squad.)

"What do people say about me behind my back?" he asked Eph, his voice course and brutal.

"Hell, I never heard anything except about how great it is to have you on our team," hedged Eph.

"I mean about my being black. My being a nigger," rasped George, his stomach burning with fire.

"I never heard nothing," mumbled Eph, almost apologetically.

George dropped it after that, but his imagination never stopped working overtime. Oh, he'd been called nigger even back in Cicero, but the term meant nothing but buddiness and sharing. Like Billy McGuire got called a "Mick" and Andy Salone got called "'Wop" and Bennie Swartz was known as "Kraut" and Tito Guizare was known as "Mex". That happened mostly in back alley play, and it petered out around the eighth grade. When they got into high school it came out only when you did something special for the guy or for the old school, then it came out as a word of endearment between guys who couldn't stand being mushy.

At Western Pacific, though, he got the full treatment from the "brothers" who sought him out in the dorm to give him the "real skinny" on life. At first their talk and efforts seemed a confused source of amusement; in the months that followed the indoctrination made inroads as he found his social life more and more isolated to the school's black community. At Christmas time he got only two short days home because his ball team played on the road, but during Spring vacation he brought the problem home to his father, and the traumatic shock of that encounter still roiled like an ugly ghost inside him.

"Hell, yes, you're black," his father said, not unkindly, at first. "You been looking in a mirror for eighteen years, what color do you think you are? But don't be bringing that "white devil" shit home to me. I won't say I'm not prejudiced, because I am. I hate dirty people, lazy people, lying people, cheating people, and I'm sorry for ignorant people. I've got some damn good friends in this town that share the same prejudices that I do. You're a man almost grown now, Georgie. In time you'll settle someplace, like I settled here in Cicero. When you do open yourself up to the people you like and enjoy being with. Let the rest of them go by and around you as you would a bunch of cars out on the freeway. You've been raised a Methodist, George, but if you want to be a Muslim, go ahead. Just don't ever bring any of that hate talk into my house is all. Understood?"

"But dad," George felt polemically prepared to give his father (who never went to college) a lesson in racial agony, "look what the white men did to our race."

"George," said his father, his face hardening to black stone, "not one white man in Cicero ever owned a slave or did the Anderson's dirt because we are black. While you read your hate literature at school, read Alex Haley's *Autobiography of Malcolm X*. That's it, now, George, and no word of this to your mother and damn well no word of it to your sister and brother-in-law."

So George Anderson went back to Western Pacific College where he starred in basketball, did well in studies, and lived pretty much to himself neither black or white. Through the four years that followed he fraternized with few people other than his teammates and coaches. He went to Pigeon Rock after graduation where he coached basketball, taught P.E. and Washington State History, lived a bit aloof from the high school faculty, and married the only black girl in town, Madge Williams, who worked at the local post office.

15

"George?" Madge's voice took on that note she used to catch the children's attention.

"Yeah!" he mumbled, coming out of his reverie.

"I said it's twenty minutes after seven, you better hurry," insisted Madge.

"Oh, yeah!" he said, towering up from the table until her head could slip beneath his armpit.

"Here," she said. "Your lunch, don't forget it. I fixed you tuna sandwiches with chopped pickles. There's an apple, too. Good for your stomach."

She helped him into his frayed tweed overcoat then watched him take bounding strides out to the street. She crossed her fingers while he cranked the starter on his ten year old Ford three-quarter ton pickup. She smiled and waved back as his big dark fist raised in a victory signal when great white clouds of exhaust blew back out from beneath the vehicles blue, much dented, bed.

While George Anderson revved over eight balky cylinders in front of him, David Huntington, III, sat at his Porsche's steering wheel and listened with a well tuned ear to that car's super-power plant tick over faultlessly. Eight floors above the big cement garage where they sat, his own spacious two bedroom condominium pad lay with accumulated clutter of a long, plush weekend party. Evelyn Miller, his most of the time chick from Castleview, still lingered in a deep bubble bath. Her teaching day at Castleview High required her presence at eight-thirty, or so, and she even considered calling in sick this morning as she had four unused days of sick leave. As she carefully finished a roach and let its clip drop to the tiled bathroom floor she giggled involuntarily, remembering with relish the ploys she tried this morning to keep Davey's slim smooth body in the satin sheets with her.

"You're an ass," she laughed at him, as he gently pushed her out of the bedroom. "What'n hell do you care about a stupid old faculty meeting."

David gave her sleek, shapely bare ass one final pat and shove, then he locked the bedroom door behind her. Moving to a grey swing rocker by his bedroom's huge white-silk window drapery,

16

he set the timer built into one chairarm's side, and he settled back for his morning twenty minutes of meditation. Evelyn, he knew, would smoke her usual joint to start her day. Well, she faced the world in her way, and he faced his world in his way.

It gave our folks a big puff up in ego when Davey came here three years ago. Hell, the Huntington's must be about the biggest in our whole damn county. Davey's Uncle Isaac goes to Olympia as our State Senator—he's been doing that for as long as I can remember. Old David Huntington the First died almost ten years ago, but old timers around here still speak of him as "The Judge." Davey's old man owns a good part of the county, and I reckon a lot of other things folks around here know nothing about. Davey got a pile of money from his grandma who died two years after "The Judge." Down at The Pastime we get to wondering sometime what a good looking kid like him with all that money finds in teaching kids and hanging around here, but we figure Davey's got his reasons 'cause he always was a kid who picked his own way.

At an early age David slowly discovered he turned on to books and got bored by the school structure. He found, by age twelve, that of all his relatives and school acquaintances only his grandfather provided conversation that held his interest for more than ten minutes at a time. Sports bored him, though he swam and played tennis. People interested him only as bacteria interest a biologist. At age thirteen he discovered pot, sex with girls, LSD, cocaine and heroin (in that sequential order), and by his fourteenth birthday he ruled out LSD and heroin (he felt he could not control them), and he branched beyond his grandfather's library of classics, modern classics, and Book of The Month selections into a world of existentialism where he vasilated between Buber and Sartre until he finally discovered Henry Miller. From that point to this, with short diversions to Vonnegut, Castaneda, Alan Watts, and finally the Marharisha, Miller remained his guru.

Detached from the drabness of classroom existence; quietly avoiding the school's social life, David put his four years in at Castleview High School, graduated with a three point GPA, scored high in his College Aptitude Test, and went off to college at The University of Hawaii. Where he had eagerly anticipated intelligensia, he found, for the most part, a continuation of the mediocrity he experienced at Castleview. By his second term he had discovered several other people bored, like himself, and, seeking, they turned to Zen and its implications—David took his sophomore year at The University of Tokyo.

In a matter of weeks he moved in with a White-Russian girl who played around the fringes of the Japanese Young Communist Party. Marx and Engels turned him off as did the whole dialetic idea and the idea of subordination to anyone, let alone The State. She did, however, get him excited about Russian history, particularly its early relationship to The Greek Orthodox Church. Before the year ended he split with his much too political mistress, and he finished his next two years of study at The University of Athens.

Two conjectures that formed early in his studies now captured his thinking as viable hypothesis. First that civilizations came into existence, grew into power, and fell into oblivion on the strength of character manifested by their leaders. Secondly that leadership characteristics evolved concurrently with the educational process employed by each civilization. A little bit of knowledge is a dangerous thing became a byword with him. He studied early power groups—the Sumerian Priest-nobles, the Egyptian Scholar-priests, the Hebrew Soldier-priests, the Greek Soldier-Statesmen, the Roman God-heads, the Russian God-heads, the early European God-heads, and finally the Western Money-gods. Communism, Hinduism, and Confucism he credited to basic human mental slothfulness and the conditioning of physical fear, and Islam he found an enigma which he relagated to some later period of study. Resolved to explore his second hypothesis, he returned to Washington and enrolled in a Master's Program at The University of Washington.

Classes and teachers proved a drag and a bore, but he put himself through the routine of History Major and Education Minor to satisfy the law that provided him with a teaching certificate. Two minor problems faced him at this juncture in his life: the professors needled by him in classroom confrontations gave him blase recommendations for his employment file (political

18

clout in his own county helped him win out for a job at Timbertop over twenty three other applicants), and the professor assigned as his Ph D advisor disapproved of the thesis he planned to write and the in-the-field manner he planned to find evidence for his work. (This second problem he overcame with a substantial cash present to his advisor.) Then, he completed the circle that took David Huntington, III from his huge old family home near Castleview around the world and back to a condominium in Timbertop less than thirty miles from where he had been born. Had the boys at The Pastime known, and understood, all this, they'd have been as happy as a bed of clams at high tide with some real juicy speculation to talk about. Had Roy Cosgrove and some of his hard nosed buddies, known—or especially Mr. W. and his buddies known, they'd have been between a shit and a sweat trying to figure a way to steal Davey's notebooks he just kept filing away in his apartment.

Old Roy Cosgrove hates Davey near as much as he does George Anderson. Roy wasn't one of the board when they hired either of those boys, and we figure down at The Pastime he run for the office two years ago just to try and get rid of both teachers. Well, he should have known it's darn near impossible to get a teacher fired, no matter how important you think you are as a school director. Those few folks that go to board meetings say Davey really slips the needle into Roy every session. Been planning to go see it for myself, sometime, I never liked that mean eyed old bastard. Maybe I'll make it this Wednesday night, if I can talk a couple of the other guys into going, should be good for a laugh or two.

Guess Old Roy doesn't hate Davey much more than Mr. W. and the coaches do, though. Bill Metzger, that's Sarah Metzger's husband (she's Mr. W's secretary), let's us in on some of the donnybrooks that happen at the faculty meetings. Seems like young Davey gets into it near everytime with Mr. W. and all the coaches 'cept maybe George Anderson. Bill says Mr. W's almost praying for Davey to get his PhD finished so maybe he'll go off and teach at college or any other damn place.

Inside the Porsche gauges at last met with David's satisfaction. He eased his sportscar into gear and rolled it toward the automatic garage door. His slender six foot frame fit snugly into a bucket seat. He checked his soft golden page boy styled hair and close clipped golden spadeshaped beard in the rearview mirror (as he would again in the mirror hung in his classroom closet). He smiled as dashlights glinted off the huge golden pendant that hung on a thick gold chain around his neck. He could almost hear the coaches grinding their teeth when they saw this one. His London Fog trench coat draped unbuttoned around him so the pastel pink skintight silk shirt showed also in the mirror.

"Now, what can I do to start things boiling this morning?" he asked his image, aloud. "Guess I'll take a shot at old fat Lisa. Haven't poked a pin in her since Orientation last August."

Fat Lisa Overstreet was more than just fat, she rated monsterous plus. A fat young girl and a fatter young woman, each ensuing year of her frustrations added further blubber until she now carried well over three hundred pounds. Over this shapeless mountain of flesh she draped a one style loose tent-like smock which she made for herself in varying flowered patterns of cotton. By habit she started each Monday morning with a clean one and by Friday it carried stained evidence of her various eating bouts and the daily sweat produced by the sheer effort of moving from one place to another.

I had Lisa for English, myself, now nearly thirty years ago when she was barely twenty one years of age and fresh out of Bellingham Normal School. Even back then it was easy to tell she hated anything that boasted male sex hormones, and, though I managed to con her out of a D because I had an easy time memorizing poetry, I was lucky, for nearly seventy per cent of the boys who have faced her grammar drills and poesy assignments over the years came away with an F in classwork and an F in deportment. Girls do well with Miss Overstreet (though most of them make nasty jokes about her when she's not around), so with three other English teachers on the faculty, now, the counselor tries to see no more than a couple of boys get assigned each term to Lisa Overstreet's sections.

Besides the dirty cracks and constant devilment the kids concoct for her every year, one mean tradition goes on year to year, and that's the loud (from hidden sites) "Quack! Quack! Quack!" that makes her face turn beet red when she walks down the hall. I did it myself, she waddles just like an old duck, but I'm old enough to know how cruel it is, now; cruelty seems to be a natural part of being a kid.

Mr. W's tried hard both as VP and as Principal to get enough documentation together so the old girl could be fired (discipline problems in her classroom takes a lot of the VP's time every day), but he's had no better luck than the half dozen principals who tried it before him. Like I said about Cosgrove wanting to fire our boy Davey—takes a hell of a lot of doing to try to get a teacher fired in this day and age. Bill Metzger tells us things are the best ever though, this year, thanks to the counselor finally getting her way about mostly girls in the Overstreet English sections.

This faculty meeting morning Lisa arrived in her classroom at a little past seven a.m. She knew, as she had always known, the administration made a great effort to try and fire her, and she never gave Mr. W. a chance to check mark her for being late in his little green book. Those men, and all administrators were men, hated her for trying to bring poetry into young people's lives. Sloppy writers, themselves, they conspired against her efforts to mold good grammatical writing habits in her pupils. Well, in two years she could retire, then the whole business could go to hell as far as she was concerned.

A second reason, too, brought her early on this one day a month. By tradition, and a near necessity, faculty meetings took place in the library, and her one faculty friend, Librarian Nola Davenport, came early so the door could be open for everyone. The two always got together for fifteen or twenty minutes before the meeting. For years they had lunch together in Nola's little office, but the library lay on the second floor and for the past five years climbing stairs proved a horrendous task for poor Lisa.

Before she left her room she carefully inspected the desk tops, the floors, her bulletin boards, and the windows. Every once in awhile a new night sweeper got hired, and she held high standards for the neatness and cleanliness of her room that got met or received a written complaint if not met. This morning she found a trace of chalkdust in one of the trays and she grimaced as the grit rubbed against her exploring index finger.

"AT probably already made a note on that," she murmured aloud, to herself. "Well, I'll be kind about it if it doesn't get any worse."

Somehow she managed to find room for her giant fur trimmed wool coat in the clutter of a personal closet to which only she held a key. Already sweating beneath the thin grey curls that straggled over her ears, between the layers of hair stubbled fat that formed her armpits, and at the heavy hair covered apex where the giant white columns that formed her legs met, Lisa waddled slowly to the classroom door, puffed her way out into the hall, and carefully locked the door behind her. She slowly traversed the long dimly lit hall her muffled grunts backgrounded by slaps from her big loose sandles on the tiled floor. Just as she turned the corner and raised a foot, painfully, to the first step of the stairway, from behind her a raucous sound echoed through the building's stillness: "Quack! Quack! Quack!"

Another early faculty meeting arrival was Heidi Vandercamp, Timbertop's brand new Home Ec teacher. Tradition, set down through thirty years of last year's retiring home ec teacher, Ethel Crudder, passed on to her the task of seeing that coffee awaited the faculty members as they came sleepy-eyed through the library door. A.T., as was his custom, set up the giant fifty cup coffee urn filled with heating water, but home ec held the responsibility of measuring out a proper amount of coffee grounds.

A tiny girl, her platform shoes barely put her over five feet, she looked younger than even some of the Freshmen girls who filled three of her five daily classes. Though her parents got married in Rotterdam, Heidi came into the world in Olympia, Washington where her father owned and operated one of the classier jewelry stores in town. An only child, she spent most of her out of school time alone or with her mother. Oh, she never missed a 4-H meeting when she was in high school, but outside of organized groups and their occasional parties, she entered into intimacies with very few girls (and those transitory), and the boys in her classes seemed to look right by her. At high school commencement she stood (scholastically) in the middle of a graduating class of 284, but she rated all A's in home ec (with the help of her super haus-frau mother.)

Living in Olympia offered the advantages of a good Catholic college, and she entered the education and home ec program there still able to live at home with her parents. If possible she lived a more alone role than she experienced in high school—though she did form several semi-close friendships with other home ec majors —one who now taught junior high in nearby Castleview. Fortunately for Heidi's job seeking efforts, home ec teachers, unlike most teaching areas, were still very much in demand, for she made a very nervous presentation of herself to Mr. W. and our superintendent, and her grades at St. Cecelias proved the minimum for graduation requirements.

I, for one, thought it was a hell of a good idea to hire a pretty little chick like Heidi into the district (Old Lady Crudder, when she retired, hadn't changed a thing in her program for nearly fifteen years). Lisa Overstreet, however, and the gaggly hens in the women's club where she played big wheel, stirred up new innuendo stories every week about Heidi and the senior boys; Heidi and the coaches; Heidi and most of the young single bucks in town, when, for a fact, nobody ever saw her out anyplace either with or without a man. About the only one they failed to link her with was Davey Huntington, and I saw her looking at him in the post office one afternoon (I'm sure he didn't even know she was there), and I got a feeling right off that Davey was one she'd like to be linked with—not just by gossip, but by the real thing. Well, she's a real blonde little beauty with that perky nose and them big blue eyes, but she's a bit too old fashioned and a bit flat in the wrong places for the kind of girl our Davey usually goes with, but I like the lift of her chin and the warmth of her smile and I hope she at least gets a chance at the boy.

Heidi was, in fact, thinking about Davey Huntington as she listened to water bubble through the grounds in the coffee urn.

23

Her weekend had been spent with her classmate girl friend over in Castleview (one of the rare weekends she failed to go home to Olympia), and the girl friend bubbled out stories about the famous pot and cocaine parties Davey held in his Timbertop pad. Shocked, and disbelieving most of it, Heidi held her feelings to herself and listened through the stream of gossip with her ever present soft mouthed smile. The information divulged by her girl friend came second hand from a Castleview High School English teacher allegedly bedding young Huntington, but Heidi's friend confided that she, herself, might get an invitation to a weekend there, soon, with one of Davey's ex-high school friends who worked as a teller, now, in one of the Castleview banks.

A shrill horsey laugh from the direction of the librarian's office turned Heidi's head, involuntarily, so that she saw the gargantuan form of Lisa Overstreet hulked above the bony form of librarian, Nola. In a little over an hour we'll have this month's crap behind us, Heidi thought, returning her stare to the metal sheen of the big coffee urn. Inwardly she sighed for the ordeal ahead, then she moved on to a more pleasant thought, her free first period for planning time. It provided her with the absolute best hour of each working day (really only 56 minutes), for she enjoyed, tremendously, the two senior girls who shared that 56 minutes as her aides. She felt, in fact, closer to the girls than she had any other person except her mother. Together they made out shopping lists, discussed clothing styles, looked through magazines featuring house plans and furniture arrangements, and gossiped about other students at the high school. Her fifth period class, however, wracked her nerves and generally ended her day with a throbbing headache. Bachelor Living, the course showed that title, brought her eighteen hyper-active senior boys who, with each passing day, took bolder liberties toward her. First they began inviting her to keggers (in a light hearted sort of way); next it was pot parties (with less joking and an air of mysterious sincerity); last Friday two of the more sophisticated boys cornered her at the class period end and, in low guarded voices, suggested she join them during the weekend for a sex orgy. Had she let things go too far? None of her education courses prepared her for situations like this. None, in fact, offered guidelines or suggestions on any of the discipline problems she faced so far in her first year of teaching. Last night, sleepless for hours in her small apartments three-quarter bed, she resolved to take the matter up with the counselor sometime today. Pat Mooney made her uncomfortable to be around, but from her years of experience she certainly had answers for Heidi.

Girl's counselor, Patricia Mooney, came late to the meeting. Besides her, only two other members from Timbertop High Schools faculty of twenty seven failed to meet the seven thirty deadline. One, Audrey Settlemeir, called in sick, and the other, Jim Bettermen, auto shop and metals man, rarely came on time if he bothered to come at all.

Pat suffered leering glances from the others (particularly the coaches) as she slipped as surreptitiously as possible into a chair near the back of the room. Mr. W. paused in his reading of a report from last Friday afternoon's administrative meeting with the superintendent to make a red pencil mark in a small green ledger that lay by his right hand. Pat's hot eyes and flushed face looked away from the authority figure seated at room middle front, and she caught a sympathetic smile from little Heidi that she answered with a sickly smile of her own.

That fat pompous son-of-a-bitch, thought Pat, as her attention returned to Mr. W., he's been documenting me for three years. This Spring I've got to make a real try for a new job someplace else. One more year in this reform school and I'll be at the end of my tether.

Pat originally taught P.E. here—came here from an Oregon school (where she taught P.E.) eleven years ago. She got into the counseling bit after three years of physical education (rumor had it she made it with old George Rutherford, our principal before Mr. W. took over). When George left she started fighting with principals, teachers, coaches, and even parents. Privileged information, she calls what the girls come to tell her. Student background information, insist the people who want to know what those girls are telling Pat. Just before Christmas they had a donnybrook in Pat's office about the Purcell girl. Seems Pat knew

25

the girl got herself pregnant, and she tried to get the girl to tell her parents, but Pat wouldn't tell them, herself. Old lady Purcell (she weighs near two hundred pounds) damn near tore the school building down on top of Mr. W.'s bald head. Then they all descended on Pat—the Purcells, Mr. W., and Boy's Counselor Greg "Coach" Patterson. Now the Purcells got a lawyer putting together a case against the district, the directors, the superintendent, Mr. W., and Pat Mooney. Who needs to go to Castleview or Portland to find excitement—seems we always got some juicy beef going between folks and The Timbertop Consolidated High School.

Pat's thoughts hovered much on the Purcell matter though both the district's attorney and the education association attorney assured her the thing offered, at best, a shady effort at legal blackmail. Involuntarily she belched, an annoying habit of her tricky stomach. A light titter of laughter came from the Overstreet-Nolan position, and Pat blushed, furiously. Once again Heidi caught her eye and offered a sympathetic smile.

I wonder if she uses coke to get through her day like I do, thought Pat, desperately. God! It would be wonderful to find someone around here I could share things with.

Her habit's cost, another agony in her life, forced her to live almost penuriously, and she no longer went to Portland for the fun weekends she had once enjoyed with old friends there. Lately she had found herself thinking about her ex-husband and wondering if he might still be interested in reuniting their marriage, as he had for a number of years after their divorce. Up until the past five or six months when her drug costs limited her traveling money, she used to meet Harry from time to time for a weekend of fun and sex at some out of the way resort.

My God! Pat, she writhed inwardly, you're not yet forty and you feel like a hundred and forty. I've just got to find someone to talk to; maybe Heidi will do.

Out in the auto shop AT ambled in to remind an already greasy handed Jim Betterman, a long, loose jointed Oklahoma boy of thirty one years, about the faculty meeting up in the library. Jim pulled his thin pointed chin head with its wild shock of black curls from underneath the half raised hood of a '51 Old's 88. Expertly he spit tobacco juice into a can by the car's front wheel then he equaled AT's wide thin lipped smile with his own.

"Shucks, A.T.," he drawled, "let them birds pick shit where they want to. I got two boys been workin' here since seven, on their own. They might need me here—them gooney birds up in the library, hell, they'll never miss me."

# CHAPTER TWO

"Schoolin' " came to Timbertop with the first white man to set down roots in this long flat stretch of tree and prairie land bordering the Cowlitz River. From that day to this "school" produced our characters, our heroes, and our socio-economical failures; gave us gossip, entertainment, and taxational anger; provided our young mothers with baby-sitters, our un-married men of thirty with an annual crop of prospective young school teacher brides, and our older population with a conglomerate proof that young people were, indeed, traveling the high road to hell.

Of course Timbertop held other names before our 1874 city charter officially placed us on a government survey map with that name. Just prior to that date, and for about seven years, loggers and sawmill men came to work for companies headquartered at Big Timbertop Camp. During eighteen years, before the logging companies came in force, people stopping through knew the place as Paradise. For many hundreds of years before the name Paradise the Indian's called this spot Toutalana (Place of Slow Waters). No one bothered to document that name for the Indians who leisurely traversed The Cowlitz to The Columbia each year placed little value on the lineal significance of history.

The Caucasion, conversely, views his history as a step ladder from the birth of his culture to the possibilities that lie ahead. Thus Hudson's Bay Company, headquartered on The Columbia River at Fort Vancouver, duly noted in journals and ledgers the formation of a subsidiary company called Puget Sound Agricultural Company in the year 1839. Detailed plans for stock raising were outlined for a broad, marshy grassland called Nisqually which lay at the south end of Puget Sound. Four hundred acres of light loam prairie land, some eighty miles south and west of Nisqually, the company platted out for a community project in raising vegetables. (They named this project Cowlitz Farms.) For two years they advertised the project, but the kind of people who populated the vast Western wilderness area lacked the sheep instinct needed for communal living.

When, after two years, Puget Sound Agricultural Company failed to generate any settler interest, Hudson Bay officials arbitrarily moved some sixteen families from their Red River Settlement in Canada and resettled part of them at Nisqually with the balance on The Cowlitz Farm. Company records religiously report each family name and each individual person's name in each family, but they fail to list the name of a non-family man who accompanied the settlers to a spot south of Cowlitz Farm. That man, Ivor Mc Ivor, a thirty five year old Scot, failed to get his name listed simply because, as far as Hudson's Bay Company concerned itself, Ivor existed as a non-person.

Mc Ivor, a sometime journalist, teacher, barrister, scrivener, and clark in Edinborough, Scotland (where his fairly highly stationed minister father disowned his son expelled by the University in a wrangle over the school's right to discipline student members for social indignities) left his native country one step ahead of the King's Justice as a working passenger aboard a creaky old cargo ship bound for Halifax. An avid student of John Locke's Political teachings, he took upon himself the task of removing from their proper place of bulletin all proclamations proclaimed by the ruling governmental power each time one would appear. Observed and apprehended by a magistrates marshal when he pulled down a new curfew order, he downed the would-be arrestor with a heavy walking stick carried for protection in the slummy district where he lived, and from that point, age twenty five, Mc Ivor became one of those itinerant shadows that constantly "move along" when anyone starts to really make note of their presence.

We know little of his physical appearance, for the only record is his "journal" as he called it (diary, I call it, as it leaves more a record of his emotional impressions than an objective record of his adventures) fails to tell us if he was tall or short, fair or dark, lean or heavy, comely featured or coarse. We assume he carried a fair amount of strength (he laid out the marshal with his cane and tramped thousands of miles through forests and mountain terrains), and he enjoyed good health (he nowhere complains of illness or the natural rigors of his existence). We know that at Red

River he looked like " a Faustian scarecrow" in self made clothes of cast off rags and poor grade trapper's pelts.

At first in the "new country" Ivor drifted from village to village working as an itinerant farm hand or a minor clerk in some company's employ. Even the loose political structure of Eastern Canada, however, he found "full of threds of pitfalls and authoritee that either drown a man in their mush of regulations or tie him up like poor Gulliver." So he drifted westward as a tag-a-long with one or another fur crew, in company with a wandering Indian tribes who he found "more crippled with rights and wrongs than the voyeers," or alone in the wilderness which he found "a satisfaction to soul's comfort but hell on the bodie." "Somewhere," he reminded himself when he found his journal voicing self-pity, "God made a place where a man can be his own man."

Red River Settlement satisfied him, for the most part, through his thirty third and thirty fourth year. Living almost like a human coyote on its outskirts, he managed a certain substance by letter writing and reading for those illiterates that made up over half the adult population and by tutoring their children for foodstuffs and a place for sleep in a barn when inclement weather held the settlement in its grasp. Though officially a non-person, according to the Provisional Government, he managed, finally, to anger the local factor by his outspoken criticism of Hudson Bay Company rules. Plans were underway to put him in the local stockade when families selected by the Company for the Puget Sound Agriculture undertaking began their trip southward. Tipped off to his danger by one of the young people he tutored, Ivor faded into the forest then attached himself to the south-moving group.

By the end of one year the Cowlitz Farm disintegrated as each farming family preferred to work a place of its own instead of a community effort. Mc Ivor, of course, still existed as a non-person unable to establish claim to any part of the Hudson's Bay land held under a Joint British-American treaty. Unruffled by legal concepts, he found a place in the valley that pleased his senses and fulfilled his meager needs. Here he built a crude log hut "four long paces by four long paces with split cedar on the floor to keep out the damp," and his few, widely scattered neighbors came to him to have a letter written or read. In time they also brought themselves or their children (for a gift of food or some useful item) to learn the mysterious arts of reading, writing and cyphering. As the cabin boasted no windows much of the "schoolin' " went on at a table outside Ivor's rough hewed fir front door, but there were times when inclement weather forced the sometime school master to "work with young Caleb Huntington inside for the rain cascades outside like a waterfall. He learns cyphering rapidlee and will likely make a mark in the world. Cabin still smells like bearfat candles. Hope I can air it out tomorrow."

In '45 he received official orders from Factor James Douglas at Fort Vancouver to vacate his premises and report to the Fort's stockade. While Ivor continued to discourage Hudson Bay messengers from coming too close to his place (several settlers gave him old guns for tutoring their children), England and the United States signed their Boundary Agreement of 1846. This put British authority on the north side of Latitude 49; and Mc Ivor immediately declared himself an American citizen (so far as his journal tells us, nobody ever questioned his questionable claim).

On December 5, 1852, according to his own records, he attended the Territorial Meeting at Monticello. Though not an invited or elected delegate, he represented himself as the chief spokesman for Paradise (his name for the place we now call Timbertop), and the discussions barely got underway before he stamped to a place in front of the assemblage and berated the men for trying to bring in more government. Ejected from the meeting by several sturdy farmers, he hiked home where he entered doomed predictions for the proposed territory of Washington.

So the name Paradise slowly passed into oblivion, though it exists as a name in dusty records of early Cowlitz, Monticello, Cathlamet, and Vancouver. It exists, too, in a faded old ledger tucked away among other old original editions in Davey Huntington's family library. The judge always meant to show it to Davey, but he put it off until too late.

So far as we can tell, Mc Ivor's school ceased to exist during 1863. If he died, got put in jail, went off to fight to free the slaves, or just went searching for a place unrestricted by law no one knows. The last journal entry, on the last page of the journal, is dated April 24, 1863. It says: "Each day I hear axes ringing on the hillside—hear giant trees crash to the hard earthen floore. This land fills with little peeple who cling to laws that breed more laws because, frightened and helpless without them, they give up freedom for what they deem security. Oh, Lord, the time draws near when not only a black man will be a slave; all men will enslave themselves in their own laws, their Original Sin."

And so the book closed on Ivor Mc Ivor, but it stayed open for the "schoolin' " of young folk growing up around Paradise and the booming Timber camps. Mc Ivor's cabin provided a bedroom for a combination church and school, the structure added on to the original through the efforts of the local family men. Parson William Jack James and his jolly big wife, Nellie, taught the 3 r's to everyone from eight year old Mary Huntington to sixty-one year old Grampa Foxley. Then, in the flood of America's post-Civil War growth, lumber demands skyrocketed, particularly in the mushrooming cities of Portland, San Francisco, and Sacramento. Talk of railroads, steamboats on the river, and the possibility of gold in the Cowlitz River's upper reaches brought farm families and itinerant loggers flooding into Timbertop.

One of the first official acts of Timbertop's new city government (1874) dealt with the building of a "real school" for the town. Though Preacher James held his regular classes at the (now) Presbyterian Church, many non-Presbyterians argued for a separation of church and state. So a one room schoolhouse, about the same size as the church, went up in a spot about a mile away, and we met our first "real honest to God schoolmaster" complete with a hickory yardstick he used to pound knowledge into the young 'uns.

That same year Davey Huntington's grandaddy was born and the following year The Presbyterian Church came down (as did old Mc Ivor's cabin now a storeroom in the rear) to make room for The Huntington House, the finest big white three story home in the valley. In another five years a lot of folks got tired of boarding their kids out in Castleview for high school, and they formed a citizen's committee for our own high school. After a battle over the tax costs folks compromised, and a new grade school went up (four rooms) to take care of eight grades while the old elementary got turned into Timbertop High School.

By the century's turn a new eight room elementary replaced the one room high school and the four room elementary school got some additions (one a big new gym) and we were hot into football, basketball and baseball teams. Our Axemen sent athletic teams to Cathlamet, Toledo, Kelso, Chehalis, and even the booming railroad town of Kalama. Then, in the prosperity of twenty seven, a new brick school went up, this one two stories high with its own gym built right into the building's middle. Here all twelve grades met together and the school population darn near equalled the census population for the town. By the thirtys, with the depression really not all that bad around Timbertop, the six year old school building already used a couple of local churches to relieve crowded classrooms, so we accepted a WPA project that built us another elementary school, a two story brick structure still used as North Elementary School today.

It was that old 1927 brick building that A.T. left in 1940 and from which I graduated in 1945. It's gone, now—South Elementary sits there low and modern like some fancy office complex or medical clinic. Our new high school got born in one of the damndest political fights that ever rocked this town. The first big explosion came over the amount of tax money asked for, and finally voted for, the land purchase and construction costs; the second battle raged when folks finally found out it wasn't, strictly speaking, "our school," anymore. Seems like two other little elementary districts lying next to us went in on the making of the thing, so "our" school became, officially, "Timbertop Consolidated High School."

Timbertop CHS sits on sixty acres of good, farmable bottom land just a short way from where the famous "Huntington House" once stood. Once those acres formed part of Huntington's original 640, and it extended on beyond the rows of spec houses built over the past thirty years by Davey Huntington's dad. Its purchase price, $300,000.00 left half the taxpayers in the valley screaming with rage, and it sent then Superintendent, Jack Lemmon, scurrying to find himself another job, put two school directors on the community shit list from which their families have not yet recovered, and brought in ultra-conservative old Miles Pettigrew as the new superintendent of schools.

Pettigrew, a master of double talk and corner cutting, bullied and harassed our building contractors to cut corners until our high school structure today (a two story brick by public demand) though barely ten years old looks much shabbier than the old North Elementary WPA structure. Windows won't open, or close completely; three times the roof had to be patched against seepage that stained most of the second floor ceilings and walls, and Jake Purdy, who contracted the plumbing, says it's just a short matter of time before all kinds of problems develop in that area.

It's big enough, though, with its two stories of classrooms shaped into a great square U. A giant double floor gym, separate from the original structure but filling in the space between its wings, serves for PE classes, ball games, wrestling matches, badminton tournaments, our girl's volleyball team, band concerts, school plays, graduation and other large student assemblies. Its Tartan floor provides one thing on the right side for old Miles, it takes a hell of a beating and don't get wrecked like a regular wood gym floor. Out behind the gym, but connected to each other and the main building els by an open breezeway, stand the extra concrete block buildings built one each for art, shop, woodshop, metals and motor shop, home ec and band. Like the gym these were built in ensuing years since the original structure—this way old Pettigrew managed to semi-hide the totality of our two point three million dollar package from most casual interest tax payers. In the building's center front sits administrative offices, counseling offices, and the building's general office (our superintendent has his own office set up down in the center of town). Directly above the offices lies the school library—the place where our principal holds his faculty meetings.

Besides a principal, a vice principal, two counselors, two secretaries, one custodian, six night sweepers and twenty nine teachers, about five hundred and twenty students meet here one hundred and eighty days out of each year. With a gross monthly payroll of almost $40,000.00 TCHS exists as the single largest business unit in the community. Add the two elementary faculties, the superintendent's office, the bus drivers, cooks and other maintenance help, and you've got a $100,000.00 a month payroll that sits on our taxpayer's back like a giant jackdaw always screaming for more. You'd think with all that building investment, all that monthly payroll and maintenance expense people would flock to director's meetings every month to see how well things were being managed. Not true, though any group of two or more people usually finds some angry comment to make about the school financial burden. Those folks who do come to the meeting come on some petty gripe that's pretty much personal. Course the directors, themselves, make the meetings as tedious (by mumbling around a table and reading off long lists of things) and the superintendent deliberately carries a closed agenda right up to the end of the meeting (sometime after one in the morning), so you really can't blame people for staying home where they can watch television, have a drink, relax in an easy chair, and smoke a cigarette.

Well, an expensive big building and a high cost educational program from the 12 by 12 foot cabin where a kid learned to read, write and do his numbers for an old winter coat, a sack of salt, or an outdated frontier musket—that's progress, I guess. Seems as how everyone agrees we got to have good schools for the kids; trouble is, as I see it, no one seems to know what makes a good school. Somewhere, though, I got a feeling, the wraith of Ivor Mc Ivor drifts around unfettered by any man made restrictions as he looks down at the place he once called Paradise and feels glad he doesn't have to help support that Garden of Eden.

In July of the previous summer, Dr. Cecil Imberlay took titular command of Timbertop's educational battle from a relieved, retiring, Miles Pettigrew. Imberlay, a man with mostly elementary school experience, came here from a suburban district near Seattle where he spent five years as an elementary teacher, six years as an elementary principal, and four years as an assistant superintendent—a position in which he dealt, principally, with elementary curriculum and elementary personnel. The same age as Mr. W., no further similarities existed between the two. Besides being a short five foot seven at a slender one hundred and thirty five pounds, Dr. Imberlay loathed any sport more violent than croquet, and he found his pleasures in reading the latest books about education, writing for educational journals, and in escorting his rather plain little wife, Pricilla, to concerts, operas, first line plays, and art exhibits. Known as a patient and often warm jovial man in his prior position, his short six months tenure experience with Timbertop CHS started an ulcer that forced him to give up his much loved morning coffee.

At his screening interviews (back what seemed like to him the longest year of his life) he early grew aware that Mr. W. and the athletic clique of Timbertop felt scorn, perhaps even a bit of fear, for his academic and intellectual accomplishments. Championed, however, by Superintendent Selection Committee Chairman, PTA leader, Velma Overholt, and vocal committee member, school director, Edna Keefer, he emerged first as one of five chosen for the superintendency from thirty eight applicants; he survived a second cut which reduced the field to himself and Mr. W., then, finally, (and it was a poorly guarded secret) he emerged with a three to two majority at a closed director's meeting. Ray Cosgrove and Bill Murchim grimly opposed him (as they took every public and private opportunity to remind any and all critics who voiced complaints against the school district). Edna Keefer proved the strongest force on the school board, however, and she teamed with pro-Imberlay, Mick Randolph, a young bank teller, to pull nervous, quiet Board Chairman, Steve Dobson (of Dobson's Hardware), along with them.

Previous to Imberlay's first screening effort old Miles Pettigrew, through a number of innuendos, warned him against taking the job, and his own boss (and close friend), Dr. Willard Parkman, urged him to stay where he was until he found an opportunity to get a State Office job or a chief administrator's post in some larger district. Imberlay, fired by his own ideas he wanted to try, heared the warning like smoke but felt no fear of finding himself in a blaze. Timbertop's curricular structure, archaic and limping along, seemed to offer the perfect opportunity for the upbeat designs Imberlay visualized. Now, too late, he found that few people in Timbertop, besides the enthusiastically progressive Velma Overholt, Edna Keefer, and Mick Randolph, wanted schools to be any different than that of their own public school experience.

Pricilla, ever a patient listener, took the brunt of his agonizing in the privacy of their bedroom (they made a special effort to assure their two small children never heard any unpleasant talk about the school business), but the past two months crowded more of his agony on her than she felt fair to her own peace of mind (particularly she resented his snash when, the two of them, alone, left town for one of their entertainment sojourns in Portland or Seattle).

This past weekend proved particularly disastrous, for its Friday produced an administrative meeting that proved super frustrating for our superintendent. As much as possible he avoided mixing into high school affairs (where he felt inept, inexperienced, and in truth, a bit frightened), but with a local special levy election just a four short weeks ahead he voiced to the three principals who lounged in his office's overstuffed chairs those things which promised to undermine their levy promotional efforts. Of first concern was the Purcell lawsuit.

"There's a lot of scut, too," he said, "about the new home ec teacher. It's gossip, I know, but Roger please check into it. Chief Braden tells me lots of drugs started to show around the high school, again, and Mr. Cosgrove called, angrily, about Mr. Huntington teaching communism in his social studies class. Somehow a crazy rumor continues to grow that I'm, in some way, opposed to our athletic program—which you gentlemen know contains not one shred of truth."

He talked on in this vein though his principals seemed obviously bored. Although he disliked and feared Roger Wellington, his biggest agonization stemmed from his inability to enthuse either elementary principal toward the curricular design he proposed. He dropped the levy problem and brought out his curricular suggestions. Once again they met with hackneyed arguments and obvious procrastination. So Friday evening as their four door Ford LTD sped smoothly southward toward Portland three hours past the administrative meeting's close, Dr. Imberlay unloaded like vomit his total frustrations until Pricilla, for the first time, ever, shouted at him in a shrill voice that closed him off for the evening.

"For Christ's sake, Cece," she screamed, her voice edged with hysteria, "Will told you not to take this job! Quit, if you can't take it. Go back to elementary teaching if you have to, at least we were happy there."

The rest of the trip, through the concert, during their one drink after the final encore, and on the long trip home, they suffered together in a mutually cold silence. Now, fifty five hours of stomach burn later (plus a pounding ache at his cranial base) Imberlay awoke to his seven thirty alarm and, still a bit drugged by sleep but in full control of his speculative faculties, he resolved to spend the next sixty days secretly hunting another job.

A bulletin from that Friday's disastrous administrative meeting gave Mr. W. the opening item for this January high school faculty meeting. None of the specific incidents Dr. Imberlay found horrendous dangers to the levy effort appeared on Zerox copy sheets passed out to each teacher. The superintendent's memo dealt in general terms with the levy's importance to one and all, quoted figures needed for maintenance and operation the following year, reminded teachers how important public relations became at election time, and offered encouragement to those who might be attempting to better their existing programs without creating greater costs. Although, as mentioned, this Zerox copy plus a mimeographed copy of the meeting's agenda went to each teacher in the room, Mr. W. ponderously read it aloud, anyway. It reinforced his power figure as an "in" part of district administration, and he knew, from experience, that half the teachers in the room would fail to read it, otherwise.

"So, you see, we got some big problems ahead of us," intoned Mr. W. "We all got to get behind his campaign if we expect to get the raises we want and the supplies we need for next year. Every one of you in this room, and your wives and husbands, if you have one at home, better be registered and better get out and vote. We got ways of knowing who votes and who doesn't. Believe me, if this levy fails because a few of our people failed to vote, I'll post those slackers on the faculty bulletin board. In district personnel, alone, we've got close to two hundred votes. Many of you got good friends in town, too, be sure they get out to the polls and mark their ballots, yes."

On that dramatic high, he slid his chair back away from the table that fronted him. He carefully crossed his legs, a signal to Mr. L. (Longfellow) to take over the agenda items. When Mr. W. served as George Rutherford's V.P. he quickly learned the byplay that existed during faculty meetings. Rutherford, a somewhat paranoic man, ran the whole show, himself, so Mr. W. found himself relegated to the background role of an observer. Bored by his position outside both the power point and the faculty circle, he keenly studied each situation that arose, watched the little teacher buzz groups that tipped off who sided with whom, and saw Rutherford constantly embroiled in an argument over issues with one little buzz group or another. Not only did his principal gather teacher enmity that way, he also missed many little sideplays that occurred away from his area of confrontation. When Mr. W. took over on Mr. Rutherford's departure, he immediately made agenda proceedings a role played by Mr. L. Not only did he gain thankful admiration from that tall young man by providing him this chance to exercise his ego, he avoided arguments over issues so that teacher enmity fell on the Vice Principal instead of upon him.

As Mr. L. rose from his seat to take a standing position by the library's bulletin board, Mr. W. caught Miss Agnes Merriweather, Typing, with a small, secretive smile on her pale thin-lipped mouth. Old WCTU bitch, he raged to himself, just squirming to get where you can talk about the dark glasses covering my whiskey eyes, aren't you? Well, you old crow, just wait 'til I get back to the extra duty roster in my office. I'll give you something to wipe that silly smile off. God damn it, what a hell of a hangover.

In fact, had he only known, Agnes Merriweather harbored no thoughts this morning about Mr. W.'s drinking habits. As of the moment she was not yet aware that he wore dark glasses. Her smile, really an involuntary one (which relaxed her usually stern wrinkled lower face muscles), blossomed as she surreptitiously watched Coach Anderson, seated next to her, join together the Xs he had drawn with a simulated half basketball court on the lower half of his mimeographed agenda copy. Joined together by ball point pen line they made a crude fist from which a middle finger extended to one lone X at the diagram's upper center.

George heard only the first few words Mr. W. read. His mind automatically traveled forward to tomorrow night's ball game, and he wrestled with a problem that had taxed his coaching skills all season. His forward line, experienced, tall strong veterans matched any forward line in the state's Double A high schools, but his two guards were first year lettermen with neither the speed nor the savvy needed to mold his team into state championship calibre. Tomorrow night, Chehalis, their opponent, brought an aggressive jug zone defense to the Timbertop gym, and the catlike speed demon young man who operated as the jug's neck could raise some hell with George's inexperienced junior guards.

From the game he backslid to a college paper written by him for a Junior Sociology class. That paper, written for a brilliant young professor who also doubled as a State Legislator, brought George Anderson more unwanted publicity than he could have ever dreamed existed. Putting the paper together, he never imagined that anyone other than himself and the prof would see it. He surely never dreamed the theme would experience public viewing. In it he backgrounded his own experiences as a black boy in Cicero, then he elaborated what a high motivation he experienced for school because of his successful accomplishments as a jock. From there he went to problems faced by black boys crowded into Seattle where chances to be recognized, to play on varsity teams, to be motivated toward school came only to one in a thousand. And in the 999 others, many athletic, artistic and academic skills

40

never found a chance for fruition, though in the many smaller towns of Washington their skills would be thought superb.

In objective style, often using his own life experience as substantuating evidence, he pointed out the easy availability of jobs (particularly unskilled labor) for one or two family heads selected for each town in this project, and he documented the ease of integration experienced by his own family. Though the paper dealt with all scholastically related skills and areas of athletic prowess possessed by these stifled 999 others, George's penchant for basketball slipped through despite his efforts to show impartiality—now, though the effort aborted at the legislative level, Coach Anderson still seriously considered a minor recruitment program of his own based upon his paper's promise.

Yet, any reminiscing about the paper brought a flood of bad memories, for the "brothers" had roasted his "Uncle Tom effort to split the people," and his white teammates (and a few white students he had come to know) turned chill shoulders to him for his design to infiltrate the still all white communities. Such a mish-mash from a paper designed as a speculative effort to answer a classroom assignment. A faint buzzer tried to warn him of some impending catastrophe as Professor Lindstrom spent an unusual two hour private session with him going over fine points of the paper. Then, like a bomb, Lindstrom announced plans to put a bill drawn from George's paper before the next meeting of the legislature in Olympia. The bill died in committee (God knows what George's problems might have been had it reached the house floor), but the publicity about it lingered on the Western Pacific campus and even followed George through his first year of coaching at Pigeon Rock. So far as he knew, now, no vestiges of the three year nightmare followed him to Timbertop. Yet, it was the fear of raising that spectre again that held him from recruiting a Seattle black family with basketball potential here to the Timbertop School District.

Across the room to his right Davey Huntington sat doodling, too. His thoughts, during Mr. W.'s long drone of reading, turned to writing his paper. This paper, however, had barely begun to emerge from the outline and stacks of note cards three years of

41

reading and recording school related incidents provided him. His doctoral thesis amused him almost as much as some of the characters he found himself locked in with on the Timbertop faculty. Currently he worked on the first draft of thesis chapter three—"School is not for The Students". His doodles formed to remind him that Mr. W.'s impassioned (no, dispassionate) plea for levy support concerned itself principally with the matter of salary raises and not at all with the increased quality of classroom education.

Back two seat rows, and to Davey's left, little Heidi Vandercamp failed to hear any of Mr. W.'s reading efforts (nor would it have meant very much to her if she had heard him). Beneath half hooded eyelids she had carefully studied Davey Huntington's bright, short bearded blonde head, admired the pink shirt that clung to his slender chest and the heavy gold pendant necklace that hung from his suntanned neck. She tried to place his beauty into the sordid picture her girl friend painted of him over the weekend. Just a bunch of jealous lies, she told herself. Dirty gossip, like they do about me. I just won't believe those things about him, not that it probably makes any difference to him, one way or the other.

As Heidi studied Davey, Pat Mooney covertly watched the little home ec teacher as her practiced ear shut out the dry, harsh explosions of Mr. W.'s voice. At seven this morning she snorted, as usual, and the rush which had buoyed her this last half hour now started to turn to a nervous anxiety. Where earlier her thoughts came colored in superiority, now they came in sequences of frustrated anger. She felt a growing urgency to get back to her office, away from this bullshit, and into the confrontation of student problems. Overriding this, however, she felt a need to reach out to Heidi and explore more deeply the tender smile she earlier received from the girl.

Lisa Overstreet, too, had her eye on Heidi. Though she found no hard evidence for it, she knew, in her own mind, that that young chit fooled around with the high school boys. Through her relationship with Clara Farmer (Fein Drugstore's clerk) she got Clara to call Mr. W. and report that high school boys were smoking out behind the home ec room. Several other girls friends cooperated by phoning their suspicions of Heidi's covert social life to the superintendent's office. Now she realized that Heidi sat secretly staring at Davey Huntington. You little slut, raged Lisa, nudging the librarian so she could point out the act of lewdness to her, you won't be back on a second contract. We don't need the likes of you here.

George Anderson mentally jerked immediately to matters of the moment as Eph Findley's size twelve loafer banged his ankle bone with a sharp knock. As his eyes focused quickly on the wall toward which his chair faced, he found Mr. L. standing cranelike near the library bulletin board. The hard blue eyes, the stern, long nosed visage pointed directly at George like a direction sign. He knew, immediately, that something had surfaced that involved him in some way, and a quick glance back down at the mimeographed agenda sheet gave him Item I—Semester Report Cards. He, with Lisa Overstreet and several other had been assigned to a damn committee on the dumb shit thing. Christ, he remembered now, they met on the matter sometime last week and he missed the meeting for a skull session with his basketball team. Somewhere behind him he heard the Overstreet titter. He straightened his hunched broad back, slowly, until he sat almost a head taller than anyone else in the room. Carl Hargraves said something to him about the meeting. What in hell had it been; he couldn't remember it, now.

"I'm sorry," he muttered in his deep voice (grew peripherally aware that Mr. W. scratched some notes on his yellow legal pad), "I missed something, I guess."

"You spoke out at the last meeting for a Satisfactory-Unsatisfactory grade mark in all un-academic classes," said Mr. Longfellow, in his practiced, pedagogical voice. "Apparently you failed to get your arguments into the report card committee's report."

"Missed the meeting," George mumbled, painfully. "Had a conflict with basketball."

"Would you like to bring the matter to the floor again?" pontificated Mr. L., his smug smile belittling all little boy coaches who involved themselves in sports instead of the important things in education.

"No. Its not that important," mumbled George, anxious to be invisible, again.

"Then we'll continue our standard report card procedures," said Mr. L., voice dripping superiority. "All cards must be into the counselor's office before you leave the building Friday night. Girl's cards to Mrs. Mooney and boy's cards to Mr. Patterson. Now, you have a place for remarks on that card, people, let's use it. Parents want to know why children get the grade they get—particularly if that grade's a C or below. Remember, cards provide a real public relations opportunity with our community. For many voters it's the only real contact they have with the school. So it behooves each of you to evaluate, carefully. Allow for the child's effort. Remember the only thing a child learns from an F is failure. (Ha-ha). If you failed, for some reason or other, to send home a poor work slip about a student, remember our policy allows for no failing mark—though you may issue an incomplete. With that incomplete, however, be sure in remarks you demand that the parent come in for a conference. We hope no F's or Incompletes occur, but, unfortunately, we all know it happens. Now, any other remarks or suggestions on the matter of grades?" (He delivered the question with his eye on Mr. W.)

"As a matter of fact, yes," Davey Huntington's humor tinged voice alerted one and all that another sacrilege lay about to be spoken. "Why don't we just make a big rubber stamp and put our mark, like a piece of stamped government beef, on the forehead of every student. You know—Grade A, Grade B, etc."

Mr. Longfellow grew red faced, and an angry murmur rose from several spots around the room. Two people, Bill Goss—woodshop and Sylvia Scanner—art, laughed appreciatively. Willard Norburton, music, one of Sylvia Scanner's more ardent suitors, joined his laugh, belatedly. With quick, angry motions, Mr. W. made a series of notes on his yellow sheeted legal pad.

"Your levity lacks good taste, Mr. Huntington," said Mr. L., coldly.

44

"Think how much paper work time we could all save," laughed Davey, unconcerned.

God, I wish I had half his poise, thought George Anderson.

I'd like to get that smart little son-of-a-bitch out behind the gym and choke him to his knees with his own fag necklace, raged Eph Findley, silently, his big fists clenching and unclenching on the table in front of him.

How very wonderful you are, thought Heidi Vandercamp, as if finding herself as the sleeping princess in a dream. Like a white knight or a fairy prince you stand alone, above and beyond us all.

God damn these people who have to interrupt a meeting and drag it on, thought Pat Mooney, desperately. Isn't it enough that I've got all those fucking report cards to process. Let's get on with things, here. Let's get on with them.

No use adding that to his file, thought Mr. W., who had just scribbled down "call Jack and see if he can get any tickets for the Blazer game next Sunday." I don't think it fits anything in the regulations. God damn it, Huntington, I do hope that this is your last year here with us.

Around the room feelings ran a gammit from amusement expressed, to amusement hidden, to patient disgust, and to vile animosity. Most felt belittled, though most hated the drudgery of report cards as much as did Davey. Yet, there seemed no solution to report cards, a fact of on going tradition. They produced a million faculty committees, occupied millions of faculty discussion hours, had, in fact, been on Timbertop agendas each year since 1921. The effort always ended at a very human point—how else can we try to keep students and faculty honest?

Such a bunch of shit for grown people to get excited over, thought Davey H. in high amusement. With our little four time a year ritual we reward those who find school work easy, punish those who find school work hard, and get ignored by that largest of all groups in the middle who recognize the thing for what it is: another damn silly adult game.

"I think our comedian has had his say," said Mr. L., stiffly, unaware that he had twice removed from and returned to the bridge of his beaklike nose the heavy black rimmed glasses that

45

corrected his myopia. "Could we please go on to agenda item number two: student actions in the halls. Some of you, I'm afraid, grow more lax each day toward discipline responsibilities outside your classroom—particularly in the matter of students in our halls. I'll not embarrass anyone by mentioning names, but I saw a teacher on Friday walk right by a boy with his arm around a girl—an arm, I might add, most intimately placed. Now, by our policies, that teacher held a responsibility to break up that tender scene, yet she did nothing about it. I found myself forced to leave my regular observation post in the hall and reprimand the boy and girl myself. Of course I made record of the incident known to Mr. Wellington, and the proper entry was placed in that teacher's personnel file. All that, however, is beside the point. The point is, when we relax our attention to duties, students relax their action responsibilities. Like the little Dutch Boy, we all and each need to keep our finger in any hole in the dike."

His eyes swept the room, and a bit of gall rose in his throat. Damn them, it had been a good simile. Several hours of his Sunday afternoon he spent working the thing out. No one offered so much as an appreciative smile, but he did see Lisa Overstreet's fat hand and lumpy arm waving high for attention.

"Miss Overstreet," his voice sharp with chagrin.

"I agree with Mr. Longfellow," she began, in her semi-shrill voice, "student hall conduct gets to be more of a disgrace every year. Gosh knows, some of us suffer real indignities because of it. But what happens in our halls is small potatoes compared to what happens behind the shops, the home ec room, the art and the band room. Smoking, drinking, and all kinds of liberties, you can bet. At last Thursday night's Ladies Literary Club we discussed writing a letter to our police chief about it. Now, as most of you know, I've sent letters to the board about this, and the Literary Ladies took a petition to the superintendent's office asking for private security police to patrol our grounds and our building. Surely the administration cannot expect those of us who no longer get around as easily as we once did to serve in the role of a police force. So far, the board failed to even answer my letters, and it's been two months since we petitioned the superintendent's office, with no reaction. I suggest, then, as a near thirty year member of TEA, that we demand our teaching organization bring pressure for action both with the board and with the superintendent."

A light splatter of applause from Nola Davenport, Patricia Armbruster, Remedial, Agnes Merriweather and Bernice Tulley, English. Mr. L. looked quickly toward Mr. W., but the principal deliberately held his head down and continued to scratch on his note pad.

"We've discussed that matter at administrative meetings," Mr. L. rushed into control of the floor quickly, before the ever ready babble of teacher small talk got it's chance to start. "Both Dr. Pettigrew and now Dr. Imberlay oppose the idea as bad school images. After all, we're not a penitentiary."

What else are we, then? Davey mocked in silent amusement. Where else besides a penitentiary are the inmates restricted to room, moved around by the sound of a bell, forced to publicly declare their toilet needs, forced to eat their lunches whether they want them or not, and forced to knuckle under to the diverse will of whatever guard happens to have duty over them at the moment?

I'm the guy in the hall, that's for sure, thought George Anderson, bleakly, to himself. Why in hell is it so terrible for children to feel affection for one another? Something gets crazy in all this that I don't understand.

Wonder if the boy fondling that girl was one of those seniors trying to hustle me? thought Heidi, and her eyes again sought out Patricia Mooney.

Pat failed to hear any of Lisa's diatribe, despite the high decibel level her screech owl voice employed. In front of her she started drawing the picture of a snowman, but she did catch Heidi's look and returned the girl's smile with an understanding smile of her own.

"Why not bring the matter to our Education Association Officers?" asked David Ross, Biology, in a stentorian voice that even got through to Pat Mooney.

"Let Lisa draw up the proposal," called Davey Huntington, "that way we'll be sure the grammar and spelling's correct."

"Come to order!" roared Mr. L., pounding the table near him with a book that lay near his hand. "We've got a full agenda and little over a half hour left to get through it."

Despite the incessant buzzing that continued to grow, Lisa Overstreet's screech managed to overcome the errant voices.

"Do I have everyone's ok to submit a proposal to TEA?" she called.

"Do that, Lisa," roared Mr. L., still unable to catch Mr. W.'s eye or pound the assemblage back to a point of order. "I'm sure we all agree with you. In the meantime (the all agree with you statement quieted most of the talkers) each of you please redouble your hall efforts, particularly about seeing that halls are cleared by tardy bell time. Far too many of our students come into classes late."

"We need an overall tough policy on tardiness," intruded Carl Hargraves, Math, now on his favorite gripe. "I've advocated one for years, but some teachers act like they don't care if students come late to class."

"We've tried different policies, Carl," said Mr. L., placatingly. "They help a bit, at first, then start to die in their own complications."

"A bit of stiffness on the part of administration would help them work," said Carl, belligerent, now as always, about the three tardy policies authored by him that had each one passed into oblivion.

"Some people could help by setting a better example of being on time themselves," piped Lisa Overstreet, deliberately hulking up to stare at George Anderson's broad back.

George felt the stare, knew that others looked side-eyed at him. How many times had he emerged from a special between class talk with one of his ball players to find Marsha Kemper trying to get his classes organized while her girls waited patiently. What the hell is all the time fuss, he thought, bitterly, most teachers waste at least a half of their class time, anyway.

One grows to hate that old bitch for the lousy job she does in the classroom, Mr. W. thought, as he finished a note "to call M.

48

about Friday night," but she knows what makes the system go, no doubt about that.

At least she can't be talking about me this time, thought Heidi, I'm always in by tardy time and only my senior boys ever come late.

Those assholes ought to have to sit at my desk and make out admit to slip classes six or seven times each day, thought Pat, angrily, and nobody made provision in my job description for the time I waste on that chickenshit program.

"Some people just take root in one classroom and sit there all day like a giant stump," said Davey, merrily, imitating Lisa's sargeant major posture and staring openly at her.

Immediately the room burst into a dozen brushfires of conversation, and again Mr. L. pounded his book on the table, more violently, this time, so that gradually from the front and spreading toward the rear the faculty members came back to order. Three minutes ticked away on the wall clock before Mr. L. again held control of the meeting.

"For the rest of this meeting raise your hand if you want the floor," demanded Mr. L., and he looked much like a mad turkey gobbler.

A barrage of veiled dirty looks provided his response to that edict, and Mr. W. saw each of them. He smiled, to himself, at escaping their enmity.

"Now, ladies and gentlemen, we all know that punctuality provides important student training," began Mr. L. in a voice showing strain. (I do, thought George Anderson. Then how come it never occurred to me?) "We've got a policy, loose, but with proscribed procedures that each of you agrees to follow. (Bullshit, thought Carl Hargrave, I'll just start locking my door again.) If each of you concentrates on applying these procedures, diligently, we'll quickly minimize student loitering. (Yes, thought Pat Mooney. The line in front of my door will get so long a lot of kids will choose to cut the class and split for a smoke somewhere.) I think you all understand what I'm saying to you, see that each of you carries out his or her part." (Longfellow, you ass, thought Davey Huntington, kids hurry to a class they feel is worthwhile,

49

and they dawdle toward one they know will be a bust, anyway.)

His upbraidment of the troops left a sullen aftermath in the room. Again Mr. W. felt smug about sliding his bad guy role off onto Longfellow. Several teachers checked the wall clock, among them George, Heidi, and Pat. Several teachers rustled agenda papers in their hands and snatched peripheral looks at Mr. W. Head down he continued to write furiously on the yellow pad in front of him.

My God, thought little Heidi, can there really be another twenty minutes of this.

I know I've told myself never during working hours, Pat said to herself, feeling her nervous hysteria grow, but I'm going to have to do it to get through this day. Thank God, I've got a little emergency bottle disguised in the bottom of my handbag.

Wonder what would happen if I just threw caution to the wind and hollered "Quack! Quack! Quack!" mused Davey Huntington.

"What time we play tonight," George Anderson whispered to Eph seated beside him.

"Second game. Eight thirty," Eph whispered back. "We'll take these guys like Grant took Richmond."

I wonder what sex with a black man would be like, thought Marsha Kemper, in an unguarded moment. Jesus! What a repulsive thought. Where in hell did that come from?

I know what all this means to me, Librarian Davenport groaned, inwardly. More noon detention cases, more after school time makeups in my library. I don't know why I have to suffer because they can't make kids behave the way that they should. Sure never had these kinda problems when I was a girl in school.

"Want to go over to Castleview tonight?" Willard Norburton, Band and Choral, whispered to the elf like, cascading black straight haired art teacher, who sat with her knee pressed against his own half bent knee.

Willie played with a three piece group at the Holiday in Castleview five nights each week. At least three of those five Sylvia went with him, and they often ended up in one of the motel's units. Both were in their second year at Timbertop, and only Willy knew (besides Sylvia) she planned not to renew on her next year's contract.

"Marry me, Syl, and you can stay home and work on your art," Willy pleaded.

"I'll never marry a schoolteacher," said Sylvia. "To me they're a bunch of men without any balls. My old man used to always say: 'Them that can, do; them that can't, teach! You quit and put your time in on music and I'll marry you then, if you think marriage is all that important."

But Willy, despite the terrible hunger he felt for Sylvia, felt an even more terrible fear of failure (two discs cut by groups of his already fizzled and cost him money). Right now they both tried to operate as if nothing had changed much for either of them; but they both knew that time slowly ate up their togetherness moments, and each felt a melancholia they could not communicate to the other.

Better get things moving, Longfellow, thought Mr. W., you're gonna run out of time and you still got a big hassle over salary negotiations.

I'm really gonna get hard assed with some of those damn hippy kids, Boy's Counselor Greg "Coach" Patterson avowed to himself. I'll just tighten up on who gets admit to class slips and park the bad ones in detention until the little bastards learn to suck eggs.

Refusing to recognize any further arm and hand raising efforts made by people who wanted to interrupt for questions, Longfellow expedited the remaining items on the agenda giving each the matter of seconds that it reasonably warranted. First a meaningless report from their curriculum committee that said, in effect, "let's go on like we are. Why should we make any waves." Marsha Kemper, Hospitality Chairman, got floor recognition to promote a faculty dinner planned for the Grange Hall on the first Saturday in February. Several hands came up over that, but Mr. L. advised them to see Mrs. Kemper after the meeting. He, himself, read the list of this week's projected activities: PTA, Basketball Game, School Board Meeting, Wrestling Match, and Girl's Basketball. There were other, lessor things: committee meetings, a student council meeting, and several community efforts.

51

Again shrugging off several waving hands, he proceeded to read a formal typewritten complaint from the sweepers about the exhorbitant number of paper airplanes that continued to daily litter the halls (the memorandum brought a buzz of angry hornets). His next memo came authored by the standing discipline committee, and it offered two suggestions for handling people caught cheating on papers or exams. (This one caused both hand waves and hot buzzing, but he stolidly ignored them and went on to his final memo).

It dealt with plans for a rooter bus to Camas on Friday night, and it came from the principal's office. All year a certain segment of the faculty bitterly fought class interruptions for rooter bus solicitations and the putting on of Pep Assemblies. The bulletin, starting out as an assurance that the best effort possible would be made to not infringe on any further classtime, went on to handle the real guts of the matter in a most dictatorial manner as it told those bitching teachers, in effect, that the matter lay not in their jurisdiction and was, therefore, none of their business. Before launching into reading the thing aloud, he had presence of mind to look at the clock. He found that only six minutes remained for the meeting. With highly emotionalized people like Lisa Overstreet and Carl Hargraves on the losing side of this issue, he knew that the entire meeting would explode and disintegrate despite any effort to chair on his part. He decided to have Mr. W. let him put a copy of the memo in each teacher's box. That would have been the proper way to handle the matter, anyway. Mr. L. continued to experience a growing feeling that Mr. W. used him in unflattering ways at times, but he couldn't quite figure out what those ways were.

"Because of the rapidly evaporating time we'll skip Agenda Item 7, Rooter Buses and Pep Assemblies (he grabbed a quick look at Mr. W., but the principal continued to stare down and scribble). Our last item deals with salary negotiations. Mr. Coleman?"

"We met last Wednesday night with all the directors but Mick Randolph," reported Tom Coleman, Business Classes, Jr. Varsity football, and Varsity wrestling. "Old Cosgrove gave us a bad time right from the go. He not only roared down our twelve per cent and the dental program, but he says the six per cent offered by the directors is more than he wanted to go. Edna Keefer seemed sympathetic, and I know Mick Randolph is always with us. It looks tough, though. We know Bill Murchim plays little sir echo to whatever Cosgrove says, and Steve Dobson's never been strong for giving teachers much of a raise in salaries. I think we might reach impasse, but we negotiators feel, along with the board and the superintendent, that the less said about salary negotiations before levy time the better for all concerned."

Before Mr. L. could open the floor for orderly questions or comments, pockets of rising voices filled the room with excited conversation. Helplessly he stood pounding his book on the table while the entire assemblage ignored him.

In three minutes I get out of this bedlam and on to something a hell of a lot better—yes, I'll snort right after the attendance lists are in, thought Pat.

Even twelve per cent wouldn't give me enough left over to get a decent car, thought George Anderson. After taxes and all that shit I'd be lucky to take home another forty bucks. Maybe Madge is right. Maybe going back to Cicero would be best for the four of us.

Whatever do people need so much money for, Heidi queried herself, in honest bewilderment. I put over a third of my check in the bank each month, now. Well, I suppose some of the fellows have got families.

On the back of his mimeographed agenda copy Davey Huntington finished printing in crude pencil form "Lisa Sucks". He planned to slip it under her door after the meeting broke up. Her classroom sat right next to his.

Suddenly the warning bell rang and in a moment a surge of bodies crushed toward the library door. Mr. W. remembered, too late, that he had failed to make a plea for their appearance at the PTA meeting tonight. Oh, well, a reminder would come in the school's regular bulletin (which a number of them would fail to read). But, then, high school teachers were rare birds at PTA meetings, with good reason; high school student parents were rare birds at PTA, too.

At last, thought Heidi almost ecstatically, I can get out to my girls and get the day started right.

God damn jostling pigs, thought Pat Mooney, as she felt the crush of teacher bodies around her and felt her own helplessness.

While most teachers struggled to find a place in the press, George Anderson sat talking quietly to Eph Findlay about the night's townteam basketball game with a visiting merchant sponsored team from Kelso. Lisa Overstreet, capitalizing on her handicap, spent the last lingering moments with her friend, Nola Davenport; letting her own first period class wait restlessly in the hall a full five minutes after the tardy bell had rung.

Davey Huntington traveled through the crowd much as a globule of mercury does in alcohol—seemingly untouched by his surroundings in passing. In his trip down the hall and the stairs, he responded with a smile and a wave to the multitude of "Good morning, Mr. Huntington's." Several girls deliberately brushed themselves against him, and he wagged a fake-anger finger at them that brought rosy blushes to their faces. At Miss Overstreet's room he appeared to bend down and tie his shoe, but the penciled words slipped beneath the door. He straightened, smiled, waved to another little group of morning greeters, then took his mandated station just outside his unlocked door keeping one sparkling eye on the hallway's activity and the other on those students who already had entered his classroom.

Upstairs the appearance of AT to pick up the coffee urn signalled Lisa that she had better start the long trek to her own room on the floor below. She smiled, condescendingly, at AT in passing, and he turned to her his ever present thin lipped smile.

What a tub of lard, he thought to himself. By God I made sure she never got one of my boys in her classroom.

Out in the hall, at the head of the stairwell, Lisa lowered one ponderous leg toward the first step downward. From someplace behind her where tall metal lockers crowded each side of the dimly lit hall, a raucous voice echoed for all to hear.

"Quack! Quack! Quack!"

# CHAPTER THREE

When Mr. W. finally extricated himself from the library, he picked his way through the slowly evolving and dissolving molecular-styled student groups that formed and unformed like flocks of chattering birds. He answered a "Good morning, Mr. Wellington" from a red lettermen's sweater on a burly football frame with a perfunctory nod, gave a second to a good morning from a thin female figure in blue jeans, and held a rock like profile dead ahead when he passed a group that laughed secretively. A Titan among little people—he felt like Prometheus headed for Olympus—his camera shutter corneas behind their smoky glasses recorded faces with hair too long, faces with radical clothing below them, and faces with far too much makeup for good taste. Sometime today he'd find the time to flip through the school annual and refer most of those faces to their respective counselors for some good, adult, advice.

In the faculty room he knew the coaches would be grabbing their last cigarette of the morning as they shared their favorite chatter about respective school athletes. The tardy bell would precede their classroom arrival by several minutes, but each had a trusted lieutenant who picked up room keys in the coaches office mail box (along with any mail or bulletins therein) and let first period students into the coach's classroom. That smoking, by anyone, was against fire marshal rules for the building; that being late to class, letting students have building keys, and allowing students in the classroom with no teacher present violated faculty policy, none of these infractions caused embarrassment between Mr. W. and his coaches. He, too, came from that special rank of people, so he knew, by experience, the necessity of bending rules for special people and special occasions. After all, faculty meetings occurred only once each month.

"Eph's not here?" he questioned through the door he pushed half open into a tobacco foggery that refused to respond to a blowout fan in this converted half classroom (the other half served as a teacher work and storage room stocked with type-

55

writer, mimeograph machine, a big shelf of AV equipment, and two walls of floor to ceiling bookcases).

"Still talking to George in the library when I left," called Dave Weydermeyer—social studies, assistant JV football and varsity track—from his lanky frame draped on top of the old red Coke machine.

"If he should stop by here before he goes to class, have him come to the office and see me," ordered Mr. W.

"Sure thing," responded Weydermeyer, then jumped back into the discussion about the potential of senior athlete, Willy Pendergast, as either a javelin thrower or a center fielder.

In the hall, once again, Mr. W. held a steady, grim appearing, course toward his office at the building's front center. He continued to nod acceptance of the "Morning Mr. Wellington", but he no longer catalogued student rule breakers—this first floor fell under Mr. L's jurisdiction.

"Good morning, Mr. Wellington," said his secretary, Sarah Metzger, brightly, as he pushed through the frosted glass door marked "H.S. PRINCIPAL". The entrance office in this complex where he now paused belonged to Sarah, and from the command post of her desk which sat to the left of his own private office inner door she kept one eye on students "sent to the principal's office and waiting on a wooden bench by her office's front wall", while at the same time she directed the efforts of two girls (different for each period of the day) who got an A or B from her on their report card for doing their work as her "office aides."

Mr. W. paused beside her desk, now, hand resting lightly on his own brass door knob that protruded from a heavy black walnut door acquired by AT especially for this office. On faculty mornings the ritual between Mr. W. and his Sarah changed just a little bit, for on regular days he returned to his office from the upper floor some ten minutes after the tardy bell (having gone there for general hall patrol from his office some twenty minutes before the first bell was set to ring). So, on faculty mornings Sarah acted as Mr. W. *pro tem* until the real wheel got back in the center of things.

"I promised you'd return several calls before noon," said Sarah, as he stood in wait of her usual instructions (no need for her to say those phone memos lay neatly on top of his huge old black walnut desk). "Dr. Imberlay called to remind us how important PTA tonight is for the levy effort, and I reminded him we always bulletinize PTA for a whole week before it happens. Chehalis called to confirm three rooter buses for tomorrow night's game. Do you want me to call for a couple of extra police auxiliaries?"

"Please do," said Mr. W.

"Mr. Cutter of School Supplies called to confirm his ten-thirty appointment this morning, and Mr. Albert from Athletic Equipment called to remind you he's taking you to lunch at twelve."

"Thank you, Sarah," said Mr. W. (he perked up a bit, at least Fat Albert provided him one bright spot in the day). "I don't want to see anyone for the next fifteen minutes, oh, except Mr. Findlay should he stop by show him right in. Would you send one of our girls out to the home ec room and have Miss Vandercamp come see me at 8:50?"

"Yes, sir. You don't want me to call her on the intercom?" asked Sarah, hating to send a girl out into the cold.

"No," said Mr. W., speculatively. "Keep this thing as low key as possible."

"Right," said Sarah Metzger, sensing real dinner table conversation for her husband (a usual bonus aftermath of faculty meeting mornings).

Roger let himself on into his inner sanctum—felt himself grow two feet taller as the door clicked softly closed behind him. Here, where polished oak floors sparkled—with little light flecks from an old iron chandelier installed on the room's center ceiling through the combined efforts of himself and A.T., he gathered together all the forces that made him Zeuslike, made this sanctum a dread destination for any summoned student or teacher, and provided him the trappings to awe parents and impress visiting salesmen or dignitaries. On his left black oak panelled wall, three tiers of a bookcase held an impressive array of books (mostly uncut and marked inside as free copies from the publishers) on educational theory, psychological studies, counseling expose's, and administrative techniques. The back wall, fronted by his great old desk and black vinyl leather padded swing chair, framed a big duotherm window that looked out onto the front lawn and bus loading zone. As he had not been here to watch buses unloading this morning, the window now stood behind heavy folds of black canvas drapes that traveled big brass traverse rods on shiny brass rings. The wall to his entrance right displayed his framed educational degrees and certification accomplishments as well as a gallery of pictured great athletic teams who brought glory to The Axemen under Coach Wellington's mentorship.

Against the fourth wall, where he now stood with hand still loose and dry on the big brass doorknob, two big wooden chairs rested their backs against black walnut paneling. The paneling, the bookcases, the drapes and the framed pictures all complimented a joint effort between Mr. W. and his good friend, A.T. Cromwell. The two mirrors which hung on the entrance wall above the wooden chairs were both A.T.'s gift to Mr. W. and his own idea.

"Saw an office like this on one of them TV shows, once," he told Mr. W. when the two started the project five years ago. "Them mirrors let you see what's happening behind anybody's back who's standin' in front of your desk and facing you. Fact is, if you got a room full of people with these mirrors you can see pretty much what each one is doing."

It had been A.T., too, who insisted on limiting the room to two chairs besides Roger's own swivel chair.

"If you got to move extra chairs in, folks feel they're imposing and that makes them nervous. If they got to stand while you get to sit, that makes them nervous, too. If they's only one or two in, they can see by them two chairs they been treated darn special, and they feel a bit nervous about the special attention you showed them. All in all," concluded A.T., "with only two chairs you're gonna keep folks on a bit of an edge. As this is your homeground, Mr. W. (A.T.'s the only one who calls Roger Mr. W. to his face), you got a right to hold you an edge."

And Roger felt that edge, now, as always, when he turned, lifted his dark glasses, and looked into the polished mirror that jutted out toward him. Most of the red seemed gone from his eyeballs except for a spot in the corner of each where the sockets abridged to the nose. That color, he told himself with a sense of real satisfaction, could be adduced to a cold, to a heavy reading schedule, or from the inclement weather outside. He slipped his glasses into a case that he carried in a front upper pocket of his suit coat. Turning back into the room, he moved to the waiting comfort of his padded swivel chair. Slowly he leafed through the call memos Sarah had placed carefully in the center of the big desk blotter that now fronted him.

The top memo, a notice to call Mrs. Purcell, he crumpled and threw into his wastebasket. A second, from Madeline Forbes over in Castleview he put into his coat pocket to be answered during his lunch break out of the building with Fat Albert. God damn, Maddie knew better than to call him at work. Crazy bitch, but then wasn't she just that crazy back when they both went to old Castleview High. His third notice, from Ray Cosgrove, he placed by the phone as his first order of phone business, and the other three different memos all contained parent names he knew from previous discipline problems with one or more of their children. These he would respond to, if he found time free to do it.

As he sorted through the telephone messages he heard the tardy bell ring, and his practiced ear marked the unwinding and lowering of thunderlike sounds that filled his building when students surged in the halls. Teachers, except for Lisa clumping downstairs and the coaches finishing off their cigarettes, would start taking role and another week of educational doing would get underway all around him. He felt the power of it all—his position at the center of a crawling people hive containing nearly six hundred warm and active bodies.

Across the room from him his black walnut door swung open and big Eph Findlay stood framed by the white plastered walls of Sarah's office.

"You wanted to see me?" asked the football coach.

"Yeah, right, coach. Come in a second and close the door, will you?" asked Roger, leaning forward with elbows pressed on the desk's cut glass top, a signal that the moment held high significance.

"What's cookin', bossman?" asked Eph, concern in his voice as he carefully closed the door behind him and approached to lean with fingertips on the desk edge across from Roger.

"Eph, we've got to cool the boys on mucking Imberlay," said Roger, voice low and hushed with conspiracy. "At least we got to get them to lay off until after the levy election. We need that money, boy; your salary increase, mine, and some new football equipment rides on that thing passing. We can't have votes against Imberlay turn into votes against the levy."

"I know it, Rog," said Eph, morosely. "Damn shame, though, I think we had that little pipsqueak bastard on the run."

"Oh, he's running, running scared, you can bet," said Roger, lasciviously. "He'll never get another two year contract here, even if he tries for one, which I doubt. So, don't let's worry about that, for now. Quit badmouthing Imberlay until we get that levy money okayed."

"Got it," said Eph, with a big wink and a smile. "How about that fag, Huntington? I could have killed that smart prick this morning."

"I've got a few coals for his crotch," laughed Roger, conspiratorily. "You leave that butterfly to me. Don't look for him back again next year."

"You got something," said Eph, with relish.

"You'd better believe it," lied Roger, knowing if Davey did leave part of the credit would be his, now, if he didn't leave he could blame the blockage on to the damn meddling superintendent.

"Hey, like, good, man," said Eph, eagerly. "I'd better dangle before old Hargraves writes me up for being late to class." (They both laughed, heartily, at that little bon mot).

"Got a party after your ball game tonight?" asked Mr. W.

"My place. Gonna make it?"

"I'll see how long the damn PTA meeting drags on. Emily's got a meeting with Bud and his millionaire buddies, so she won't get home before midnight," said Roger.

"Wish that brother of yours would cut me in on some of that dough," sighed Eph Findlay. "What a bastard, he won't even cut you into the pie."

"Takes all kinds," said Roger, uncomfortable with this tact of the conversation.

"Hey, I'm gone. Know you're rushed," barked Ephriam, and he bolted out the door on a fast march toward his classroom.

As his door closed, again, Mr. W. consulted his super electric gold bracelet Sieko wristwatch (Emily's last birthday present to him), and he noted that six minutes remained until his scheduled meeting with the home economics teacher. From a lower right hand desk drawer he took out four different bottles of vitamin pills, and one special plastic jar that contained some prescription tranquilizers. (Once, long ago, he started to bring some of these things home but Emily's derision drove them back to his secret vice). With five pills cupped in his hand, he poured a glass of water from the tureen Sarah always filled fresh for him every morning. Secretly he harbored a wild hope that these chemicals might somehow reverse the decay process rapidly destroying his once powerful, muscular body. Dr. Felton, however, prescribed less booze and more exercise, a diagnosis Roger chose to ignore. Lately, however, he began to have second thoughts about the pills he kept taking, and he promised himself a stiffer physical regime as soon as the weather warmed up in the Spring.

With his daily medication down, he quickly scanned the day's activity list which Sarah placed new on his desk each morning. At nine AT came in for his weekly meeting on maintenance (this left him only ten minutes for Vandercamp). At nine thirty he planned a teaching observation on Mavis Parmenter, math, and at ten thirty he had promised Joe Cutter thirty minutes to talk over next year's supplies. Eleven looked open, but that was Huntington's free period so he needed that time for the genius boy. At eleven-thirty the two counselors and the attorney planned to meet with him on the Purcell bit, and he planned to enjoy a long, leisurely lunch with Fat Albert from Athletic Equipment from twelve until at least one thirty. At one thirty a scheduled teaching observation on Mike O'Malley, Agriculture & Driver's Ed showed, and at two committee members for the one thousand dollar annual Huntington Scholarship planned to meet in his office.

"God damn the Huntingtons," he mumbled, aloud, then looked up quickly, guiltily, to make sure he sat in the room alone.

Well, it looked like he might find some slack time around three just to poke around the halls and look in, casually, on a couple of classrooms. School ended at three thirty but he faced a four o'clock meeting with an irate parent and Mr. Longfellow. Well, he'd gone the route with the parent, Ed Kalifonte, several times before, so it might be good to let Ed feel like he won this one, for a change. Give him, maybe, a reason to vote for the levy on election day.

Shit, he thought, to himself, why sit here and ruin the thought of lunchtime fun with old Fat Albert and a games-we-play phone call with little old Madeline. The trouble with you, Wellington, is that you worry too much. Quote, unquote, Dr. Miles Pettigrew, retired superintendent of Timbertop School District. Well, Miles, you old bastard, if I'd worried just a little bit harder about getting close to Mick Randolph and been a little less sure about the help I never got from you, I might be superintendent, today, instead of that freak, Imberlay. By God, I'll get it next time if I have to kiss every ass on the school board.

On the desk in front of him a buzz and a flash of red light warned him that Sarah wanted his attention.

"Yes, Mrs. Metzger," he said, tripping the speaker's toggle switch.

"Miss Vandercamp's here," said Sarah, primly.

"Send her in," ordered Mr. W.

From the time the office girl delivered an order for her appearance at the principal's office to the time Mrs. Metzger signaled her to pass through Mr. Wellington's holy portal, little Heidi suffered horrible agonies of the bumper jack syndrome. At first she only lamented the fun time lost with her student aides, but that quickly panicked toward the way she was summoned at this unlikely time. As the seconds ticked up she moved from a

62

routine possibility dealing with her accreditation (a more likely matter for the superintendent's office), through a discussion of her work in the classroom (not too likely as Mr. Longfellow had observed her only two weeks ago), to the possibility of formal censor for her lack of disciplinary action for those senior boys who got really "fresh" with her last Friday. Now, as she let the heavy door shut behind her, she moved almost catatonically to a place in front of Mr. W.'s desk where she stood, trembling knees pressed together, fighting not to wet her pants.

"Miss Vandercamp, Heidi," Mr. W. began, sternly, slowly, "uh—why don't you pull one of those chairs over here by my desk?"

My God, I forgot how little she is, thought Roger. Can she even lift one of those chairs? Maybe I should do it for her—no, that makes me servitudinal to her. She's smaller than my fourteen year old Betty with half as much tit and three times as little ass. Who did Imberlay suggest she was fucking? Young Huntington? Christ, I've seen some of the gulls young Davey flies with; he'd never look twice at this flat chested little bird.

He's so big and so angry looking, Heidi thought, weakly, as she struggled to pull the big wooden chair into a position across from her principal. Look at all those big books he reads, and all those awards on his wall. I never read anything but home ec magazines, and I don't even know what's become of my 4-H awards. Maybe I'd just better turn in my resignation, right here and now. I don't think I'm good enough for this school thing, anyway. Maybe a junior high, someplace, where I won't have such big boys.

"We're going to talk off the record, Miss. . .ah. . .ahh. . . Heidi," said Roger, watching her perch upon the chair like a sad eyed little canary. (God, he thought to himself, I hope she's not going to cry.)

"Yes, sir," she whispered, barely audible to him, and she knew by his confidential tone something dreadful waited her in the, moments ahead—her father always talked very confidential to her mother when things were bad at the store.

"Dr. Imberlay's office received some disturbing calls this past week about your—well, your private life," Roger began, clumsily.

(My God! her eyes are brimming up already. How big and blue they are. I can't believe that she's real.)

"Disturbing?" whispered Heidi (her throat seemed constricted almost to numbness). She tried desperately to think of something bad she had done. Played her record player too loud in her apartment, perhaps? Let too many of her girls come to visit her and stay too late in the evening?

"Yes—ah—personal things, you know," Roger stumbled onward (ready to abort the whole thing should the tears start to rush). "It seems some of the ladies in town feel you've not been very. . .very. . .discreet in your private relationships with—er—men—you know what I mean."

"No," whispered Heidi, hoarsely, "I don't know what you mean."

"Well, that's your private right and privilege, of course," said Roger, a bit angry with her suddenly because he felt a growing anger with his own blundering self. "We can't tell you how to live your personal life, though morality certainly plays a large part in being a teacher. Our example to the community rates as highly as our example to our classes. Believe me, those outside of school activities play an important role in Timbertop hiring processes." (She seemed stunned, not even breathing, and the tear drops that had originally formed at the corner of her eyes still hung there like diamond droplets.) "Anyway, I suggest you be more careful in your conduct—for your own good as well as our own public image. These things reflect themselves in voter attitudes, you know, and we do have a levy facing us."

"Mr. Wellington," her tiny voice croaked the words, and she coughed, discreetly behind her hand to clear her throat. "Mr. Wellington, I've never had a date with a man."

"I said that's your own business," said Roger, gruffly, (God damn girl could very well be putting him on, he thought. It was no secret that women wanted equal rights but when it came to confrontation they quickly took to women's wiles. What kind of shit did she think he would swallow? Never had a date with a man!) "Look, I'm just carrying out the superintendent's orders; there is nothing personal in this for me. I do have one thing of

64

mine to say to you, however, (the total helplessness of her seated bolt upright in front of him gave him a target for all the anger Emily had built in him during their morning session) and that concerns the smoking that goes on out behind the home ec building. That area is your responsibility, Miss Vandercamp. You get freed from hall duties because you are supposed to police around your building. Now, I want you to put a stop to the smoking out there, understand?"

"Yes, Mr. Wellington," whispered Heidi, and the two tear drops she could no longer control slipped down the sides of her classic Grecian nose and ended in the corners of her cupid bow mouth.

"Good," said Roger, brusquely. (My God, she is crying. Thank God that's over.) "Then we understand each other. Fine. If you've nothing to add, that's all I've got. See you at PTA tonight. (His face dropped toward the desk blotter in front of him and he made pen marks on the paper that lay beneath his right hand.)

Somehow Heidi found a reserve strength inside her never tapped before, and she used it to rise, gracefully nod a goodbye to the bowed head across from her, and return the chair she sat on to its original position with much less apparent effort than she used to move it to the desk. Without looking back she opened the big black walnut door, and, wet eyed but shoulders squared in a military manner, she marched unblinking past Mrs. Metzger, her office girls, and a wet, muddy clothed, waiting boy on the detention bench. As the opaque door with its H.S. PRINCIPAL closed behind her, Sarah Metzger decided that poor little Miss Vandercamp's problems were none of her damn husband's business.

In the big, silent gloomy hallway, Heidi met Mr. Cromwell, and he smiled at her in a warm way that helped relax the chains of tension that bound her chest.

"You should be more careful 'bout runnin' between buildings without a coat, Miss Vandercamp," said A.T., as she stopped almost face to face with him trying to decide whether to go left to the counselor's office or right to the corridor that led toward her own classroom.

"You sound like my mother," said Heidi, almost absently, but warm again inside through communicating with another real person.

"You listen to what I just told you," warned A.T., still smiling and warming her more, "or you'll be home with your mother drinking hot chicken broth instead of here with our kids giving all them good learning things you're a doing."

"You're right, Mr. Cromwell," she said, thrilled with her first compliment from anyone on the staff at Timbertop. "I'll remember, next time."

His short moment of recognizing her both as a person and as an important part of the school re-kindled her earlier determination to bring the senior boy problem to Pat Mooney. Quickly, before her resolve could melt, she made her way to the Girl's Counselor Office where she got waved by the line of girls waiting there for admit to class slips (the privilege of by-passing lines of students still made Heidi feel guilty, but everyone else seemed to accept it).

"Gosh, I can't squeeze you in now," whispered Pat, indicating the body shifting, gum chewing, giggling line of waiting girls. "Look, how about dinner at my place tonight? Six o'clock. Nothing special. Just of the two of us and we can talk our heads off."

"Oh, wonderful," breathed Heidi, all her stars seemed ascending at the same point in time. "You live just a few blocks from my apartment. I'll be there at six sharp."

As she returned to her classroom, wearing seven league boots in place of the ball and chain she had drug on her way to the office, she thought to herself how Pat Mooney and A.T. Cromwell must be the nicest people in the world—except, of course, for her mother and father.

Back in her office Pat Mooney got such a lift from the idea of Heidi coming to dinner that evening that she decided to forego the snort of coke she had planned. That, in turn, made her feel doubly good that she had not yet broken the rule of on campus abstinence she had set for herself. Things definitely seemed to be taking a move in the right direction. Perhaps she should have second thoughts about finding a job someplace else for next year.

With one friend in her corner she could face down any damn principal in the business.

At his desk, Mr. W. completely put the Heidi incident out of his mind with the same ease as he had scratched her name off the list of things to do in front of him. A.T. came into the office, moved a chair up to the desk (back rungs in front of him) and astraddle the chair's seat he swapped the latest winter steelhead fishing information with his boss. From steelhead they got into the latest report on A.T.'s boys (who always asked after their old coach, Wellington), and finally they discussed a salmon hole they planned to explore this Spring on the upper Cowlitz. While they talked Mr. W. signed requisition forms for supplies that A.T. carefully stacked on the desk between them. The principal took no time to read the requisitions, A.T. knew what he had to have and knew the best place to buy things. As he put his RW on the last one, he looked up to find A.T. eyeing him with the kind of a look most unfamiliar to him.

"That little Miss Vandercamp's gonna be a mighty fine teacher one of these days," said A.T. slowly. (That jolted Roger who figured, suddenly, that A.T. knew some things that he, Roger, ought to know.)

"What brought that on?" he asked, cautiously.

"Nothin'," said A.T., with just the trace of a shoulder shrug. "It's just that, most of the young teachers we get these days don't really act like they come to stay—you know, like they're using us for a step stone to someplace else—like Bic Morton's young attorneys go through his prosecutor's office like a dose of salts, and them young doctors that come to the clinic are gone before a man even finds out their names. Well, you look at the teachers that come and go here, and it's pretty much the same way."

"What's that got to do with Miss Vandercamp?" asked Roger. (He respected the custodian's opinion on teaching talent more than any one else in the district except, of course, himself.)

"She's a giver—not a taker. She likes kids—I mean, she really likes them. Takes them home with her. Does all kinds of extra things to help them. You know how it is, she likes what she's doing so the kids like doing it with her," said A.T., his smile bordering the angelic as his eyes held Roger's penetrating stare without displaying a trace of guile.

Roger continued to study the sturdy figure in milkman bibbers who shared an equal sixteen years of Timbertop experience with him. No small amount of personnel notes that hid in teacher files were penned by Roger Wellington out of Arthur Theodore Cromwell. What passed here, now, promised a definite influence on the future of one Heidi Vandercamp.

"Spit it out, A.T.," said Roger, flatly. "Don't walk around like you was barefoot in a cow pasture."

"Okay, Mr. W. (A.T.'s the only person who ever calls Roger Mr. W. to his face), though it's, of course, none of my business," said the custodian leaning forward on the back of his chair. "Miss Overstreet and some of her gang are out to get Miss Vandercamp, which, I imagine, you already know. Now, like you I've seen teachers come and go from here for sixteen years and either way the school goes on. But the longer I work here the more I see the good ones go and the lesser ones stay. Now, I'm not suggestin' Miss Vandercamp's gonna be a great one, she's like a frail flower now it's hard to make out the bloom, but she's got everything going for her to become a real good one. That tiny little flower, though, 's gonna need a lot of protection an a lot of encouragement. Way I see it they's only one gardener in this place who can make sure that little violet grows. That's you, Mr. W., that's you."

For a matter of long seconds the two old friends studied each other as two opposing bull elks might on meeting outside the rutting season. Then, as if by mutual agreement, they dropped the topic of Miss Vandercamp and got down to the business of changing locks in the gym (Mr. Anderson had mislaid keys, again), some possibilities for better supervision in the cafeteria during lunch time, and the amount of overtime A.T. should plan to ask the district for because of the many night events that would demand his special attention during this week.

As the principal and his custodian began their discussion of Miss Vandercamp, Lisa Overstreet began the study hall portion of her first period sophomore English class. The class, this morning, lost seven of its allotted fifty six minutes because they spent it standing in the hall waiting for Lisa's return from her faculty meeting. When she unlocked and opened the door, a small, skinny, dark haired girl with many fast nervous habits slipped into the room first. It was she who spotted and gave to Lisa the message Davey Huntington had placed under her door. Though Lisa suspected some personal indignity, she felt compelled to look at the outrage, anyway. The "Lisa Sucks" blinded her with consumate rage, as she banged several desk-arm chairs out of her way as she lunged toward her desk like an arthritic elephant.

"There will be absolutely no talking in this classroom," she shrieked at those students still sliding and shuffling into their seats. "Anyone caught doing so will get a theme to write on politeness."

With the nineteen girls and three withdrawn undersized boys seated at last in their prescribed seating order, Lisa spent four more laborious minutes calling each student's name, making an X for present in the attendance book, and offering some remark (generally uncomplimentary) about that particular student's progress in her class. Because Lisa came late to class, the girl from the counselor's office who picked up the attendance slips had become a part of the group waiting out in the hall. Now she stood by Lisa's desk, self-consciously trying to ignore the other girls in the class who made secret signs at her.

"What a stupid bother," said Lisa, at last, handing the girl her report slip. "No absences in my class so why did you have to be here and interrupt me?"

Speechless, and blushing, the girl moved swiftly toward the door. In her near blind eagerness to escape she banged, painfully, against a desk-arm chair skewed out of line by Lisa in her passing. The incident evoked a general round of laughter in the room—with the loudest brays coming from the direction of Miss Overstreet.

Another few minutes passed before order again returned, then, on Lisa's instruction, out came grammar books with today's lesson confined to prepositions. While the majority of the students followed along in their books, Lisa read the same material to them from her book. In a few more minutes the students supposedly knew how objects change their relative positions through a change in prepositions.

"Now you know what a preposition is, what it does, and you've got a list of prepositions in your book," Lisa bleated at them. "I want each of you to write twenty simple sentences, and no cheating by looking at your neighbors paper or you'll get forty to do. Write the sentence, underline the subject once and the predicate verb twice. Then encircle the preposition. Papers due at the end of the period."

I'll bet that damn Davey Huntington put that thing under my door, Lisa thought dourly to herself as she painfully lowered her bulk into a chair that faced her desk. Had to be a teacher on that meeting agenda memo. Little son-of-a-bitch, wait until I tell the girls he's trying to put the make on our little home ec teacher.

As her students turned their efforts and energies to the task at hand, Lisa dozed at her desk with practiced eyes open like two blue agates. It had been an extremely trying morning, and she had three more classes like this before her free planning period. A little snore escaped from her throat and a subdued titter ran around the class. Carefully students started exchanging papers; you could never be sure that Miss Overstreet was not just shamming sleep.

Next door, in Mr. Huntington's Senior World Problems Class, the decibel level made normal conversation impossible. Six different groups of four students each vociferously argued about the constituents of power. To a stranger, coming in the door, the room smacked of bedlam, certainly testimony to the truth of Mr. Ray Cosgrove's vilification of Mr. Huntington.

The trained observer, however, sensed immediately that many strong things were happening here—that the conversations, like the cartoon covered bulletin boards and the far out posters on the walls and ceilings, held real meaning for these students. One foursome dealt with power at the high school student level, one quartet explored possible power structures in the city and county. A third group argued factors that made for economic power while a fourth planned an expose of techniques used to build up military power. Group five argued about power functions and failures from a historical point of view, while unit six, led by Billy Lane, ASB President and debater extraordinary, made predictions about future power envolvements. Through this maelstrom, cool and unruffled, David Huntington moved from group to group adding reinforcements where an argument appeared to be weak and poking with a sharp intellectual needle to explode what had first seemed by that group an irrefutable argument.

"You know better than to try and slip by with an ad hoc argumentation," he teased Billy Lane who had forwarded, what he believed to be, an iron clad proof for the ultimate power of the free market place.

"By God it sounded perfect in Harry Browne's book," said Billy Lane, stubborn but enjoying the put down.

"Sounds equally as good for Marx if you want to go that way," laughed Davey, other conversations in the room slowed and attentions turned to the usual stars in the room.

"Well, you'd better be ready for us by the end of the week," vowed Billy Lane, and his three cohorts shook their heads in agreement. "You just heard our first opening round, today, wait until we get all our bullets in the barrel."

"Okay, troops," called Davey, lightly, as he moved to a podium at the front of the class.

One by one the groups shifted their attention to him and cut their own conversation to a standstill. The last to give up single effort for group instruction was a senior girl who finally gave up trying to impress Billy Lane and turned her best Farah Fawcett Major smile on Mr. Huntington.

"You've got the idea," said Davey, cool but still enthusiastic, as he noted that each person's eyes touched with his own eyes in passing. "Let me review the ground rules with you again so we can be as sure as possible you work in the right direction. Remember, if you have any question; if I use any term you do not understand, stop me right at that moment and let's set that matter straight. Okay?"

A general nod of approval rocked the young heads in front of him.

"Our project deals with power," continued Davey, "and I want you to continue on from our last week's study of Michael Kordas' book. Most of you memorized the axiom: 'We live in a mass society, like members of a herd, and conventional wisdom teaches us that safety lies in following the herd. But my friend is right; man is not a herding animal; his safety lies in his skill as a hunter, his ability to act and be alone. To *understand* the herd is part of the hunter's skill, to hide in the herd is useful deception, but he cannot *join* it without sacrificing his essential nature.' Now—your assignment for the week is as outlined in the mimeo copies I passed out to you when class started. You must determine, as objectively as possible, how you would react, or would have reacted, to the forces in your assigned categories of research. I supplied each of you with reference source lists for your categories—try to cover as many sources as possible. I've reserved the library for our class period tomorrow, so meet with me there instead of here. On Wednesday I want to go over with you your individual progress, and we'll use Thursday and Friday to hear, criticize, and argue your reports. Okay?"

"How about those of us with student power?" asked a cute little blonde in the first row. "Suppose the people you've suggested won't talk to us?"

"Hey, now, Elaine, what boy or what man teacher's not going to want to talk to you?" gibed Davey (several class members laughed, appreciatively).

"Seriously," he continued, "most of those people are going to be mighty flattered by your attention. It's not often people get a chance to really talk about themselves to someone who shows an honest interest."

"Can we put our stuff on tapes instead of writing it out?" asked one of the boys (a three time loser in English).

"Sure," said Davey, "just like any of our other assignments. Be sure, too, any of you who need film projectors, record players, overheads, or any of that stuff let me know by class period Wednesday so I can get them checked out through AV."

"Will this grade get on our this semester report card?" asked a tall, slender auburn haired girl who sat alone in the back room's.

(She traditionally gets A's in all her classes except Marsha Kemper's PE where she comes away with a C.)

"If you agree to let me give the final grades on Wednesday," said Davey. "My report cards have to be into the counselor's office by the end of Friday's school day."

"Who cares about the grade?" asked Billy Lane.

"Anybody care?" asked Mr. Huntington.

No one voiced a yes nor showed a hand. Several side discussions started from the assignment papers each student held. A bell rang and a few students got up and made slow movements toward the door.

"Get out of here, you guys," Davey shouted at them in a mock theatrical voice. "You want to waste next period waiting in line for an admit to class slip?"

"Mr. Huntington," said Elaine Perry (the little blonde in the front row) as she stopped with her perky nose almost touching the gold pendant that lay against his chest.

"What is it, Elaine?" asked Davey, careful to hide the special emotion that wanted to creep into his voice when he talked to this fresh faced senior girl.

All year from her chair almost directly in front of the podium where he often stood, Elaine Perry's quick, throaty laughter and unusual green cornead almond shaped eyes trapped Davey into childhood memories of his mother. He knew, in fact, that Elaine was a second cousin of his (of sorts) as her mother had been a distant cousin of Davey's mother, Angeline. Angeline, more older sister than mother, with her Alpha-Romeo sportscar, her jumping horses, and her super daring feats on skis that resulted in her death fall into a crevass when Davey was barely ten years old. Yes, though Elaine stood barely five feet tall to Angeline's five foot six, and the high school girl's long golden hair looked nothing like his mother's remembered short, auburn curls, some magic existed there that tied the two of them together in Davey's mind. A number of Timbertop people were related to Davey through one side or the other of the union between Davey Huntington, II and Angeline James, both third generation growths in the Cowlitz Valley, but Davey found no chemistry with any of them except that which flowed from little Elaine. Neither Elaine, nor any other of the Timbertop shirttail relatives attempted to openly claim kinship with Davey, but a few (like Tom Coleman's wife, Frieda) used their relationship in name dropping (Frieda felt it gave her a special social standing in her position at the bank, and she grew angry at any show on Tom's part to join the coaches in their malingerment of "Cousin" Davey.)

Beyond the mother-image transferences Davey experienced from Elaine, he felt also very much aware of her sexual attraction for him (perhaps, he reasoned, that was part of the mother-thing, too). Several times he considered dating her (he knew other teachers who dated, sureptitiously, their eighteen year old senior girls). The possibility of public censorship detered him in no way, but the enormous advantage he enjoyed over her in his pseudo-godlike role of "teacher" promised to make the relationship a too one sided adventure. ("Like shooting pigeons on the ground," a graduate school buddy of his had remarked several summers ago when the topic of teacher student dating came up at a party. "Same big edge as good old 'doctor' has, or that divorce attorney, or a minister with a hot feeling to save more than just souls.)

So the feeling that gradually evolved, for Davey, in his relationship with Elaine Perry was the feeling commonly felt by an older brother for a very pretty little sister. Incestual, but super controlled. A cool feeling that made his understanding and her naivity a warm bond of communication between them.

"Do you know Miss Vandercamp very well?" asked Elaine, now, with the same lack of restraint and social concern she might show to an older brother in a place of high authority.

"No. Only that she teaches home ec," answered Davey, in a manner as unsophisticated as her own.

"Mr. Huntington," said Elaine, and now her eyes raised from his pendant to stare deeply into his own dark brown eyes, "Miss Vandercamp's got a lot more trouble out in that home ec room than she's able to handle at this time. I'm her aide during fifth period, and some of those senior boys give her a real bad time."

"So?" suggested Davey, knowing she wanted something from him, but not sure what that something might be.

"So, I think she needs help, right quickly, and I think you can help her more than anyone else."

"Why me, Elaine?" asked Davey, honest amazement in his voice. "That's Mr. Wellington's job. She should take things to him."

"Miss Vandercamp's too nice to try and get anybody in trouble," said Elaine, her mouth now as determined as her stare, "besides, Mr. Wellington's just a principal; Miss Vandercamp needs some help from a man."

The boy's locker room cleared only seconds before a tardy bell rang, and George Anderson sighed emphathetically for those last stragglers who must face counselor Greg "Coach" Patterson for an admit to class slip. Two boys with long hair had tried desperately to towel their wet curly hanks dry enough to comb; these two, George suspected, would arrive at the counselor's office to find themselves already on the bottom of Patterson's shit list.

After checking to see all showers were closed from dripping, he picked up a few odds and ends socks, two soiled jock straps, and a dirty T shirt left lying between the floor bolted benches. These he placed in a big canvas basket half filled with dirty towels deposited, one each, by his 34 first period Freshmen boys. By the end of the day two baskets would brim with dirty towels, and the gym sweeper would take their loads to a washroom for cleaning and drying. George much appreciated this improvement over Pigeon Rock where he supervised towel washing and drying by boys picked for their lack of athletic coordination to serve as locker room managers (and where he very often ended up doing the towel wash himself).

He enjoyed, too, the near luxury of having his own office here in the locker room instead of sharing a corner of the basket room as he had done at Pigeon Rock. His office, plus an extra locker room exclusively used by organized athletic teams, meant more to George (when not considering his family) than did the few thousand dollars a year more he made here at Timbertop. As he closed his office door behind him this morning, he felt himself reborn from the straw man who left a barely touched breakfast, fought an old pickup on his drive to work, and knew loneliness and humiliation at the morning faculty meeting. The change came through strongly to Madge in the tone of his voice as he spent five minutes on the phone with her in his traditional morning call. With the phone instrument back in its cradle on his desk, he felt the cavernous silence of those heavy cement walls around him as a contented child feels the encircling strength of his father's arms. With a small sigh of pleasure, he pulled his grade book from its place in the desk's wide, flat middle drawer then took a stack of report cards from the deep lower right hand desk drawer where they had lain in two copies each since the third copy had gone home with his students at the quarter report. With a second sigh, this one resignation, he opened his grade book to page 3, 9th PE—and he grimly found the card which matched his first named entrant there—Acorn, Donald.

When he first arrived at Pigeon Rock George employed an intricate formula for awarding marks based upon a suggested reporting system he came across in Education 401-PE—Teaching Physical Education. For each physical accomplishment it offered a certain point reward and a certain total score announced the student's accomplishment at Levels A, B, C, D, or F. The total score, however, got modified by leveling factors before transition to its letter counterpart. Into the leveling factor went statistics on the boy's age, weight, height, apparent coordination, attendance record, attitude, efforts at leadership and tendency for improvement (each category carried its little *psi* factor [h, w, a, ac, ar, at, el, and ti] with advice on how to handle those subjective areas of the formula).

That first year George spent multitudinous hours filling in student charts, running out mathematical totals, agonizing over the subjective leveling factors, and explaining, under remarks on the report card, why a boy received a D, a C, or a B (the leveling factor made it possible for him to transpose from score to letter grades so that nobody failed and the el factor gave most of the A's to varsity athletes). At summer school that year he explained his grading efforts to one of his classmates who had five years of P.E.

teaching experience. When his classmate got over a more than mild fit of hysterical laughter, he pointed out to George the amount of hours spent by Anderson on meaningless shit to resolve a grade already pre-determined by each boy's attitude. From that day to this, report cards, for George, were a seat of the pants operation he resolved in one or two planning periods every quarter.

Thirty minutes after opening his grade book to Acorn, Donald, he concluded on page 10, Advanced PE—with Wuxtra, Alex, and his report cards lay ready for the original copy to go to the counselor's office and the second copy to go to the students sometime next week. His grade book now showed Acorn, Donald—First Quarter, C, and Semester Grade, C; as did Wuxtra, Alex and 89 other Timbertop boy names. 31 showed B's and 29 showed D's. Though his eleven varsity jocks with their A's skewed his Bell Curve unbalanced by F's, his percentiles would still satisfy the counseling office and administration concerned themselves only in case of failures. George leaned back in his vinyl covered padded swivel chair, stretched and yawned with satisfaction. A picky job, he thought; thank God it only happens four times each year.

A rap on the glass windowed door on his left jerked him out of his yawn and hurried his big hands to shove records and report cards back in their respective drawers. The rap came, again, and the desk top cleared, George uncoiled his nearly seven feet moved to his left and found Alvin "Kit" Carson, one of his junior guards, staring, anxiously, through the glass.

"Come in, Tiger," called George, opening the door and letting it swing inward slowly.

"Thanks, Coach. Hey, I bet I'm bothering something," said the slender redheaded boy in a rush.

"Not a thing," said George, affably. "Fact is, I was getting kinda lonesome. Pull up a chair man. What you doing out of class?"

The boys heavily freckled bony hands trembled a bit on the back of a folding chair as he scooted it up beside where George again sat ensconced at his desk. As the boy seated himself, George tried to capture and hold Kit's blue eyes with his own dark brown ones, but the youngster shifted his gaze from one spot to another above and to each side of George's smiling face.

"Hey, Kit, slow it down," soothed the coach. "You didn't kill somebody, or something like that?"

The deliberate loosener garnered a short, dry mouthed laugh from Carson, then the boy started a nervous finger drum on George's metal desk top.

"It's my old man," Kit blurted out, at last.

George knew the older Carson, vaguely. Remembered him mostly from his cat calling of referees during Kit's play in junior varsity games last year. He recalled talks with Eph about the man's drinking, his penchant for tavern brawls, and some trouble with another man over Kit's mother.

"So, what does he want, a free season ticket because his son made the varsity?" asked George, with levity.

"He's no good, coach. He's rotten. He said some things about you, yesterday, I wouldn't take, so he pitched me out of the house," said Carson, his voice edged with a sob.

"Hey, man, that's a bear," sympathized George (play it cool—play it cool). "So, where you staying now?"

"I bunked over with Kelly last night (the other junior guard), but my mother called the office this morning and said if I don't come back home she's turning me over to juvenile," choked out Kit, and the tears did form in his eyes.

"Slow, boy, slow," said George, laying one big hand compassionately on the youngster's bony trembling shoulder. "You talk this out with Mr. Patterson?"

"He's the one who told me I have to go home or else," said Carson, bitterly.

"Or else what?" asked George.

"Or else get locked up in juvenile home until the court decides what to do with me," lamented Kit. "God! And us with that tough one with Chehalis tomorrow night."

"Maybe your old man's over his mad," suggested George.

"Not likely," said Kit. "He's been building it for a long time. Seems he's got this thing about blacks. I don't understand it."

78

"Neither does he," said George, softly, encouragingly. "So, what do you want?"

"I don't want to go back there and I don't want to go to juvenile," said Kit.

"You talk to Mr. Wellington or to Mr. Longfellow about this," persisted George.

"Not really," said Kit, his voice trembling noticeably, now. "It was Mr. Longfellow who sent me to the counselor, and Mrs. Metzger told me Mr. W. was too busy to see me today when I asked. Hey, Longfellow's going to kill me when he finds out I came out here without a pass."

"Don't worry, I'll write you a pass in case anyone says anything," assured George. "Look, Kit, I'm no lawyer, but I got this suggestion to make to you. Don't panic on this thing and take off from school. Don't try to run; you've got everything going for you here and nothing to run to out there. I suggest you talk to Mr. Huntington. He knows a lot about the law and especially about student rights. If you don't want to talk to him, well, I'll have some answers for you by ball practice time after school tonight. Okay?"

"I'll talk to Mr. Huntington," said Kit, already the optimism of youth brightening up his voice. "I've got U.S. History from him fourth period, and he's easy to talk to, like you, coach."

George felt that familiar lump of sentiment rise in his throat as the boy's open love and admiration came pouring out around the word "coach". He squeezed the boy's shoulder where his big fingers lay, then he took them free to dig out a building pass that insured Alvin "Kit" Carson of safe passageway back to his second period chemistry class.

During third period Davey usually kept to his room, the library, or the teacher's work room. This planning period he needed more ditto copies for his U.S. History classes, so he made it to the work room where a few minutes sufficed to get the job done. In an unusual instance, for him, he felt desire for a bottle of Coke, so a stack of mimeo sheets in hand he left the work room for the empty faculty lounge next door. He'd barely uncapped his cold little retrieved bottle when Mr. W. came through the door as obviously as surprised to see Davey as Davey was to see him.

"Buy you a Coke?" asked Davey, pleasantly, exhibiting a shiny quarter in his free left hand.

"No. No thanks," rumbled Mr. W., "damn weight, you know." (He patted the bulge above his sagging belt line.)

"Don't indulge in sugar often myself," said Davey (pleased to contrast his brown slender body with Roger's white portly one).

"I'm glad I caught you, though," said Mr. W., moving on into the room until he stood a few feet from Davey. "Save us trying to get together for a formal meeting on the thing."

"What thing?" asked Davey, blithely.

"Well, it seems some damn fools in the community got it in their heads that you're teaching communism in your classes," said Mr. W., his attempt to be matter-of-fact came off with a supercilious officiousness. "Dr. Imberlay asked me to talk to you about it. Can't have that kind of talk at levy time, you know."

"You mean Ray Cosgrove bitched about me, as usual, and Imberlay's afraid to talk back to him or bring up the matter to me," said Davey, lightly. "You've got my sympathy, Roger, it's a shitty stick you keep trying to climb."

"Now wait a minute!" (Mr. W. didn't like the tone Davey used for the word, Roger. He also realized a tactical error in not having Huntington in the principal's office—though it seemed to make little difference in their previous confrontations.) "Nobody's trying to stifle your academic freedom, Huntington. (Big drag on the Huntington.) Doctor Imberlay knows you're no communist. Is it too much to keep things cool in your classroom until after the levy election?"

"The Huntingtons (Davey mocked Roger's drag on the name) never acquired the tag of chickenshit," said Davey, "though we've rightly been called bastards, assholes, and many other like names in this community. Why doesn't your Dr. Imberlay just tell Cosgrove to fuck off, once and for all times? Why don't you tell him, Roger? You've got tenure up your ying yang."

"Okay, Huntington, so you're a big shot with your money and your smart mouth," snarled Roger, his wattles turning very red. "God damn you, sometimes I'd like to. . . ."

"Take a swing at me?" laughed Davey. "Hey, go ahead. I'm curious to see how a black belt karate stands up against an overweight college football player."

Wellington spun on his heel, abruptly, showing the remains of grace and balance that had once made him an excellent athlete. Messing up Huntington would be bad for his image. He talked to the man as he had promised the superintendent. He needed, badly, to get back to the strength center of his private office—make that call to Cosgrove and go to lunch with Fat Albert.

Poor son-of-a-bitch, thought Davey, watching the principal almost trample on the two coaches who had entered as Roger sought to exit. He's got a hell of a lot to learn about the real use of power.

"Bossman," Eph had said, aloud, as Mr. W. stormed by him.

"What mad dog bit him?" asked Tom Coleman, the second entering coach, as the principal passed both men without speaking a word.

"I think it was a skunk not a dog," said Findlay, as he caught sight of Davey still lounged against the Coke machine.

"Hi, David," said Tom Coleman (hating the role his wife forced him to play as a Huntington non-hater).

"Hello, Tom," said Davey, watching the coach light up a cigarette. "See the noxious weed still beats you at its game."

"God, yes," laughed Coleman. "I spend all week cutting down until by Friday I maybe smoke three. Then Saturday and Sunday it's beer and cigarettes, and by Monday I'm back to a full pack again."

"Bettern' smokin' junk," said Findlay, pointedly. (He smoked neither.)

"Less illegal, anyway," said Davey, amiably.

"What'd you say to old Rog that sparked him off like that?" asked Tom, stretching his muscular frame into the contour of a shabby old donated reclining rocker.

"I implied that he and Imberlay took a chicken-shit attitude toward Ray Cosgrove," said Davey, not attempting to avoid a stare of either man.

"You sure got the fucking gall, Huntington," grumbled Findlay, dropping his 210 pounds onto a scarred old stuffed maroon colored davenport that groaned beneath his weight. "Or, is it just all that money that gives you strong balls?"

"Maybe you'd like to try me out sometime, Findlay," said Davey, softly, watching his stiletto prick anger from the football coach's ego.

"Hey, come off it, you two guys," laughed Tom Coleman, trying to peace make. "You'd think you two are on different sides."

"Oh, we are, Tom. We are," said Davey, emphatically. "You try to stand in the middle, Tom, so to you it looks like we both believe in a real education for kids. Findlay and I know better, though. Don't we, coach?" (The coach sounded like something lewd or unclean.)

"Hey, David, you sound like what's left of a bad weekend," kidded Coleman, trying hard to still the waters. "Own up to it. This little old school ain't so bad as you try to make it out to be, sometimes. Bet it's as good as Castleview, where you went to school."

"Yes, I suppose it's as good as Castleview was ten years ago," admitted Davey."I imagine it's like you said, Tom: 'not so bad.' That is, it's not so bad if we compare it to something like Lucy Jefferson's picture of a school in Studs Terkel's book: 'It's a disgrace to keep calling these places schools. I think the best thing we can say about them, these are meeting places where people get up every morning, give their children a dollar, seventy five cents, or whatever the heck they give 'em, and these kids go off. Schools you learn in. They could take a store front on Roosevelt Road or anywhere and clean it up, put some seats in there, and put some books in. But see, you can't learn anything where there is no books.' In my world, Tom, a certificate doesn't necessarily make a teacher and a school building doesn't teach much of its own accord except oppressiveness. Yeah, Timbertop ain't a bad little old school. Course, it ain't a very good one, either."

"Whyn't the hell don't you get out of it, then," snarled Eph, who had watched Davey through his soliloquy as a mongoose might stare at a cobra.

"Maybe I will, Findlay," laughed Davey, finishing his Coke and racking its bottle. "Then, again, maybe I won't."

He turned from the door to look back at Findlay's crimson face and Tom's big wondering eyes, then he laughed, deliberately, and let himself out through the door. Pausing just outside he smiled as Findlay's voice gained volume and an angry timbre. With ten minutes left in his planning period, he remembered little Elaine's plea for Heidi Vandercamp, and he considered going out to the home ec room.

Oh, hell, he told himself, it's nearly lunch time. Maybe I can catch her in the cafeteria.

Heidi failed to show for lunch in the cafeteria, and he learned from George Anderson (who had brought his sack lunch in search of Davey's advice about "Kit" Carson) that she ate in the home ec room with some of her girls and the occasional teacher who stopped in there with a sack lunch. George laid the Carson problem out in front of David, making no bones that blackness lay at the center of things.

"I know that shit, Carson," said David, in a low, guarded voice so students might not overhear. "My old man fired him for laziness, and he tried to burn down one of our outbuildings. The old man caught him at it; he got a warning from somebody, and spotting that lazy bastard almost fifty pounds, my white collared, accounting minded, forty five year old (at the time) father chewed this thirty year old slob into a hamburger face. Yeah, you don't have to tell me about Carson, George, no matter what color he came in he'd still smell like puke."

"How about Kit?" asked George, anxiously. "I know it's not very altruistic, but I need that kid in the game tomorrow night with his head screwed on right."

"Never apologize for objectivity, or try to hide it under sanctimony," said Davey, softly. "Of course you need that kid, and he damn well needs you and that game more than anything else in the world, at this time. You say he's going to talk to me

83

next period. I'll tell him you talked to me, and I took care of things. I'll arrange for him to stay with the Kelly family the rest of the week. No problem, George. Thanks for asking me to help."

God, what a Tiger, thought George, catching the wink Davey dropped him as he slowly made his way through the "Hi, Mr. Huntingtons" on his way to the dirty tray return. Wouldn't I like to be able to make a few phone calls and straighten some things out. Come to think of it, I've seen my old man do that more than once back home. More and more it seems like that's where I belong—working for him.

After the unhappiness experienced during her first period planning period, Heidi gradually regained her composure. Experience slowly taught her that students generally behaved better on Mondays than on other days of the week (most grew really bored and restless by Friday), and she used that knowledge to bolster her along with the excitement of Pat's dinner date offer and A.T.'s wonderful compliment. During second period she shared her sewing skills with her ninth grade girls, and her obvious enjoyment of the tasks they tackled together made the students feel good and eager to learn. Her first period sophomore girls fixed a lunch for invited guests, and the happiness there bubbled on through the lunch period. During fourth period an exciting discussion on family planning by her junior and senior girls carried her completely out of her plan book, but the near hour grew so stimulating she felt the deviance very worth the time spent.

Then, like an ugly creature let out of its hiding place, her bachelor living group of senior boys poured in for her fifth period trial. As usual, the three boys who caused her the most trouble with their lewd suggestions came into the classroom after the tardy bell quit ringing. She knew they deliberately did that to taunt her, for she saw them loitering near the door between fourth and fifth period class several times. Today, as it had been for weeks, she lacked the courage to order them back through the cold to get an admittance slip from the counselor. Before Christmas she did send one boy for a slip, and Mr. Patterson reminded her after school that the boy had a long trip from the woodshop to her classroom.

With a near heart in throat feeling, she took her place in front of the class while her aide, Elaine, busied herself marking the attendance in her grade book.

"This week we plan to study, discuss, and prepare menus for a single person that are both economic and nutritious," Heidi began.

As her eyes swept the classroom (utilizing techniques from Education 240), one of the naughty boys caught her eye on him and drooped one of his eyelids in a suggestive wink. Heidi felt a flush of blood flow at her neck, tried to stop it and ended in a full, furious blush.

"Do we get to cook a dinner for the girl of our choice?" another of the naughty boys called out, innocently.

"Next week we plan and make an intimate meal for two," Heidi stumbled on, and the small ripple of laughter near the rear of the class told her someone had made a slur of the word intimate.

"Please quiet down," she said, sharply, but the words carried little authority, even in her own ears.

"Now, today I have a slide film for you on nutrition, and you will each receive a chart of basic foodstuffs showing type, calorie content, and vitamin-mineral contributions from them," she felt her voice rising toward shrillness as the back row conversation continued in unabating competition with her word efforts.

"Gentlemen, please," she pleaded. "Could we please have it quiet so I can background you on this filmstrip."

"Couldn't we have one on sex instead, teacher," called one of the naughty boys, and a general laughter ensued.

"Sex comes up much later in the course," stammered Heidi, and realized she had made a monumental booboo as hilarity grew from almost every seat in the room.

"Quiet!" she heard herself shriek, and it shamed her. "Quiet! Do I have to send Elaine to get Mr. Longfellow?"

A sullen quiet descended slowly on the group. Her communication loss with them made bile rise from her stomach until her mouth and her throat felt fetid and sour. Stiffly Miss

Vandercamp moved to where the slide projector sat ready for operation. She realized the film strip needed her explanational background, but she lacked both the strength and the courage to face down her audience and try to deliver the needed words. As the lights dimmed and the record that accompanied the film strip started to play, she heard low hums of conversation start in little pockets around the classroom. She hated herself for throwing Longfellow (the Bogeyman, as they called him) at them, but what else could she do? After all she only weighed a bare 92 pounds.

# CHAPTER FOUR

Most Timbertop CHS students accepted sixth period each day as their agony hour. Had they enjoyed adult status in the community, a general strike would have long ago reduced the classroom day by about half—no intelligent adult could have withstood six hours of restrictive boredom day after day—week after week. That whole concept, in fact, gave impetus to the best educational theme Roger Wellington produced as an undergraduate at Western Pacific. In his paper he devised and created a totally fictitious school where students spent a half day with intellectual pursuits (in a comprehensive not a fragmented situation), and a half day at the school enjoying personal or social pursuits. His instructor (a young doctoral candidate) gave the paper an A rating, agreed voluably with Roger's concept, and urged him to put it into practice someday should he find himself in a position where he might do so. Though sold on his own idea way back then, our principal (who had long forgotten his 'leftish' effort) would today snort derisively at any effort to alter his instruction's status quo.

"We need to get back to basic 3 r's," Ray Cosgrove would roar.

"By God, but you're right, Ray, and that's just what I'm trying to do," promised our Roger.

His phone conversation of this morning with the truculent school director had left him hung somewhere on dilemenic horns. If he read Cosgrove's verbal bombast correctly, the director planned to scuttle the levy election anyway that he could. No concrete avowal to this end had been made; Ray offered inuendos, implications, and possibilities. One possibility had come through clear enough, however, Ray felt the inconvenience to Mr. Wellington and the district resulting from a levy failure at this time would turn strongly to Roger's personal advantage when the time came to recontract a superintendent.

As the school clock ticked on toward three-thirty, he took another tranquilizer while he tried to recall Fat Albert's jokes so he could share them tonight with the boys drinking beer at Eph's house. His phone conversation with Maddie had been stimulating, but much too short. Her husband had swing shift at The Castleview Plywood Friday night, so she would be free to play a bit—at least until two a.m.

In her office which lay left of the principal's complex, Pat Mooney, skin beaded with moisture and a mouth that tasted foul from her gassy stomach, listened with a practiced look of sympathy while sophomore, Debbie Fairweather, unfolded another story of misguided teen-age love.

"So I had this one joint with him," she said, her voice low and her eyes fixed on her own long white fingers entwined upon her lap. "I told him I never even smoked a cigarette before, but he told me it'd be alright—it would just make me feel good—and how could I say I loved him if I didn't even trust him in a little thing like that."

She paused to seek some kind of reassurance or criticism from Pat who merely nodded and smiled encouragement at the story's break. My God, I'd like to get out of here and roll a joint for myself, she thought, feeling a growing exhaustion from the electrical play of nervous energy that kept exploding against the extremities of her body.

"That was the first time and it did make me a little high though I didn't tell Arnie it made me a little sick, too," Debbie continued, eyes downcast again and voice in a monotone. "Then the next time I tried two with him, and the third time we rung in a six pack of beer some guy got for Arnie. Well, that's the time it happened—the, you know, and I ain't had a period since. My God! My ma will kill me if she finds out."

Debbie started to cry, softly. A husky girl with long hanks of corn colored hair framing a broad, white face with rather vacant, pale blue eyes, she seemed all at once (to Pat) to disassemble into a huge lump of white, pasty bread dough. Her tear ducts were open faucets; water flooded down each side of her nose.

"Go ahead, cry a bit, baby," encouraged Pat, handing the girl her ever ready box of school district paid for Kleenex. "Cry it out; you'll feel better."

88

"Won't change nothin', though," sobbed Debbie, mopping at her shapeless white face with a gobbed handful of tissues.

"No, but then the world hasn't come to an end, either," said Pat, sending out her opening hook.

"Easy for you to say," sobbed Debbie. "For me, it's ended."

"Only your little girl world, Debbie," philosophied Pat. "We all lose our little girl worlds at one time or another and in one way or another. Losing it's not so important; the important thing comes in how we handle our new life."

"I could get Arnie to help me find an abortionist," said Debbie, helplessly.

"I think you should tell your mother this afternoon," said Pat, firmly.

"Oh, no, Mrs. Mooney, I couldn't do that," sobbed Debbie, and a new flood of tears stained three more school tissues.

"Have you told Arnie yet?" asked Pat, setting her pincer movement in action.

"No, I'm scared to. He'll just call me stupid. He wanted to put on one of those rubber things, but I wouldn't let him," she blubbered.

"Why not, Debbie? You knew the chance you were taking," said Pat, having heard the answer to that one from a hundred other Debbies who preceded this one.

"It just didn't seem right, that's all," sobbed Debbie. "Like cheating—like being mechanical about something so beautiful as our love. Oh, really, Mrs. Mooney, I do want to have Arnie's baby."

"How will Arnie feel about that when you tell him?" asked Pat, and she pulled her big guns into position for the final assault.

"I don't think he likes babies," Debbie sobbed, softly and without tears, now. "He planned to go on to college after he graduates in June. I don't think he'd be very happy about having to put up with a family right now."

"And what about you?" asked Pat, setting the firing pin ready to go. "You've got two more years of high school after this year. Parties—ball games—fun with your girl friends; maybe other boy friends, who knows."

"I could never love anyone but Arnie!" wailed Debbie.

Oh, shit, you're so pitiful, Pat moaned inside of herself. We are all, all of us, so pitiful. Silly stupid little girl with your mixed up emotions and your unreal movie-colored view of the world. How in hell am I going to get you a clean honest abortion? That's the real world we both face sitting here.

"Well," she said aloud, "Arnie is an attractive young man, but things do happen in our lives, you know."

"I could never give my body to another man after having made love to Arnie," said Debbie, stubbornly and without tears.

"Perhaps," said Pat, softly, letting off her first big salvo, "I'm a woman, too, you know, and I had the same thought about the first boy with whom I experienced sex."

"And there were others?" Debbie reformed magically from a shapeless dough creature into a sharp featured girl about to share a fabulous secret.

"Why, yes, quite a number, in fact," chuckled Pat (if I carry this act though this late in this day, she thought, I deserve at least two academy awards). "Do I look like I might not be attractive to men?"

"Gee, no, Mrs. Mooney," breathed Debbie, now stareyed and breathing a bit more rapidly than normal. "You look real nice, I think, for an older lady." (Pat winced but kept smiling at that one.) "And did you—did you ever get into my kind of trouble?"

"Sure. A girl can't be bright all the time," lied Pat, lightly (she learned early in her marriage to Fred that she could never expect to have children). "Haven't any of your other friends had the same trouble?"

"Not that I know about, but I heard some of the older girls did," said Debbie. "What did you do about yours?"

"Talked it out with my mother and had it taken care of by a good doctor," said Pat, matter of factly.

"Oh, no, my mother will kill me," groaned Debbie, but the agony this time was more staged than real.

"Would you like me to tell her for you?" asked Pat, firing off her final gun.

"Could you—I mean—could you just be there and I'll tell her," pleaded Debbie.

"You bet I can," assured Pat, letting her own broad, long fingered hand with its telltale liver spots come down lightly on the girl's head which now stretched across the desk toward her. "Why don't you come in after school and I can leave by four. We'll go to your house in my car and have that talk with your mother."

"Oh, gosh, Mrs. Mooney, you must be the most wonderfulest person I've ever known," said Debbie, in a full rush of fifteen year old emotion.

You see, Mr. W., Pat said to herself as the now completely re-generated girl sailed back to her sixth period class, like I keep trying to tell you and Longfellow, man, I did learn some things from the Purcell fiasco.

At 3:55 Mr. W. saw Pat Mooney leave with the Fairweather girl. He made a mental note to jog her about leaving before four p.m., then thought, more angrily, "I hope she's not going to get us into a mess with this one like she did with the Purcell girl." He watched her little blue Maverick slip out of the faculty parking lot, then continued his vigilance on the other teacher's cars parked in the lot from his vantage spot in the empty second story chemistry lab. At four he had to leave and join Longfellow for their meeting with Ed Kallifonte, but in the meantime his teachers knew that any early exit effort by them would go down in the principal's green record book.

From his eagle aerie he could also see the two shops and the home ec building. Now, to his surprise and somewhat murky speculation, he saw Davey Huntington come out of the main building and walk to the home ec door with the little blonde Perry girl. Maybe, he mused, there may be something to that rumor about them after all. You really couldn't tell about those rich kids; they developed all kinds of kinks in their sex.

Visting Heidi Vandercamp after school was the farthest thing from Davey Huntington's mind as he wound down his classroom day helping a half dozen students who dropped by for after hour's help. About ten before four the last struggling U.S. History student departed, and a surprised Huntington saw Elaine Perry waiting patiently in a desk chair at the back of his room. As he got up from his desk, she rose from hers and came to the front to stand with the desk between them.

"I think we should go out and see Miss Vandercamp, now," she said, quietly, and he seemed to hear his mother's voice as she quietly gave him instructions.

"Maybe she won't want to see us," he said, defensively.

"She needs your help," said Elaine's final word on the matter.

So it was this condition that existed, not an amorous one, as Mr. W. watched the home ec door close behind the Perry girl and Huntington. Had Davey thought about it—had he been less concerned about the unknown confrontation that lay ahead, he would have paused at the doorway, stared up at the blank dark windows of the chem lab, and saluted the unseen figure there with the middle finger of his right hand.

"I've brought Mr. Huntington to see you about those awful fifth period senior boys," said Elaine, without ceremony, as she led Davey directly to a sewing machine where Heidi sat doing a demonstration for three Freshmen girls.

The four sew-involved females looked up at the male who had invaded their warm feminine nest. Individually, and as a group, using the word "cool" or whatever their particular bent, they agreed in kind that: 'goodness, he's a mighty good looking fellow.'

"This is Elaine's idea," said Davey, softly. "I hope we haven't upset you, Miss Vandercamp."

"Oh, no," said Heidi in a rush, the soft blush rising in her fine featured cameo face like a poet's tribute to a special pink rose.

What do I say to him? thought Heidi, desperately. Should I ask him to sit down? Have a glass of lemonade from the frig? Offer him some of the student's cookies? Throw myself into his arms and cry?

"Elaine tells me you've had problems with some of our senior boys," said Davey, quietly. "Somehow she seems to think I can be of help to you."

"Well, I. . ." Heidi's tiny hand flew involuntarily to her slender throat. She rose from the sewing machine bench and felt her knees tremble as they had earlier that day in Mr. W.'s office. "I—maybe we'd. . .better go back in the corner and talk. I—I don't know whether other students should hear this, or not."

"Whatever you say, Miss Vandercamp," said Davey. "I personally believe in letting everything hang out when you've got something to say, but I guess there must be some good arguments for secrecy, too."

"No—well, that is. . .I don't mind talking in front of the others if you don't mind," said Heidi, her voice faltering away almost to a whisper.

"Tell you what," said Davey, lightly, finding her delightful in her fresh almost unbelievable naivety, "why don't we compromise and go sit at your desk. That way if these pretty ladies want to eavesdrop, they can, and if they don't, our talking won't disturb them." ('Pretty ladies' got some happy giggles from the three ninth grade girls and a look of approval from Elaine Perry.)

"Well, it's like this, Mr. Huntington," Heidi began when she got perched on her chair behind the big blue and pink metal desk with Davy on a chair placed for students beside her desk. (Elaine discreetly moved to the sewing machines and started helping the novices do their work with the needle.)

"Call me David—or Davey—or Dave—or whatever," laughed Davey.

"Alright, David, then you must call me Heidi," she said, in a burst of social courage.

"Tell me about the naughty boys, Heidi," said Davey, seriously.

"I'm sure they don't mean anything bad," confessed Heidi. "It's my fault because I didn't stop them when they first came tardy and when they first started making those cracks to me."

"That's not quite true," said Davey, "though your educational textbooks probably told you that. Many young people today question authority today just because it's authority. They equate authority with evil, the evils inherent in conflicts like Vietnam; the evil of price gouging that we continue to experience from government protected big businesses; the evils of political filth we constantly expose in Washington, D.C. and other seats of government—evils their parents seem to accept as a matter of life. They feel their parents gave up a birthright of true freedom to become sheep trusting themselves to crooked shepherds as long as those shepherds continue to see that the sheep get fed. They resent an outpour of legislation and laws from people who announce that people are too stupid to run their own lives, even know what their life is all about. And they ask themselves: 'What justification do stupid people making laws have to tell stupid people like us how to live our lives.' These boys who have challenged you—they're not really challenging you, they're challenging your position as a symbol of authority."

Heidi heard him speak and understood the words up and through the "educational textbook" part, then she lost herself in a wonderment she experienced from the sound of his voice; his words simply flowed over and around her like magical warm incantations. In all her secret daydreams, and many involved vague, unrealized young male figures during these past two or three years, she had never envisioned anyone as fantastically wonderful as David Huntington, III. Don't ever stop talking, or looking at me like that, she thought, now, as her own eyes clung steadily to the moving tip of his golden haired Van Dyke beard.

She's a Dresden doll, Davey thought, as he carefully laid out his philosophy on youth versus adult authority. So tiny, so petite, I guess I've never seen her as a real human being because she seems so unreal. Yet, she walks, talks, looks warm when she blushes, and has the most heavenly blue eyes I've seen in my entire lifetime. Wonder who her boyfriend is? Some straight arrow, I'll damn well bet on that.

"Did I confuse you?" he asked, as silence continued to hang between them.

"I'm afraid I'm not very intellectual," said Heidi, a note of sadness in her voice.

"Hey, don't knock being that way," laughed Davey. "I'm too much the intellectual, and it doesn't win you any friends in our business, believe me."

"About the boys," said Heidi, with her penchant for details, "I'm having dinner tonight with Mrs. Mooney, and I hope she can give me some answers."

"Tell you what," said Davey, "let me think on this thing a bit, too. If you'll have dinner with me tomorrow night, I may have some answers for you."

Had a bomb exploded beneath her chair, Heidi would not have felt a greater pressure grab her than she felt from Davey's dinner invitation. She tried to fight her way through the tongue tying maze of emotions that gripped her, but it proved an impossibility—she sat, speechless.

"I'm sorry," said Davey. "I've embarrassed you by moving too fast. You probably have a date with a boyfriend, or something planned with someone else. Say it like it is. I meant it when I said I believe in letting the truth of a thing hang out for everybody to see."

"The truth is," said Heidi, laborously. "I'd love to have dinner with you."

"How are you on Japanese stuff?" asked Davey.

"Sounds fine," said Heidi, numbly—or a hamburger or a tuna fish sandwich.

"Great," enthused Davey. "I picked up some good recipes when I was in Japan. I'll pick you up about seven."

"Sounds fine," Heidi repeated herself.

"See you tomorrow, then," he said, his smile flashed a rush of warm clinging honey that brought blood to her neck and cheeks and goosebumps to her arms and legs.

"Tomorrow," she echoed tonelessly.

There's a lot more to that girl than meets the eye, thought Davey, walking carefully to where Elaine leaned over one of the Freshman girl's shoulder coaching that novice in the arts of a Bernina.

"Come on, Blondie," he said (bringing a titter from the ninth graders) "I'll give you a lift home in my hot car, and we can start another rumor for the Ladies Literary Guild."

"Everything going to be alright with Miss Vandercamp?" asked Elaine, smiling and waving her goodbye to Heidi.

"Everything's going to be alright with Miss Vandercamp," assured Davey, adding his smile and goodbye wave to the parting.

It had been a half hour of revelation and warm communication for Miss Vandercamp and Mr. Huntington, but it had been a half hour of teeth grinding and stonewalling in the encounter between Wellington-Longfellow and Mr. Kallifonte who had awaited the principal by Mrs. Metzger's desk. He preceded the two tightlipped men through his big black walnut door, and he dropped heavily into his padded black leather swivel chair as though totally exhausted by the day's trying moments of decision. Longfellow and Kalifonte pulled hard, straightbacked wooden chairs to the two extreme corners of Mr. W.'s broad shiny desk. Now the three men made a triangle, but one in which only Mr. W. could see two other points of the isosceles at the same time.

"I want my kid back in school," said Kallifonte, without preliminary. "Not next Monday, like your letter says, but tomorrow at 8:30 a.m."

"We can't make special rules for your boy, Mr. Kallifonte," said Longfellow, pendantically, and by drawing Kallifonte's attention to himself he left Mr. W. in the position of benign observer. "He knew the penalty for skipping school. After all, this is not the first time."

"The boy's got problems," argued Kallifonte. "He don't do too good with class work as it is. How's he gonna learn anything if he can't come to classes?"

"He'll learn, hopefully, that he can't break rules at his own convenience," said Longfellow, Mr. W.'s slumped chair position signalled he was to continue carrying the ball.

"Look, you think that kid cares that he comes here?" persisted Kallifonte. "He's got his rinky dink buddies that hangs around the bowling alley. You think he feels bad that you kick him out of school? I'm the one, Mr. Longfellow, me and his mother; we want him in the school."

"Then why don't you forbid him the bowling alley?" challenged Longfellow, and he caustically exhibited his superior reasoning to this calloused handed man of minor educational accomplishments. "Maybe he won't be so happy about being kicked out of school, then."

96

"Forbid him?" cried Kallifonte, raising those calloused hands as if in a plea to heaven. "He's seventeen years old, a foot taller and twenty pounds heavier than me. Forbid him? Why don't you make this school more interesting to him than the bowling alley is? He should want to go here, not have to go."

"We can't tailor our school to fit five hundred and forty seven different students, Mr. Kallifonte," said Longfellow (acid dripping from each word, now). "The law says you are responsible to see your son stays in school—not us."

Kallifonte's face hue changed from bronze to red to a deep shade of purple as Longfellow drove in one telling spike after another. He sputtered, pounded the desk top with his hard, clenched fist, then stared at Mr. W., his last court of appeals. It was time for God to come forth and mitigate human strife.

"I think Ed's got a point here, Mr. Longfellow," said Mr. W., rising slowly in his seat until he seemed to tower above the other two men. (His chair sat on a four inch high platform, another of A.T.'s innovations.) "Brad seems to have some real problems with his school work, and he very probably should be here for semester tests this Wednesday, Thursday, and Friday. Tell you what, Mr. Longfellow, if it's not going to cause you too many problems, I suggest we let Brad have a kind of a probation in this thing. You know, suspend three days of his punishment for good behavior, or that kind of thing."

Now the drama spotlight switched to Mr. Longefllow. He let his presence be felt very much by Mr. Kallifonte. The making or breaking of a school administrator seemed to be riding on this great decision Mr. Longfellow pondered. Actually, earlier in the day he and Mr. W. had discussed the case and agreed that a partial victory for Mr. Kallifonte might mean two yes votes at election time. This conversation preceded Mr. W.'s phone call from Ray Cosgrove, but Mr. W. decided, anyway, not to reverse their earlier decision. He could not divulge his new suspicions about Cosgrove's antipathy to the levy to Mr. Longfellow. He could not, in fact, entrust the matter to his wife, A.T., or even his close confidant, Eph Findlay.

"That sounds fair and in keeping with good school practices," Mr. Longfellow announced, at last.

"Thank you, Mr. Wellington. Thank you, gentlemen. My wife thanks you, too," bubbled Mr. Kallifonte, tasting the triumph he would enjoy when he brought news of his victory home to "the little woman."

"Glad to do it, Ed," said Mr. W., towering now above the big black walnut desk (a signal to these lesser mortals that the great ones must ever rush along to solve another crisis, someplace). "Mr. Longfellow will show you out. And, don't forget, Ed, we'll be needing a little help from you come levy election time."

It was five fifteen before Mr. W. finally got to his car in the faculty lot. Besides his own battered cream colored Pinto, only Eph Findlay's big new black Ford pickup and George Anderson's much dented old rig remained in the faculty lot. Well, that was what coaching was all about—long hours, low pay, and a bunch of shit from those who knew your job better than you did because they had never done it.

George Anderson, too, noted the time of day at five fifteen as he glanced toward the gym's big wall clock with its hands timed exactly to Mr. W.'s gold plated Sieko. On the other court Eph slowly wrapped up his JV practice, but the varsity would pound on until six, maybe even a little later.

George felt particularly good about Kit Carson, for the boy seemed to have suddenly found himself and tonight showed real varsity savvy and capabilities for the first time this season.

"Should'a fought with your old man a long time ago," kidded George, as the red headed junior guard faked the man checking him practically out of his shoes, drew the second string center on him with a quick penetrating dribble and a vertical leap as if to shoot. As the defensive man made his move on Kit, the boy passed neatly to varsity center, Hunk Anderson, and that six ten behemoth dropped the ball easily through the hoop.

"That's no kiddin', Coach," said Kit, returning to his place on the offensive point, and the smile on his sweat covered face could have lighted a ten room house.

Eph's whistle blew his team to the showers, and a new excitement gripped the varsity boys—it was time for full court scrimmage.

"Okay, men, let's get with it," said George, and he handed his whistle to the second string center. At the jump ball circle, George faced Hunk Anderson in a tip off. The scrimmage would rocket from one basket to the other for a grueling half hour without pause. To the boys it consisted of an all out effort that left them exhausted but with a sense of well being; to George it consisted of a half physical effort affair in which he held the second team group together in a jug zone simulating what the varsity would experience from Chehalis tomorrow night, called out constant messages of approval or correction for certain varsity player action, and used the power of his own scoring presence to force his own three big men to double and triple team him with their shifting man-to-man defense.

When George's pickup (last car of the day—wrestling coach, Tom Coleman, rode to school with Eph each day) pulled out of the faculty lot, it was past six thirty and A.T. Cromwell had already started walking from his home to the North Elementary School. The domain there was not strictly speaking his immediate responsibility, but as the district's senior custodian he felt impelled to make sure everything there sat in proper readiness for tonight's PTA meeting. At George's house, Madge held dinner on the stove for the quick dash through her husband would make between his high school basketball practice and his town team basketball game (she fixed pot roast, potatoes, and carrots with a lime jello salad chilled in the frig). Mr. W., too, involved himself in dinner—waffles and ham for which he congratulated his daughter, Betty, profusely. Lisa Overstreet took her dinner at Bingo's Restaurant with two friends of hers from the Literary Guild who would later drive her to the PTA meeting, and Davey Overstreet restricted his dinner to a bowl of green seedless grapes and a plate of diced sharp cheddar Tillamook Cheese which he ate while he worked on his doctoral thesis spread out on a big glass topped desk in his apartment. In Pat Mooney's apartment, Heidi's coat had been stored in the bedroom and the two women were carefully getting acquainted with each other.

"And I don't know why I didn't think about asking you to dinner months ago," Pat gushed along. "We're all—all of us—so bound up in our own little day to day worlds we tend to treat everyone around us as if they were aliens. Don't you agree?"

"Yes. Oh, yes," said Heidi, who had said, in her half hour here, little else beside yes or no.

"But we'll make that different between you and me beginning right tonight," Pat bubbled on. "We'll just be the best of friends, and we can do things together—and we can help and comfort each other. You did say you had a problem to discuss with me. Right?"

"Yes," said Heidi. "About my fifth period class."

"Oh, heck, I'd hoped it would be more personal," pouted Pat, playfully. "You know, a sort of girl to girl kind of thing—not some old on the job dull thing."

"It's a problem," began Heidi.

"Of course it's a problem. You wouldn't have said it's a problem if it wasn't a problem," rambled Pat (she had snorted just before Heidi arrived and for the past ten minutes her rush held her charged with excitement). "After all you're an educated professional woman and I'm an educated professional woman, and we do have educated professional problems."

"Well, I thought maybe you might give me some advice," began Heidi, cautiously.

"Of course I'll give you advice," laughed Pat, gaily. "After all, that's what counselors are all about, isn't it? Advice. I spend the whole day handing out advice for better living—except, of course (he he) when I'm making out admit to class slips."

"This has to do with some senior boys," Heidi tried, again.

"Watch out for those senior boys," said Pat, merrily. "Those beautiful young bodies—those strong young hands and arms—those unbridled young sex urges (he he)—of course, I'm only kidding about that."

"These three boys keep giving me a bad time," Heidi pressed on.

100

"Well, give the little bastards a bad time right back," rambled Pat, gesturing as if to toss those senior boys around. "After all, you're the teacher and they're the students—let them damn well behave their little selves or get the hell out of your classroom. I've met some of those smart mouthed little boys with their grubby minds and their grubby hands. Some of them aren't that young anymore, either, been out of school for as long as twenty years. They're grubby—all of them. Grubby, grubby, grubby!"

"I don't think they really mean to be naughty," said Heidi, desperately.

"Naughty? It's good to be naughty once in awhile," chattered Pat. "Take that from a professional lady counselor. Be naughty, once in awhile. Good for the liver; good for the soul; and particularly good for the spirit. When was the last time you were naughty, Heidi?"

"Well—I—" she blushed, furiously, wondering if her thoughts about Davey Huntington should be confessed on Sunday.

"You see, you need some naughtiness right now, that's what you need," said Pat, reeling a bit as she lurched up abruptly from her seat at one end of her davenport. "Would you like a little cola?"

"Well, yes," said Heidi who didn't generally drink soda pop because her mother worried about tooth decay (but who could also make adjustments when she felt that the circumstances warranted it).

"Good," said Pat, and she made for the bedroom where Heidi's coat lay.

What a funny place to keep soda pop, thought Heidi, looking around for the first real inspection of Mrs. Mooney's three room apartment. The nine by twelve rugged rectangle where they sat conversing on a big overstuffed sofa joined a short stretch of vinyl where Pat's compact kitchen lay half with and half without a room divider. The room seemed austere, lonely, a bit sad to Heidi whose own very similar apartment glowed with the warmth of a hundred Heidi made knick knacks.

"Here we go," called Pat, who came back into the room carrying a small bottle that seemed to contain white crystals and a mirror on which rested a razor blade.

"What's that?" asked Heidi, in amazement.

"Cola," laughed Pat, excitedly. "Coke, cocaine, you know, baby, a snow storm full of good feelings. We're going to be naughty tonight."

"It's against the law!" cried Heidi, jumping to her feet, horrified.

"So's driving over 55," laughed Pat.

"We could lose our teaching certificates," cried Heidi.

"Or go to jail," laughed Pat.

Like a humming bird headed for home, Heidi darted past the housecoated Pat who watched the speedy exodus dumbfounded. She still stood, mirror in left hand and bottle in right as Heidi burst from the bedroom struggling with her coat. She tried to say something, anything to halt the exploding moment, but words slipped through her mind as if coated with oil. With the slam of a door the little home ec teacher was gone. Pat moved to the kitchen table, sat her treasures on its polished surface, and tried to feel anger about the dinner in the oven that would not get eaten tonight.

"You're alone, girl," she said, to her image in the mirror. "You came into the world naked and alone, and you'll go out of the world the same way. Better make the best of this nightmare you live in, maybe someday you'll awaken to something that's a hell of a lot better."

During her wild, half blinded terrorized five block dash to her own apartment, Heidi slid and stumbled twice on icy patches that showed up as nothing but darkened places along the dimly lit city street. In her second slip she nearly hit the ground, and it was this second near catastrophe that Lisa Overstreet, riding to PTA with her best buddies from the Literary Guild, Cecil Asbrenner and Mavis Trenchard, witnessed from her usual place on the front rider's seat in Cecil's big Olds 98. (Lisa gave up her own car five years ago when, after four minor accidents in as many months, her insurance company cancelled her out. Though she complained

102

about the cost of cab fare to work every morning, she shrewdly knew it amounted to far less than her insurance would have cost her let alone the price of owning and keeping up an automobile. After school provided her no transportation problem because one of her friends waited on her as is the wont of all special royalty.)

"There's that Vandercamp girl out on the prowl," said Lisa, triumphantly, as Heidi righted herself on the black ice at the last perilous moment. "Looks like she's been drinking this time. Did you girls see the way she's staggering?"

"Disgraceful," snorted Cecil Ashrenner.

"It's time something was done about that little snip," vowed Mavis Trenchard.

"It will be done, girls. It will be done," Lisa promised, grimly. "Right after the levy election we'll take this whole matter to the school board right over the superintendent's head."

"How do we ever get such disgraceful teachers?" asked Cecil, querously.

"Men make the choice; that's why," snarled Mavis.

"It's a wonder a decent woman ever gets hired," said Lisa, sucking in her lips as if suffering some deeply felt pain. "Well, we know how Pat Mooney got her job here, and I wouldn't wonder if Vandercamp didn't pull the same kind of shenanigan."

"It must hurt you terribly, Lisa, to see our children exposed to these kind of creatures, and you so dedicated yourself," said Cecil, sympathetically.

"Oh, I've had some nightmares about it, you can bet," sighed Lisa,"but I don't expect any help from Mr. Wellington when it comes to censoring bad teachers."

It was ten after seven and Mr. Wellington arrived twenty minutes before the PTA meeting's scheduled beginning time. (He found that being early gave him a chance to hang in back of the room, converse with people who sought him out, and spot his teachers in attendance without the need of rubbernecking.)

Tonight it surprised him to find a very nervous Dr. Imberlay in early attendance, and the two men exchanged pleasantries, were joined by A.T. who brought more banal remarks about the weather and such, then finally all three came under the powerful personality of perennial PTA President, Velma Overholt.

"Well, Dr. Imberlay, you can just bet I've got my girls organized for phone committees, coffee clatches, putting up posters, and getting people rides to the polls on election day," vowed Velma, beaming on Imberlay who she considered a great educator and ignoring Wellington, as obviously as possible, for she classified him as nothing more than an athletic bum.

"You are a wonder woman, Mrs. Overholt," said Dr. Imberlay. "No one will have contributed more to our success in this levy matter than you will, of that I'm sure."

"No need for flattery, Dr. Imberlay," said Velma, coyly. "I consider it all part of my civic duty. Could I take you away for a moment, Dr., I don't believe you've met Mrs. Penington from our Mountainview Elementary PTA group."

So Imberlay sailed off under the captaincy of Velma Overholt, and A.T. grinned and shrugged his shoulders at Roger. His bibbers had been replaced by a khaki shirt, regulation thin black tie, and khaki pants. On his feet brown GI issue shoes shone with a mirrorlike sheen. His big fur parka hung down in the furnace room where he had, earlier, run over a checklist with the South Elementary custodian.

"Sometimes I wonder if it's worth the price," Roger murmured, aloud, as he watched Imberlay bob his head to Penington and another small group of women.

"Gonna be interesting to hear what young Lane says about the levy," said A.T., changing his tact as the dark, slender intense young A.S.B. President made his entrance with four other senior students.

"They're just kids," said Mr. W., bored. "Just more fun and games, A.T. It don't mean shit in the end."

"They ain't kids long at this age," said A.T., slowly, "the Perry girl's already a registered voter—turned 18 before Christmas."

"So they turn 18 and maybe they vote once or more likely they don't vote at all," said Wellington. "I've played student council games for sixteen years—I know how little these kids ever follow through on anything."

"Times are changing, Mr. W.," said A.T., softly. "Look out for boys like Billy Lane, they might have something to show us all. I went to school with Billy's old man, and he was one guy who wouldn't back down from a chargin' bull."

"Well, he's a two bit newspaperman now," said Wellington, disdainfully. "He can't even handle John Barleycorn let alone a tame heifer."

The two men spoke about Kevin Lane who worked for the Castleview *Daily News* as a combination reporter and circulation manager. Once, it was rumored, Kevin worked for some big paper back East at the end of World War II. Something happened there to send him crawling back to Timbertop and the deep six of a whiskey bottle. Married in 1949 to Agnes Perry, Elaine's aunt, he fathered one child, Billy, who worshipped him as the father adored the son.

By the time he was ten years old Billy Lane knew his father was an alcoholic. He knew it because his father told him so. His father also told him, in graphic terms, about the real world that lay outside the Eden of Timbertop like a gigantic jungle full of self seeking and power seeking human animals who smiled at your face while their talons ripped the testicles from your sack. For long hours, in the Lane kitchen or out fishing on the river in Kevin Lane's old kicker boat, father and son explored philosophy, psychology, sociology, literature and economics at a level far above the pitiful pontifications of the average American college undergraduate student. By age twelve, though he got top marks, school bored Billy to tears. By age fourteen he decided the ninth grade would be his final year, and with the blessings of his father on this idea he grimly counted off what he figured would be his last 180 days in the academic prison.

Then a magical thing happened to him in late August of that year as, with no thoughts to plague him about returning to classes after Labor Day, he swam lazily out to a float anchored in Lake Merwin and crawled up on its deck where he stretched out in the sun by the golden skinned figure of David Huntington. Though the two had never met before, Billy found himself, with amazement, unfolding the difficulties of his life to this young man who introduced himself as a new social studies teacher at Timbertop High School. They spent two hours in the 85 degree sunlight exploring each other's minds as they might pick shreds of meat from a walnut. For the first time Billy found tenets he believed inviolate ripped into shreds by a logic far superior even to that he worshipped in his dad. The two young men met again, this time by design, at Davey's new condominium apartment in Timbertop. From that day on, with his father's blessing, Billy placed his life's direction in edicts of Davey Huntington.

Back in school as a sophomore, though still bored with all but Huntington's Sociology class, Billy dug into things instead of letting them passively roll around him. He challenged the most popular girl in his class for the position of class president, and he emerged as a solid victor. That year too, even as a first timer, he captained the debate team and won a number of forensic trophies. His junior year proved a personal triumph, too, for he won regional awards in debate and national awards in forensics. In a most unusual student election he stepped outside the hackneyed traditional type of poster campaign and party platform to promise himself as a gadfly in the side of the school administration.

"I'm going to make it in politics," he announced to Davey when he got more votes as student vice president than the two opposing student president candidates polled together. "I'll tackle law school, that seems to be the easiest way to get youself there."

"The hell with law school," said Davey, flat voiced with a strong taste of dislike. "We've got too damn many lawyers screwing up the government now. Be another Tip O'Neil or Peter Rodino. Be a man who respects the law instead of one who is constantly using it to his own advantage. Start out right here in Timbertop as soon as you're 18 years old. Run for school director or city council member—learn by experience. Hell, you're an organizer, and nobody really campaigns for those thankless offices. Get yourself elected then move into the political party of your choice bringing your own power with you. Never forget, Billy, the game winner is one who best knows how to use power, not necessarily the one who seems to hold the most power. Learn politics from the ground up—and the ground is the people your power controls."

Billy listened, and he decided to do things Davey's way. Not that he always agreed with David; not the he always followed his direction. Tonight, for example, the speech he planned to give in support of the levy did not meet with Huntington's approval.

"You're talking over people's heads, Billy," admonished Davey, as he read the text placed before him on his desk. "People don't act according to their heads; they act according to their guts. Junk all that talk about professional expertise and sound more modern educational practices. People don't care what children learn in school—they care about what children do in school. Remember your own mother when you were little—yes, maybe even your dad. Did they ask: 'Billy, what did you learn in school today?' Of course not. They asked: 'Billy, what did you do in school today.' When you get up there tonight pound the podium and threaten to take away their kindergarten; take away their athletic teams and their band and choral groups. Warn them that a part time school means more baby sitting time at home for mother. Scare the hell out of them with the unknown evils that will catch up with children with too much time on their hands. You sure as hell won't reason them out to vote."

And there, in front of him, as he rose after a flowery introduction by Mrs. Overholt, he saw the truths he denied from his mentor by not changing his script. As he pointed out the need to follow professional leadership in the matter of needed finances for the budget year ahead, as he talked to them of the possibility of overcrowded classrooms where individual help could not reach student need, as he pointed out the need to have adequate books and supplies and he enumerated point after point for the levy's necessity, he saw his audience sink slowly into the apathy of boredom, watched them turn him off until he realized he'd even lost the superintendent, and he felt empathy for the aching asses the folding tin chairs generated.

And these are the good guys, he thought, sardonically, how in hell will we ever motivate the other 90%?

As Billy Lane finished his talk to a mild spatter of relieved applause, A.T. craned his neck around the room searching for Heidi Vandercamp. Through the opening flag salute, the pastor's blessing upon the meeting, and the droning of the secretary's minutes, he had kept his eye on the door. After Billy got introduced and started his pitch, A.T. relaxed his vigil, but concern for the little home ec teacher still troubled his mind. That something very unpleasant had happened to her in Mr. W.'s office this morning he knew without being told that it had. He had seen her tears when they met in the hallway, and he had tried, with his quick compliment, to give her a little good cheer. Now he felt concern because she never failed to make the PTA meeting, and he knew from her constant punctuality and the neat care she gave her classroom that, like him, she was a person who generally followed a pretty constant routine.

Pat Mooney's missing, too, he thought, and she usually comes to these things. Maybe the two of them got together; they both certainly need somebody to hold hands with at this time in their lives. It'll be wonderful if they did, but I hope Pat doesn't try any of her coke on that little girl. Not that I think there's much wrong with coke, some of the best guys in my outfit snorted it, but the thought of something as far out as that would scare the pants off the little Dutch girl. Poor old Pat; she goes on thinking nobody knows her secret. Well, I just damn well hope she never gets caught up on the thing.

Mr. W., too, had wondered briefly why Miss Vandercamp and Mrs. Mooney failed to show. Both women were most popular with mothers of girls in the district, and they generally received more attention at the meeting than the principal did. He missed them, mostly, because they were two of the six to eight he could generally count on to represent his building here. Even Longfellow, who refused to accept Mr. W.'s viewpoint on the importance of PTA appearance, limited his meeting night to the first one of the year where faculty members were introduced. Two rows in front of him, and off to his left, sat one ever faithful PTA attendant he could do without—Lisa Overstreet. As he watched her, covertly, he saw her suck her lips in and out as if suffering some deep pain while she nodded to whispers directed to her ears by one of the old girls who sat on either side of her—presumably the whispers contained some comments on the text of young Lane's levy speech. Agnes Merriweather sat near Lisa, too, as did Nola Davenport and Patricia Armbruster. They made his total faculty contribution for the evening, four old single women and not one man. In contrast a number of both men and women teachers represented the elementary faculties here tonight. They, of course, would find here parents of children in their classes, something a high school teacher could expect but upon rare occasion. Mr. W. failed to locate Ray Cosgrove who usually made these meetings, and he wondered, uncomfortably what the school director might be doing or thinking at this time that would undermine the levy effort.

"So it will take each of us bringing a voting friend to the poll on election day if we are to succeed," concluded Billy Lane. "As you did when you were a student—give your all for your old alma mater—this time do it with your vote."

The kid sure doesn't have much enthusiasm in his voice for somebody who's supposed to be a hot shot speaker, thought Mr. W., as he clapped politely. Well, it's bullshit bringing kids into this thing, anyway. What do they know about education?

"And now we'll hear from our own Dr. Imberlay," announced Velma, triumphantly.

"Let me thank this young man, and all young people, for their continued support in this major educational crisis we face," began Dr. Imberlay.

As he swung into statistics and figures needed to give the district a sound program, most of the audience began to shift, uncomfortably, in their tin seats. A.T. concluded that Miss Vandercamp and Mrs. Mooney had, indeed, managed to hit it off somewhere, and he wished them both well. He wished, not objectively but wistfully, that his youngest boy, Tom, were not married. He'd like to get him together with Miss Vandercamp. Oh, he thought, almost guiltily, there ain't nothing wrong with Tom's Ruthie. It's just, well, there's something kind of special, something a little classy, about a girl what's got an education.

109

Lisa Overstreet, an educated girl, looked at Imberlay and thought to himself: "Just another man pushing his damn authoritative weight around." She felt herself start to doze off—pulled her bulk upright on the metal squawking chair.

"Poor Lisa," whispered Cecil. "Does it hurt too bad?"

"I'll make it though," Lisa whispered back. "I know my duty."

Go ahead and have your little play, thought Mr. W., finding Imberlay more and more feminine as the superintendent gesticulated to his lecture points with soft, floppy white hands. If they had hired me, as they should have, this levy would pass like a breeze.

Look at them, Billy Lane told himself, as he studied the vacant faces and twitching bodies around him, and remember, always, the things Davey Huntington taught to you. From now on you play politics on the gut string and keep your intellectual gymnastics for forensics and formal debate.

The superintendent finished with his charts and his visual aids to a light applause equal to that accorded Billy Lane. Velma Overholt offered to excuse any non-voting members who didn't want to stay for room count, PTA voting business and cookie and coffee time afterwards. She announced a five minute break in the schedule, and the much relieved asses got a chance to stretch relief for their growing aches.

"Better catch young Lane before he gets away and tell him how much you enjoyed his talk," A.T. suggested, quickly, to Mr. W.

"What the hell for," shushed Mr. W., almost a little angrily with his old friend. "He's just another kid and he don't talk all that great."

"He wins elections for himself, though," A.T. continued, in a hushed monotone. "And I understand he plans to take on Bill Murchim for his spot this fall. Murchim, if you remember, don't get too much backing, unopposed."

Thus it was that a very surprised Billy Lane got some effusive compliments from Mr. Wellington, a man who had never spoken to him before, nor who had, to Billy's remembrance, even bothered to acknowledge that young Lane was alive.

110

"Thank you, Mr. Wellington," he said, playing the game very well, himself, "All of us students want to help in any way that we can."

On that note Billy and the other students left the room along with a number of men who would smoke outside in the cold and then return for the room count. Mr. W. would stand up for his two children and be the only one there representing the Freshman class as a parent.

As competition for the vaunted traveling P.T.A. banner awarded each meeting for room count continued, a red hot conflict involving hot, harsh breathing bodies charged and banged its way up and down the South Elementary Gym. Here the Timbertop locals clung to a slim lead over a traveling Kelso Hardware five. With four minutes left in the game, George Anderson felt like he'd absorbed enough elbow smashes to last him for the rest of the season. Peripherally he saw Eph Findlay duck his left shoulder toward the forward guarding him then go straight up in a vertical leap. At the apex of his jump he released the basketball on a flat, floating trajectory toward the Timbertop offensive basket. George swung his hips low and around the big bearded man guarding him, and he timed a leap that perfectly coordinated his interception of the ball in flight. Hanging high in the air, ball and hands high above the basket, he stuffed the pebble grained sphere through a metal ring so it swished into the netting below it. A light applause from the sixteen faithful fans on the sideline rewarded his effort—the fans were mostly wives and girl friends.

Madge had not come with him this evening as she usually did; one of the girls showed a runny nose so she insisted on staying home to take care of her. (Their finances made a sitter a luxury they reserved for very special occasions—like the Chehalis game coming tomorrow night.) Though she never mentioned it, in so many words, George got the feeling that maybe Madge had grown a little tired of basketball games.

As he drifted rapidly back to his defensive position with his other teammates, he realized that this thought about Madge had been the first thought about anything but winning this game since the opening tipoff. Here, on the basketball court, he grew into a whole man with no hidden fears or creeping misgivings about himself and his real worth. Here black and white existed only as the color of a man's jersey. That's where loyalty, support, comradeship lay—with your teammate who had no race, color, or religion.

He expertly blocked a shot attempt by the towering bearded man he guarded, and he saw Eph recover the ball and start a fast break. Charging down the court George filled with the total joy of contest. A perfect bounce pass came to him from Eph, and he cross stepped by Kelso's last defender to lay a soft left handed cripple into the basket off the glass backboard. When the final horn blew, and the post game victory talk in the shower room was over, he'd return to a white man's world as a suffering, self-conscious black. At the moment he was the greatest player out on the court with the full admiration of friend and foe, alike.

Hunched above his thesis Davey, too, wrestled with the problems of black and white—with the problems of all minorities, all little people caught in the crush of oppressive traditions. In front of him the pile of notecards slowly formed along the pattern he planned to follow in a futile, but for him self-necessary attack, on the status quo in the vast wasteland of Western education.

"I think a little wine might come in handy right now," he said aloud, to himself, as he rose from his chair and adjusted the satin Oriental smoking jacket he wore when he worked with the thermostat at 65 degrees. "I'll read them through just one more time, but I think, Davey boy, you are ready to write."

# CHAPTER FIVE

By eight fifteen Tuesday morning three conversational groups held forth in the high school faculty lounge. At the rickety old davenport that this morning miraculously held up over six hundred pounds comprised of George Anderson, Eph Findlay, and Tom Coleman, the topic focused on tonight's game with Chehalis (after some standard opening hangover remarks attributed to Eph's beer bust of the night before). At the moment the group's main speaker was Coach Dave Weydermeyer who had scouted Chehalis on the previous Saturday night.

"You've got to work hell out of the base line," said the young, blonde unmarried track coach (who had been a hurdler in college). "They got this kid, Penbrook, who's hell on wheels in front of their jug."

"Well, I think Carson's found himself," said George (of the five coaches gathered here for their regular morning conflab his position as varsity basketball coach gave him the power center unless his team started to lose). "I had Sparky press and foul the hell out of him yesterday, and he kept his cool through the whole pounding thing."

"I figured Kit would have it when I had him playing ninth," said Coleman, who, two years ago, had coached the ninth grade team.

"Hadn't been for that stupid old man of his screamin' from the sidelines the kid would have done a hell of a job for me on the jayvees last year," growled Eph Findlay, and the others nodded in sympathetic agreement.

Toward the room's midsection, seated on metal folding chairs around an old donated coffee table (scarred from a hundred cigarette burns), a compatible group of married women teachers sucked on their morning cigarettes and exchanged their usual common felt agonies about their triple roles as breadwinners, mothers and housekeepers.

"I told Alvin last night," said Audrey Settlemeir (English), "he'd better start doing some things around the house while he sits home and draws his unemployment. It's getting so every year construction shuts down for two or three months and he just sits home on his ass doing nothing. Well, believe me, I told him this year things would be different, or else."

"Joe's always been good helping around the house," said Mavis Parmenter (math), as she stabbed her cigarette butt into the pile already forming in a large grey school art class made pottery ash tray. "It's keeping the kids in line where I get no help from him. My God, the way he backs away you'd think he's afraid of his own thirteen year old son."

"I know what you mean," said Bernice Tully (English), as she wagged her carefully coifed head in sympathy. "Ralph treats our Emily like she was an honored guest in our house, or something, and he looks right by me, sometimes, like I don't exist."

A fourth party to this smoking bee, Agnes Merriweather (typing) sat just apart from the others with her attention centered on stock reports in her *Oregonian*. Each morning she brought the paper from home with her, and she sat reading it here with the other three girls oblivious to their conversation. An old maid, she knew none of the frustrations that beleagured her colleagues, but she enjoyed the physical fact of having someone around, and, besides, she couldn't enjoy her paper and smoke at the same time if she took the news to the desk in her room.

Our third group, poised by the door as if ready for flight should an administrator chance to poke his ugly head in the door, consisted of polyinterest people whose names and faces changed from morning to morning. Usually they came to this spot on completion of some kind of task in the teacher's workroom next door, and they rarely stayed more than five or ten minutes before hurrying back to their own room, or to a visit in the room of one of their friends. This particular Tuesday morning they just all happened to be from the science department, and each of the three taught a section of ninth grade general science. So, having just completed the mimeo work on their semester exams for that week, they retired, momentarily to the lounge to compare notes on the instruments with which they planned to "level the troops."

"I suspect more and more as the years go by," said David Royce (biology and ecology with his general science), "the elementary school teachers give our students less and less science."

"It's the aftermath of that Vietnam thing," said Marvin Kemplar (who also taught chemistry I and II). "We're getting a bunch of kids taking over those classrooms who are anti-scientific and pro-sociology. I don't find the interest for chemistry I used to have in my classes five and ten years ago."

"It's the same way with my physics class," agreed Stephen Boyd (who also taught surveying). "Would you believe I've got only five students this semester? Of course part of that's the way the administration lets kids pick and choose their subjects now; we didn't have that kind of laxness when George Rutherford was here."

Now, if the dozen people gathered here obeyed school rules, as they expected their students to do, each and all would have been in violation of the code of work conduct agreed to by them when they signed a contract agreement to teach in the Timbertop school district. The manual stated, explicitly, that teachers would be in their classrooms from eight to eight-thirty each workday morning to help individual students who might seek out instruction or counseling. This part of the code, however, rarely experienced enforcement (exceptions occurred when the principal sought to harrass some particular teacher into resigning). Mr. W.'s predecessor, George Rutherford, had, in fact, openly defended a need of teachers to rub shoulders with each other from time to time during the course of their day.

"It's a damn lonely job," he would say, to anyone criticizing the faculty room klatch, "a teacher's a one of a kind in a room full of young egos who, more often than not, resent the fact that they have to conform to rules they had no hand in making. Though a teacher may be less than a decade apart from the kids in her classroom, she's a generation apart no matter how you slice it. Yeah, I'm for them getting together every chance they can to reinforce their feeling of oneness with a faculty. After all, even a policeman usually travels with a companion, or he has a constant contact with one or more of his colleagues. I say, if we can't get that damn rule out of the manual, the best thing my office can do is ignore it."

Mr. W., however, did not openly share the view of his former principal, nor did he openly defend teacher time in the faculty lounge. He chose to act as if such happenings did not exist, and if they did so, they happened so seldom and so clandestine that its occurrence seemed an unlikely detection.

"I damn well get this gut feeling that some of my young teachers, like Huntington and his type, loiter there before school sometime," he told Ray Cosgrove, confidentially. "Checked the damn place every morning this week and didn't find a soul. Well, you can bet, I will keep on checking."

Now, Davey Huntington never came to the faculty lounge before or after school. There were others, too, who didn't leave their classrooms open and unattended (another no-no) while they joined their buddies for a before or after school jive, and though some of those others (Lisa Overstreet, Carl Hargraves, Bernice Tully) opened their doors at eight and promptly re-locked them behind them, there were many like Davey Huntington, Heidi Vandercamp, Sylvia Scanner, Willy Norburton, Bill Goss, and sometimes others who might come as early as seven or seven thirty to help from one to thirty or more students who sought them out for advice or help on a project.

The rest of the teachers, as well as librarian Nola Davenport and our two student counselors, pretty well satisfied the letter of the law as their jobs, by their very nature, started with the arrival of the first school bus about three minutes after eight a.m. Mr. Longfellow, too, came precisely at eight, and he stationed himself in a strategic position on the lower floor where he served as chief constable for that first half hour of hectic traffic. Mr. W., on the other hand, arrived at seven thirty (giving the impression that he had more problems facing him than anyone else), and in that nice, quiet, comforting half hour before the first bus arrived, he took his vitamin pills and his tranquilizer while he answered an occasional phone call from some student calling in absent or some teacher calling in sick. George Rutherford, as principal, never had

116

come before eight or eight fifteen, and Ray Cosgrove was quick to point out Mr. W.'s special "dedication" to his job as a leader. At eight a.m., with Mrs. Metzger ensconced at her desk and manning the now constantly ringing phone, Mr. W. departed for his constabulary station up on the second floor where his harsh, foreboding visage helped cool the nervous enthusiasm of our hyperactive ninth and tenth grade boys and girls. An envelope of hushed voices always seemed to surround Mr. W. wherever he moved in the hall.

It was toward the south end of that hall that Coach Tom Coleman found our principal at a little before eight thirty this morning. Two more of Tom's varsity wrestlers had quit after practice the previous day, and his already skeleton thin squad (with not one team victory for the year) seemed close to total disintegration.

"Talk to Rog," Eph had insisted, when Tom cried his blues on their way home from work yesterday.

He had tried to bring the matter to his chief's attention at Eph's beer bust last night, but Mr. W. fobbed him off with a "fun tonight and problems tomorrow." Now Tom had left the coach's klatch early in hopes that his leader might offer some magical solution to the growing mess (and possible disgrace) he faced.

"It's a bummer," Mr. W. agreed, but as Tom waited no sorcerer's formula emerged.

"It's the double A competition, Chief," said Tom, plaintively. "We're just too small for that level competition in both basketball and wrestling."

"I know, Tom," sympathized Roger, "it's a bitch. It's just as bad for Eph in football, too. The fans just don't understand we're a little double A school instead of a big A school, now."

"Can't you petition us back into A competition, at least in wrestling," pleaded Tom, knowing even that wouldn't take away the twelve more matches that spelled twelve more nights of defeat for him.

"Look Tom, you know how long I held down our October attendance reports so we could stay with the A's," said Roger, conspiratorily. "I've got about as much chance with a petition to the State Athletic Association as Lisa Overstreet has to become a Playboy Bunny. Those boys linger on forever, and they don't forget."

"Okay, then, just tell me what to do," an edge of desparation sharpened on Coleman's words. "A couple of more quitters on my squad and I might as well forfeit every match."

"Now, there's a possibility," said Roger, not quick to perceive answers in himself, but often quick to pick up answers from others. "I've got a principal's meeting Friday, maybe I can rig something up with the boys—most of them owe me a favor or two. Suppose we forfeit our remaining league matches; the other coaches won't like it but who cares about them. We'll finish out our schedule with some Triple A C squads and work in some matches with some A's and some B's. You can pick up Gorman's JV squad for personnell and we'll junk out our JV schedule."

"Dave may not like that very well," suggested Tom.

"Dave won't give a damn," said Mr. W., fiercely. "I don't think he even wants to coach—he's certainly not one of us. Remember, he was Imberlay's choice, not mine. Besides, if I tell him to button it up what can he say? He gets his money, anyway."

"Hey, Chief, if you can pull all that off for me, you can bet I'll never forget it," said Tom, fervently.

"I promise nothing," sotto-voiced Roger. "Just keep this under your hat; go ahead as usual with your Thursday night match, and I'll let you know over the weekend how I make out at the principal's meeting."

"You can count on it," Tom assured him.

"Remember," said Roger, "it's damn near levy election time. Something like this, if it got out, could muddy things up with a lot of voters."

Lisa Overstreet talked the levy over with her cab driver, Gordon "Mudge" Taylor on the way to school that morning. Mudge, who would be forty on his next birthday, never officially graduated from Timbertop High School because he failed in all four sections of Miss Overstreet's English classes. That was over twenty years ago, however, and Mudge, a happy-go-lucky character (who had jumped from welfare to Timbertop's only cab owner when a familyless uncle died two years previously leaving the business to Mudge) held no grudges against Miss Overstreet (though he discussed her as a ridiculous, monstrous, fat old figure who practically broke him up inside with her occasional ten cent tip). Though he had every opportunity (as a taxpayer and her sole sure means of transportation every morning) to vilify her to her face, he felt no rancor and continued to feel a loyalty to Timbertop High School and all the people therein.

"How do you think people will vote on the levy, Gordon?" asked Miss Overstreet, this morning. (She never called students by their nicknames.)

"Like always, Miss Overstreet," said Mudge, lightly, "cussin' the high cost of taxes."

"Still and all, we've got to keep our schools in top shape for our children," insisted Lisa, doing her part for politics.

"I guess you must be right, Miss Overstreet," said Mudge. "Got four or my own in school now, and I always try to remember to vote for them levies."

"How many girls do you have now, Gordon?" asked Miss Overstreet.

"All of them boys," said Mudge, his chest swelling with pride. "Got one boy playing center on the eighth grade basketball team, and Mr. Anderson says he's gonna be a dandy."

Silence settled over the back seat of the cab, so Mudge drove on humming idly to himself. Miss Overstreet must have a lot on her mind this morning about English and all, he told himself. He felt no surprise when she failed to leave him her usual ten cent tip.

Heidi saw Miss Overstreet arrive in her cab as she stood near the window showing one of her early girls how to trace from a pattern. Like Miss Overstreet she experienced the sharp pains of heartburn, but hers came from three aspirin she had taken earlier at home to combat a pounding occipital headache gained during a fretful night in which she hardly slept more than one hour at a stretch. Twice she got out of bed to take a warm bath and drink a warm glass of milk, but each time, as she returned to the crisp coolness of her sheets, she closed her eyes and saw Pat Mooney coming toward her with a bottle of cocaine extended ahead of her.

My God, she told herself, over and over, my mother and dad would die in disgrace if the police had carried me off to jail. I'll have to confess this on Sunday to Father Mueller, and I might as well make a clean breast of my thoughts about David Huntington, too.

Now, working closely with her girls on a very difficult part of their program, she found momentary relief from her own problems by concentrating on theirs. Her door opened off to her far right, and she half turned to see a smiling Elaine Perry approach with a little hello wave of her hand. In a rush she remembered her date with David Huntington—the dinner tonight—his Oriental recipes, he had said. That meant he planned dinner at his apartment. Her mind went under siege of bombardment from her girl friend's last weekend stories. The orgies—the dope scenes—the wild David Huntington. Her mental storm made her shake so uncontrollably she clung to the edge of the cutting table in fear that she'd faint dead away.

"You alright, Miss Vandercamp?" Elaine asked, with concern, as she placed her round firm young arm, still in a sleeve of her heavy wool blazer, around her teacher's trembling shoulders and held her close for support.

"It's nothing, Elaine," murmured Heidi, a twist of torture in her stomach that ground empty, with no food having entered it since noon of the previous day. "I think I'm just hungry. It seems I forgot to eat breakfast this morning."

Pat Mooney, too, skipped dinner the previous night and breakfast this morning. A quarter to eight snort, however, brought her an eight o'clock rush that fired her with ambition to get everything going at once in her office. Her first customer of the day, Debbie Fairweather, dropped by to report all things copacetic at home, and that tribute to her ingenuity as a counselor so elated her that even an early morning rush for admit to class slips could not dampen her good humor.

Davey Huntington, too, felt charged with energy this morning, but drugs played no part in his special reservoir of feeling. Things went well for him last night as he worked on his thesis, and his morning meditation found itself interspersed with some special, novel, possibilities for his evening dinner with little Heidi. To top off his sunshine cake of happiness, an early morning call from Billy Lane paid a plaudit to his ego.

"Well, you were right, as usual," said the self disgusted voice on the phone lines other end. "I put them all to sleep—even my own faithful little group."

"So? Big deal," Davey chided him. "Now you know what not to talk about when you start your campaign for the board in the fall."

All of the present school directors were very much in A.T. Cromwell's thoughts when he found a large pool of water backed up from the six urinals in the boy's first floor restroom. He swore once, aloud and alone, at this importune break in his morning schedule, then he shut off the water to the closets, put a padlock on the door, and laid out plans to attack that problem, later. He knew from other asking occasions that no reservation in this or next year's budget allowed for major expenses in plumbing repair and maintenance. In August, given signs to suspect the winter might bring some very serious problems, he took the matter to Mr. W. and got his okay to take the matter on to the new super-intendent. It provided his first experience with the district's now supreme executive, and he came away shaking his head from the bland replies and blank looks he received in Dr. Imberlay's responses.

"He don't know his ass from a hole in the ground about takin' care of buildings," A.T. confided to his round, soft wife, Barbara. "I ain't gonna pass that headache along to Mr. W., he'll have enough besides that before this year's very old."

For five consecutive board meetings, A.T. petitioned the superintendent's office to put a discussion of the high school plumbing on his agendas, but to date the matter had never appeared. Well, thought A.T. this morning, that pool of water makes it necessary the matter get discussed tomorrow night. Poor old Mr. W.'ll just have to include it in his principal's building report.

So with A.T. laboriously framing a memo on plumbing to the office of his principal, Timbertop Consolidated High School got off to its official 8:30 a.m. start with a twenty second long bell. Mr. W. and Mr. Longfellow prodded the slow and reluctant into their classrooms, Mrs. Mooney and Mr. Patterson hurriedly made out admit to slip classes and filed away excuses sent for yesterday's absentees from their homes. Mr. Anderson urged his Freshmen boys to hurry into their gym clothes; Lisa Overstreet ponderously began her call of the roll with appropriate snide remarks about those named therein who had angered her on some occasion; Davey Huntington pinned a reminder note to his door for his class to meet that morning in the library, and Miss Vandercamp, in the luxury of a private restroom she enjoyed with her home ec building, sobbed out her mental pain on the verge of mild hysteria as she tried until 9 a.m. to resolve her dilemma about David Huntington.

By the time Heidi got involved with her second period class, her personal problems might never have existed at a conscious level. George Anderson, however, on his second period planning time found himself, once again, a victim of his own self deprecation.

The contrast he had seen during first period between his own P.E. class of Freshmen boys and Marsha Kemper's class of Freshmen girls forced him, now, to call his own efforts at being a teacher a shoddy pretense to satisfy his working arrangement. Her efforts showed a planning effort and organizational expertise—his showed neither. Her program offered girls substantial physical undertakings that could benefit them for a lifetime—his merely provided fifty minutes of baby sitting.

While his group had shambled into some kind of line order along the wall that sided their small sized basketball court, her girls quickly aligned themselves along their opposite wall with each squad leader briskly giving an accounting of any absentees in her command. While a half dozen of his boys still in street clothes (gym clothes forgotten, stolen, or deliberately left somewhere else) sat as a desultory group in one corner, her one-in-clothes miscreant stood against a wall doing isometric exercises (which she would continue for the balance of the period).

When his class finished a sloppy session of standard exercises, George took some of the better ninth grade boys under his wing for basketball instruction at one of the four baskets his class enjoyed. The rest of his boys fractured themselves into groups at the other three baskets where they played three on three scrimmage at their own speed and own fun. Marsha's girls, on the other hand, started with a routine of belly dancing exercises which they did to the controlled record sound of middle Eastern music. This portion of their classwork completed, they moved by squads into separate stations under direction from their own squad leader. At one station girls practiced poise walking, posture exercises, and worked with light dumbbells; and at a second station steps to a disco dance were practiced to controlled record music; a third station provided practice in proper strokes in badminton, while at a fourth girls practiced shooting free throws. At the final station girls performed basic gymnastics on a mat, a horse, a balance beam and a parallel bar. It was here that Mrs. Kemper gave direct supervision though her eyes constantly recorded happenings at the other four stations. At regular eight minute intervals she blew her whistle for squads to change stations. When she blew, again, five minutes before the bell rang to end the period, both girls and boys scrambled to the showers, and the two teachers followed their charges in like cowboys bringing their animals home to the barn in the evening.

Now that the last of those Freshman boys had left his locker room (the two long haired boys destined to be late to their next class again, of course) George took out a lined sheet of paper and pointed himself at the problem of planning something more organized for his classes. Either I ought to clean up my program, he thought, or get the hell out of the business. For awhile, then, he sat and daydreamed about how things had been back in Cicero. He conjured up his father's warm, honest, undevious face, and he smiled, unconsciously, at some of his mother's little foibles. He could play basketball with the Cicero town team and make twice what he made here by working for his father. Yet, would he be quitting because he wanted something more for his family, or would he simply be walking away from a challenge he didn't have guts enough to handle?

While George escaped in the world of his daydream, Pat Mooney felt her good humor and her charge of energy begin to dissipate. She had listened to junior, Pricilla Martin (one of Lisa Overstreet's pets) complain about the unfairness of Mrs. Kemper's P.E. class where a threatened B could spoil Pricilla's chance for a perfect semester report card.

"That's life, Pricilla," she said, suddenly, in a manner much more characteristic of her counterpart, Greg "Coach" Patterson than it was of ever patient and consoling Mrs. Mooney. The girl across from her stiffened in her chair, surprised.

"Mrs. Kemper sets standards for her P.E. class in the same way Miss Overstreet does for hers," Pat continued. "If you can't meet those standards, whose fault is that?"

Maybe Patterson's more right with his approach than I am with mine, she thought, almost angrily. At least he shifts the load onto somebody else instead of trying to carry somebody else's problems for them.

"But Mrs. Kemper's so picky about things," protested Pricilla.

"Then why don't you talk it out with her?" suggested Pat, abruptly, knowing Mrs. Kemper didn't waste time talking to any of her students.

"I tried to. She told me to go see the chaplin," pouted Pricilla, resigning herself to a minor loss in an institution that, generally, provided her the best melieu for her success.

"Well, you've seen me and there's nothing more I can do for you," said Pat, in a flat voice of dismissal.

"You're not feeling too good today, Mrs. Mooney?" asked Pricilla, in a warm voice of concern cultivated since the first grade to make brownie points with her teachers.

"Yes, that's right," said Pat, suddenly feeling a surge of guilt and shame for her brusqueness with this pliant, charming girl. No matter what I think, she told herself, I'll never be a Counselor "Coach" Patterson.

The world of Mooney and Patterson promises to help young people find their way through trouble and into a way of life with their best chances for happiness, but the world of Mr. Wellington and Mr. Longfellow promises dire consequences to any young person gone far enough astray to come under the awesome disciplinary force of that office. Into this second world, for the second morning in a row, came a scrawny 81 pound Freshman boy, Reuben Schwarz, who, muddy and wet, again, waited on the bad person's bench in Mrs. Metzger's holding area. Because yesterday Mr. W.'s cramped and crowded schedule made it impossible to work on this pitiful miscreant, Mrs. Metzger fobbed him off to Mr. Longfellow's office, and she bridled with disgust as she saw him returned to her again this morning almost identical (but some minutes later) to his appearance of yesterday. Now, at her signal, the cowering little creature moved his wet muddy self on in to see Mr. W.

"So, Reuben," said Mr. W. to the bedraggled figure who left light traces of mud on the polished oak of his floor, "what kind of lame excuse do we have today?"

"The girls pushed me down in the mud at the bus stop and the driver wouldn't let me on the bus, 'cause she said I'se too dirty," whined the boy through a nose that continually trickled a thin white line of snot. "Had ta' walk to school."

"Yesterday the boys, today the girls," intoned Mr. W. in a priestlike voice, after examining the detailed report from Longfellow that lay before him. "You don't have many friends here, Reuben, do you?"

" 'Guess not," sniffed the boy, then blotted snot from his upper lip with the back of his hand.

"Who's fault is that?" asked Mr. W.

"Mine, I guess," admitted little Reuben who long ago learned that adults treated you more lightly when you readily admitted that you were the faulter.

"So, why didn't you go back home and get some clean dry clothes?" asked Mr. W.

"My old lady would kill me if I come home like this," whined Reuben.

"How'd you get clean yesterday?" asked Mr. W.

"Commie helped me," said Reuben.

"Mr. Cromwell," corrected Mr. W.

"Mr. Cromwell," repeated Reuben, diligently.

"And what did Mr. Longfellow say to you yesterday?" asked Mr. W., though the evidence of that lay right in front of him.

"Said next time he'd send me home," sniffed the boy, again applying the back of his hand to his moist upperlip.

"So, what else can I do but send you home?" asked Mr. W.

"Bust me a couple of times with a paddle?" offered Reuben, hopefully.

"You're a little old for a paddle, aren't you?" asked Mr. W.

"Coach Findaly still uses one on the guys," said Reuben, more hopefully, and this time he cleaned his upper lip with the tip of a whitish coated tongue.

"Then you want Coach Findlay to bust you a couple of times?" suggested Roger, the snot business starting to make his stomach queasy (like Heidi and Mrs. Mooney he missed breakfast—Emily, very late from her meeting in Castleview, took the occasion to sleep late).

"Hey, that would be better than goin' home to face my ma," said Reuben, now growing eager to resolve the thing.

"Well, I'm sorry," said Mr. W., tired now of toying with the boy and sickened further by a second run of the tongue right up to the nostrils. "Mr. Longfellow already called the play. I'll have Mr. Patterson run you home."

With a shrug of his shoulders Reuben turned and slunk out of the principal's office to where Mr. Ray Cosgrove of the Timbertop School Board stood, having just arrived, at Mrs. Metzger's desk.

"Send the boy with a note to Mr. Patterson," Mr. W. ordered Mrs. Metzger. "I want him taken home, immediately."

A few minutes later the note lay crumpled just inside the firehole of Mr. Cromwell's furnace. In the aura of heat at the furnace's front Reuben Schwarz stood drying himself. At home he knew the house would be cold as outdoors and probably locked. His mother, whose welfare check couldn't cover very much oil for heat, went immediately from her bed in the morning to a local tavern where she nursed a glass of beer (more if somebody else bought) enjoying the commercial heat in that establishment. Several weeks ago Reuben stole a key from Mr. Anderson's ring that fit this door to the furnace room. He knew Mr. Cromwell's habits well—knew it would be close to eleven before he returned to check on the automatic furnaces. By that time he would be dry and safely out in the warmth of Mr. Goss' Woodshop.

Back at the principal's office Mr. W. graciously offered his special black leather swivel chair to the comfort of Mr. Ray Cosgrove. Over the board member's weak objection, Mr. Wellington protested that he, himself, thought and conversed much better when he stood on his feet and moved about. Cosgrove, his pink domed head still shining from stimulating exposure to the cold outdoors, let Mr. W. help him off with his big brown tweed overcoat, but he insisted he couldn't stay long enough to warrant the removal of his big rubber overshoes.

"I just wanted to have this little talk with you this morning, Roger," said Cosgrove, settling his portly, khaki clad body into the chair's soft embrace. "I felt you read me right on the phone yesterday, but you never know who listens in down at the one horse honky tonk telephone office of ours."

"Smart, Ray, smart," agreed Mr. W., moving so that records of his accomplishments that garnished one wall framed his real person with his publicity background.

"I listened to them damn teacher negotiators and their I want this and we want that, until I wanted to punch the four of them in the mouth," snarled Ray, doubling his two big rough ex-stump logger fists upon the desk top.

"I know what you mean, Ray," agreed Mr. W., letting a little heat enter into his words, also.

"Afterwards, and all weekend, I got to thinking: it's got to end somewheres. Someplace it's got to end. Somebody's got to stop it," said Ray, through a very grim mouth. "Sometime a halts got to be called before it gets too late."

"Better now than when every taxpayer faces bankruptcy," inserted Mr. W.

"That's right, Roger, that's just the way I thought it," said Ray (who had said it aloud, a half hundred times beore). "I figure if we give them a set back this year—I mean an all the way set back— make sure no levy gets passed at all—they'll be damned scared about their demands next year—'specially if we got to let a few teachers go."

"Smart, Ray, smart," agreed Mr. W.

An even more fierce countenance masked the school director's face. Like an aged bull out to rip things up with his horns, he hunched himself forward above elbows braced against the desk top. His eyes, dark, purple huricanes of pent up anger, flashed at Roger who came to stand in front of the desk.

"In the meantime what backlash we'll get should pretty well close out Imberlay's chance for a contract renewal and leave you with the inside shot you should have had last time around," Ray concluded. "With all them fancy type teachers weeded out by a budget cut, you could get the district on a basic education program where it belongs."

"We've got to walk on eggs with something like this," said Roger, confidentially, and a quiver of fear eroded part of the confidence he wanted to create for his role in this undertaking. After all, he thought, a backfire, at most, meant the loss of a non paying thankless political office to Cosgrove, but the loss of his position meant a loss of a job source of finance, a loss of his power position, and probably the end of his career as a school administrator.

"That's why I thought we ought to put our heads together here this morning," said Ray, and he leaned backward in the chair until his eyes focused in a speculative manner on Roger's unique chandelier.

As Roger groped, rather hopelessly, for some trail that might offer both a way to success and a cordon of safety for himself, he found nothing that offered enough import to be felt, noticeably, by the select voters who would bother even to go to the polls. To cover his inadequacy, he moved slowly toward the undraped windows where he stared out toward the snowy horizon as if seeking some answer there.

"I thought about talking things out with Bill Murchim," said Ray, as their silence continued, "but that little bastard never had an original idea in his whole damn life."

Murchim, that's it—that's the answer, thought Roger, and once again his great reflex thinking process responded to a single trigger. A letter to the editor of the Castleview *Daily News* condemning the levy and signed by a Timbertop School Board member—Bill Murchims. It would give the loyal opposition something to rally around, and it would split up the undecided electorate who never felt too happy about voting taxes on themselves in the first place.

"Well?" asked Cosgrove, as Roger returned to his earlier position across the desk from the again hunch shouldered school director. A bell outside announced the end of another class period.

"I think I've got us the answer, Ray," said Mr. W., softly but with plenty of dramatic undertones. (He leaned forward from his side of the desk balanced on his fingertips so the two men now held faces close enough to each other to kiss.) "Let me type up a letter to the *Daily News* editor; I may need a couple of days to work the whole thing out. Then you get Bill Murchim to sign it, and you mail it in. It can turn the trick and leave us both, very innocent, on the outside looking in."

Although getting a crew of boys to mop water out of the restroom put A.T. behind his scheduled morning, he still took time at the bell to check for smokers behind the home ec room. Via the Metzger grapevine he had learned that Mr. W. laid smokers in that locale as a hard issue on little Miss Vandercamp. Between first and second period he flushed out two senior girls who laughed at him but ground their cigarette butts out under their heels because they loved and respected him. In the break between second and third period, the grounds behind the home ec building stood empty (the 'word' already circulating), but he picked up a smoking sophomore boy, Bert Terwilliger, who slouched against the back wall of the woodshop. Bert, whose only distinguishing feature was the super abundance of acne on his face, owned more rule infractions (minor) than any other student in school.

"Hey, Bert, what's this?" asked A.T., as the slender, thin hunched shouldered, long hanked greasy brown haired boy took a long, deliberate drag before gounding out his weed.

"So, turn me over to the Bogeyman," said Bert, two slow trails of smoke drifting out of his nostrils.

"Not me, you'd like making more points with the administration," said A.T. "I ain't going to help you play the big man role."

"What's that supposed to mean?" asked Bert, angrily. "You think they don't know who I am, already?"

"So, if you think so, what's the big thing about makin some scene for yourself again?" asked A.T., fixing the boy with a penetrating look.

"Look, Mr. Cromwell, I don't want no trouble with you if you don't want no trouble with me," said Bert, uncomfortably.

"Hell, Bert, you get yourself a mess of trouble whether or no anybody helps you to it," said A.T., affably. "You carry it around like one of them old comedy advertising sign carriers with the thing slung over them front and back: Bert Terwilliger, it says, one bad hombre."

"Come on, Crommie, I got to get to class," muttered Bert, as he pulled his hunched shoulders away from the building.

"What's your hurry? Either you got a teacher who don't care or you got to see Patterson for an admit to class," said A.T., matter-of-factly.

"Got O'Malley," (agriculture and driver's ed), mumbled Bert.

"And he don't care whether you come or not," said A.T.

"Right," said Bert.

"So, sometimes you show signs that you might have a brain," said A.T.

"What's that supposed to mean?" asked Bert.

"It means you won't get boffed for being late to class, but you still played hot shot fool smoking out here where you could get caught when you know a half dozen places no one would ever spot you."

"So, it's my life," mumbled Bert, eyes shifting as he sought the best way to slip away from the force of A.T.'s presence.

"So, it's also your mother's life," said A.T., softly. "One of the nicest persons in Timbertop's got to get shit thrown at her all the

130

time 'cause her little boy can't never do enough to convince himself that people know he's alive."

"What in hell's ma got to do with it?" asked Bert, desperation in his voice.

"You're killing her, that's all," said A.T., his words cutting with the clean force of a feller's axe. "All this time you keep trying to prove you're one real bastard, like your old man was, you keep killing your mother a little bit more each day. Better get on to your classroom, big man, maybe you can push O'Malley into sending you in to see the pincipal."

When the bell rang for lunch, Davey Huntington considered grabbing a tray in the cafeteria and taking it with him for further explorations in the home ec room. Just as he prepared to leave his room, Billy Lane descended upon him with his little coiture of political seniors. They felt it necessary to report last night's PTA effort in detail and to discuss some of their plans for the Wednesday night School Board meeting.

"Something's going on with Ray Cosgrove that doesn't smell good to me," said Billy Lane, for openers, and the give and take that ensued after that kept David from enjoying any lunch.

So Heidi, who had secretly expected him with mixed thrilled anticipation and dreadful trepidation, found herself, instead, eating her usual salad seated across a table from George Anderson who had brought his bag lunch here to escape the pre-game pressure that would generate among the coaches gathered in the faculty lounge.

The teachers gathered in the home ec room for lunch were young, and, except for George Anderson, they ate here regularly. Some brought soup to heat on the electric range, others made tea, and some even, occasionally, brought a casserole to heat in an oven. They were not, however, a socially cohesive group, and though a comment concerning salary negotiations or some other such related item might get a few moments of general conversation from time to time, for the most part they paired together at separate tables and shared a pretty intimate lunchtime relationship.

Sylvia Scanner and Willy Norburton formed one constant team; Jim Bettermen and Bill Goss formed another (occasionally joined by Mike O'Malley). David Royce age 31 and Marvin Kempler age 32 made the oldest, and the most academic, team. Both being of scientific bent, they abhorred the cloud of nicotinized pollution that hung heavy in the faculty lounge, or they would have eaten there by prestige preference. One loner, Dave Gorman, ate his ever constant can of soup at a table by himself (though he many times considered sitting at a table with Heidi Vandercamp, if he could only think of something to say to her).

Conversation, today, followed its usual one on one pattern with Willy and Sylvia recapturing their previous nights gala moments at the Castleview Holiday Inn; Jim and Bill grew deeply involved with a discussed rebuilding of an old farm tractor Bill had bought over the weekend at a local farmer's auction. Our two scientists mutually shared an ecology article both had read recently in the library's last issue of the Science Digest, and Dave Gorman, with no one to talk with, of course, glanced covertly from time to time from his bowl of beef vegetable soup to where tiny Heidi sat with towering George.

Conversation between George and Heidi was not something either of these two shy people would normally instigate. But Heidi, desperate in the dilemma she faced concerning tonight's dinner invitation from David, felt compulsed to reach out and establish some kind of relationship with another person.

"Would you like a cup of tea?" she asked George, in a rush of boldness.

"Why, yes, thanks," answered George, both pleased and surprised. "Sounds real good, sounds different. My mother used to serve us tea at dinnertime."

Now, even after such a dramatic breakthough things would have normally died right there, but for Heidi, facing the most terrifying and agonizing mental moments of her life, there was a need, somehow and with somebody, to make David Huntington something more than just the projection of her feelings and the sum of her girl friend's wild verbal perambulations. Here was

George, a colleague of both she and David's; married, a man of the world, and certainly a strong man who could have no fears about speaking the truths as he saw them.

"It's Japanese tea," she said, carefully, trying not to stumble or expose the caldron of emotion bubbling dangerously close to the surface of her demeanor. "I'm very interested in Oriental things. In fact, Mr. Huntington who, I understand, spent sometime in Japan, invited me to an Oriental dinner at his place this evening."

George, still a bit amazed that Heidi had spoken to him at all, sat dumbfounded through a speech that contained more words than the total number of words he had heard come from her during their nearly five month's acquaintanceship. Now he tried to put some perspective on this unusual happening and he recalled rumors heard recently about Huntington and Vandercamp. Were they supposed to be having some kind of an affair? He couldn't remember. He rarely heard gossip or small talk even when it was addressed to him, and he never repeated it, which often made a little contention bone between him and Madge.

"Sounds exciting," he said, helpfully.

"You don't think it might look bad to people? A girl in a man's apartment, I mean?" asked Heidi, in a tiny, hushed voice.

"What difference could it mean, girl at boy's—boy at girl's?" asked George, sensing the girl held some very real concerns. "Anyway, you're an adult with a right to your own private life. Why should you care what some lousy backbiters say?"

He almost laughed, sarcastically, at himself, as he heard his own words—words that his father, his wife, and his friends threw at him when pressures grew too great inside himself and he spoke, with concern, of his own personal or professional image. Like a Sunday morning quarterback, he thought, it's easy to call the right play when the game is over.

"What do you think about Mr. Huntington?" whispered Heidi.

"He's a one hundred and ten percenter," said George, with a force that surprised himself. "I'd like to be sure I had just one friend in this world of David Huntington's calibre."

His stress of the name as his voice timbre grew brought heads swinging toward them with questioning eyes, and Heidi's neck and cheeks grew pink with warm blood as she felt herself the unwanted center of attention. David Huntington, thought Sylvia Scanner, and she openly reached across the table to press the affection of her hand on top of Willy's. The thought of two more young lovers in the world made her feel soft and warm inside. She thought she might do a picture of David and give it to Heidi as a surprise.

Had Davey been an eavesdropper to that home ec room by play, he would have been mighty flattered by George's testimonial and mighty amused by Sylvia's casting him in a valentine role part. His thoughts, however, lay far from George Anderson and Heidi Vandercamp; the small political klatch had, by the end of the lunch period, expanded into a room full of sophomores, juniors and seniors all concerned about the upcoming levy and its personal effect upon them.

"Look," shouted Davey, above the conversation buzz that greeted his answer to the last question addressed to him, "it's almost time for the bell. Billy plans to set up some regular town hall things starting next week. He'll bring in panels of school directors, teachers, coaches, businessmen, farmers, loggers, you name it. He'll take one, two, three whatever amount of nights you need to find answers to the questions no one person can answer for you here today. Okay? Now, get out of here and get to your classes. Responsible citizens don't need admit to class slips."

With much talking, some friendly shoving, and a little horseplay from a couple of sophomore boys, the room slowly cleared of all but Davey's junior U.S. History students. When the tardy bell rang all thirty one of these sat expectantly in their respective seats. Davey scanned the room, quickly, noted that all in his register were present, then smiled to himself about a total incongruity—instead of sharing his lunch period with Heidi, as he had planned, he ended up with a bunch of kids and not one bite of lunch.

"Mr. Huntington," the long, thin, but muscular, arm of Kit Carson waved at him.

"Mr. Carson," he said, signing his attendance slip and handing it to a front row girl who would hang it outside his doorway.

"I'd like to ask a question not about our present subject matter before class gets started," said the lanky red head.

"Lay it on me, friend," said Davey. "No answers are guaranteed, you know."

"That's part of the question," said Kit, squaring up in his seat and leveling bright blue eyes on the teacher. "I'd like to know how come our class is so different from Mr. Findlay's U.S. History class?"

"What brought that on?" asked Davey, curiously, and he draped himself (gracefully) across the top of his podium, his attention extended totally to the questioning boy.

"Well, like, I'm staying with Dingus now (Everett "Dingus" Kelly—the other Timbertop junior basketball guard)," said Kit, carefully. "Last night he's studying for semesters in Coach Findlay's U.S. and he's got about two hundred questions to answer from a textbook. I'm trying to help him, but there's a lot of things I don't know about Dred Scott and The Federalists and things like that. (Kit seemed to have lost himself, and his look appealed to the teacher for help.)

"And you wonder why, in the same school, in the same course for guys in the same junior class, how two different things could be happening because of two different teachers," concluded Davey.

"Yeah, that's right. Not knocking it," he continued, hurriedly, "just wondering."

"Fair enough question," said Davey, and he now eyeswept the class to let each individual know that the answer forthcoming was meant for them, too. "Each teacher presents material to students in the way he feels those students might best prosper from that material. In social studies, especially, there's a wide variance on what has historical significance and what does not. Mr. Findlay, in his class, feels that Dred Scott, The Federalists, and the answer to those two hundred other questions are most important to his students. He may or may not be right—that's not important. The important thing is that's what he believes, so he gives his presentation a maximum effort for his students. I, on the other hand, happen to believe that all historical records are a form of

135

fiction—incidents and accidents reported from the viewpoint of one or several like thinking people. I believe its real value is its continuity and its relationship, personal relationship, to you, to me, to everyone. That's why, instead of a textbook like Mr. Findlay uses, I encourage you to read the historical fiction of Jakes, Roberts, Mason and others who give you well researched looks at your country's history in a way that draws you into its unfolding story. I chose White's "Breach of Faith" as our text for this class because I believe it best represents, in a scope you can comprehend, a most dynamic picture of your and my U.S.A. as it really was and really is. I think understanding the California syndrome in modern politics and knowing about Clem Whittaker and Leona Baxter will mean much more to each of you than will an acquaintanceship with The Federalists and The Dred Scott Decision. I don't exaggerate when I say I've read extensively into history, and I've found no other author, and certainly no U.S. History textbook that so aptly makes a person aware of the true power picture in American politics and American government. That, last week, you were all able to discuss, and hopefully comprehend, the contradictions that exist between our Bill of Rights and the executive power of our president; were able to voice your own opinions on how those contradictions became instrumental in destroying Richard Nixon, is, I believe, far more important to you than the facts about our glorious wars or the biographies of our 'important' people. I, like Mr. Findlay, may or may not be right—that's not important. The important thing is by presenting what I believe you get the maximum effort from your U.S. History teacher."

In the room next door, Lisa Overstreet's efforts to get her class underway finally succeeded. The girl who picked up her attendance slips this period had long ago grown wise enough to wait outside the door until the always tardy missile came forth. Better to risk a mild reproof at the office for returning late from her rounds than to expose herself to one of Miss Overstreet's ever ready barbs. In this fourth period class Pricilla Martin always carried out the absent-tardy report. She sat directly in front of Miss Overstreet's desk, and she often got summoned by teacher to write lesson instructions or special pieces of poesy on the black-board (Miss Overstreet had a growing tendency to scrawl on the board, besides she didn't trust turning her back even on a class of junior girls).

"Now, class," Miss Overstreet began, unctuously, "please open your books to page 131. Today we continue our study in the works of our beloved Emily Dickinson, foremost among America's great poets."

(In this semester of literature catalogued as "American Writers" in the Timbertop Student Directory, Miss Overstreet spent two weeks on Anne Bradstreet's, *The Tenth Muse*; two weeks on the writings of Abigail Adams; three weeks in Margaret Fuller's, "Women in the 19th Century"; three weeks on Hawthorne's "House of Seven Gables", two weeks, each, on the works of Sarah Orne Jewett and Mary Greeman, and four weeks on the letters and poems of Emily Dickinson.)

Today, as the class members finally got past the noise of digging out and opening their books to page 131, she took a deep breath, then read, aloud, with deep passion and full dramatic elocution:

"IT IS NOT DYING HURTS US SO, by Emily Dickinson. 'It is not dying hurts us so,—'Tis living hurts us more; But dying is a different way, a kind, behind the door,—The southern custom of the bird—That soon as frosts are due—Adopts a better latitude. We are the birds that stay, The shiverers round the farmers doors, For whose reluctant crumb—We stipulate, till pitying snows—Persuade our feathers home.'"

As Lisa, hushed, husky voiced, brought those "feathers home," a stillness held her class as if each student there had been deeply tranquilized. As teacher's popping blue eyes swept over the faces before her, those faces made every effort not to draw her attention by the trace of a movement or the blink of an eye. If no one attracted teacher's attention, they knew, she would hand the chalice of analysis to Pricilla Martin, and they could hide their own unfeeling, unartistic stupidity under the disguise of their classmate's ever ready blanket of sop. So, as Lisa laid on her students the haughty look of a diva who has just cast her pearls into a crass herd of swine, not a breath stirred in the classroom, not a sound came from a seat.

"Now," exploded Teacher, returned again to her crow's caw voice, "who first would like to explain for us the meaning in this poem. Pricilla?"

"Well, Miss Overstreet," Pricilla began, sweetly, "Miss Dickinson wrote this poem for her cousins who had lost their father through his death, so she tries to reassure them that death is painless to the one who dies, and only their sorrow of being left behind him is painful."

"Beautiful—beautiful, Pricilla dear," gushed Miss Overstreet. "And we must see the images—mustn't we? The image of the poor birds who cannot migrate when the cold winter comes. The soul of the departed one wings away, but the birds left behind in a world of reality must suffer the daily agonies of physical living. So beautifully done. So—Emily Dickinson. So—feeling for others and the artistic beatitudes of an inner world trapped in the soiled world around it. I'm sure all of that is as evident to all of you as it is to me when I read it. Any questions?"

Everyone waited on Pricilla, but today she sat mute apparently having shot her all on the first go-around. There were, then, no further questions or discussions.

"Please copy this poem out of your book, neatly, and mark in the meter and the syllable signs," directed Miss Overstreet. "When you complete that, and on the same page, write a poem of your own about death. Make it no shorter than six lines and no longer than ten. Mark out the meters on your poem, too."

Again the shuffle of getting out paper; each student diligently started to make her poetic copy. (Three girls had forgotten to bring pencils to class—an unforgivable sin in the eyes of Miss Overstreet—so they hunched over as if writing and thus avoided losing the five credit points Miss Overstreet would have charged them for their errant ways.) As the room sounds reduced themselves to a rhythmic pen or pencil scratching, Liza dozed with her blue eyes popped open. She felt particularly drowsy from the lunch she had consumed; macaroni and cheese was one of her favorites, and she had sent Mrs. Tully back to get her seconds.

138

When, at last, her soft snore joined the scratch sounds, those three write-faking girls managed to borrow working tools from friends in the classroom, and they got quicky into transposing their assignment.

Fourth period was the last period of that day when most of the students at TCHS gave much attention to teachers, classwork, or convention. Heidi's fifth period boys got so noisy she did have to send Elaine after Mr. Longfellow; and Mr. W. got called to stop a near riot in the typing room. With the exception of the coaches (who, except for Eph Findlay generally ran pretty loose classroom discipline), Mr. Huntington's class who got deeply involved in a discussion of the energy problem, and Jim Bettermen's class where the rest of the school world seldom made any impression, the classroom scenes reversed their general orderliness and became almost scenes of bedlam where, certainly no learning took place. (The Bogeyman ended the last twenty minutes of the period bulldogging Miss Overstreet's class while that old girl retired to the Lady Faculty Toilet.)

Had a form of madness brewed during lunch period finally come to a head? Had the long oppression and boredom here at school felt by so many students finally erupted into a volcano of dissent? Neither of these occurred, in fact, nothing really far from the ordinary had presented itself. Tonight the Axemen met the Bearcats and at ten to three—fifteen minutes into sixth (agony) period, a bell would announce a chance to let off steam in the shrieking malestrom of a pep assembly.

For each of the major employees at TCHS, the explosive din and the colorful pageantry that would rock the gymnasium held slightly differing significances.

Mr. W., that old storm trooper, would feel goosebumps rise on his flesh as the band blared forth "Glory to Timbertop," and he would, later, nostalgasize both as an ex-player and an ex-coach when cheers from the student packed bleachers greeted introductions of the characters who held leading roles in tonight's scheduled athletic drama.

Mr. Longfellow saw the whole thing as a pain in the ass, for not only had his disciplinary energies been tapped fifth period and the early part of sixth, he now prowled the building halls and outbuildings to be sure that teachers assigned by him to patrol special areas not only appeared in their allotted places but that they actually "wrote up" any transient students who wandered there.

George Anderson, of course, held a starring role in the undertaking, and his emotion choked voice would find difficulty introducing his varsity stalwarts and presenting a "pep" talk that would guarantee a victory to the waiting assemblage. When they screamed their belief in him his throat would choke on a knot of feeling (though he'd been this same route over a hundred times before).

For Marsha Kemper it would be a bitter experience. Not that she didn't like pep assemblies, and not that she resented her minor role of birddogging the Freshman Class section where she stood. No, Marsha resented the fact that all this hoopalaa got staged for the boys as often as twice each week, while her girls, who played their games on Thursday afternoon, never got a pep assembly.

To Eph Findlay the pageant beat spending the last half hour with a squirming ninth grade Washington History Class that generally bored him to tears, anyway. He enjoyed all pep assemblies, but with varying degrees of excitement. He liked to see young people flushed with exploding energy, and he joined in with the cheers like he was one of the gang. But basketball pep assemblies failed to turn him on the way the football and baseball assemblies did; today he was just a second team sort of guy, in the Fall and the Spring he was Star. Then, too, he got a handout assignment from Longfellow. Today he was designated a watch dog on the senior class section.

Tom Coleman, like George Anderson and Mr. W., found himself choked with emotion and goosepimpled by the brassy blasts of the band. He wasn't so old, either, or so completely involved as a jock, to be blind to the cheerleader's lithe and shapely showing of a lot of female pulchritude in their cute little frilly tu tus. He found it difficult to share his attention both with them and with the junior class section where it was his responsibility to help keep conduct under control.

David Weydermeyer, too, had some attention problems with the cheerleaders. Especially one, a senior girl who had accompanied him on an all night outing in Portland over the Christmas holiday. So far, on their return, she managed to keep the decorousness that put her in the troops and him in the officer's club, but several times she caught him alone in his classroom and pressured him to take her again—this time for a weekend—and despite the fear of consequences he felt himself beginning to entertain the idea. Now, as she deliberately bounced in front of him on her gym floor spot, he looked away to shout at two sophomore boys in the section under his charge.

"Hey, you guys, knock off the pushing," he demanded, and he felt a pool of perspiration form in each of his two armpits.

For Billy De Haven the mob scene seemed unimportant, immaterial, and a happening that, like much of school life, went on around him but did not involve him. As a tennis team member in college, his competition, as fierce as any contact sport, fought its battles in an aura of silence and good manners. Being ninth grade basketball coach, as well as varsity tennis coach, occurred as an accident attached to his acquisition of a teaching contract in social studies. Unlike Marsha Kemper, he felt glad that his team (which also played on Thursday afternoons) did not go through the convolutions of a pep assembly. To perform like George Anderson would perform, today, would have made Billy feel ridiculous. His assignment to keep an eye on the locker rooms pleased him. Here the thick concrete walls cut out nearly all sounds of the kid's celebration.

Dave Gorman, though coaching a soon to be defunct JV wrestling team and scheduled to assist Eph Findlay with baseball in the Spring, felt none of the standard little boy aggressiveness so common to most every natural jock. Single, and a very private person, he got into weight lifting and wrestling more as a means of self exploration than as an outlet for competitive drive. In high school he played a rather good, steady shortstop to satisfy an often spoken wish of his father who, at age 45, still played for the local town baseball team. But Dave never really enjoyed the game, and he dropped out of that sport when he continued on

141

into college. Of all the other coaches in their faculty, he felt drawn only toward George Anderson. It was so typical of our society that these two young men, who could have found a bond of feeling and understanding between them, were both too shy to expose themselves first to the other one, so they had not, in fact, exchanged any more words than an occasional, unscheduled, good morning. Today Dave had volunteered for upstairs hall duty during the assembly, and he leaned against a window casing looking down and out across the much trampled snow that surrounded black wet patches of parking lots. This winter he had started to learn how to ski, and he looked anxiously toward every weekend opportunity to get off to the mountains.

A.T. saw young Gorman at the window as the custodian (who, by union edict, should have left for home twenty three minutes ago) came to the second floor locker section to fix a reported balky combination lock. The two men smiled at each other, and A.T. thought to himself: 'another good one—he really makes those business classes of his come alive for the kids. Well, 'spose we'll lose him in a year or two. Wonder how he might get along with the little Vandercamp? Maybe I can figure some way to get those two opened up to each other.'

Heidi, who would have been thrilled and partly terrified by the pep rally antics, hosted fifteen girls in her classroom who had, the day before, got her written permission to come there during assembly time to work on their individual projects. Being in charge of a group in her room excused a teacher from other pep rally obligations. Lisa Overstreet, too, entertained in her room— Pricilla Martin and two Freshmen girls (the minimum group a teacher could stay in her room for was three). Lisa's appearance at a pep assembly was beyond anybody in Timbertop's memory. I can't remember her ever coming to any of ours, and that was over twenty years ago.

Audrey Settlemeir, who disliked pep assemblies as much as Lisa, volunteered and got a spot policing students in the library with friend Bernice Tully and librarian, Nola Davenport. Twenty two students opted for that out from the assembly, today, and most thumbed their way through magazines or gathered for a bit of a conversational buzz someplace in the aisles formed by the bookcases, at the pencil sharpener, or in a recess of the room not visible from the librarian's desk.

Davey Huntington, on the other hand, sat in the thick of things with the senior class where Longfellow had assigned him to duty. Privately Huntington thought the whole mash of raspberry was a bunch of overdone hokum (as a junior and a senior high school student he had managed to play hooky from every pep assembly), but he recognized the impact teacher interest in things at school had on those shadowy student figures who drifted around the edges of the central theme. Pep assemblies, Davey was wont to muse, like the flag, apple pie and mother love may be a bunch of unmitigated shit, but they all provide strong pivotal points that keep our society from flying apart like the rickety one hoss shay. As he joined in the cheering, physically, now, he hoped that those fringies who thought Mr. Huntington "one cool cat" joined in because he did. As shades most of them flickered constantly on the edge of trouble, even disaster, if school could hold their interest until they acquired a little substance of their own, expenditure of taxpayer money for schools would be a lot less than society would have to pay for those lost to the criminal element.

Henry Crenshaw, the one male member of our English department, drew the downstairs hall as his assignment. He accepted his fate without a feel of emotion one way or another. Twenty years ago, when he graduated from a fine, small New England private college, he faced the world with a burning desire to right wrongs with his pen, fire the world's intellectuals with his poetry, and write the first, truly epic, American novel. Today, he felt very thankful for his school tenure, his monthly paycheck large enough so that wife, Sophie, need only work part time to help support their two kids, and the hours of free time school teaching afforded him for reading and dreaming about how things might have been.

In the typing room, Agnes Merriweather dozed at her desk while four Freshmen boys (none from her typing classes) collaborated on making a pornographic black and white picture with an old Royal manual typewriter. Carl Hargrave, on first floor hall patrol with Henry, looked in through her door once in search of a sympathetic ear. She appeared to be busy at her desk near the back wall, so he returned to the dim hall and his own angry brooding. He hated pep assemblies and rooter bus scheduling. As often as he shared this hate with others, he never tired of seeking another available ear.

Steve Hutchinson and Mavis Parmenter always sympathized with Carl's constant rankling on both these issues and tardiness to class, though they didn't really find any of the three matters quite as inconvenient as he did. Today Steve was not an available ear for Carl, for Longfellow assigned him the Freshman group with Marsha Kemper, and Mavis, too, was beyond Carl's reach, as she drew the junior section with big Tom Coleman.

David Royce, Marvin Kempler and Stephen Boyd drew blue chip assignments for the affair, because they got to hold a departmental meeting. Each pep assembly one or another department (on a rotating basis) met officially to discuss, supposedly, curriculum improvements and other such heady stuff. This piece of sop to that community splinter that felt that "teachers should do more than just baby sit" evolved as a brain child of Mr. W.'s. Its inception won him praise from old Miles Pettigrew, who had recognized its PR value, immediately, and, at the old now ex-superintendent's suggestion and prodding, Mr. W. doctored the truth a bit and used the concept for an article in an educational publication. Notes were kept of the meetings and turned into Mr. W., so, should the occasion arrive (which it hadn't yet in five years) the administration could show any doubting Thomases that little time was wasted by teachers because of student activities at Timbertop High School.

Out in the woodshop Bill Goss, too, entertained a crew of five boys busy on projects (mostly due before Christmas), while Jim Bettermen (who wouldn't have accepted any Longfellow assignments regardless of conditions) worked closely with three boys rebuilding an old Reo found in one of the boy's grandfather's barn. Patricia Armbruster received special dispensation to work one on one in her remedial reading clinic, while Mike O'Malley got an early start with his four students in the driver's training car.

Involved with some students who absolutely had to finish their art projects before the semester ended Friday, Sylvia Scanner chafed beneath restrictions that made her be here in the art building as a baby sitter while Willy Norburton played a starring role at the assembly. As the faint sounds of his trumpet leading "Glory to Timbertop" drifted through an open window louver, she closed her eyes and visualized him there in front of his sixty piece band—a young god with flaming staff, a magician waving a magic wand—a strong hard penis demanding the ultimate from his straining crew. She felt a moistness in her labial palps and smiled, dreamily.

"Glory to Timbertop" thought Pat Mooney, as she watched her male counselor counterpart hurry off to his much loved position as overall director of the pageant. "He gets his jollies, along with the other coaches," she thought, bitterly, "while the rest of us are supposed to bow down and holler amen and hallelujah!" For one harried moment she thought about trying to slip out early so she could get a fast start on the evening ahead. "Sure as hell, Wellington would catch me up in it and get me down in his little green book," she figured, with resignation. What she couldn't figure was why or how Longfellow missed scheduling her into some picki-ass job. Could it be a chance moment of good luck for her, or did the omission carry some ominous undertone? The effort to analyze caused a nervous tic to start at one corner of her mouth, and she hurried from her office toward the growing malestrom sound in the gym. "One thing about a pep assembly," she told herself, "with all that blast of noise you don't have an opportunity to think."

# CHAPTER SIX

Thirty seven separate bell clappers simultaneously vibrated the school day's end, and an explosive sound of young voices and bodies bursting through our gym's outside double doors carried to Heidi's home ec room where she began goodbyes to eleven of her fifteen girls, then moved among the other four encouraging them to close shop for the day. During the sixth period's last ten minutes a growing feeling of unease had built inside her by geometric progression, for her conscience began to nag that she might very well soon face David Huntington and, despite George Anderson's blue ribbon certification of her projected date with that young man, she harbored a number of frightening reservations.

"Can't I just please finish hemming this skirt, Miss Vandercamp?" pleaded a thin little sophomore girl she tried to push toward putting things away.

"Please, Deborah, not this afternoon," sighed Heidi, and her voice, too, carried a note of plea. "I've got a terrible headache, and I'd like to go home right at four, if I could."

She told no lie; her head felt like a walnut caught in the grip of a nutcracker. Behind both ears, her pulse pounded with dull, throbbing aches, and her mouth and throat, constricted and dry, joined an intermittent sharp cramp in her stomach to further add to discomfort. For Heidi, who rarely knew a moment of illness, her situation grew more impossible by the minute, and more terrifying as the clock ticked onward.

It took David Huntington fifteen minutes to extricate himself from an exhuberant senior mob who meant to claim him as their own. (Seniors, allowed to bring cars to school, found themselves freed of the school buses exorable time schedules.) They continued chanting "Go! AXEMEN, GO!" as they serpentined around the gym, through the faculty and student parking lots, and finally ended on broad cement porch steps that fronted their red brick building. Though anxious to get himself away from the kids, David found them a source of psychological amusement, too. The greatest fever of excitement, he noted, came upon the five thinly clad cheerleaders who danced through cold slush in the parking lot in their flimsy white boots of soft (hardly waterproof) suede, while the least show of emotion came from five cool boys scheduled to star in tonight's drama.

Free, at last, from hands that clung to him and the worshipping eyes that held him even more fast, David got through the front door and made it down the hall to his classroom door. As he passed along the lower hall he saw Longfellow holding three small boys boxed into one of the corners. From the VP's chopping hand motions those young miscreants found themselves in bad trouble, and Davey hurried by not wanting to hear what words flooded out in the administrator's strident voice.

"The Bogeyman strikes again," he muttered, under his breath. "Paste up another gold star on the side of law and order."

Carl Hargraves and Henry Crenshaw had deserted their lower hall posts precisely at 3:35 (as per scheduled agreement), and they waited, now, in their rooms for a 3:57 exodus. In the faculty room coaches smoked and discussed tonight's best game strategies, and the sympatico married teachers shared their last cigarette and complaint of the day (Miss Merriweather still dozed at her desk with the pornographic typewriter picture now raggedly thumbtacked to her bulletin board). Up stairs Mr. W. herded a few lingering freshmen and sophomore bodies on their way (they were second bus people and were supposed to wait in the bus loading zone below), and in the girl's counseling office, Pat Mooney, with a "Back in a Minute" sign on her closed, locked door, sat at her desk with a window partly open behind a drawn shade as she sucked nervously on a most illegal cigarette while she watched seconds tick by on the hands of her clock.

David shook off a childish impulse to knock on Lisa Overstreet's closed and locked classroom door before he stepped through the door to his own room, but he let it go for he felt she'd probably had enough razz for one day and, besides, would probably ignore the knock, anyway, as her girl friends who came to pick her up usually awaited her in the faculty parking lot. He got his topcoat from his closet, checked floors, chalk boards, bookcases and chair alignments to see the room looked fairly neat and orderly for the sweepers, adjusted the upper and lower window blinds to near perfect alignment (as per teacher instructions from the principal), then locked the door behind him as he headed on down the hall and out across the faculty parking lot to the porch of the home ec building.

When he walked through the door, the world stopped turning for Heidi Vandercamp. She found herself unable to breathe, unable to move, and unable to feel her headache or the beat of her heart. He came moving toward her, a broad smile on his face, and she knew should he touch her—here, at this moment—she would flame up and die in a burst of sheer pleasure.

"Hi, there," he said, looking down on her as Gulliver must have looked at his first Lilliputian. "Thought maybe I could follow you home, if you're not staying too late. That way I can find where you live, and I can figure how much time I've got to work on our dinner before I come pick you up."

She continued to stare at him, stupidly, her tongue latched to her parched mouth's dry rooftop. What kind of idiot he must think I am, she thought, wildly. I've got to say something, anything. Can I beg out of the whole thing with an excuse of my headache?

"What's the matter?" he asked, gently, "you're not feeling so good? These pep rally afternoons raise hell with all of us."

His warm sympathy thawed her numbness; she felt her heart beat again and moisture return to her mouth to free her tongue. In an unprecedented movement, for her, she placed one tiny hand on the rough cloth of his coat sleeve.

"Why don't you sit down," he suggested. "Let me get these girls moving on their way."

"Please, could you?" she whispered, hoarsly, and the hand flew from his coat sleeve to her ivory forehead where crevasses of pain had returned to plague her.

With jocularity and a big brother manner that pleased the girls and bemused their teacher, David got things packed away and closed her outer door behind the last chattering sophomore.

"Now, what is it?" he asked, returning to Heidi, who had watched the antics from a seated spot behind her desk.

"Just a terrible headache," she said, apologetically, but pleased that she felt relaxed, now, in speaking to him. "I'm afraid I didn't get too much sleep last night, and I'm usually out of it by ten or so."

"Mrs. Mooney's dinner party turned into a bash," suggested David, and a secret sharing, boyish grin made him seem even younger and safer to be with.

"It turned out to be a disaster area," Heidi confided, feeling a confidence with him now as she did with her father and with Father Mueller. "She brought out some cocaine for us to use, and it scared me half to death, I'll tell you."

"That's too bad," sympathized David, and his mind grasped a vivid picture of the terror such a moment would create for this naive little girl. "Don't judge Pat too quickly or too harshly, Heidi. You won't find many with empathy like hers in this business of ours."

"I don't know what that means," said Heidi, and an involuntary shudder shook her shoulders. "I just know I don't want to get mixed up with any kind of dope."

"I understand that," said David, "and I'm sure Pat never dreamed you had such strong feelings that way. I mean, she's the kind of a person who really feels and understands the problems of others—perhaps too much so, for her own peace of mind. You've got to realize that she's very lonely, right now, and she wanted you to meet her most constant friend—cocaine."

"Well, I don't want to meet her friend again," said Heidi, and she trembled visibly. "I'm not sure I even want to be alone with Mrs. Mooney again."

"Live as you feel you must," cautioned David, "but I wouldn't shut her out of my life, if I were you. Don't put some kind of a barrier between you that someday, later, you might regret. Right now you've been scared and like a turtle you want to pull yourself into your shell. That's okay. Nothing wrong with that. Just don't block your exits so that you can't get out again when you get tired of the little world with only you in it."

All this philosophy proved too much for Heidi, but his words sounded beautiful and she smiled to show her appreciation.

"How's that headache now?" he asked. "Good enough to herd that little Honda car of yours home? It's almost four o'clock."

Amazed at her suddenly bouyant feelings, she touched slender fingers to her temples and her forehead. Listening to David the squeezing pressure that had agonized her had somehow slipped away.

"Much better," she assured him, and she gave him another smile, this one in thanks for the wonderful relief he had brought to her.

"Then let's close this place and get away from the madhouse," he said, laughing lightly. "I got woks to heat, hibachis to fire, tea to brew and some incense to burn."

By the time school buses left on their first run, A.T. had repaired two combination locks and had run a big hand crank snake through the main lower floor sewer line in a third effort of the day. With the gymnasium cleared of bodies, at last, he made a round there picking up a half dozen discarded lunch bags, two jackets for the office lost and found and a pom pom left behind by a cheerleader. At four he used Mrs. Metzger's phone to call Barbara and ask her for dinner at five (he would return to the school at six to let in Eph Findlay's JV boys and the team and the coaches from Chehalis High School). Then he waited, watching Mrs. Metzger close down her business for the day, until Mr. W. returned from his vigil in the chemistry lab. With a "Mr. Cromwell" for any chance listener who might be around, Roger marched through his big black walnut door with A.T. trailing behind him. As the office door closed Mr. W. sank into his chair with his usual sigh of exhaustion; the lesser Titans may have been embattled for the afternoon, but from his spot on Olympus, Zeus held responsibility for all.

"Hate to bother you with this thing," said A.T., placing his painfully worded plumbing memo on the glass surface that glinted in front of his chief. "Believe me, Mr. W., I tried since last August to get Dr. Imberlay to move on that plumbing. The guy just don't hear us peasants talking."

"I know," said Roger, delighted by the expression he, himself, would repeat to any of his friends who wanted to discuss the superintendent, "he doesn't pay much attention to what I say, either. What can I do?"

"Get my memo into your building report tomorrow night," suggested A.T. "Try to get Mick Randolph or Edna Keefer to move on it—nobody else on that board's got the brains God gave to a titmouse."

"No money's been placed for plumbing, you know that," said Roger.

"Superintendents always got a special contingency fund," said A.T. "I seen old Pettigrew pull that one a half dozen times when he wanted somethin special, or we really had ourselves some trouble. You tell that to Mick, and you tell him we got real trouble. Enough to close us down if somethin' ain't done pretty soon."

"Got it," said Roger. "Hey, you want me to run you home? Kinda late in the day for you, isn't it?"

"Thanks. I got plenty of time," said A.T. "Gonna try that rest room one more time. Hopin' we can make that thing get by a bit longer. Some of them boys got a hell of a time tryin' to make classes when they got to make it all the way upstairs every time they got to go to the pisser."

The urinals flushed without backing up, so A.T. retrieved his padlock and returned it to its spot in the furnace room. Zipped up in his mackinaw and feet warm and dry in his mukluks, he locked his outside door behind him (the Schwartz boy had a key to the inside door) and started across the faculty parking lot toward home. Looking old and tired, George Anderson's rig stood alone in the center of the lot; only Mr. W.'s Pinto, in his marked spot near the door, remained to keep it company.

Damn kid should be home resting for the game tonight, A.T. told himself, then he did an about face and let himself in through the boy's outside lockerroom door. He found George Anderson alone in his office slowly studying his way through the varsity score book.

151

"Hi coach," said A.T., poking his head through the half open doorway.

"A.T., what's up?" asked George, looking up quickly, pleased and surprised.

"Wonder if you could do me a favor?" asked A.T., glibly.

"Whatever," said George, closing his book.

"Well, seems I'm running a bit short on time," lied A.T., "and I thought, maybe, if you was leaving soon you could give me a ride."

"Gosh, yes," said George, eagerly, glad to do a favor for this man who did hundreds for him. "I was just fixin to leave. You ready, now?"

"Sure am," said A.T., jerking a thumb at the mackinaw he wore.

George grabbed his overcoat, with no further word, and with the tall young man in the lead (like Mutt and Jeff) they headed for George's old car.

It surprised, and greatly pleased, Madge to find George home before five o'clock. She fussed over him, insisted they share a martini in pre-celebration of the victory she assured him for the evening. His little girls, too, got an unusual chance to "play with daddy," and the three of them romped in horsey play on the living room rug while Madge called encouragement from the kitchen.

"All in all," thought George, as he pretended to be in stitches of laughter from the girls tickling him, "it's pretty great to have time for your own family. In Cicero every night could be like this. Saturday or Sunday I've got to have a long serious talk with Madge on the thing."

As the Anderson family gathered around their dinner table, Roger Wellington arrived home to find Emily not yet started with their evening meal. Both of his kids lay stretched out in the rumpus room numbed by overdriven decibels and flickering color from the 21 inch Zenith TV. With them out of earshot, Roger grabbed the chance to take off on Emily for her late party of the night before.

"You sleep in so I don't get any breakfast," he stormed, "now it's after five with no dinner started. You know I've got to be back by seven for the game."

"Look, big shot," Emily snapped back at him (even a half hour of extra sleep, two Alka Seltzers and a light day at the office failed to alleviate all of her hangover), "I'm not your kitchen slave, you know. I go to work everyday, too."

"You play games with a lot of poor suckers trying to get fleeced buying a house, and flunky for a couple of minor con-men who mask under the disguise of real estate salesmen," he said, acid voiced.

"Con men, is it?" snashed Emily (whose father's Irish brogue caught up with her when she got her dander up), "Con men, is it, you bit of hasty pudding. It's you, the pot, callin the kettle black, it is. Con men, indeed, and yourself as slippery as a pond full of frog eggs."

"Look, Emily," reversed Roger, swiftly, remembering the next level of her explosion involved throwing things in his general direction, "I don't want a quarrel; I'm not looking for a fight. I just think it looks pretty bad in the community when you come home, alone, from Castleview at three o'clock in the morning."

"It was business," she mocked him, "and the bars closed at two. How many hundred thousand million times have I heard that statement from you on your five nights out each week while I stay home awaiting your pleasure."

"Not my pleasure," he argued, stiffly. "After all evening work is part of my job."

"Your job, my ass," she said, "George Rutherford didn't baby sit ball games, and wrestling matches, and school dances, and PTA meetings, and go to Boosters, Kiwanis, and a dozen others, like you do."

"George ran a sloppy ship," he said, lamely.

"But he was lucky to have a first mate like you to keep it from capsizing," she said, caustically.

"Somebody's got to keep things under control," he argued, stubbornly.

153

"Then what about Longfellow; the first mate you chose?" she accused. "How come he's not the big 'Athletic Director' you were as V.P.? How come he doesn't ride herd on the cheerleaders and see our students behave when they go away to games?"

"God damn it, Emily," he roared, angered beyond reason (as she generally made him when they clashed to this point), "Longfellow knows nothing about sports and sport schedules."

"So what's to know," she said, caustically, "that any competent ninth grade boy couldn't learn."

"I do my job the way I see it needs to be done," he shouted, loud enough for Betty to hear above the roar of the Adam 12 car (she nudged Bobbie, ducked her head in the kitchen's general direction, shrugged her shoulders and grimaced so he knew exactly what she meant).

"Your job, my ass," she said. "You love walking tall in that world of sweaty little boys and screaming little girls. You like to have those mealy mouthed teachers genuflect even when you know they've just been sharpening knives to cut a hole in the middle of your back. You love playing Little King to the local goody two shoes—you love it all, you fourflushing bastard. Don't tell me about your work, Roger Wellington, you're still backin' the line for old Castleview High."

He wanted to grab her in his big, still powerful hands. Hold her choking in front of his face, and shake her as a pit bull might shake an aggravating toy poodle. Every word she said; every nerve she needled, made him feel that he shrank smaller and smaller while she seemed to grow like Athena before him.

"Be careful of your heart, Roger," said Emily, now cold voiced, as he stood fists rage clenched in front of him and his face turning more, each second, a deep plum-like color. "With all that fat you're carrying, you could go down any second for the count of ten."

"Arghh!" was all he could force himself to reply.

"Which reminds me," she said, now matter-of-factly, "I wish you'd see about getting another fifty thousand dollar life policy; your brother just did. Raising kids these days costs a lot of money. Pretty hard for me to make it alone with them even on the good salary Bud pays me each month."

The unpleasantness that grew in the Wellington kitchen, though not desirable, at least expressed a clean, honest sentiment on each participant's side. The sentiments, however, lying behind a dinner conversation going on at that time between Lisa Overstreet and her friend, Cecil Ashbrenner, stemmed from vile, pus filled pits of human frustration that we find bubbling inside every person who secretly hate themselves for what they are, but who also lack the moral fibre to do anything about the things they hate in themselves. So, as these two girls sat together over plates full of steaming stew prepared and left to simmer on a burner by Agnes Mulcahy (Lisa's present Tuesday and Saturday housecleaner and cook), the context of their conversation belonged more properly in that slimy place where devils caretake the souls of evil dead gossip mongers.

Lisa lived in a modest two bedroom brown frame house on a quiet backstreet near what had grown to be downtown Timbertop. For almost 18 years she lived in this same location, and in a little more than two years her mortgage would be paid in full. The first five or six years at this address she spent hours on yard work, days and nights decorating and cleaning, and many afternoons and evenings hostessing lunches and dinners for her girl friends (memories of these affairs provided a core for the power position she continued to maintain with her Guild, though she no longer played an active role as an officer or entertainer).

But the past ten years, as she grew more obese and plagued with tiredness and pains, she turned her yard over to the twenty five and fifty cent ministrations of small boys and small girls who sought pin money with their efforts from time to time, and the interior upkeep became the enterprise of a continuing series of welfare mothers who, for a "few dollars under the table" came in twice a week to clean the outward show of her messes and to cook a stew, a pot roast, or a big pan of chili that could be warmed again by Lisa for her subsequent meals. Though the "cleaning ladies" kept things tidy on the surface, years of filth accumulated in hidden spots under furniture and in dark corners. These decaying eating spots for silverfish and cockroaches gave the rooms a sour, unpleasant smell that escaped Lisa who had accumulated a tolerance for odors by close association with them. Cecil, Mavis, and others who came here to visit, however, always brought packages of incense which they insisted on burning.

"I do so love the smell of that sandalwood," Cecil was saying, now, as she stopped her slow, careful chewing on a piece of stew beef to take deep sniffs from the haze that rose from a smouldering black cone on the table in front of her.

"Nice," grunted Lisa, through a huge helping of boiled potato and carrot she ground together with her strong yellow teeth. "Something genteel about it (as the food cleared her throat with a noisy gulp) something mystic, like the Orient—you know what I mean, Cecil."

"Oh, I do, I do," breathed Cecil, her fork poised to pick up another dainty bite. "I love the East—wanted always to visit Hong Kong and Singapore" (her voice grew reverent in deference to all that colorful mystery and ancient culture).

"I, too, love to think of Kubla Khan," moaned Lisa, sadly, "but I'm afraid I'll not be strong enough to travel that far by the time I can afford the opportunity."

"Poor Lisa," sympathized Cecil. "You've given so much of your life for the children of Timbertop and got so little back from them in return."

"One does not teach for money, recognition, or reward," said Lisa, solemnly. "One teaches because something bright and forceful inside forces you onward to do the things that you must do."

"Oh, I know," breathed Cecil Ashbrunner. "A call like our famous evangelistic preachers. Like Amy Semple Mc Pherson, and of course, Billy Graham."

"But we've false ministers in our midst disguised as teachers," said Lisa, ominously. "People out to distort the minds and corrupt the bodies of our young under the pretense of doing them good."

"Heidi Vandercamp," said Cecil, grimly.

"Yes, and Pat Mooney," agreed Lisa, her voice grown conspiratorial. "Our little drunken home ec teacher staggered

156

home from Pat Mooney's apartment when we saw her last night. Worse than that, I'm not sure that she wasn't high on drugs instead of filled with alcohol."

At the word drugs Cecil exploded a startled "No!"; now, it took her a few stunned seconds to regain her voice.

"Drug addicts," she said as if the words were excrement in her mouth. "Right in our school. Teaching our children. Lisa, dear Lisa, we've got to do something."

"I wish it stopped there," said Lisa, hushed voice, "but it seems there is also the possibility they may be. . .lesbians."

Cecil sat bolt upright in a proper catatonic silence. The word lesbian was no stranger to her for the girls had mulled it around after reading the "Well of Loneliness" and other like literary exposes. But this was "lesbians," for real. Real people with faces she, herself, had seen; real bodies that had been (horrors) in close proximity to her own. Her mind froze at the picture of horrible doings and secret sins pushed by these two depraved women on the young girls of Timbertop.

"Whatever are we going to do?" she asked, at last, in a frail, trailing voice.

"Nothing, of course, until after levy time," said Lisa, dispassionately. "Then, I think a little anonymous phone call to the sheriff first from me, then from you, then from Mavis, and perhaps one or two others letting him know those women harbor dope rings in their apartments. If the phone calls won't get Buck Peterson off the shiny seat of his big wide backside, then I think a letter to the F.B.I. in Portland might just be the ticket to clean out their foul little nests of perversion."

Had Lisa been able to see Pat Mooney at that moment, she might have sent Cecil immediately to the phone—special levy or no special levy. For Pat, spaced out from long hours without food, groggy and unbalanced from lack of sleep, and raw nerved from the many demands on her understanding and felicitations during the day, lay naked in the middle of her living room rug. Feet flat on the floor but knees spread wide and high, she held a Playgirl Centerfold in her left hand while her right busily worked in masturbation.

"Oh, God!" she moaned, softly, over and over. "Oh, God! I'm so lonely. Please make it all end."

By now George Anderson had ended his dinner, and he relaxed in front of TV with two quiet little girls cuddled in the warmth of his lap. As he stared, uncomprehendingly at the impossible situation Captain Kirk seemed unlikely to overcome, his mind occupied itself with offensive possibilities against that very dangerous, explosive jug zone his boys faced in a matter of hours. All at once he sensed Madge standing behind his chair, then he felt her soft hands smooth heavy grooves that sought to erode permanent wrinkles in his forehead.

"Got a baby sitter coming?" he asked, hopefully.

"Sure thing, man of mine, you don't think you get out of this house two nights in a row without me," she joked, lightly.

"What time will she be here?" he asked, and already tension for the night ahead started to build in in bowels like a pressure cooker.

"She'll be here at seven, so we can see some of Eph's game," she promised him.

"Madge, I really do love you," he blurted out, spontaneously, for no reason, at least, he could think of.

"We've got a beautiful family, baby," she said, pressing a kiss where her hands had smoothed away at his forehead skin.

"I've been thinkin' about that a lot lately," said George. "Yep, I've been giving that matter a lot of my thoughts."

"She's truly unbelievable," thought Davey Huntington, as he held the passenger door of his sports car open so that Heidi could slide in upon the leather seat. "Like one of those virgins in a Victorian gothic novel, or some special little princess raised in the shelter of an old sultan's harem. Sister Mercy! That's who she reminds me of. At last I've figured out that, at least. God! I haven't thought about Sister Mercy in almost twenty years."

It had been Sister Mercy, a wizened old nun, who gave him music lessons on his mother's demand. She visited, often, with Davey's grandfather at the old Huntington place. There, in the awesome quiet of grampa's study and library, Davey sat at grampa's feet and watched the radiant face of Sister Mercy as the two old people discussed people, ideas, and places far removed from the mundane county that surrounded the Castleview city limits. Davey III, by the age of five, heard the summa of Thomas Acquinas challenged by the haunting imagination of Kierkegard. He knew that politics, American as well as others, provided greater temptations of sin to the bodies and minds of men than did the wiles of a woman or the profits of a business. Sister Mercy took them with her when, as a young novitiate, she served with the world's kindest man, Father Delaunay, among the poor and diseased out in Pakistan. His grandfather took them exploring up the Amazon River, and Sister talked of the ancient treasures of Rome while grandpa described a holy city of the Incas. As if speaking about old friends the two old people, unaware of their incongruous relationship to a very small boy, quoted Shakespeare, Moliere, Mark Twain, Henry Miller, and a hundred others. Small wonder when David started public school he felt his teachers a little retarded.

"You're a Catholic," he said, their first conversation since he had said "hello" at her door (surprised to find her dressed and coated as she opened her room).

She turned in the car to face him as he inserted his key in the ignition.

"Yes," she seemed a bit surprised by the question note his voice had inflected into his statement. "Is something wrong with my being that?"

"God, no," laughed Davey, "it's just that you remind me of a nun I knew years ago."

"Well, I thought very seriously about taking my vows," Heidi admitted, confidentially, "but I just didn't feel that strongly about giving up the things of the world, nor of remaining celibate."

"Is that what being a nun is all about, celibacy?" teased Davey, forgetting, momentarily, the total depth of her naievity.

"That's part of it," she said, seriously, "and being dedicated to God and to the service of others."

"But you're serving others now," persisted Davey, as the Porsche moved smoothly along. "I'm sure you're very dedicated to going to church, and I'll bet my last dollar you're celibate, too."

"I've not been all that faithful since I came to Timbertop," she said, almost in the way of an apology, "but, of course, I never took my holy vows."

He let it drop there realizing she got easily lost in the spider web of his logic. In a thumbnail sketch he presented her his experiences in Christianity, Zen, the Muslim faith, agnosticism, and his present exploration into Hinduism. It helped fill the three miles to his condominium, and though he felt she understood very little of the points on religion he continued to make, she seemed starry eyed in the light from the dashboard as if she just enjoyed the sound of his voice.

At his place she did an "Oh" and an "Ah" about the big drive in and under garage, and the plush lined elevator that deposited them effortlessly a few steps from his door. By the radiant sparkle in her heaven blue eyes, and the eagerness that flowed around her like a spiritual aura, he knew she found his apartment something extra experientia, even the makeshift Oriental center he had constructed around a low glass topped coffee table in the center of the room where a brass pagoda on a tall brass serpent column emitted incense smoke above the silken cushions he had placed for their comfort around the table.

"Let me help you with your coat," he suggested, when she finally stopped flitting around the room like a humming bird from his large sombre Matisse, to his wall cased with books, to his still work cluttered desk, to, finally, the big undraped picture window that exposed a light show from the residential and downtown districts of Timbertop spread out below.

With a gay laugh she unbuttoned her grey fur collared coat of maroon mohair fibres, and he lifted it from her shoulders to see a perfect size 3 in a silver metallic short cocktail dress.

"How very, very nice he is," she thought, as he carried her coat away into another room she judged to be his bedroom, "and what wonderful taste he has in decorations and furnishings. I wonder if he'd let me bring my fifth period boys here on a field trip when we start our section on apartment planning next semester?"

In what was indeed his bedroom, Davey laid her coat carefully on the satin comforter that covered his queensized water bed. The mirror that closed off the four poster's top into a canopy reflected the coat lying there, all alone. "A strange new sight for you, huh," thought Dave as he caught the reflection, and he let himself smile an indulgent amusement at himself. From the bed he moved to a big walk in closet from which he emerged carrying a small, heavy, colorful deep red and yellow flowered raw silk Japanese kimono and its accompanying obi. To his knowledge the garment had never been worn, for he bought it just before leaving Japan and Heidi proved to be the first possible wearer he had brought to any of his subsequent apartments. He wondered, as he made for the bedroom door, what reaction she would expose to a proposal she wear it for the evening. Never one to avoid truths or put off actions, he moved steadily ahead until he once more stood where she stared out through the white gauze curtains into the night beyond.

"A view from on top," he said, lightly, and she turned, smiling quizzically, so he knew his bon mot had escaped her again.

"How lovely," she exclaimed, on seeing the kimono draped across both his forearms. "How absolutely exquisite."

"Would you like to wear it for the evening?" he suggested. "I can join you, then, by wearing mine."

"Oh, could I!" she exclaimed, breathlessly. "Where can I change?"

"You take the bedroom, he said, indicating the door through which he had just emerged. "I keep mine in my sauna bath. It's just down the hall."

A.T. strolled into the locker room where an excited, exhuberant, shouting victorious Chehalis Jayvee team horsed each other about as they splashed and soaped in the hot steamy showers. Although coaches supposedly watched their boys so no vandalism occurred (according to page eleven in the league handbook), A.T. knew from years of experience that, more often than not, a young jayvee coach found more interest in replaying the game verbally with the referees or with one of his buddies who had carefully charted game statistics. Though boys who won were must less likely to rifle lockers, unscrew shower heads, steal towels than the boys who lost, A.T. took no chances with either, for he found it simpler to make his presence felt by the boys before the fact than it was to deal with the coaches after the fact. He didn't, of course, worry about their varsity locker room where Eph's boys verbally demeaned themselves for their many mistakes of the evening. He knew Eph held tight control of his sophomore boys at home and abroad; they would no more think of vandalizing with him around than they would think of murdering in broad daylight under the watchful eye of a policeman.

So, in the visitor's locker room, A.T. seemed to move aimlessly about doing little things, totally ignored, openly, by the boys in occupancy, but each secretly felt the custodian's eyes were on him. In the same manner he patrolled locker rooms A.T. covered out of the way spots in the gym and the two rest rooms for public use that lay at each end of the outer lobby (he used an old mop and bucket trick to enter the Ladies for regular checkups). He expected, and got, little trouble from his own high school students; his main problems stemmed from Timbertop drop-outs, a few one or two year alumnae (who, having done nothing while in school now returned to public events with booze hidden under their jackets, grass and papers stuffed in an inner pocket, fish knives or brass knucks which they fondled in their jacket pockets, and a feeling that, somehow, a display of these things might prove that they were somebody doing a real something, now). These, as their visiting counterpart from the challenging school did, made him feel at times that he might be back on the islands under fire while all around him lay hidden Japanese mines. Visiting students, like their Timbertop brethern, rarely caused trouble (especially those who came on a rooter bus). In the last few years, however, he noted with no small amount of distress that more and more high school girls came in cars with the would be hot shots who were looking for trouble. Though he usually tried to handle situations himself, bringing in Mr. W. if it did happen to be one of their high school students, he made it a point to turn the mixture of out-of-school boy and in-the-school girl over to one of their auxiliary policemen on duty.

162

Tonight, so far, things seemed quiet and pretty well under control. After letting the boys and their coaches into the gym at six, A.T. made an extra round of all the not-to-be-used doors and assured himself if they stood chained and locked. At 6:30, when both JV squads hustled out on the floor for their pre-game warmup, he began his slow, measured patrol of locker rooms, under bleachers, in off shoot hall recesses, and into their two public rest rooms. Finally he joined Mr. W. by the admissions door (he noted Agnes Merriweather supervising girls in the ticket booth and wondered how she had brooked Mr. W.'s displeasure).

"They got five rooter buses come'n in," Mr. W. informed him, cryptically.

"Big game," said A.T., his eyes studying each face and form that came in through the turnstile.

"Winners goin' to be in first place," said Mr. W., and a note of boyish excitement made his voice younger, not so flat.

"How many cops we got outside?" asked A.T.

"Two on regular traffic and patrol, and Buck promised a regular car would park here unless it got a call," said Mr. W., voice toneless, again.

"See we got young Ryan and his old man on the inside," said A.T.

"I knew you wanted it that way," said Mr. W., laconically.

"Hi, Mr. Cromwell," called a couple of Timbertop ex's, as they pushed their way past where the custodian and principal stood.

A continuous stream of greetings got answered by his wide smile and nod, and Mr. W., too, occasionally had a graduate stop by to talk briefly with him. In the influx of healthy, happy young bodies that flowed by, he detected several Timbertop blights familiar to him; then two, far out couples, apparently from Chehalis, pushed their way in laughing loudly and displaying their flaunted affections for the world to see. A.T. put them at the top of his suspect list; he hoped the girls, ages not distinguishable from their hanging hair and sloppy jeans, were not Chehalis high school girls.

By tip off time (seven p.m.) his mind recorded and catalogued the location of nearly two dozen tinderboxes most capable of starting a blaze. Through the jayvee games next hour and twenty minutes, he made patrols at fifteen minute intervals being careful to see if any of his twenty four happened to be gone from his or her seat. Though he saw little game action, he did keep track of the score, so he knew Chehalis took an early lead in the game and pulled ahead by ten points when the claxon rang half time. Shortly after half time he missed seeing the four Chehalis suspects, who had returned from an outside intermission trip to the parking lot, and had resumed their same seats in the stands. Acting on a hunch he turned back from his trek toward the locker room, and he made his way quickly to the men's public rest room. Pushing inside he found two small high school boys cowered and cornered by a urinal. Facing the boys, in lounging but menacing poses, stood the two hoods from whom he had earlier translated potential trouble.

"You boys better get back to the student section and stay there," A.T. told the relieved sophomore boys. "I'll handle any beef these two hippies might think that they have with you."

"Hey, now, pops, whatcha' hot about?" sneered one of the hoods, swaggering toward A.T. with thumbs tucked into a bright blue beaded belt (the high school boys split for the door).

A.T. caught the odor of marijuana that clung to the boy's denim jacket, short shaggy beard, and long greasy hair. He shot a quick left hand forward, grabbed the boy's oily chin whiskers and jerked the thin, blackhead pitted face close to his own.

"I suggest," he said, his voice like a thin garrote wire, "you take your friends and get the hell out of here. If I don't tear you apart, myself, I may be forced to have the local Johns shake down all four of you, and your car."

As a young schoolboy, Art Cromwell wanted desperately to be a football player or a basketball player, but he had neither the size nor the speed (one must have one or both early in life to attract the attention of a coach) desired in those sports. Had Timbertop had wrestling, then, as they do now, A.T.'s whole pattern of life might well have changed (not that he particularly wanted any change), and he certainly would have left after graduation with a legal, signed diploma. Out of school, as a young bar room fighter, he quickly learned to hit first and talk afterwards—the guy who got in the first lick won better than 90% of his fights. That same quick aggressiveness—the lack of hesitation when a dangerous situation surfaced, helped him stay alive at Guadalcanal, Saipan, Iwo Jima and later Korea. It meant the difference now as the scared, washed out grey eyes of the kid in his grip built a head of panic that brought tears to his lashes.

"You poor little bastard do-nothing," thought A.T. as he slowly loosed his grasp, but not the powerful stare from his eyes. "Maybe if you'd been bigger or had some speed they'd have found a place for you when you went to high school."

"We ain't hippies," mumbled the boy, as the pain in his jaws subsided a bit. (He knew his buddy behind him had a big fish knife in his pocket, but he also knew, as he knew about himself, when it came to a physical showdown his buddy was chicken shit.)

The mouthful of unwashed teeth that affronted him destroyed any sentiment A.T. might have felt brewing. A twenty year Marine Corps tradition of cleanliness, attention to duty, and respect for rules and regulations blotted any empathy he might have entertained for the boy's unfortunate background.

"You're slime, hippies," said A.T., and his two hands came half port as if to grab the boy again.

"Easy, man, easy," begged the boy. "We didn't do nuthin. We was jus' horsin the kids."

"You horse your ass on out of here, like I said," warned A.T. "You got five to collect those two chicks of yours and fly."

Now, as the first game of the evening ended, the four were gone, but he still knew of twenty or more potentials like them. He hoped the cops stationed outside were not screwing off the job, and the regular car sat parked under a light somewhere so it could be easily seen. His four ejects might easily vent their anger on cars in the lot or windows in the outbuildings. "'maybe," he thought, "I should go out and take a look for myself."

A raucous blare from their scoreclock claxson announced opening ceremonies for the varsity game. The last of a 63-51 victorious Chehalis jayvee team hurried out to see if their varsity teammates could repeat the triumph engineered by them. As a muted Star Spangled Banner forced its way in under the locker room door, A.T. moved around slowly gathering the few odd towels not thrown, as requested, in a basket set out for them. In George Anderson's office he saw the jayvee officials slowly putting on their clothes—heads still sparkling wet from their trip to the showers. He recognized one, a slender, wirey man. Amos Twofeathers played basketball at Castleview High when A.T.'s oldest boy played guard for the Timbertop Five.

"'Rough out there tonight, Amos?" asked A.T., coming to the half open door.

"Hi, A.T. Rough, well I guess. You know all Eph's boys play rough. Hard for that old boy to remember where football leaves off and basketball begins," laughed Amos.

"Well, somebody's got to make you guys earn your money," kidded A.T.

"Sometimes," said Amos, wearily, "I think I'd just like to get me a nice quiet custodial job like yours."

The gymnasium promoted a growing deafness in both Mr. W.'s ears as, at his station just inside the entrance to the student section, he kept one eye on the fast moving ball game and the other on student maggot-like movement, into, out of and through the bleachers. Since the Jayvee game began, he had ejected three Freshmen boys from the gym for rough housing, sent Miss Merri-weather, twice, into the ladies restroom to bring out high school girls he knew had gone in there to smoke, talked briefly with a dozen jock happy dads and ex-ball players of his own during half-time in the lobby, and had some brief, whispered words with Ray Cosgrove assuring him the letter to the editor was underway (Cosgrove came just before the varsity game commenced—he first checked the parking lot to see if he could find any students drinking).

Now, with the first varsity quarter ended 18-18, Mr. W. found his mouth and throat dry from excitement, and he longed to go someplace for a tall, cold glass of beer. He felt Anderson's team looked well coached during their first eight minutes of play—a credit to his whole athletic program—and he particularly found an extra edge of excitement in the play of the Carson boy at guard. Several times, when the boy made some spectacular move, Roger waited to hear the fog horn voice of the senior Carson, but apparently the man was off someplace drunk, or something, tonight, (a rare circumstance) for no sound of his came from the adult section which lay across the floor from where the students sat.

On reviewing the quarter with Eph, who had come to stand, momentarily, with his chief athletic man, they agreed that if Hunk Anderson could get started hitting with his game ability, The Axemen might well emerge number one in the league.

"Too bad about your game," Roger sympathized.

"Damn referees just kill us," said Eph, grimly. "Particularly that damn bow and arrow, Amos. He's been on my ass ever since I blackballed him as a football official three years ago."

A horn's blare brought two teams of hard working cheerleaders back from the gym floor to their place bouncing in front of the stands, and it brought Willy's ear deafening brass section to an uncoordinated halt. Back on the floor again the white shirted Axemen returned to action against the blazing traveling orange of Chehalis' speedy Bearcats.

Hunk Anderson took an under the basket feed from Carson and put the Axemen out in front by two as the gym rocked with cheers of joy. "God!" thought Roger. "I'd love to be going up and down that floor with them, now!" Sweat poured from his armpits, ran down his back, and puddled up in the ridges above his eyebrows. "Maybe I should start playing in the over 35 league. I'll lose some of this gut working outside this summer and get started right out with them next season."

In high school Roger played a competent, steady forward— jayvee in his sophomore year, varsity sub as a junior, and a starter during his senior season. Not too big on scoring, he proved big and strong on the backboards where the same reflex agility and hard, powerful, muscles that made him an outstanding football linebacker won him respect from other basketball players who tried to physically compete with him for the leather oval coming off the glassboard or the iron.

As a college jock he played a little gym rat ball off season from football, and, as coach at Rapid City he played a lot of town team ball for that logging town. When he came here to coach football for us, he sparked our town team in two city league championships, but after he became V.P. at the high school he didn't come out for the team anymore. Me, and a couple of other old boys who still puffed our way up and down the court on rubbery middle thirty legs, tried to talk him into coming back, but it seemed his new job just took up too much of his time. It was after that he started getting fat; me, I still work out at the YMCA thirty minutes every day.

Now, as Roger watched the trim sweating young men strain their muscles and tax their lungs, he regretted not having stayed in shape over the years (the trainer warned him when he left college lack of regular exercise would bring on blubber). Plain exercise, however, bored the hell out of him, and he never learned tennis or felt like giving up his fishing boat for a set of golf clubs. Jogging, just the sound of it, disgusted him fully, and Emily long ago gave up trying to get him to do a lot of dancing (though he did dance, some, with Madeline on some of their clandestine dates).

The red headed Carson boy scored, brilliantly, on a long looping lefthanded pushshot deep in the left hand corner baseline. Now, four points ahead, Timbertop's stands screamed: "Give 'em the Axe!"

Emily used to come watch him play on the town team, he remembered; she cheered louder than anyone else in their sparse loyal group. They used to swim together a lot every summer, too, especially when Betty and Robbie were small. Where had it all gone, those exciting good times? She never came to a ball game with him anymore, and neither of them had crawled into a swimsuit since his big white tire started to inflate beneath his chest.

Chehalis scored, but the Axemen countered right back with another. Then a pause in the action for some Chehalis free throws. From the corner of his eye Roger saw Ray Cosgrove talking to some young people grouped near the door on the adult side of the gym. For a moment, in a quandary, Roger felt torn between the force of stability his presence at the student section made, and the possibility of making more points with Ray by siding him if the director found himself in trouble. Just starting to move that way, he saw A.T. emerge from the mill of people by the door, say something to Cosgrove, then beckon three long haired, bearded young men to follow him out into the lobby.

"Good old A.T.," thought Roger, "what in hell would I ever do without him. Think I'll give him that salmon pole Bud gave me for Xmas as a birthday present next month. Don't like the damn thing, anyway, and that pole of his gets more worn and shabby everytime we go out."

Chehalis picked up one point at the free throw line and now only trailed by three. "Go! Axemen!" the students screamed, almost shattering glass in the gym skylight far overhead. Kit Carson cooly dribbled the ball deep left into the forecourt and the screams implored him to: "Get that score!"

"If Emily would only take a more active part in school things with me," Roger continued thinking, "maybe we could get back to the way we once were together. Christ knows, I don't really want this thing with Madeline, but a guy's got to know that some woman appreciates him just for the way that he is."

With a move like a magician's hand, the orange shirted speedball, Pennbrook, who made the neck of the Chehalis jug, stepped in behind Carson and stripped him of the ball. Quick reflexes sent Kit diving after it, and he and Pennbrook got whistled to a face off.

"Foul!" screamed fans on both sides and for both teams, but the referees implacably ignored criticism of their call. In a scramble for the tip, that same speedy jug neck got a feed on a break, and the Bearcats, back in things again, now stood just one point behind.

"Hi, Mr. Wellington," said a whiney voice down near the buckle of his belt.

He glanced down, vaguely recognized Reuben Schwartz (by sight, not by name), and nodded his scowling visage glowering down at the boy as a reminder that he belonged in the student section until released at half time.

Across the way, to the left of the timer's table, he saw Coach Anderson hunched on the edge of his substitute bench where seven other gangling boys screamed encouragement to their teammates out on the floor.

"I know what's happening in your guts, old buddy," he thought, emphatically. "I took on jayvee basketball those three years at Rapid City, and I'm still carrying ulcer scars in memory of that. Give me football where a coach at least has some control over the game. For all you can do sitting there and watching that footrace go on, you might as well be at home sending in substitutes by telephone."

At half-time the Axemen went to their locker room trailing the Bearcats by four big ominous points.

As Coach Anderson led his (momentarily) dispirited warriors to a bench in the cool varsity locker room, Heidi and David delicately set down tiny eggshell cups from which they had been sipping hot saki. They looked, companionably, at each other across the culinary remains on the coffee table's glass top, and both shifted ever so slightly in their unaccustomed cross legged sitting position on pillows close to the floor.

"Delicious, David, everything is just delicious. I'm going to have to include a section on wok and tempura cookery in both my advanced cooking class and my bachelor living class."

"I worried a bit about the Choan Mushi," he admitted.

"Well, you didn't have to worry about anything," said Heidi, "though I think you made enough Oyako Donburi for eight couples instead of one."

"I did get carried away," he chuckled. "Maybe I'll bring it to school tomorrow and we can invite some people to lunch with us."

"How exciting," bubbled Heidi. "I've got plenty of room in my refrigerators."

"The important thing, though, is that you enjoyed yourself," said David, simply.

"All of it," she breathed. "Even the hot saki which I thought sure I could never drink."

"It's really not much good cold," he said.

"My father always makes mother serve wine at room temperature," said Heidi. "I usually like the sweet ones, but the sour ones taste like vinegar to me."

"How do you like my Japanese music?" asked David, as a particularly strident one string passage burst forth from the stereo then shattered like fine shards of glass with the interjection of brassy cymbals.

"Mostly it's noise to me," Heidi admitted, shamefaced. "I told you I'm not very intellectual."

"You got a darn good appetite for a little girl, and a damn honest attitude as a human being," said David. "That's the important things in a dinner companion."

"I did enjoy your Japan stories and pictures, though," she said. "Someday I want to travel all over the world and see how other people live."

"You don't want to settle down and have a family and all that kind of thing?" asked David, trying not to tease.

"I don't think I ever want any children—though I might adopt some, sometime. Far too many children in the world now, I'm afraid. One more by me would just add to their problems and hers."

"I thought you weren't intellectual," he chided her, softly.

"You don't have to be intellectual to read and understand facts," she said. "Dr. Ehlrich's work was part of my undergraduate study, and the girl friends I talk with realize the truths he and others keep trying to make. I don't have any close girl friends who plan to have children."

"How do you explain that to your Pope?" he asked, pushing a little.

"I don't, and I'm sad about that," she said. "Father Mueller agrees, however, the Pope is wrong in this matter. Historical pressure, he told me, makes all great leaders act sometimes in a manner they know wrong for them and wrong for the common good. The future, he told me, will justify my decision not to bring children into the world. To do so just to conform to a highly questionable edict now, to bring a child's life because our leader made a historical mistake, would be a sin against mankind if not against God. I truly believe in what Father Mueller says."

"And who's Father Mueller?" asked David, politely.

"My priest and confessor," said Heidi. "I've known him since I was a girl."

"You're not much more than that, now," laughed David, tenderly, "and already you've decided you'll never get married."

"I didn't say that," she said, fixing him squarely with her deep blue eyes. "If I found a companion I wanted to be with, live with, and that person happened to be a man, I suspect I'd want to marry him, for otherwise I might make my parents, my priest, and the school people I worked for very unhappy persons."

"Suppose, for the sake of discussion, the man you chose wanted to have a child by you?" he asked, curiously.

"We should understand how I feel on the matter and how he feels on the matter before we formed a permanent partnership," said Heidi, matter-of-factly.

"And you don't believe in love?" David asked, almost archly.

"The only real love I've ever seen, that I can be sure of, is the love my parents share, and it's a pretty wonderful thing," she said. "They could have had other children beside me; I'm sure, in fact, my father would very much like to have a son. They've seen the world, however, where hunger really exists; they've known what happens when populations outstrip their sources of nourishment. Long before I ever heard about Dr. Ehrlich, before, even, I talked these matters out with Father Mueller, my mother and father explained these things to me, and I have some pretty grim pcitures about what the world can hold in thirty or forty years for a child who is born today."

"Never again say to me that you're not an intellectual," said David, his amazement with her growing at each self revelation she made. "Let's talk now about something much more mundane— those senior boys who give you the trouble. Tell me who they are and what they do, and I'll see if I can help you find some relief."

The standing and stretching relieved some of the minor back and shoulder aches that plagued Madge after sitting nearly two hours on a hard eight inch wide bench. As she settled back down again she watched the cheerleaders perform a routine to the band, and she secretly told herself this actually provided the best part of the evenings entertainment. As she leaned back a little, sitting up straight to better see the tableau below her, she heard a quarrelsome, unhappy voice remarking on the games second quarter course of action.

"Why doesn't he press those bastards right up against their backboard," the voice demanded, loudly.

"Anderson's a conservative," answered another, less rasping voice (both men sat behind her and she had not as yet seen their faces). "He plays the percentages. You wait; the game's not over yet."

"Well, if them kids don't get off their backsides and start scrapping for that ball, it'll be over by the end of the third quarter," said the first voice. "You don't see Eph's boys pussy footing around."

"You don't see Anderson's boys fouling out all the time, either," claimed the second voice.

Both speakers got drowned out by a howl from the rooting section that greeted The Axemen who returned floorside for a quick pre-second half warmup. At the sideline George hunched like a big shepherd's crook above the sinewy red headed form of Kit Carson. No emotion showed in the coach's face, and he seemed to be speaking, low, deliberately, pausing from time to time to indicate with his gestured hand a particular place on the tartan floor. The boy, looking up into his face then away as the gestures indicated, nodded from time to time (his mouth and chin seemed very grim for one so young). When the two parted company, they each gripped the other at the bicep. The boy swung out on the floor to shoot baskets; the coach started slowly toward the timer's bench.

Madge saw George's eyes search the crowd where she sat, saw them locate her, saw a big smile and slow wink. He raised his big hand, his left, and she knew what to expect—a circle formed with the tip touch of his thumb and first finger.

"Coach says we're going to win," she said, turning and startling the two men whose knees almost touched her shoulderblades.

After quick surprise, they both smiled recognizing her as the coach's wife.

"I never doubted it for a moment," and she recognized the second voice, a skinny bald headed man in his fifties.

"Your husband's the finest basketball coach we've ever had," said a round, fat little man whose shortness of stature made basketball unlikely for him. (She recognized, though the tone had changed, the voice of the opening speaker.)

As the second quarter got underway and Timbertop muscled the tip off, Madge paid little attention to the game's progress action, for her eyes fixed themselves, for the most part, on the back of her husband's curly head.

"I'll have to tell him this weekend," she thought, "perhaps he may want me to have an abortion. After all, we've got two children, and that's plenty for anyone in this crazy world. Besides, we sure can't afford to raise a third on his teacher's pay, and he gets pretty damn mad when I mention going to work with babies at home. Poor George. Poor George. You'll just have to make your girls into tomboys, I guess."

By the end of the third quarter the score showed 56-56, and the Penbrook boy, a lightning rod attracting basketballs at the head of the jug, showed four fouls in the scorebook as he tried to keep Kit Carson outside.

"We've got 'em now, guys," said George, quietly, from his kneeling spot in the center of a team huddle. Around him five sweaty bodies puffed, panted, showed the wearing edge of tiredness that had strained their young muscles, and stood in ready alert for his next instructions.

"Shall we go full court?" asked the Carson boy, sponging his face with a cool, water soaked towel.

"Not unless they lose Penbrook, or we get two baskets behind," said George. "If I think differently at any time, I'll signal for you to call a time out. In the meantime keep working along that left sideline—they're more vulnerable there than they are on the right. Stay out of the free throw lane; we can't stand any three second violations with the score this close. Anybody need a longer rest?"

Negative head shakes, and the buzzer brought them back out on defense.

"God, what a great bunch of kids," George thought, hunching himself forward again on the bench. "Aren't they all, though—the Chehalis kids as well as my own. Great kids with a real American spirit working together for team glory. Oh, sure, there's always the once in awhile screwup who's in it just for himself, but he doesn't get what the others get—the wonderful, complete, self satisfied feeling of being an integral part of a team."

As early as his fifth and sixth year in school, George's male teachers sensed great athletic prowess in this shy, skinny, often asthmatic boy. They knew, also, that though he tried to hide himself in the classroom and in schoolyard organized play, on the back lots and in the back alleys and side streets of Cicero he emerged a fierce competitor with his roughhouse friends where he excelled in kick the can, run sheep run, and stick ball.

It was Mr. Dolliver, George's fifth grade teacher and one block away neighbor, who got George's dad to fasten a basketball hoop on the front of his garage and buy George a new, genuine copy of NBA, basketball. Between Mr. Dolliver and George's dad the boy found both a great deal of encouragement to spend time shooting baskets and help from both men in improving techniques. Mr. Dolliver (then 23 but seeming very old to George) spent a lot of time with the boy at the expense of many angry words from his young wife who rebelled against her spending time home alone with TV while her adult husband spent his time "playing games with a bunch of little boys."

Star of his sixth grade basketball team; then seventh, eighth and ninth grade teams, as a sophomore George led his high school team in scoring and went on to make All Conference at the tender age of 16. Folks in Cicero remember George as an All Stater in basketball, but they tend to forget he also made all conference offensive end in football two years, and he was rated the best first baseman the Cicero High School baseball team ever had. But it was basketball that put George Anderson as a leading citizen in his own home town, and it was basketball that provided him with a mighty plush ticket for his college education at Western Pacific College.

Next to the deep attachment he felt for his father, George's feelings for other men lay primarily with the coaches he had known. His personality, his little outward physical habits, the way he walked, the way he talked, and the basic pattern of his thinking were reflections of what he most appreciated from each different man, and the conglomerate was a total of George's coach hero-worship. He still corresponded, sporadically, with all of them (even Mr. Dolliver who never really became a coach), brief informational letters—birthday or Christmas cards—totally devoid of any sentiment or emotional outpourings. Just man to man objective things that could never cause anyone any embarrassment.

He treasured, also, many what he called his "good buddies." Jocks who shared a total love of sports with him in common. Some, from high school, still worked around Cicero, and he looked them up immediately everytime he and Madge went back to his home. Others, from college, he saw from time to time at tournaments, clinics, or on a drop by visit at their business or his. Each meeting took place as if the participants parted only the night before. One thing George knew, however, was that with these people he neither felt black or white—he felt like a man. Some of them were black; most of them were white. The color of their skins never crossed his mind, either.

Now it was a pale, freckle skinned boy with a shock of red hair who carried pinned to his jersey George's search for The Golden Fleece—the Double A State Basketball Championship. With less than four minutes to play, Kit put his team ahead by a point on a foul shot that sent the Pennbrook boy out of the game. With his bonus, Kit put the Axemen up by two, then he and Dingus jumped on the Pennbrook sub with a flurry of pressure that immediately caused a Chehalis error and put the Timbertop team up by four.

From that moment on the game turned into a rout, and a shrieking mob stormed out on the floor as the final buzzer rang it up: Timbertop 91—Chehalis 75. Before he got towed away by his boys, George got one last look at Madge up in the stands. She grinned, widely, winked her eye, broadly, and she made an O with her left thumb and its adjacent forefinger.

For Madge and George, in an aftermath of excitement which they shared in their own bedroom; for Mr. W. and Eph Finlay who drove to Castleview for a couple of victory drinks in a little out of the way place they knew, and for a lot of Timbertop students and adults, the night's excitement extended on for hours. For George's victorious jocks, however, (training for their long hard road to the state's highest award) the night's activities were ended and, mostly by the honor system, they took their exhausted bodies off to bed. Lisa Overstreet (who could care less who won the silly ballgame) sent Cecil home at about this same time, then she lowered herself, groaning, into her bed (though she secretly admitted to herself she should probably take a bath). On the floor of her apartment Pat Mooney, finally at the point of total exhaustion, fell asleep where she lay and would not awaken until after 3 a.m. when she grew blue with cold. A.T., who made sure proper switches were thrown and who got a "volunteer" group of young boys to sweep under the bleachers and push them back to the walls, turned things over to the sweeper with several specific instructions, then accepted a proferred ride home in the sheriff's car where he invited the boys in for a cold bottle of beer.

Little Heidi Vandercamp found herself delivered home a little after the ten o'clock bedtime she had mentioned earlier in the day to David Huntington. No headache any more, she felt more wonderful than she could ever remember feeling physically. The food, the wine, the atmosphere, and the warm intimate conversation had promised a solution to her school discipline problem. Still and all, she thought, as she showered her trim little body for bed, I think I really expected something more— something exciting if perhaps a little sinful. Do you suppose he found he really doesn't like me? I'm sure he found my conversation pretty boring—maybe even silly. But what a nice person—what a very nice person. And he let me bring home the Japanese robe so I can show it to my girls tomorrow.

For David Huntington III the night proved to be a very different adventure from any other undertaking he had ever experienced. His half-in-fun plans to seduce the little Vandercamp grew ridiculous with the growing feeling of "big brotherly" emotion he found himself unable to stifle in her presence. He sensed in himself a deep wonder of her that was vestigital to his Sister Mercy memories. He found himself considering her, as she sat like a bright plummaged bird in his Japanese kimono, with the same kind of feelings he felt toward Elaine Perry. All these things went through his mind as he drove home, slowly, keeping a chary lookout for the horn blowing teen age cars out on a celebration.

At home he filled a small clay pipe bowl with some special hashish, took the Japanese tape off his stereo and put in an old favorite of his featuring Roy Orbison. In the room the Japanese motiff now seemed kind of silly to him; still he felt a real glow of pleasure that Heidi seemed to enjoy it so much. Later, much later, he slept naked on his waterbed remembering, as he turned out the bed lamp, how her little fur collared coat had lain here on the comforter where he slept alone.

# CHAPTER SEVEN

If we liken our high school to a learning "factory", (as people have continued to do for the near past one hundred years), production reaches its classroom peak at Timbertop Consolidated High School on Wednesday of most weeks. Physically, and mentally, students present their best potential on Mondays, but their taskmasters feel sluggish after a weekend of play and, more often than not, they find themselves not yet organized or oriented towards the week's work which lies ahead. Tuesday things start to come into focus for our educational learning facilitators, and by midweek the stars of both teachers and students conjoin at last in their proper houses. By Thursday boredom begins to errode student interest, and on the fifth day they (and their now near frazzled nerved guides into knowledge) greet their morning alarm clock with one single cry: "Thank God It's Friday!"

I remember it like that way back when I went to school, and I listen to my boy, Stanley, ramble about school things at the dinner table, so I gather things remained pretty much the same even after a twenty five year elapse of time. Now, I've gotta admit that sort of sets me to thinking, now and then, for the other things around me sure made a hell of a change while my old high school went on the same as it was. Christ! when I started at Timbertop the word television wasn't even in our physics textbook let alone the number one entertainment center of the whole U.S. of A. Cars changed so much my old 41 Chev now rates as an antique, and we got boats that go on a column of air instead of on water while somebody besides Flash Gordon and Buck Rogers really took a trip to the moon and back. People eat different, dress different, talk different and think different—except (for that last item) in our school house where everything seems designed to lock the kid's thinking into the mold of their daddy and his daddy before him. Why, my Stan comes home with the same themes to write for English that old fat Lisa Overstreet gave us to do, and my daddy did in the eighth grade at the old Timbertop elementary from where he graduated. His math problems I wrestled with in the old high school, and, so far, he's memorizing the same names and dates I did in my history classes. Funny, you know, I can't remember one single theme I wrote for a teacher, not a biology experiment I did, nor a history test that I took. Come to think of it I don't think, since I left the ninth grade, I ever spoke another word of Algebra to anybody. I do remember, however, the ball teams I played on, a school play in which I did a minor role, and some of the girls I used to dance with at school dances and the junior prom. When I put all of them things together in my head at one time, it makes me wonder if them bright educational people like Dr. Imberlay, and others, really know what's important to a kid going to school. As Stan, who works at Parmenter's Hardware on Saturdays, told me the other day: "If we treated our customers at the store like us kids get treated when we go to school, old Timbertop would be out of business before the end of the year."

Despite this sentiment, shared consciously and unconsciously by Stan and his fellow classmates, almost all of them continue to attend classes on a pretty regular basis, and not just because the law required it of them and their parents backed up the law. Scrawny little old Reuben Schwarz, for example, felt himself drawn to school like a moth drawn to a flame. Had his feelings been explored by an analyst (who would certainly wonder what reason the boy felt for continuing acts of almost total failure), Reuben would be able to offer him little help. At best he might shrug his thin, partly hunched shoulders and whine: "I gotta go or the old lady'll kill me." Not, exactly, a truth on Reuben's part, for his mother cared little or nothing about what the boy did. She entertained, in fact, a hope that he might run away from home and, thereby, divest her of what few shreds of social responsibilities still harboured in her maudlin mind. Reuben did attend, in fact, (albeit somewhat irregularly) for reasons more real than his practiced coverup about his ma. He went because the classrooms enjoyed heat while his own home did not. He went because he got a free lunch ticket through welfare, and the school lunch provided his one solid meal of the day. Finally, like most homo sapiens, he naturally gravitated to the proximity of others similar to himself (because of his undersize and whiney ways, the bowling alley bunch let him know, forcefully, they didn't want him around).

This Wednesday morning Reuben hung around the outskirts of the youngsters grouped at his school bus pickup point. A light, cold drizzle fell on them this morning, and he wanted no trouble that might keep him off of the bus. Several girls, and one of the smaller boys, watched him cautiously knowing, from experience, Reuben's role as a troublemaker. But he threw no muddy iceballs this morning nor did he offer to heckle anyone with derisive name callings. When the bus at last stopped for them, he loaded on with the others and arrived, for the first time that week, in time for his first period gym class.

Now Reuben, like the others at his bus stop, could have walked the less than two miles to school had they started in that direction at the point in time they started waiting for their ride. Reuben, in fact, with a little hurry in his getalong, could have made school on time on Monday or Tuesday after being ejected by the driver for the wet and mud on his clothing. He chose as a walker, however, to poke along and explore interesting looking places along the way. Yesterday morning he had, in fact, stopped in the Richfield Station crapper for a leisurely shit (the rest room enjoyed steam heat—quite a luxury after the ice cold seat he straddled at home). A more accurate measure of his travel speed showed in the 22 minutes it took him to come home by foot on the near darkened streets after last night's basketball victory (in which he, vicariously, shared as a star).

Now, back in that same gym where last night he daydreamed his triumph, he felt anything but a victor as he hunched down in a corner on some old wrestling mats with three other boys who, like himself, took a "Fail" for the day because of no gym clothes to "suit down" in. Although Reuben long ago passed by the number of "Fails" allowed before total failure in Coach Anderson's class, he knew from older, experienced heads that he would not, in fact, get a report card F, for the lowest grade coach ever gave anybody was a "D". That D, he knew, comprised the only passing mark he could expect on his next week's report cards. Second period, Mrs. Settlemeir would award him an F for his lack of effort in English;

Mr. Goss would hand him an Incomplete for a project he would never complete in third period shop. Coach de Haven would explain the F on his fourth period Washington History report card as: "Reuben fails to join in discussions, hand in assignments, or get passing marks on his quizzes or in his tests." His fifth period general math teacher, Mr. Hutchinson, would accompany his F with the terse observation that: "Reuben could do this work if he would only try." Mr. Hutchinson sensed the truth of the matter, Reuben realized, for he could, if he wanted to, do all the book's problems with more ease than could Mr. Hutchinson. He realized also, though, should he start getting A's in his math classes (as he did in grade school before he got wised up), the counselor would be on him like a duck on a June bug insisting he get the same kind of marks in other classes (which, for the most part, he found quite incomprehensible). By maintaining a perfect failure (PE didn't really count), he created an image of himself more to be pitied than censored. Poor Reuben, a trashy boy with no support at home, would likely drop out of school as soon as he arrived at the legal age of sixteen. Why waste a counselor's time on him? Leave him alone to seek his own level. A failure in school, Counselor Coach Patterson reasoned, needed only enough learning to sign his name on his welfare checks for the rest of his life. Had he been a girl, Pat Mooney's treatment of him would have been a much different thing. As a boy, however, he accepted full responsibility for his own direction in life where you either "toughed it through" or "folded up like a little white fairy."

This morning he could have avoided a "Fail" by wearing the gym suit Coach Anderson last Friday salvaged for him from the locker room lost and found. He chose, however, to sell it to Buster Cole (who had left his at home) for twenty five cents of Buster's lunch money that now felt warm, wonderful and smooth as Reuben fingered the quarter in the tattered front pocket of his mustard colored woolen pants bought by his ma for a similar quarter at "Sallys". Most of Reuben's clothes (as did his mother's) came from the Salvation Army Store, so for the young man to have money all of his own (and unknown by his mother) gave him an opportunity to daydream a little about the Twinkie, or something, that would help fill the hole that grew in his stomach while "ma" sat in the tavern at night waiting for some "friend" to buy her a beer and maybe a basket of popcorn.

He watched Coach Anderson working near the basket with six foot two Eddie Grimes and six foot three Allen Dewait. In his fantasy he stretched his own five one into a lithe supple seven foot. A combination of Bill Walton, Karim Jabar and Dr. J., he slam dunked the Axemen to a national high school championship. He felt good about it; modestly accepted acclaim from his teammates and gave public credit in his TV speech to the coaching of Mr. Anderson.

"Without his help I'd be nothing today," he said, aloud.

"What ja' say, Ruby?" asked another "Fail" huddled near him on the mat.

"Nuthin'," said Reuben, his voice curt and surly.

"Yes, ya' did. I heard ja'," argued the interloper, and the two other boys now sat up from their on the back prone position in hopes that a fight might ensue.

"I said nuthin'," snapped Reuben, and, leaning toward his antagonist from the waist, he balled two skinny fists into sharp knuckled weapons. " 'Ya want a mouthful of knuckles?"

"Shit, Reuben, I don' want no stuff with you," exclaimed the cringing "fail" boy.

He let it go, then, with a sneer on his face that put the other two spectator boys in their places, too. After all, he thought, Coach Anderson approves of a guy who stands up for his rights, but he lets the other guy back down graceful, like. That way nobody goes away from a beef feelin' stepped on too hard.

"This kind of tolerance shows the stuff real heroes are made from," Reuben told himself, in the after moments of the incident. (Quite a psychological insight for a boy whose 87 recorded Stanford-Binet IQ test from the sixth grade proved only that he spent part of the time daydreaming instead of working on the test.)

The real hero of Timbertop High this morning, Kit Carson, floated on a cushion of air from the time his alarm pulled his slightly stiffened and sore body out of bed until he settled, among the worshipping faces of his fellow students, in Mr. Hargraves advanced math class. Two days ago, at this time, he went to the office where his spirit got reduced to the nadir of his life's existence. This morning, only a matter of forty eight hours later, his star stood at the highest peak of its ascendancy. This wonderment would have awed, even humbled and frightened, the average adult whose lives rarely knew such depressions or peaks, but to Kit's teen-age world such moments existed as a normal part of their lives, and they accepted each moment for that moment's sake.

What he did find incomprehensible were the reasons for several radical changes in his life, but as they were incomprehensible, and he was not a particularly sensitive or deeply imaginative child, he accepted them as "the way things are" and directed his attention to things of more immediacy. Another's life change made his life change occur, although he would never see the relationship of the two. For some reason, which entailed mild curiosity on Kit's part, his father left suddenly for Venezuela and a construction job. He was not to return until Kit graduated from Timbertop (with both athletic and academic honors) and went on to Western Pacific where he repeated his high school triumphs. The abortion of the senior Carson from his son's life gave the son the one ingredient he needed to raise his talents from grade B plus to grade A—self confidence. No longer twisted inside by the fear of making a mistake, Kit now used his mind and physical aptitudes to their utmost with nothing held shakily in reserve. From a 3.2 scholastic effort (his total school GPA at this time) to a 4.0 production would be accomplished by him with an ease never experienced by him before. Likewise, in basketball, his performance would grow more outstanding with each ensuing game, as he did things he always felt that he might be able to do but never before had the confidence to undertake. Kit would be known by his friends and his employers as "a winner", and he would give credit to a lot of teachers and coaches when, in fact, credit belonged to his absentee father.

After last night's smashing victory over Chehalis, Kit had gone straight home with Dingus so as to be in bed by ten-thirty as training rules dictated. In the Kelly's front room he found his nearly teary-eyed mother drinking coffee with Mrs. Kelly (Mr. Kelly having adjourned to the Pastime with me and some of the rest of the boys to rehash the game and compare it to some we won when we was in high school).

"Kit, I want you to come home with me," his mother begged, a bit tremulous as she dabbed at her eyes with some crumpled Kleenex dug from her open purse beside her. "Your sister and I are all alone in the house, and we need a man to protect us."

"Where's pa?" he asked, not too gruffly, he hoped, for he wanted Mrs. Kelly to see him as a boy who was always good to his ma.

"The Huntingtons hired him for some job they got going down in Venezuela," said Kit's mother, her voice a bit choked so that each word came out a bit packaged in pain. "He left this mornin' on a plane out of Portland."

"When's he comin' back?" asked Kit, who really preferred his own bed at home to the one he shared here with Dingus.

"Huntington's personnel chief said something about a year, maybe two," said his mother, now reaching for his wrist and drawing him closer to where she sat. (He smelled whiskey on her breath and knew that she and Mrs. Kelly were drinking "Irish" coffee.)

"Okay, ma," he said. "I'll get my stuff out of Dingus' room."

"You boys can play awhile, if you like," said his mother. "I can just sit here and visit with Mrs. Kelly."

"We got to get to bed, ma," Kit informed her, solemnly. "We got to stay in training, you know."

So, he got to drive the family car home, received the squealing approbation of his ninth grade sister who left her TV seat to rave about his actions in the game, and he got to drive the family car to school this morning—a first, for him, and a fitting tribute to a man who rose, in one day, from mediocrity to the stature of a great Olympian.

All through his school career, in the classwork he did, or the athletic action he performed, Kit had split his attention in two directions—one toward the task that lay before him and the other toward his father's roar of approval or disapproval. When he did something right he showed the world that "he could do things the way that his old man did." When he failed to excel in an undertaking, the world and he learned that he was a "weak misgotten pup, an abortion from that 'bitch' the old man lived with." But basketball had long been the greatest trial of his life, for he grew old enough to interpret the smiles of tolerance he received from his teammates when his old man's voice exploded from the stands. And it exploded, often, at the referees, especially: "Get that blind robbin' bastard out of there. Somebody ought to kill the bum."

His split from his father turned Kit's attention in a singular direction (though vestige memories under crucial pressure haunted critical ball play for several subsequent years). Hence his "arrival" as the coaches and the avid jock fans called it, began with the Bearcats on the previous night. Beyond even this, Kit's family doctor would later note that Kit no longer trembled at the sound of loud noises, and he, himself, would gradually grow to realize he no longer awoke, damp and cold with sweat, from a nightmare that tormented him in the middle of his deepest sleep.

"And so we arrive at the same answer by utilizing angle co-signs," Mr. Hargrave concluded his explanation that preceded each day's assignment. "Any questions about the process?"

Several hands went up and the teacher very carefully reiterated information to help solve specific difficulties. As he continued this, most of the other students, Kit included, rustled out notepaper and found the assignment in their textbook as listed in bold chalked handwriting on a front blackboard. Some five minutes later, deep in his calculations, Kit grew aware that Mr. Hargraves leaned like worsted bark tree above him. He smelled odors that remained from a morning brush with Brut, and he paused his handwriting motion to lean back and look questioningly into huge brown eyes magnified behind dark, horn rimmed glasses.

"Understand you had quite a night for yourself," said the teacher quietly, so as not to disturb others working around them (he leaned down even farther as he softly spoke, as if he were examining Kit's paper on the desk arm before him).

"We beat them," said Kit, his voice hushed, too.

"Played some basketball myself when I was in school," Mr. Hargrave confessed, as if unloosing a classified document.

Kit sought a proper answer that would both please Mr. Hargrave yet not make a fink of him with his classmates. Mr. Hargrave had, in Kit's memory, never spoken to him before, other than to call his name as a questioner or a responder to some oral classroom exercise. "Strange," thought Kit, "that he should speak to me now. God, I had him as a freshman for algebra and as a sophomore for geometry."

While Kit Carson pondered on a possible response to his situation, out in the band room, Pricilla Martin fought a nagging pain at the base of her skull as she continued to blow into her clarinet. Her mouth and throat, too, continued to quickly grow dry and rotten tasting sending her to the side wall fountain for a drink of water everytime they experienced a musical break. She suffered, as she had a number of times before, a hangover from too many long pulls from a wine bottle she had shared with some of her pep band playing girl friends after the Chehalis victory.

A most physically attractive girl (by young American standards), Pricilla combined her appearance with a quick, perspective mind that made her a desirable addition to a group of young people or a group of adults. Her career long successful experience with playing "the school game" won her a spot among "the top five students" in her junior class. Only PE kept her from being a 4.0 student, and her willingness to help teachers and students with learning problems became legendary from her fourth school year onward. Not just an academic success, she also served as class secretary during her ninth, tenth, and this eleventh grade year, and this was her third year as a "Pep Band" member as well as her third year as a soprano with the "Tonettes". Already forces underway promised that she could expect to be Junior Class Princess in this year's annual May Timbertop High School Spring Festival, and next year, though no one thought about it now, she would find herself Queen of that same event.

187

With all these accolades, Pricilla lacked one thing other girls of her age treasured highly—boyfriends. Though she went through bundles of girl friends (much as a wheat thresher tours the sheaves in a field), not once in her three years at Timbertop had a boy approached her offering her a date. In her Freshman year (and particularly through the trying, blossoming female emotionalism of her eighth grade year) she carried the pain of this inside her like a heavy lead weight tugging stomachward on the strings of her heart. Then Mr. Norburton appeared in her sophomore year, and thoughts of any other male (except for her robust lawyer father whom she adored) ceased to plague her. Last night, as she sat drinking from a half gallon of Chianti with three of her girl friends, she felt amused as she listened to the girls chatter their evaluations of boys from both the jayvee and the varsity ball teams from Chehalis as well as Timbertop. Had her feelings of superiority, for the four of them were in her car (a Christmas present from her father), not abstained her from joining their silly drivel, her daydreams of Willy Norburton would have. Though she sat in the car apparently in a world with her girl friends, in fantasy she shared a bright theatrical stage where she and Willy Norburton entertained the greats of the world with duets on his trumpet and her clarinet that brought audiences to their feet with tumultuous ovation.

This morning she blew a not too professional lead through a passage in "Camelot", and she blushed to her hair roots feeling Mr. Norburton's questioning eyes on her face. He rapped the play to a stop, seemed about to say something to her, then raised his baton in a signal to start the passage over again. This time, despite her reed that felt like a piece of rough lumber against her tongue, Pricilla managed to bring her notes out clear and true. During the next break she turned, mouth full of water, from the fountain to find him standing immediately behind her.

"Not feeling too good this morning, Pris?" he asked, and her heart began to bang like a triangle in her chest.

"Too much after the game celebration," she admitted, after a pause to make the water go down her emotion constricted throat (most band members shared the same comraderie with their teacher that athletes enjoyed with their coaches).

"You tell that boy friend of yours, whoever he is," kidded Mr. Norburton, "he'd better take good care of my star clarinet player. After all, I'm counting on you to bring us all fame and glory at contest this year."

"Oh, there's no boy friend," said Pricilla, lightly (wanting to add, "except you").

"Well, whatever, Pris," said Willy Norburton, patting her shoulder in a companionable way, never dreaming that his touch on her bare skin left an invisible imprint of his hand like the sear from a hot branding iron.

She went back to her place in the center of the reed section; he took his place center front of the band. This time when the clarinet ran through its trill, it was as if a great virtuoso magically stepped down into their group. It was this quality of Pricilla—this perfection she seemed able to display almost at will—that surrounded her like a cellophane bag that no high school boy wanted to chance breaking through.

One person at Timbertop, however, felt unimpressed by Pricilla Martin, Kit Carson, or even the awesome Mr. W. Bert Terwilliger, as had always been his practice, failed to attend the great athletic event of the night before. Had he gone (a very, very vague probability) the play of Kit Carson would have been "a bunch of shit," and the music of Pricilla Martin's pep band "a bunch of dumb noise." In a cynic's world, Bert stood out as a cynic's cynic.

This morning he carefully did an assignment in Mr. Crenshaw's first period sophomore English class. The work called for his reading a short story: "The Gold Plated Guns," then composing a written theme of approximately one hundred words in which he, from his own opinion, assessed the actions taken by the protagonist. Bert felt the bastard played things out pretty damn stupidly, but he knew Mr. Crenshaw didn't want to read anything that came out like that. So he patterned his essay off the old adage, "pride before the fall," for he needed a plus from this paper to assure him a C status when report cards came out.

189

Since his year in the fifth grade, Bert easily maintained an almost constant 2.0 GPA. It took much less savvy than his to figure out, from the first week of class, what minimum effort the teacher demanded for the reward of a C grade at the end of that semester. Prior to his fifth year in school, Bert's name appeared at the top of the list as a most outstanding student in each school area of undertaking. The summer, however, between his fourth and fifth year the boy's father, tall as a giant and wise as a prophet to Bert, skipped town with a transient waitress working at Dino's and carrying almost six thousand dollars taken from the safe at Angelo's Foundry where the father worked as a bookkeeper. Oh, he didn't get far, and he wound up residing at Monroe where he's about due for parole, now, providing he's behaved himself there. To a worshipping son, he became a symbol of society's unfairness, and, as societies are composed of people, Bert decided that he would hate everyone. For the most part his intricate mind and forceful imagination made this kind of a hatred possible. Two people, however, existed outside the real pale of his bitterness (though he barely admitted it to himself); one of those persons was his mother, Milly, and the other was our custodian, A.T. Cromwell.

Yesterday, although he, himself, didn't realize it, A.T. got to Bert with his crack about the boy killing his mother. It hung with him through the boring day at school, and he took it home with him (walking the three miles as he despised the proximity of so many students crowded into a bus) where he brooded on it all through his silent dinner. Painfully he introspected himself, in a way he never considered doing before. He saw, too, his mother's work roughened hands (she now worked as a cook at Dino's), and he saw harrassment lines in her mid-thirty year face that made her look ten years older than he knew her to be. In a move that surprised, and embarrassed, both of them, he had got up from his chair, moved across the kitchen floor, and put his arms around her as she washed their dinner dishes in the kitchen sink.

"Well, that felt nice," she said, choke throated, as he released his squeeze.

190

"You're gettin' a bit fat around the middle," he chided, fighting back tears that threatened to spill from his eyes.

"It's all that grease fuming up down at Dino's," she played back to him. "Might do that skin and bone frame of yours some good to spend a little time in them grease smells with me."

He laughed at her not very amusing joke, and she smiled her appreciation for his letting her into his world if only for a brief moment in time. Then, again, he surprised them both. Instead of heading out for the bowling alley where he "fringed" with the guys who hung out there, he messed around putting dishes from the strainer into the cupboard while she cleaned the sink. When she finished he followed her into the front room where, without words between them, they watched the pitiful offerings of their black and white TV until the eleven o'clock news sent them both off to bed.

"Fuck! Fuck! Fuck!" Bert thought, now, as he slowly ground out his cigarette and field stripped it so no evidence could tip off one of his better smoking hideouts. It was, he figured, about six minutes into second period, and he needed, if he were going to be consistent with a new kind of Bert he hoped to evolve, a way to con himself into Mr. Royce's second period Biology class without getting demerits for an unexcused admit to class slip from the counselor. He could stay here in the dark secrecy of Mr. Bettermen's steel supply room until the period ended, but with Friday the last day of this semester, he felt a little unsure of his C in the science class. "Coach Anderson," he thought. "He's got a free period, now, and I bet I can con a pass to class out of him. I'll just tell him I left my cap in the gym after the game last night, and I came out after first period to try and find it."

He slipped outside into the slushy storage pen, let himself out through a well camouflaged slit in the heavy chicken wire fencing, then headed for the gym almost at a trot.

From a vantage spot in the laundry room's recessed outside doorway, A.T. worked with cold, aching fingers repairing a door return unit broken in last night's victory celebration by some over-zealous fan. He saw Bert slip through the wire and jog toward the gym. The boy's hiding place was well known to him, but he never, before, had seen Bert move in any other manner than his hunched, shuffling style of walk.

"What in hell you 'spose got into that boy all the sudden?" he asked himself. "Leastwise he hid his smokin' today; that's a plus for him, at least. Got a lot of real brains that Terwilliger kid—hope he learns how to use them. His old man was smart as a whip, too; hell the price some people have to pay in this life for losing their head just once in a lifetime."

Debby Fairweather, whose sexual mistake with her Alan would now be easily, and clinically, aborted, sat frowning and chewing a pencil eraser at a table in her second period bookkeeping class. In one of those rare moments we like to consider as insight (but which, more often than not, are wishful thinking results) she saw, really saw for the first time, her bookkeeping teacher, David Gorman. This morning she had come to class angry with herself, angry with him, and angry with area of study, in general, for she had gone home directly after last night's ballgame particularly to get her bookkeeping problems done (at least that excuse she gave Alan for not joining a party with him), but the careful explanations, the step by step interpretations from the accounting text presented on Tuesday by Mr. Gorman either eluded her where she sat home at the kitchen table or seemed so much gibberish as she tried to recall it. After nearly an hour of total frustration, she finally took a Sominex and crawled into bed. So much for putting school work ahead of a date with Alan, and an opportunity for a safe sex experience before she went in for her abortion on Saturday.

Now, here she sat at her table wtih ledgers open before her and no computed data to put into the proper columns. She watched as Coach Gorman moved slowly from table to table toward her, showing first one student then another a way to solve their minor problems. "If I flunk bookkeeping on top of the other things I've done to my mother this month," thought Debbie, painfully, "I might as well forget having any social life until I move away from home."

"What's the matter, Debbie?" asked Coach Gorman, in a concerned but slightly amused tone of voice. "Too much basketball game for you last night?"

"Not really, Mr. Gorman," she replied (and she experienced a strong, new awareness of his male proximity, and the delicate scent of his aftershave lotion). "I worked on these dumb problems for hours at home, but I just couldn't remember how we was supposed to do them."

"Let's see if I can help," he offered, sympathetically, and he pulled a chair alongside hers. There he sat as he carefully read her first problem, aloud.

"Now, your company predicated its wholesale price on sixty per cent of its suggested retail," he said. "Your problem statistics show actual costs to the company. These must be entered into the debit columns for manufacturing and marketing. See, here's a labor cost figure and a percentile to pro rata it to that particular product. Just multiply those figures out so you can enter them into your ledger under the 401 account."

She watched his brown, competent hands make careful Arabic numerals whose neatness defied description. Covertly she appraised a blue shadow on his cheek where his morning's close shave already showed signs of stubble growth. She thought of Alan's ridiculous efforts to cultivate a few scraggly chin whiskers, and she almost giggled aloud. Then, he started to stand, and she moved quickly to keep him by her side.

"I guess I'm just dumb, Mr. Gorman," she said plaintively. "When you do it, it looks so easy. When I try the same things, I can't get them to work."

"You're not dumb, Debbie," Mr. Gorman assured her. "You're a very bright young lady who's not yet quite found the key to unlock our bookkeeping door. Let me go through it with you once again, and if you have any questions as I go along, stop me right at that point."

He sat down, again, on the chair alongside her, and she fought off a desperate urge to snuggle her head of long soft hair against the blue worsted sport coat that covered his shoulders. Somehow Alan seemed not quite so important in her life, anymore. After all, as Mrs. Mooney pointed out to her Monday, a woman, a real woman, often has many heart affairs in her lifetime. "This could be one of the most important mornings of my lifetime," Debbie thought, as she seemed to accidently brush her left breast against Mr. Gorman's right elbow. "Maybe even the most important moment."

Elaine Perry's morning seemed, until third period at least, designed wholly for her own singular pleasure. Before school began, in her usual morning visit to Miss Vandercamp in the home ec room, she found her favorite little teacher and friend alive to a new kind of excitement with shiny stars in her big blue eyes. The two exchanged appreciative comments about Mr. Huntington's Japanese kimono, which Heidi now hung in prominent display, and Elaine listened, eagerly, to a description of his dinner menu, his apartment funishings, and a short narrative of the evening's affair. With Heidi she shared an appraising taste from the different left over dishes Mr. Huntington had brought earlier that morning to store, until lunch period, in the home ec refrigerator.

From that early high she reached even more spiritual elevation when, in first period World Problems, her display of inductive reasoning from data gathered by her cousin Billy, herself, and the other two members on their committee won high praise from all her committee members plus a special commendation from Mr. Huntington. During second period she and Billy pinned Mr. Boyd neatly into a rhetorical corner, and he finally admitted that his alleged mechanical laws (before which he seemed constantly ready to genuflect) were, in fact, nothing more than highly probable hypothesis like the other laws of physics. This singular defection by him (he usually shut off, immediately, any challenge to his pattern of thought) made a landmark for all five of his senior students, and particularly edified Elaine who led most of the student verbal challenge.

This unusual flush of victory she felt, or perhaps, more than that, the pyramid of a mornings success, stimulated her toward further aggressive thought and action (normally Elaine offered little resistance to the wills of her teacher being content to accept their offerings without comment no matter how she might feel about those offerings personally). But this morning she went on from her second period challenge for a third period face off with one of Timbertop's most hard headed mentors, Mr. David Royce.

Royce, still a bit disturbed by the late appearance last period of Bert Terwilliger (a boy he loathed on general principals) with a legitimate admit to class from George Anderson (who, Mr. Royce felt, had no right to excuse any student), faced his eleven ecology students with a show of peevishness they had come to expect.

"Young people, more than any other group," he said, acidly, "are the world's greatest wasters. They waste food, waste gasoline on silly, pointless driving around, waste the goods parents sacrifice to give them, and waste the most important thing they ever have in life, time."

He flung the gauntlet, defiantly, into their faces, but no one picked up his gage. Elaine, however, felt herself build toward an emotional boil. "It's about time somebody twisted that long snotty nose of yours," she thought, studying the famous Royce beak.

"Let's open our text this morning to page 173, young people," said Royce, heavy sarcasm on the 'young people'. "We'll take a look at what happened when DDT went to war against the Asian mosquito."

"Why?" asked Elaine, suddenly, aloud.

"I beg your pardon, Miss Perry," exclaimed Mr. Royce. (Her ten classmates sat like marionettes divested of strings.)

"I asked: Why?" said Elaine, clearly. "Why should we bother to read about DDT ten or twenty years ago when we've plenty of real ecology problems right here in our own community."

"Are you trying to tell me how to teach my class, young lady?" snapped Royce.

"I'm suggesting that things like our need for a sewage treatment plant here in Timbertop might be a better study project in ecology for us than is a look at twenty year old DDT results in a country six thousand miles from here," she said, firmly, and she sensed an awakening in her classmates—a growing eagerness to back her in the scrimmage line she had opened between her and Royce.

"You don't need a science class to explore the politics of our sewage treatment project," said Royce, heavily, a note of 'back off girl' entering into his voice.

"Perhaps," agreed Elaine, "but we do need expertise like yours to help us formulate judgments on the basic issues involved. We need you to take us, too, out where the county okayed that slash cutting. You can help us decide for ourselves if that kind of thing should be continued or not. Taylor Brothers plan to spray their reforestation project for moths—we hear about these kind of things on the radio or read about them in the paper—but you never bring these things up in class, so how can we decide for ourselves what the truths are?"

"That's quite enough, Miss Perry," stormed Mr. Royce. "Now, I've given you a page number; let's get into the book; we've a semester exam on Friday."

"I don't think so, Mr. Royce," said Elaine, "unless you'd rather explain to my father why a Timbertop class in ecology can't study our own ecological problems."

Ed Perry, a local gyppo logger, stood six three, two hundred and twenty pounds in his wool stockinged feet, and community members knew that, next to his wife, this bear of a man adored and doted more on his blonde lovely daughter than anything else in his life. Several school board meetings ago the directors, superintendent and one elementary principal felt his anger because of an (in his opinion) injustice done to his seventh grade boy. It took little imagination to conjecture some of his possibilities if he felt his daughter had been afronted.

"I'm cheating a bit, using daddy's name," Elaine thought, as she watched Mr. Royce start to squirm. "Old Royce cheats everyday, though, with his threats of a test and holding that grade book over our head like a big wooden club."

"Is that some kind of threat, Elaine?" asked Royce, his voice a tight wire.

"Come on, now, Mr. Royce," disembled Elaine, sensing victory and not being one to crow over losers, "you know me better than that. A simple question I direct to you because my father asks the same question of me all the time. What's going on with our local ecology? After all, my dad works with ecology everyday in his timber business, and I think it's only natural that he, as well as those of us here in this classroom, should know what goes on ecologically around Timbertop."

A murmur of approval came from a half dozen other now intent students whose strings seemed to have pulled them upright in their seats. Mr. Royce, an old campaigner who seldom lost control of either a classroom full of students, or himself, knew when it was 'better to join 'em than to beat them.'

"You've a darn good point, Miss Perry," he said, no trace of animosity in his well trained pedagogical voice. "Let's do it this way, if it meets a majority agreement. Let's finish out the remaining three class periods of this semester as I've previously designed. Next semester we'll put our texts aside and study ecology, live, right here in our own community."

This time an almost unanimous ripple of agreement and rumble of approval from the students who nodded their pleasure one to the other. Elaine Perry, who seemingly should have voiced the most enthusiasm for their "new look," failed to respond in any manner (a situation that not even Mr. Royce observed). Somehow what a few moments ago she envisioned as a crusade she planned to crown with a great victory seemed but a petty sniper effort against the establishment in which her opponent gained new favor with his class while she became (as she knew from overheard remarks between other teachers): 'that smart ass little Perry bitch who, thank God!, we get out of here come June graduation.'

Billy Lane, too, enjoyed his morning immensely. Pleased by the efforts of his committee, first period, he felt a glow of pride for his cousin as Mr. Huntington praised her assessment of their findings. Second period turned into a real gasser for him. Lane's greatest passion lay in tormenting people with pretended power positions, and the route of Mr. Boyd, through efforts of his and Elaine's, left him adrenal charged as he sat down for his third class period of the day.

Today things started in their usual innocuous manner (as did all Mr. Henry Crenshaw's English classes, but particularly this well conditioned Senior English Class). Most of the entire period wasted away on the clock as first one person, then another (according to the sequence of their seating) read from the text of Milton's "Paradise Lost." In general class members used this period just before lunch as a kind of light naptime, and they carefully policed their own ranks to make sure no one disrupted the smooth flow of class activity.

"Let not my words offend thee, Heavenly Power, My Maker, be propitious while I speak. Hast thou not made me here thy substitute, And those inferiors far beneath me set? Among unequals what society Can sort, what harmony or true delight?" (Adam asked these things of God, but the voice now here presenting the plea came from the throat and mouth of Edith Zarb, Editor of our High School's paper, 'The Tall Firs'.)

As those few who conscientiously followed the script awaited for her to continue with: "Which must be mutual. . ." she brought a shock that disturbed the pacific moment in which all seemed to exist. With only ten minutes left until the noon dash to freedom, Edith said:

"Mr. Henshaw, wasn't John Milton a heavy about censorship of newspapers?"

Now, no one in his or her right mind risked changing the gentle flow of Mr. Henshaw's classroom program just to seek some kind of personal answer. To do so was to invite a writing assignment, a quiz, and possibly some kind of research for homework. To let things idle along meant a chance to nap, daydream, write a letter to a friend, or read something you wanted to read while others droned on reading the oral assignment. Each class period spent most of its 56 minutes in the rotation reading of its twenty eight seniors from Avery, Mildred to Zarb, Edith. Now, endangering them all was the damnable ever inquisitive school editor who could have just as well held her question for a brown nose job on Crenshaw after the class ending bell rang. Some of the more religious breathed a silent prayer that perhaps Mr. Henshaw (himself known to be a daydreamer) might not have heard her question.

"Uh! Why, yes," he answered, at last (shattering that hope). "He wrote a tract called Areopagetica, a very famous and passionate plea for freedom of the press."

"You think that Milton had a good thing going?" persisted Edith (in the back rows several audible groans arose).

"Why, yes, of course," mused Mr. Henshaw. "One of the strongest supporting pillars of our federal constitution."

"And you would agree with Milton on freedom for our presses," Edith continued onward, uncaring for the groans or her own non-sequitor.

"Why, yes, of course," said Mr. Henshaw. "Witness Watergate, as proof of our need."

"Then how come you cut my editorial out of last week's paper?" asked Edith, bluntly, and over half her classmates moaned softly in pain.

"Why, yes, that's the faculty advisor's prerogative," said Mr. Henshaw. "I felt that Mr. Wellington, as well as Dr. Imberlay and members of the school board might well be embarrassed by your parallel of our school to the state prison farm you visited over the holidays."

At Edith's first outbreak, Billy Lane secretly groaned with the others. Milton bored him enough in the classroom without being forced to do outside work on some of his other poetic or narrative productions. As the exchange between the two continued, however, his indignity toward the establishment for its high handed treatment of someone as traditionally un-radical as was Edith Zarb brought him out of his seat with his forensic forefinger pointed at Henshaw.

"You felt the editorial embarrassing," he said, in his best oratorical voice (all other class members but Edith Zarb sank into a depression of gloom). "Who made you God the super censor? Who, for that matter, gave Wellington or Imberlay the power to subvert this student's legal rights? Why are most of the students in this class, in this school, in this country, and their parents, too,, for that matter, indifferent—even ignorant—of our Constitutional First Amendment? Because of educators like you Mr. Henshaw—because of school administrators like Mr. Wellington and Dr. Imberlay, our people early get conditioned to censorship in the very institution designed, supposedly, to widen not restrict their horizons. All during a person's school years no one learns that free speech and free press has anything, personally, to do with them. They all learn, instead, to keep quiet so they won't aggravate a teacher or a principal. Fantastic training for a person destined to become a citizen in a democratic country. Well, hopefully, Mr. Henshaw, the facism you and your colleagues practice now wavers under heavy attack. With the Supreme Court, the Student Press Law Center, and the A.C.L.U. to help them, more and more students risk the heavy hand of school administrative displeasure in an effort to tear down the Berlin Wall of school censorship. Granted, tens of thousands of school officials continue their self-conceited disregard of our Supreme Court and our other legal institutions, but the crusade by young people grows—and we will overcome in our efforts to have what is legally already our right. Mr. Henshaw. . ."

The bell rang and bodies immediately shuffled in their seats.

"You're not excused yet," roared Mr. Henshaw, now on his feet. "In the light of interest in this subject, I'm assigning you to read *Areopaegita* outside of class then evaluate it in a five hundred word essay due at the beginning of classtime on Monday."

As Mr. Henshaw gave the dismissal signal, Billy and Edith realized that only the civilizing of society made it possible for them to leave this room alive and not covered with bruises.

While Billy and Elaine staged their third period brushfire battles on behalf of enlightened learning, Lisa Overstreet spent most of that 56 minutes hulked over her desk; scowling, often; chewing (from time to time) the eraser end of a yellow number two pencil. She mumbled, sometimes coherently, sometimes incoherently, as she tackled each new name in her open grade book. Four times during each school year this process with numbers taxed her slim mathematical capabilities, but she meticulously added the line of numbers that followed behind each gradebook entry.

Each student in a Miss Overstreet English class received fair warning about her grading procedures as a standard part of the first day's lesson. Each student, could, she explained, garner up to one hundred points behind their name in her gradebook by the simple expedient of achieving perfect marks on all daily work, all quizzes and tests, all homework, essays, poetry recitations, book reports, or what have you. To the uninitiated it seemed most simple on first encounter, but as the class progressed they learned the situation easily became more complex. Extra points, for example, by production of 'extra credit' work (a series of possible 'extra credit' tasks went to each student in the form of a mimeographed sheet); on the other hand, certain classroom infractions meant a subtraction of points in the book (five points minus for late to class; five for no pencil or paper; ten for backtalking the teacher or throwing things in the classroom; fifteen for profanity, *etc.*—Eunice Underwood, for example, fouled up badly enough to lose twenty points the day before, and she dropped from a C to a D on her extrapolated letter grade).

It was this extrapolation from the numerical to the letter wherein strange things seemed to happen in Miss Overstreet's grade book. It was quite possible, for example, to put together one hundred points (a seemingly perfect score) only to find yourself with a B instead of an A. As Miss Overstreet persisted in using a curve ratio (of her own erratic design) to establish at what numerical point a grade became an A, B, C, D, or F, and as she persisted in never having more than ten percent A's in a class (where people like Pricilla Martin might stockpile as much as 100 *extra* points) the two or three super-eager beavers in the class walked off with A's leaving the around one hundred percentiles to fight over a place in the B category. In the old days (before Pat Mooney and Greg Patterson started scheduling boys into English classes other than Lisa's), her curve in a class of thirty usually reflected 3 A's, 6 B's, 9 C's, 2 D's, and 10 F's (at least nine of the F's would be boys). Today her curve shows a closer bell formation, and she proudly praised the fairness of that system as well as her own 'extra credit' innovation which she believes causes real 'student motivation.'

Today, when Lisa finished her arithmetic, she began to transfer her number totals as letter grades onto report cards stacked in her right hand lower desk drawer. The task, a tedious one (and sometimes a perplexing one for her to decide just where the line fell between B and C, or C and D) took most of her usual free period nap time the last three days of each quarter and each semester. Though her final examination for the semester would be held on Friday, she got around the ten points allotted there by crediting each student with a perfect score at this time (the papers for the test would end in the school incinerator unweighed by teacher's eye).

What other papers her students handed in during a grade period either received correction by other students during classtime, under Miss Overstreet's direction, or they more often were corrected and graded by Pricilla Martin who, during Miss Overstreet's 'planning period' served as a Teacher's Aide for which she got a regular curricular credit.

Pricilla Martin enjoyed her work as a Teacher's Aide, though, unlike most TA's at Timbertop she worked continuously, and hard, during this assigned third period in the English room. Most aides ran a few errands for their teachers, did a little mimeo work, corrected an occasional quiz or entered scores into record books from papers graded by their teacher. For the most part they experienced a casual, loosely supervised fifty six minutes—a time to read magazines, books, assignments due in their own classes, or, if they happened to be adventurous, they slipped away to secret hiding places for a smoke or a visit with other T.A. friends. (For some reason the ratio of girls to boys in the T.A. area stays around 10-1. One thinks, with a certain lasciviousness that grows with age—depending upon who one is,—of the infinite possibilities should boys ever stop to think what a sexual split of fifty fifty might mean to them.)

I think such an awakening on the part of Timbertop's young men, however, will not likely occur as long as the student handbook persists in supplying them with the rhetoric it utilizes: "Under close supervision," claims the book on a 1/2 credit for T.A., "a student does those tasks which help the teacher better expedite her own efforts freed from mechanical and routine undertakings. During planning periods, teacher's share the philosophies and techniques employed to structure and motivate classes with their T.A.'s, and they further serve as unofficial counselors for the student who shares this period with them. It is the hope of our faculty and school administration that, through this course of study, students find their own inducements to attend college in search of their own teaching degrees." (As an honest survey of Timbertop boys would not expose one in ten eager to become a school teacher, or perhaps seriously want to go on to college, T.A. provided little macho appeal).

Before we condemn this purple passage on T.A.'s for its obvious misrepresentation of reality, we must consider most of the other entries in that student handbook which mask their real educational offerings. U.S. History, for example, claims: "A course of study to acquaint each student with his cultural heritage. Projects that lead to a deeper understanding of one's role as a citizen, and an opportunity to read and understand the lives, actions, and thoughts of America's great leaders." As we earlier got an insight in to what really happens in Mr. Huntington's and Mr. Findlay's U.S. History classes, we can shake our heads over that handbook rhetoric.

A few classes, though, come very close to their course descriptions, and among these less floridly described offerings we find Bookkeeping I and II, Business Math, Business Machines, and Accounting I and II all taught by Coach David Gorman. David, too, enjoys third period for his planning time, and his aide, senior Deborah Pennypacker finds her 56 minutes generally as occupied as does Pricilla Martin in Miss Overstreet's room. Unlike Lisa, however, David meticulously corrects all work handed in by each student. He marks a letter grade on each paper and it is Deborah's job to see that letter grade gets into the record book.

"Will you need some extra help with report cards, Mr. Gorman?" asked Deborah, this morning, as she finished one stack of papers, clipped them together and got another batch from his OUTGOING basket.

"I sure could," he said, warmly, "but I hate to ask you to give up your own time after school."

"It's alright; I enjoy it," said the dedicated Miss Pennypacker. "When would you like to start?"

"Tonight, after school, if it's alright with you," said Mr. Gorman. "My Jayvee wrestling practices are cancelled until after semesters. We don't have another match until a week from tomorrow."

"That'll be fine," said Deborah, returning to her corrected papers.

As the two resumed working, Deborah studied her teacher noting an abstraction about him foreign to his usual intent concentration. "Something's really bothering him today," she thought, "he's always a little nervous but never like this."

At his desk two rows of tables in front of her, Dave Gorman automatically checked a batch of business math papers which lay in front of him. His actions came without any thought, for his forebrain wrestled with some improbable possibilities. This morning, before school, in a gesture without any preliminary explorations, David Huntington, who he hardly knew, had invited him to share Japanese food for lunch in the home ec room with Heidi Vandercamp, Pat Mooney, and George Anderson. So far in his part of a year at Timbertop he found no opportunity to socialize with any of these young people, and he felt unsure as to how much he wanted them to come into his generally private world. He felt particularly excited, however, about forming a closer relationship with the quiet little Vandercamp. He felt, on the other hand, the same force of misgiving about exposing himself to the flamboyant intellectuality of David Huntington.

David Huntington, too, used third period for planning. Like George Anderson, Jim Bettermen, and one or two other teachers, however, he offered no encouragement to having a T.A., preferring to do his own thing in his own way. Today he brought some levity and giggles to Miss Vandercamp's third period home ec class as he spent the last part of the period with her girls readying a table for his Japanese luncheon.

# CHAPTER EIGHT

Most Timbertop High School classrooms, by their day to day appearance, present a lot of insight into the teacher who spends a greater part of seven hours each day, for 180 days each year, commanding activities that take place in that enclosure. For example, Mr. Huntington's far out posters, banners, construction paper backed contemporary cartoons, and black and white collaged headlines advertise a pendant who feels learning is very much alive and who relates to the mores of the young people in search of that learning. Miss Overstreet's room, on the other hand, seems to carry a musty (though it's cleaned and air-freshened as regular as other rooms) atmosphere, while its generally barren walls and untarnished blackboards break in their monotony only for an upper border of construction paper cut out flowers placed on a background strip of other construction paper (the work done by Pricilla Martin under direction from Miss Overstreet). This room, subsequently, speaks of a person who, though boasting twenty eight years on the faculty, seems merely to be passing through with little interest in the effect of the room upon students attending. I could go on, but suffice this narrative to say, that from the complete clutter of Mr. Bettermen's near impossibile to get into shop office, to the antiseptic math room where Mavis Parmenter grimly puts in her hours, a kaleidoscope of all other differing rooms in between those extremes offers irrefutable proof that no two of our teachers feels toward their professional calling in the same manner.

Miss Vandercamp's room mirrors her personal habits and scopes of interest far better than I could ever describe them through the limited medium of words. I might describe the symbols: a macrame hanging, a decorated seasonal area, a bulletin board devoted to fashion, or diet, home decoration, or some culinary effort, but these words would only name something and not deal with the generality of feeling created by the rooms "neatness, cheeriness, cleanliness, warmth, hominess, femininity, comfort, friendliness, etc." Besides that, my labels would also fail to give an idea of the personal things each individual found with relationship between something in this room and something in the past or present of their life.

When Heidi took over this area late last August, she found thirty years of clutter and a shabby, slowly decaying facility. A housecleaning sent dozens of cardboard boxes stuffed with outmoded kits, projects, filmstrips, abandoned student efforts, and demonstration materials off to the incinerator with the cheerful help of her students and Mr. Cromwell. When Mr. Wellington advised her that no money existed in his budget to brighten the room, she got permission to buy paint and material from her own pocketbook, and her first advanced home ec class project enjoyed an exciting practical experience of painting, making curtains, refinishing furniture, and arranging decor. At first the walls showed off weaving, macrame hangings, and other decorative projects done by her, but now those projects had all been replaced by similar other ones done by her students.

This setting, then, provided a backdrop for the Japanese luncheon David Huntington hosted this Wednesday during the schoolday's noon break. With a pink cheeked Heidi (coaxed by David into wearing the kimono) serving as hostess, the invited teachers gathered at one Orientally decorated table to which the other, uninvited, teachers offered varying compliments before they went on about the business of their own eating and their own personal conversations. David saluted his hand picked group with a cup of green tea, as, with a chuckle, he apologized for school rules which forbade the addition of saki to his luncheon offering.

"Second day in a row for me to drink tea," said George Anderson, with a grateful look at Heidi. (Warmed by his inclusion into what appeared to be a most exclusive little group, he felt a strong inclination to help make conversation with some other topic than basketball.)

"Food's delicious, David," bubbled Pat Mooney, close to hysteria with this rare opportunity to share in an 'adult' world, for a change.

"Just dig in, friends," laughed David, urging them to second helpings. "What's left we poison and feed to Miss Vandercamp's fifth period class."

Pat joined Heidi in a light laughter of appreciation, and though Anderson and David Gorman knew none of the quip's background, they, too, added their nervous get acquainted laughter.

"Must be quite an experience living in another country," said George, hoping his statement didn't make him seem gauche.

"Much like you experience by being a black in a mostly all white community," said David, easily (the others, except for Heidi, stiffened noticeably). "At first you're something of a novelty, then, in awhile, you find yourself accepted into most things but not quite acceptable to any particular person. Finally, after a long settling period, you end up with a few friends, a few enemies, and the bulk of the neighborhood's people who are indifferent toward you as they are toward most of the rest of their neighbors."

"You think things are that way for me here in Timbertop?" asked George, and he hated himself for the formality he detected creeping into his voice timbre (he also grew acutely aware of his attention from the others around him—even felt, wrongly, that others away from the table now stared at him).

"I'd lay bets on it," said Huntington, "though maybe you don't see it that way. You know we all tend to see the world in our own different way, and we ourselves in a way, that nobody else does. I've got a little trick I play on my students the first day of class each year. I have each of them write a short evaluation of each student in class, including him or herself, on an unsigned piece of paper designed by classroom role seats. The next day I hand each back his own paper, with a rare mistake, and they grow amazed at my seeming magical insight."

"But a comparison of their paper against what others in class say about them clues you to the author of each paper," said Pat, shrewdly. "It works, too, I use similar self-profile tests in helping students work out personality problems."

"You're into psychology and sociology, Pat," said George, eager to extricate himself from the unaccustomed spotlight under which he seemed to have placed himself. "You think David in Japan parallels me in Timbertop."

"Theoretically, yes," said Pat, who loved to have the floor, "but I think the concept oversimplifies the black-white situation. Our culture, particularly, reeks with emotional overtones concerning the color black. Prince of darkness; black mass; bogeymen in the dark; hell, I could go on for volumns and you could still add something. It's a cultural thing, like, for example, the blacks found themselves big medicine with the Indians, particularly our coastal Indians, where black connoted big power and mucho macho kind of thing. But in most of the so called Christian world, regardless of the ethnic people's skin coloring, black meant evil since the first preachings of Saul of Taursus. God, even black people, themselves, torn away from their native African religions and exposed to Christianity, began to treasure a lighter colored skin. Had Christianity, instead of Mohammedism, become the chief religion of Africa, it's hard to say if that continent would ever have sought to throw off the yoke of white domination."

She paused for breath, realized her monopoly of the conversation had been too heavy for this kind of meeting, and trilled off a laugh in the form of begging their pardon.

"I'm sorry," she said, "I got carried away with my own erudition. Hell, George, I think David probably had a ball in Tokyo compared to the kind of crap you put up with here in Timbertop."

"Then, that's terrible, if it's true," said Heidi, whose admiration for Pat's command of the moment made it possible for her to forgive and almost forget Monday night's debacle. "Mr. Anderson's an educated man—a teacher—a father—an American—a credit to himself and to the rest of us. What possible difference can the color of his skin make?"

Gorman thought he had never seen anything more beautiful than the blue sparks that flashed from her eyes. Anderson felt her sincerity and wanted to reach out to clasp her hand—tell her how much he hurt for friends like he enjoyed back in Cicero. Pat Mooney smiled at David Huntington, and they mutually mentally agreed there was much more to the Vandercamp than that which generally met the first inquiring eye.

208

"You're a Catholic in a so called Christian civilization, Heidi," said David, and all eyes (except Gorman's still on Heidi), swung now on him. "Don't you sometimes find yourself ostracized, abused, at least bitterly criticized for your beliefs?"

"Perhaps," she admitted, "but it doesn't bother me. I feel anyone has a right to belief in her own religion."

"That's the point I'm trying to make," said Huntington, and they found nothing facetious in his manner. "I suggest that the philosophy you just espoused applies to Mr. Anderson, or anybody who entertains paranoic thoughts because they feel themselves different from a majority in which they need to exist. If people give some one a bad time for religious, racial, philosophical, or any other characteristic which does not, of itself, injure others, then I think the best mental repose that person can adopt is the stoicism of Marcus Aurelius. He can say: 'So I am, so let them be.' Grant everyone the right to his own skin color, own religion, or what have you."

"Easy enough for you to say, white boy," thought George, in the bitter language of his soul brothers. "You don't have to live through it, honky."

"I, for example," David continued, still holding their attention, "get labeled a fairy by some and a satyr by others. To most I'm a dope fiend and to all I'm a rich snot nosed smart alec." (He paused to bark laughter at himself.) "Perhaps the secret of a serene mind is a multiplicity of non-conformity."

"He certainly uses big words," said Heidi to David Gorman, with a little laugh (she had grown increasingly aware that he was staring at her).

Huntington heard her and laughed again, brightly. Pat, too, joined in David's merriment, and George, relaxed by Huntington's amusing self deprecation, relaxed into a grin backed by an inside silent chuckle. Gorman, aware of the attention he shared now with Heidi by virtue of his eyes fixed on her, felt compelled to enter his first words into the flow of the table conversation.

"I think the relationship of black and white will eventually level itself to a position of a minor social problem," he said, inwardly cursing the light flush of embarrassment that, uncalled for, flushed out his neck and jawline. "It can never be perfect, nor will the relationship between rich and poor, young and old, even thin and fat."

"Bravo!" said Huntington, enthusiastically. "Spoken like a true realist."

"And what are you, David Huntington," said Pat Mooney, almost coyly, "a romantic?"

"First, last, and always, my dear, Pat," said David, with a flourish of his ivory chopsticks. "To me, life without a romantic glass is a cold, dead moon where I feel no desire to exist."

"He really is something," Dave Gorman confided across the table to Heidi.

"Yes," she dimpled, "he certainly is."

"Say, David, thanks for the great food," said George, uncoiling himself upward until he towered over them at the table. "Sorry I got to split, but I left some unfinished things in the gym I'd better get to before my troops start trailing in."

"God, man, but you sure are a big one," laughed Davey, waving off the thanks with his chopsticks. "What say we start doing this lunch thing once a week or something like that? Beats hell out of that cafeteria slop."

"Great with me," said George, unconcerned about food but hungry for this kind of companionship.

"I'll host the next one," volunteered Heidi, quickly. "I'll make Hollanders out of all of you."

Pat applauded, and Dave Gorman suggested his desire to be their third host. Five most different people drawn together, even momentarily, into an island where each could touch and find succor from the personality of another. Like fissioning cells they drew strength from each other's psyche—Heidi would sail through her Wednesday fifth period class as if she had never experienced a problem there; Pat Mooney would find seemingly unlimited emotional reserves to bolster her acceptance of minor problems from a dozen girls and the traumatic outpourings of two near hysterical girls; one whose father raped her the night before and the second, a senior, whose impending failure in Mr. Royce's sceince class meant a strong possibility she could not graduate with her classmates in June. Dave Gorman's generally stern young visage would, for no apparent reason, break into an occasional warm smile at students during the afternoon, and those students would excell their usual efforts thrilled that, despite what they previously imagined, Mr. Gorman really did like them. Nothing tangible changed the outward actions or appearance of Mr. Anderson for the rest of the day, but he went home at seven (after basketball practice) and amazed his wife by eating the largest dinner she remembered him consuming since the start of the school year back in September. As for David Huntington, author of this party and guru to its aftermath, his mind for the afternoon bent toward the school board meeting that evening and shut out, consciously, any memories of the home ec room affair. His students, as usual, found him sharp, concerned about them, and mentally demanding of them, but he did that on an automatic level of psyche, for his forebrain concerned itself with a specific problem for the night ahead to which he had not, at this point, found himself a completely satisfactory answer.

Others besides David Huntington bent their chief thoughts on the director's meeting slated for seven thirty this evening. Two particularly, Dr. Imberlay and Director Cosgrove, talked of nothing else at the Kiwanis luncheon at Dino's and later in the privacy of Dr. Imberlay's office. At lunch, with others involved, they spoke mostly about the levy effort the board and its promotional committee, chaired by Mrs. Overholt, planned to undertake, but the office conversation grew personal and dealt primarily with issues involved in the rough draft of Dr. Imberlay's agenda for the evening.

"Those damn teachers likely to be there in force," said Ray Cosgrove, concerning the item listed immediately after building principal reports. "Maybe you should just forget to list them."

The two men studied each other across the superintendent's seven foot long polished mahogany desk top. The desk, plus six very expensive black leather covered heavily padded swivel chairs had been bought by Miles Pettigrew out of the superintendent's emergency fund. To them Imberlay's wife, with her unfailing artistic touch, added just the right amount of their best leather

211

bound books in a highly polished period bookcase, three small mid-period Goya prints framed on one wall, and a carefully groomed Christmas cactus that gave a splash of color from one end of the big desk to the otherwise hushed tones of the room.

"They have a right to be heard, Ray," said Imberlay, trying to offer a friendly tone when he felt only despisement for this stupid, small minded man.

"You got 'em too early in the meetin', though," argued Ray, his voice heavy and demanding. "Could be a lot of folk there, at that time. Damn Coleman's a smart ass young guy, for a coach. Could start of lot of rumors floatin' around that'd hurt some votes on the levy."

"Perhaps you're right," mollified Imberlay, not wanting anymore spectators than possible when the inevitable evening's clash between Coleman and Cosgrove occurred.

"Wanted to talk to you about Wellington, too," said Cosgrove, his voice dropped now to a low, conspiratorial rasp. "Last night at the ball game I got the feelin' he's laxin' off on the kids. Lets 'em run around—lets in a lot of hippies what should be kept out. He needs to tighten the screw."

"You want me to tell him that at an open board meeting?" asked Imberlay, stiffly.

"Naw," said Cosgrove, "just pass it off on him in your regular administrative meeting."

"I'll make a note of it," said Imberlay, gorge rising in his throat.

"Another thing about this here agenda, too," continued Cosgrove, "I don't think we oughta' 'low this complaint by students about our cafeteria food. They don't got to eat it if they don't want to. 'Sides, they're just kids."

"Students have a right to be heard at board meetings," Dr. Imberlay reminded him (a situation the administrator disliked as much as did his director).

"Bull pucky," snorted Cosgrove, "them's just words in the news and in them letters we get from Olympia. What them kids gonna do if we just don't let 'em speak out at the meetin'?"

"Get a lawyer—sue us—get a demand by the court placing us in a contempt position," said Imberlay, fighting to hold down his frustration—caught between his base desire to support Cosgrove's position and his educated responsibility to the law and a sense of fair play.

"Sue us? For what? I talked to Ned Perkins on that student stuff when I was over in Castleview for some legal work on Monday," said Cosgrove, gravel voiced and hunched toward the superintendent, as if set to charge the front of his desk. "Hell, according to Ned, the way the law works, and particularly the way old Judge Finney and some of the other judges in our district feels, them kids could get growed and have kids of their own 'afore they'd get a judgment of any kind out of the court."

"Even so," said Imberlay, and he couldn't keep the distaste out of his voice, "the students could cause a lot of dissention in the community and damage our levy efforts. I've managed to stall them off for a couple of months on this cafeteria thing with one or two technicalities, but the boy, Billy Lane, is in to it now, and I can't bluff him or put him off with trivialities."

"Lane," snorted Cosgrove. "Just another pansy like his old man and that Huntington fairy he pals around with."

"Those are pretty strong words, Ray," exclaimed Imberlay, in a half-hushed, nervous voice, and his eyes flickered around the room as if searching for some possible bugging device.

"Shit, Imberlay," snarled Ray, "strong men use strong words." (He rose from his seat, stiffly, and leaned against the front of the desk—a trick learned from Wellington that impressed him.) "Maybe you ought to get a bit of iron into your words instead of peddling that soft soap you keep spreadin' around."

Dr. Imberlay still smarted from that sally when he left his home six hours later for the monthly school director's meeting. Sick to his stomach after Cosgrove left, he had thrown caution to the wind and called his former boss (despite the possible leakage in the one horse local telephone office) and asked to be considered for any administrative opening that district might offer. The sympathy received from that phone call was not at all reassuring; school politics, like governmental politics, tended to take care of the ins and sluff off the outs. It also felt, often, a cool attitude toward anyone who tried to alter or break out of the pattern.

The superintendent, as usual, found his car the first in the faculty parking lot when he reached the (now) old North Elementary building. Though by modern standards the W.P.A. monstrosity offered poor heating, lighting, and student facilities, Dr. Imberlay felt a nostalgic warmth for this old structure as did most of the over thirty fives in the community. A multi-purpose room at the newer South Elementary provided a much more suitable place for directors (as it did for the PTA) to meet, but forty years of tradition outweighed comfort and convenience. Even had the superintendent wanted to change, the school directors (except Mick Randolph) would have nixed the project.

Imberlay found the front door open, listened as his heels rang hollow sounds down the cavernous deserted halls. From the hallway a door let him into a space originally designed for a band room but now occupied only by director's meetings, programs for the whole student body, and the annual Spring performance of the North Elementary band concert. One end of the room opened onto a floor and wall battered old stage which long ago lost its heavy sagging theatre curtain. In front of this stage, and at ground floor level, a long cafeteria table with seven captain's chairs awaited the stars of the night's performance. At the back of the room, tall wooden folding doors closed off a middle section of theatre seats like the ones in the band room section. These, once utilized as a makeshift study hall location, now opened only when (on rare occasion) the board meeting overflowed its usual seating capacity, or the other mentioned activities took place in the school. This section, too, closed off at its back with more tall folding doors, and behind them lay the school library which could also be used to extend auditorium facilities. The front two sections inclined slightly from front to rear (as in a movie house), but the

library section floor flattened out making the folding seats used in that area a very undesirable kind of spectator position very seldom used. Tonight, with both back sections cut off (and unlikely unneeded as no major controversies raged in the school district), Imberlay found A.T. Cromwell, as usual, seated alone in the top back row of seats.

214

The superintendent smiled a bleak "hello", and got a brusque nod from his custodian in return. As neither man had much use for the other, recognition of the other's existence sufficed for communication. With no further look at Cromwell; or the scratched and battered theatre seats that rowed in the badly lit room like a series of wooden grave markers, Imberlay marched to the incongruously new fibretopped cafeteria table with its round, grey metal tubular legs, and he plunked his fat bulging leather briefcase on top of it. From the briefcase he took copies of correspondence, one for each director; agenda copies, one for each director; copies of last month's minutes from the director's meeting, one for each director; and a short narrative of each of the four administrative meetings held by him since the last director's meeting—one copy for each director.

He barely finished placing these in front of their appropriate chairs when his office secretary (who also served as recording secretary for the board) marched in carrying her official ledgers, notebook, and the list of bills to be paid. Mrs. Sebastian, sixty years young come next March, took superintendents and board members in her stride (seven superintendents and over a hundred board members), and, so far as least I or anyone else knows, she has never missed a board meeting in the thirty one years she's been running the district office. She placed her bundle down in front of her chair at one end of the table (Dr. Imberlay would sit at the other end), and she waved a cheery "hello" at A.T. Cromwell who waved back at her and sent her one of his very best admiring smiles. Seated, she nodded at Dr. Imberlay (who she considered the lesser of two evils between him and the possibility of Mr. Wellington), then she examined her four pens and four pencils to assure they were operable before she parcelled her paper work out in the order that it would be utilized. A short, pouter pigeon breast and legs kind of woman, her granny glasses and grey bun of hair made her look like a TV commercial "grandma". In real life (away from this illusion she maintained on her job) she swore like a truck logger, chewed snoose in the privacy of her own home, and ran her husband, her three grown children, and seven grandchildren with the same efficiency she made things happen in her office.

Her papers barely laid out, Mrs. Sebastian felt the hand of her friend and favorite board member, Steve Dobson, Chairman, fall lightly on her shoulder while his voice whispered playfully in her ear:

"Hello, there, beautiful."

She scoffed a laugh at him and they exchanged their monthly "family talk" (Mrs. Sebastian was Mr. Dobson's mother's cousin), then he moved on to say his hellos to Dr. Imberlay, and she went back to her process of organization.

With the entrance of Mr. Wellington, and the two elementary principals, the musty old room began to take on some sound and show a rebirth of life. Ray Cosgrove entered (like a Superior Court Judge Mrs. Sebastian always scoffed to herself), and he waved a patronizing hand at the principals, spoke deferentially to Mrs. Sebastian, then sat down to study the papers in front of his chair with a black scowl of concentration grooved into his face.

Mr. Wellington left the room as Stan Coleman, leading in a contingent of seven teachers, stopped by his principal and whispered "Micks in the hall" into his ear. Several questioning eyes, chief among them Dr. Imberlay and A.T. Cromwell, followed the movement of Roger's exit. A student group burst in, noisily, headed by Billy Lane and Elaine Perry. Then, in ones, twos, threes and sometimes fours, assorted parents, non-parent adults, teachers, others students, began to fill the seats beginning mostly from the back of the room and gradually edging toward the front. As the room clock's big hand hit seven-thirty, Edna Keefer rushed into the room looking her usual harried half-mussed self. She said her hello to Mrs. Sebastian, in passing, gave a big smile and a "how are you" to Dr. Imberlay (who rose from his seat as she neared the director's table), and tried to ignore the scowling visage of Ray Cosgrove who glared up from his paperwork study.

"Guess we got our quorum now," Steve Dobson said to her, softly, as she dropped into her seat and bobbed her windblown hair at him.

"This meeting comes to order," he continued, lifting his home made oak gavel and rapping it sharply on the table top. "Secretary please read. . ."

"Move dispense minutes," interrupted Cosgrove.

"Second," said Edna, automatically.

"Correspondence," mumbled the chairman.

As Dr. Imberlay, on cue, began his near sotto voiced plodding through a seemingly irrelevant letter from somebody in the Office of Public Instruction at Olympia, few spectators in the room were aware the meeting had begun. The chairman's gavel sounds reached only the first two rows, and the superintendent's mumble could not be heard beyond the first row (particularly above the hushed individual conversations alive in the audience). Steve Dobson, learned quickly that though the letter dealt in some manner with Driver's Education, its contents said nothing about safety. As a result, his attention left the table and wandered outward into the spectators.

Partway back and up in the slightly tiered seats he saw his neighbor, Mel Potts, whisper something to Mrs. Potts. Steve winced, involuntarily, pretty sure that Mel said to Edith (as he had said to chairman Dobson many times):

"They deliberately read those God damn communications so's nobody can hear them. That way people don't know what goes on, they get bored, and leave so the board can then do what it wants to do. I keep asking Steve why he just doesn't have that super make copies for each board member. Hell, I hope they can all read."

Each time Mel hit him with this, Steve promised to bring it to Imberlay's attention. Several times he got himself almost up to making that point (in the privacy of Imberlay's office), but at the last moment his voice dried up as did his forwardness. His awe for a school administrator, to some extent even for a teacher, drilled into him by his parents and his own schoolday's experience, rendered him helpless when it came to a confrontation with an educator.

Beyond his schoolmarm fixation, Steve's natural relationship to others early earned him the adult appelation of "that shy little

217

Dobson boy." Nobody was more surprised than me when old Steve run for the board twelve years ago (he's in my voting district), because I knowed him all my life and never knew him to take a public stand on anything (except the one time his kid got hurt on the school grounds). Though he was three years ahead of me when we went to school I got to know him pretty well. Seems he liked to play with us younger boys instead of the ones his own age.

Steve never held no office in his class nor the student body, and he turned out for no sports nor did he take a part in a play. Though I don't know, being younger, whether he ever went to school dances (least he never talked about them), I do know he thought girls was icky like us younger boys did. After Steve left school I kinda lost track of him for some years, then one day, surprising like, he came back home having been in Korea, and brought a mighty meaty California gal to live with him and his folks out on the old Dobson place. Steve and Delores (she must tip the scales at 300) soon had two kids of their own, and they treasured them kids like they's made from spun gold. The oldest one, now, works for his daddy at Dobson's 76 Service, but it were the second boy, Dwight, who got Steve elected to the board.

That boy's a regular A.T. Cromwell, he is, 'cept I guess a bit more unlucky than A.T. was as a fast drivin' kid. Right now young Dwight, him aged twenty, lays in the hospital over in Castleview with a big cast on his leg (and his car sits totalled out at Renfro's Wrecking Yard). It was thirteen years ago that he lay with casts on two busted legs in that same hospital when a spin out motorcycle run him down here on the elementary playfield. Seems a bunch of the young bucks from hereabout used the playground for an obstacle course on the weekend, and young Dobson defied their orders to stay away from the happenings. Well, you can just bet that Delores Dobson screamed about that precious Dwighty of hers so she could be heard as far as two counties away. Steve he starts talking around town, the first time ever, and he's white mouthed about the kid's accident blaming the thing on negligence on the part of the school. Next thing he gets to be a permanent fixture at school board meetings, and he jaws safety in this and safety in that until pretty soon old Dick Garvey, the chairman, won't even recognize Steve from the floor. Well, by God! Garvey's up for election that fall and damned if Steveboy don't just go out campaigning and whup him. He got quite a few safety things done around the school that year, but I guess he ain't done much in the last eleven except attend meetings and vote now and then.

The Driver's Education letter, it turned out, dealt exclusively with financial matters, so its contents passed unheard by Dobson's ears. Not so Edna Keefer who digested every word of it, for her business oriented mind with its flair for figures found interest in most everything of a financial nature. (Secretly, too, she felt "sweet" or "soft" on Dr. Imberlay's erudition and fine manners, so she found her attention riveted on him any time he happened to be the center of activity for a meeting.)

When he finished the first letter and got into the second, however, she found this one (dealing with student rights for high school students) ambiguous and unrelated to any of her interests. Her attention started to wander to the last of her post Christmas sales at the shop that she planned to advertise for this Friday and Saturday. From here she continued on to look, mentally, at some plans she entertained for a revamp of her store in preparation for Spring lines she would soon introduce.

If us adults held a popularity contest in Timbertop, the way the kids do in school, Edna Keefer, thumbs down and going away, would be voted the most popular woman. Our ladies just sort of gravitate to Edna—get advice on things to buy in her shop, use her menus to feed their families, and take her advice on how to raise their husbands and their kids. Menfolk pay attention to her, too, (though she's not much of a looker—tall, bone thin, with a sharp nose, bold eyes and hair that's always flying a loose strand or two), for they can't forget how she hung by and took care of Carl (her now dead husband) through the hell of his bowel cancer and the big medical bills that plumb busted them into bankruptcy. Nobody ever saw her other than cheery, lugging those (then) two baby girls around with her while she cleaned other folks houses and anything else for a dollar. She planted Carl (it was a big funeral) in a splash of tears, wore black and a long face for a month, then hit into things cheery again. With a couple of hundred bucks Davey Huntington's dad loaned her on the strength of herself, she put together Edna's Femme Nook which today is the nicest little money making business in town. Edna's still on the run, though, for besides schoolboardin it for her two little girls (grades five and seven), she leads the cancer drive every year, chairs the local library committee, and acts as secretary to our chamber of commerce. Tall enough to look most men straight on in the eye, she got the men's votes as she did the women's when she run for the schoolboard three years ago in an effort, she said: "to bring our elementary instructional program out of the dark ages."

Now, as Edna visualized how she could decorate one wall of her shop by draping the bolt ends from yardage goods growing old in her inventory, Dr. Imberlay droned on with the student rights letter, and the culture of his diction recaptured her wandering attention. Until her girls entered high school, at least, Edna felt little concern about what took place in that building. Her life's forte found its success in dealing, wearing horse blinders, with one major problem at a time. Her school related problem, as she saw it, involved her all out attempt to help Dr. Imberlay overcome the elementary administrative and faculty lethargy toward curricular improvements at that level. For that reason she had placed her name (uncontested when it became known) for school director three years previously. Until that issue resolved itself to her satisfaction, she felt little interest in any other part of the school's activities.

Meticulously Imberlay closed out letter number two and placed it to his right. The next missile he began to read, his voice now sonorous, came from a Castleview contractor and concerned some proposal for repair to South Elementary's multi-purpose room. Ray Cosgrove had ignored the reading of the Driver's Education letter, scowled and made muttered deprecations about parts of the student rights letter, and with the tedious sterility of the third letter he started to fidget with the papers in front of him. A man long accustomed to the ways of the outdoors (his language and general courses of action tuned to the problems faced in short logging), the formality of directors' meetings (loose though they were by Robert's Rules) frustrated and exasperated him. Particularly he dreaded these open hearings, for despite his "bluster, blow and hang spring cleaning" inside he cringed at the thought that people laughed at his social clumsiness. Acutely aware of his limited eighth grade education, and openly proud that despite it he had never taken "one damn cent of welfare in his whole life," his own four children learned life's discipline from a strap of bridle harness waiting on the wall of his tractor shed for just that purpose. He felt he accomplished his role as their father when each of them, dutifully, graduated from high school somewhere in the middle of their class standard. He let the world, at large, know that his kids: "Knew if they came home from school after getting a licking they faced a harder one from the old man." Today's schools, he reasoned, bitterly, provided children with a playland where they, not the teachers, seemed to be in charge. He resented this, bitterly, blamed the State Department of Education, the laxness of a new breed of school teachers (as he saw them), and, in the case of Timbertop High School, he blamed George Rutherford, Roger Wellington's predecessor who, because of his lax discipline toward students (according to Cosgrove) prompted Ray to run for the board where he worked to get that principal fired. The fact that, even as a board member, he could not get Rutherford fired, further angered him (as it did about Huntington and other teachers he would like to get rid of), but he did find his position gave him some weight in the hiring of personnel, so he remained a goad in the side of "the liberals" as he saw Imberlay, Mick Randolph, Edna Keefer, Vera Overholt, and others of their ilk.

Now, as he lost his last vestige of interest in Imberlay's reading, he spotted David Huntington, III, seated near Billy Lane and a group of students toward the center of the audience. Huntington looked like a Playboy ad for men's clothing with his light cream pants and open throated sport shirt. As the room had not yet reached its usual overheated situation, he still wore a dark brown corduroy jacket with a wide soft gray fur collar.

221

"Fairy!" thought Ray, furiously. "You fruit! You with your money suckin' a big salary out of us poor God damn work back-breakin' tax payers. You, with your fancy education playing games with our little boys and girls. God, but somehow I'm goin' to getcha'. Somehow me and Wellington's gonna have your skinny ass."

As Cosgrove's face started to purple from the explosion of emotion bombarding his mind, Imberlay concluded the contractor's estimate and proceeded onward in a letter from Purcell's attorney. At certain emphasis points in the letter, he paused to extempore for the board incidents and information leading up the those points. As the superintendent droned on (and the audience, unable to hear him whispered among themselves), Mr. Wellington re-entered the room in company with our fourth director, Mick Randolph. Roger's brief nod and wink to A.T. assured the custodian that his instructions to our principal had been carried out. A.T. smiled back his appreciation, sure now, at least, of some action by a very capable man.

Mick Randolph, as he slid into his seat at the table to join with his fellow school directors, was the youngest, the newest, the best educated, and the most affluent member of the board. He was also the only member who had not either been born in Timbertop or attended Timbertop schools (a condition which Ray Cosgrove constantly used as an ad hoc argument against some point Mick tried to make). In our last school election, Mick kind of set the community on its ear by actually staging a campaign for the position in which he put out posters, bought newspaper advertising, made some speeches at grange and other club meetings, and held a big downtown rally for himself. The novelty of all this effort, more than anything else, gave him a 218 to 196 edge over Bev Hickeroy who, herself, told everybody who kidded her about her lack of campaigning before election time: "Vote for that cute banker—maybe he can figure a way to operate our schools without running no special levy elections."

Actually Mick knew very little about school finances, and obviously he found no way to stop our special levy effort. But he was learning, monthly if not daily, about school budgets, taxes, student problems, bus problems, maintenance problems, personality problems, personnel problems, and a hundred other minor school related things. He found the challenge of it very interesting, and he wished he could find more time to involve himself in some in-depth study of these problems. Prompted to run for election by remarks (when he moved here at the beginning of the last school year) from his second and fourth grade daughters that their classes were "dumb", he faced down angry administrators and teachers and inspected those classes in person. He found, after several times in attendance that he agreed with his daughters. Based on their previous school experience in Spokane, Washington, the girl's classes of study were indeed "dumb".

"I'm going to run for the school board and see if I can't help my girls get a better education," he told his wife.

Elected he found himself paired in most of his efforts with Edna Keefer, though he also developed a great respect for Roger Wellington, Dr. Imberlay, and, to a lesser degree, some of the elementary and high school teachers he had come to know through teacher negotiating procedures. He found a deep dislike for Ray Cosgrove, a disdain for Bill Murchim and Steve Dobson, and a great deal of exasperation with the elementary principals who he suspected of being more lazy than reactionary.

As he joined his fellow directors, now, his jeans and sweater made him look extra-boyish in this older, more conservatively dressed grouping. He realized as he looked around the table at them (as a result of his just completed conversation out in the hall with Wellington—who had called him at the bank to ask for a bit of his time before the meeting) how very limited, some of them even stupid, these people were for the great responsibility toward the community, particularly the young, they held. The high school plumbing situation, of which Wellington had just given him his first bit of knowledge, presented just another bit of evidence on the shortsighted, self-centered, pennywise and pound foolish manner in which the district's business got transacted. Besides this explosive little issue slated for tonight's meeting, he planned, also, to make himself vocal on the cafeteria issue. On advice from Billy Lane (a young man he hoped to proselyte, eventually, into the system of his own banking concern), Mick visited the elementary cafeteria for lunch several times this month. He found, quickly, why his own daughters demanded sack lunches each day. He no longer argued the need of hot lunches on cold winter days.

Product of a smaller community even than Timbertop, Mick Randolph got into local civic affairs almost as soon as he got into long pants, for his father, a Methodist minister, saw a preacher's role as the conscience of his community *albeit,* he acted accordingly. From his father Mick early learned that he was, in fact, his brother's keeper. That same spirit, made manifest by him in high school and college, put him at the forefront of student government, student protests, and finally the dynamics of student action.

It was the final events—the efforts that exposed a bad misuse of taxpayer funds by the administrators of a public college he attended—that brought him to the attention of Bill Emerson, President of Evergreen National Bank, a young concern clawing for its place in the financial world. A Washington State based corporation, the less than twenty year old operation pitted its youth and energy against the near stranglehold of the older banking concerns, and in the nine year new look presidency of Emerson, Evergreen jumped from one Tacoma main bank to, now, some sixteen branches in fifteen different cities. Bill personally courted young Mick Randolph—outlined for him a glowing future with Evergreen—brought him in for one short year as a head cashier in a Tacoma branch, gave him six years as assistant manager in an equally large branch in Spokane, then gave him his own managerial position sixteen months ago in the Timbertop branch. Barely thirty years old, as manager of Timbertop's Evergreen Branch, First National people (who laughed at their competition's first two years of feeble effort) already secretly credited him with a substantial inroad into their list of solid accounts. Planning, efficiency, and a goal of common betterment for all provided the trilogy upon which Mick Rancolph based the daily decisions he made for himself and for others who turned to him for advice.

Publicly, for the sake of the bank, he tried generally to maintain a calm, dispassionate demeanor appreciated by customers of their "banker". Tonight, however, he felt extremely pissed, first by the cafeteria situation (which he felt affected his own two children), but secondly, and more fiercely, by the plumbing situation fobbed off on the high school kids by Imberlay and his precedessor, Pettigrew. If Wellington spoke the truth, and the principal had quoted Cromwell whose reputation in the community credited him as an unfailing authority, the high school could well be closed down in a matter of days or weeks to the detriment of over five hundred young people. "Well," Mick thought to himself, as he tried to make some sense from the Purcell lawyer's letter Imberlay began to conclude, "wait until Roger makes his principal report, Mr. Superintendent. I may just peel a little hide off your ass along with the butts from a few of my fellow directors."

"What a handsome boy Mick Randolph is," thought Velma Overholt, appreciatively, as Imberlay came to the close of his correspondence. "That black curly hair and that big black mustache make him look more like some dashing pirate in the movies than like a little old small town banker. Oh, Vera, how you go on, sometimes!"

"Any additional correspondence?" Steve Dobson asked the directors (there was none).

Dobson's last words were the first heard and understood by most of the audience, and the whispered exchange around the room sputtered out, first in the front and then diminishing gradually toward the rear. In front those around the table shuffled papers and moved in their seats. (Five long foolscap sheets listing bills to be paid moved from member to member for their officiating signatures; some time later in the meeting, a curt motion to pay them would be validated. In the thirty some years Mrs. Sebastian prepared and circulated these sheets, only once had any member questioned them. Mick Randolph, at his first meeting, asked to see the accompanying invoices, and he refused to sign until he did see them. As three other members did sign, it made no difference in the process, but the next day Mrs. Sebastian

225

felt very pleased to go over the invoices with Mick in her office. She felt he stood out as the finest director in her memory.)

"The chair now calls on Mrs. Overholt, chairperson of our levy committee," said Steve Dobson.

Mr. Overholt rose to her feet by her front row seat, and her heavy busted well padded frame swayed dangerously until an enforced partial paralysis from the hard seat she had occupied at last left, with a tingling sensation, from her badly vericosed vein legs.

"Mr. Chairman, members of the board, and friends of Timbertop School District," Mrs. Overholt began, in her best PTA president's voice. "It pleases me to report an eager group of people already have begun their campaign to get out our levy vote for next month. Seven of our PTA ladies volunteered to call everyone in the phone book on election day; our door to door campaign volunteers already number in excess of twenty ladies, and the young people from the high school promise to more than double our number. Our Legion Auxiliary, Royal Neighbors, and the Literary Guild all promise bake sales for the money needed to pay for posters, newspaper ads and radio spots. Our student body president, in conjunction with myself, plans a series of public forums to bring the message to our people for answers to their questions. We invite each of you here this evening to join with us in whatever way you best think you can help to assure the passage of this very critical money issue. Thank you."

A light smattering of applause followed the lead of hand clapping by Velma's two closest friends who flanked each side of her seat. She blushed beneath her heavy pancake makeup then lightly waved her appreciation of the audience recognition.

"Sounds like you've once again got things well under control, Velma," vouchsafed Steve, as the PTA president worked her wide, corseted rear back into the hard seated backbreaking theatre seat. "We'll hear building reports from our principals now. South Elementary—Mr. Gant."

"Son-of-a-bitches! They moved us down the agenda," hissed Tom Coleman into Bailey Miller's (South Elementary Sixth) ear. "We should be in committee reports."

226

"Cosgrove!" Baily hissed back to him. "We'll be here 'til after midnight. Somebody ought to nail that bastard's balls to a stump and push him over backwards."

"South Elementary went through the Christmas holidays with a minimum of wear and tear," said the tall, slender, stoop shouldered John Gant. As usual, his opening remarks, with a still somewhat nasal down-Easter accent, raised spots of comic relief laughter from some of his teachers and parents in the audience. "Attendance for December's last school week and January's beginning school week showed better than twelve per cent absenteeism, but we're back to our normal cold weather six per cent, and I 'spect we'll pretty well stabilize there. We got hot water, again, for showers, so the town team members should vote yes on the levy (ha-ha from a few in the audience), and I guess you'd say things seem smooth as a new baby's backside (several women tee-hee this time). We figure to throw in with North this Spring for one big carnival instead of two different weeks like in the past. We agreed on this thanks to the effort of Mrs. Overholt's PTA committee study (and he smiled his best professional smile for her). Want to remind any of you folks here who got kids at South that you're always welcome to come visit ('Don't bet on that,' thought Mick Randolph). We're particularly proud of our new math program ('You mean some new math books,' thought Imberlay, bitterly), and we got a new program in folk dancing with Miss Cunningham, one of our new teachers ('More waste of time for the kids,' Cosgrove told himself, as he frowned his displeasure). Guess that's about it, unless somebody might have a question for me."

No questions were voiced aloud, though several people whispered something among themselves. Gant dropped slowly into his seat at Wellington's right, and from the seat on Mr. W's left Ralph Miles rose and stuffed his wrinkled shirt waist down into his belt.

"North's got about the same attendance story," said the stocky, rotund very red faced young man. "We're happy, too, about this going together with South on a carnival. So far as I know we got maybe one minor problem, that about a slide on our playfield. I see on the agenda the matter comes up later, so I'll skip saying anything about it at this time. Hey, it looks like we'll have the county eighth grade basketball champs this year (a few half-hearted cheers from some fathers in the audience), and that wraps it up for me if there are no questions (there were none)."

Wellington waited until the seat beneath two hundred and twenty six pound Miles stopped groaning and squeaking, then he rose to his feet with a white standard note card held loosely in his left hand. Regulars at the meeting settled back in search of a little comfort from their ancient "opera" seats, they knew (from their previous experiences) the high school report often took as much as a half hour or more.

Roger spoke first to attendance, and he quoted statistics similar to the elementary reports (the three principals established what figures they would present after the adjournment from the super-intendent's office following last Friday's administrative meeting; at that time they also arranged a time to meet in the North Elementary hall so they would come into the meeting together in a show of solidarity). Following his attendance report (more statistically detailed than his collaborators had voiced), he went on to talk about the rash of broken windows at the high school during the past weekends and holidays. He made a strong point both of the cost to the taxpayer and the extra labor effort placed on A.T.'s shoulders, and he suggested that those present in the audience make a special effort to report any suspicious youngsters (to him) they might see loitering around the school grounds. He reported, in some detail, on three expulsions from the school during the past month, and he described the reasons and procedures and administrative actions on several suspensions (including a descriptive, self-aggrandizing version of the Kallifonte case). He paid an almost passionate tribute to George Anderson and his still victorious five (firmly believing that winning teams meant successful levy efforts), then he presented a totally fictitious report of an unnamed committee supposedly studying curriculum improvement (information that jarred hell out of Cosgrove), and he gave a short, hard pitch on the need by the school for levy money that concluded with a big verbal bouquet for Velma and her crew.

"Finally," he said, and that word drew back to him most of the attention in the room which had, generally, wandered away from him at one point or another, "we face a very serious problem in the condition of the plumbing in our high school building. With my pardon to Dr. Imberlay, and others not here at that time, this is a matter I brought to the board's attention over three years ago."

"Maintenance matters come through the superintendent's office," snapped Dr. Imberlay, angered by this covert diversion from protocol. "You said nothing about this to me last Friday."

"Again, I apologize, Dr. Imberlay," mollified Roger. "I didn't realize last Friday how critical things had become. The flooding, this week, of our boys restrooms brought the matter to a head of immediacy. It obviously had to be a part of my building report, as Mr. Cromwell referred the matter to me. My real concern stems from a possible continuation of these floodings. The next one could well bring a visit from the health department and a closure of our building."

"We'll take the matter under advisement," said Imberlay evasively ('And I'll eat your butt over this, Wellington, as well as give you both barrels on Cosgrove's discipline complaint').

"I hope you can move rapidly," said Roger, his voice ingratiating. "Mr. Cromwell (the name brought a murmur of appreciation from the room's upper fringes) warns me the matter is most critical."

"We'll do what we can," said Imberlay, lamely, unaccustomed to handling a public challenge of this magnitude.

"Exactly what does that mean, Mr. Superintendent?" asked Mick Randolph, and he picked up the ball allowing Wellington to gracefully retire from a sticky confrontation with his boss. (Roger sat down.)

"Well, Mick, I, ah—," Imberlay stumbled, helplessly, feeling himself into something beyond his experience of learning or training.

"Yes," continued Randolph, mercilessly, "what do we do about this problem, tomorrow?"

"Well, ah, there's the matter of money," Imberlay stumbled on. "We've—they've—the budget—I didn't make up this year's budget—it doesn't allow for any large maintenance expenses."

"Does it allow for a school shut down?" Mick persisted, cruelly.

"Hold on, Mick," Steve Dobson attempted to smooth troubled waters, "you're a bit new at this business."

"So?" Mick shot at him, then eyed all those at the board table. "How long does it take to know that one day of school closure disrupts about six hundred families in this community? How many times do the people responsible for avoiding these closures have to be warned before they do something about a possible cause? I want that plumbing checked into tomorrow—by an expert plumber. I want it repaired, brought up to standards, as soon as possible. In fact, right now I make a motion that we see that it gets done."

"Your motion is first, out of order," said Dr. Imberlay, stiff lipped, "and I presume, secondly, dies for the lack of a second. Maintenance, Mr. Randolph, is an administrative matter, not a policy matter. This concerns my office and does not concern you except as a fiscal matter."

"Look, Imberlay," snarled Mick, and the superintendent visibly shrank right before the audience's eyes, "don't quote your little book of rules at me. The voters elected me, elected us, to see that this school gets properly run. I say it's improperly run if the doors get closed for health reasons. Do I make myself clear?"

"There's still the matter of money," Dr. Imberlay argued, weakly, reaching for any straw that might float him out of this storm.

"Use your superintendent's emergency fund," ordered Mick, and the other directors looked at their newest colleague with varying degree of feelings.

"Yes," exploded from Edna Keefer, who found Randolph magnificent, if a bit caddish for attacking her favorite educator.

"Sounds like a railroad train to me," growled Ray Cosgrove, his dislike of Mick Randolph somewhere between his loathing for Davey Huntington and his disgust for Dr. Imberlay.

"Sounds like a good idea, Dr. Imberlay," Steve Dobson suggested, quietly, with no feeling on the issue one way or another as it did not deal directly with safety.

"Very well," said Imberlay, in a voice that carried only to where, in the first row of seats, Wellington sat with the elementary principals and Mrs. Overholt. (Roger craned his neck around to give A.T. a victory wink.)

As the directors abruptly ended their discussion, Chairman Steve looked to Mr. Wellington, got his signal of being finished, then introduced the next matter which dealt with the proposed purchase of a new school bus.

"We need one to replace old number three," said Dobson. "It's ten years old and if we don't trade it off we stand to lose some state monies."

"We have different road needs, now, than when Three was purchased," said Dr. Imberlay, crisply, his confidence returning with a rush as they moved into his real love and expertise, transportation.

Immediately the group at the table dissembled into an opinion offering buzz session with no order or direction from the chair. Their mingled mangled words, lost to the audience, sent people in theatre seats back to whispered conversations among themselves. From a middle area, the Carmichels, husband and wife, rose and said their goodbyes to several friends on their way out. Perhaps a dozen others, bored now but able to boast the next day that "they were keeping track of things down at the school" eagerly followed a lead they had waited for some more bold person to make.

Into this minor, but nearly ten minute time of disorder, Bill Murchim, our remaining school director made his hand signalling hello to friends way down the aisle from the room's back entrance and took his seat at the director's table some hour and fifteen minutes late (one of his cows had a difficult time calving). Murchim, a part-time farmer, part-time installer and cleaner of septic tanks, carried a low public image as a person to socialize with, but a high public image in his ability to make and hold on to a buck. In the seventeen years since he inherited one hundred and twenty acres of hillside stumps from his dying alcoholic

231

daddy, he grew that spread up to a full section of pretty damn good pasture and hay land which he fought, bitterly, to keep on a low tax basis. It was Cosgrove who talked Murchim into running for the board where he might keep his eye on that part of the public tax dollar, and Bill looked to Ray for which way to vote though he always voted no on any request for extra expenditures.

A small, wiry man, who could still wear his high school graduation suit (and did), he looked a sun wrinkled sixty though he was, in fact, just turned 43. A bad set of dentures set in shortly after his maturity forced a crooked pattern to his mouth and jaw that a recent set of dentures seemed unable to correct. As a result, Bill seemed to constantly sneer at the people and the world around him when, in reality, he felt good about most everything and generally agreed with anyone who addressed their viewpoint toward him. Murchim, then, presented a many faceted personage to the people who came to know his acquaintance. New acquaintances thought him "a nasty little man", old timers called him "a good old boy with a real hand for a dollar", and the casual person who experienced his amiable syncophanticy found him a "pretty sharp guy". (After all it was an old sage who said: "He's a wise man; he thinks as I do.")

Now, established in his seat next to Ray Cosgrove, Bill found himself first agreeing with Ray that old number three would best be replaced by a big new diesel, while on his other side he agreed with Mick Randolph that "they'd better get a gas engine and keep their fleet consistent."

"Let's get back to order!" shouted the voice of Steve Dobson, above the bang of his gavel on the tabletop.

"I move we ask for bids on an eighty passenger gas pusher," said Mick Randolph, loudly.

"Second," called Edna Keefer, and the gavel rapped for either discussion or a vote.

"We need to start getting into diesel," argued Ray Cosgrove. "More reliable and cheaper to operate in the long run."

"Right," agreed Bill Murchim, through his bobbing choppers.

"I agree with Ray," said Dr. Imberlay, now proving he could speak loud enough to be heard above whispers in the back of the audience. "Surveys done on diesel fleets of West Coast school buses show decided operational advantages over gas rigs."

"We've got eight gas engined buses, maintenance parts for gas buses in stock, and a bus mechanic who understands gas engines," argued Mick. "A diesel would be out of step with our operation. We'd have to install another tank and pump for fuel, stock a bunch of diesel parts just for one bus, and send Cox off to school to learn about diesel."

"We got to start someplace," interrupted Cosgrove.

"Right," agreeed Bill Murchim.

"Mick's arguments are sound," warned Edna Keefer.

"The advantages, future advantages, for starting a diesel fleet far outweigh its disadvantages," countered Dr. Imberlay.

Though all participants spoke loud enough to be heard, now, most of the audience slumped in boredom tuned them out or carried on their own conversations. During all this verbal interchange our two elementary principals slipped out, unnoticed, through the side door as if, perhaps, they might be going out for a smoke.

"We could go on like this all night," said Mick Randolph, in a commanding voice that stilled the directors and began to close down conversation patches in the audience the way a rain storm puts out ground fires. "Call for the question."

"Question is yes for bids on a pusher gas operated 80 passenger bus," read Mrs. Sebastian, and her seldom heard sharp old voice stilled the remainder of conversations alive in the room.

"Those for say aye," said the chairman.

"Aye," from Mick.

"Aye," echoed Edna.

"Them against, no," said Dobson.

"No," snapped Ray Cosgrove.

"No," lisped Bill Murchim.

A long pause at the chair, and a near stillness fell over the audience. Steve tried to avoid the demanding stare of Dr. Imberlay, felt Ray Cosgrove's hard eyes bore into him. On the other hand he knew what Edna Keefer might say to his wife when she came into the Femme Nook, and he, himself, never knew when he might need a quick signature bank loan from Mick.

"Seems we got us a deadlock," he said, at last. "The chair ain't made up his mind on this matter one way or the other, so I'll entertain a motion to table until we come back here next month."

"So move," said Randolph, with disgust.

"Second," echoed Murchim (while Edna and Ray glared at each other).

"We next got a request from Maple Creek folks for a nine tenth of a mile extension on that bus run," said Dobson.

Again disorder broke out at the table and the directors loudly exchanged viewpoints without benefit of chair recognition.

"My God," Elaine Perry whispered to her cousin, Billy Lane, "if you ran a student council meeting like that old Wellington would tear you apart."

"Do as I say, not as I do," Lane whispered back to her. "The number one axiom of so called adulthood."

"You think you can straighten this mess out when you get elected?" she asked.

"You can bet we'll get rid of this correspondence reading thing and the complete ignoring of the audience," he promised her. "With Randolph and Keefer to team with me, I think we can straighten out a lot of things in this district."

"Just look at them down there," she sighed, shifting on her hard, creaky seat. "Our great educational leaders."

"Don't knock it," said Billy, wisely. "As Huntington says, they may be wasteful, even stupid, but they beat hell out of being at the mercy of one person's whim on how things should be run."

"What's cousin David up to tonight?" she asked, peering past a shoulder that fronted her vision to the place where their favorite teacher sat two rows ahead and four seats to their right.

"He's out to challenge Tim Nelson's expulsion," whispered Billy.

"Oh, that's why he's sitting with Tim's folks," said Elaine. "I didn't think they were buddies or anything like that.

Below them Dobson banged, loudly, with his scarred old oak gavel.

234

"He probably thinks Robert's Rules is another book of Hoyle for a card game," giggled Elaine.

"Likely as not, he's never heard of either," Billy shushed back at his cousin.

"Let's get back to some order, here," said Steve, banging three more times for an emphasis. "Chair recognizes Dr. Imberlay."

"As I've said before on these kind of requests," Imberlay began, pendantically, "we can't continue supplying taxi service to families in our district with only money enough to run a specific bus service. State funds subsidize a substantial part of our bus operation, and the state auditor can be very rough on us if we fail to meet state standards and abide by their rules. You directors know, as well as I, the state allows for us to run our buses so that no student need walk further than two miles to get on board. In the case of Maple Creek Road, we already come within one point three miles of the last family on the road. Our turn around we managed to establish that closely by law because no suitable area for it existed between its present location and the two mile marker. Besides the state's interest, we have a local interest for the continuing stretch from our present turn around to the next possible turnaround means negotiating one point three miles of very steep hill that will require a driver to traverse it in first gear using a great deal of extra fuel and putting a great extra strain on the bus. Under the second condition, particularly, and also to keep our position good with the state auditor, I must strongly urge that this extension request be denied."

"I so move," said Ray Cosgrove.

"Second," echoed Murchim.

"Just a minute," said Edna Keefer, and excitement in her voice hushed audience conversations in the first five or six rows. "Ruth Miller's widowed and living up there with two little girls in the first and third grade. Since that car wreck that took her Joe, Ruth doesn't get around too good, or she would never ask us for anything. Rules or no rules; hill or no hill, we're darn poor neighbors if we can't help her out when she's got all the troubles she's fighting with now. I know that bus route and it's past dark this time of year when Ollie gets his bus to the turnaround. Those

235

two little girls darn well shouldn't be out on that road alone after dark, and I know Ruth's in no condition to navigate up and down that hill."

"Let her move into town," snapped Ray Cosgrove.

His words and manner created an angry murmur in the crowd. In the audience center, Keith Parmenter rose and waved his arms trying to attract attention from the board. Carefully the chairman avoided seeing or calling on him. Dobson could not, however, stop Micky Randolph whose emotional heat now reached an even higher level.

"You clown," Mick snarled at Cosgrove. "What kind of man are you, anyway?"

"Man enought to know right from wrong!" roared Cosgrove. (He banked with the First National, so Mick's connections meant nothing to him.)

"I say you're no man at all," Mick raged. "Even a half man protects children and crippled widows."

"Gentlemen!" shouted Dobson, banging a half dozen hard swung blows on the table top until the directors finally slid back into the chairs from which they both had lifted themselves. "Let's get back to business and away from personalities."

"Question," called Murchim, loudly.

"The question asks yes for bus route extension and no for no extension," canted Mrs. Sebastian (who had her own system for framing a motion).

"Naye," chorused Cosgrove and Murchim, after a quick exchange between them to figure out how a negative vote supported their position on the matter.

"Yeah," said Keefer and Randolph; they, too, needing to take a second look.

Caught in the middle again, Dobson knew that his options here were closed off. If he failed to vote with Edna Keefer on this issue, he might as well pack his bag at home and move out the the Timbertop Motel.

"Chair votes to extend the bus line," he said, heard Cosgrove snort, maliciously, saw Imberlay grit his teeth, and heard a light applause in the audience that bolstered what little confidence he held in himself.

"The next matter deals with a slide on the North Elementary playfield," Steve continued, as applause lightly spattered to a stop. "How does the board feel about this issue?"

"Mr. Miles assured me that it was quite safe," said Dr. Imberlay, looking for support in the front row and finding his elementary principal gone.

"Bastard!" he thought, to himself. "Left me to play the bad boy without getting a bit of mud or shit on himself."

"What a bunch of hokie," Billy Lane thought, as the directors again began to chatter amongst themselves. "No wonder people stay away from these meetings. Hell, everything they've done so far tonight could have been done in no more than a half an hour, and it's already nearly ten thirty. Jesus Christ, three whole hours! Most people who came are so bored who could ever talk them into coming again. Like David said, I'm sure, part of it is deliberate so that people won't stay or won't come. Guys like Imberlay and Cosgrove really hurt now they can't do their business behind closed doors. By God! I dedicate my life to pushing every political meeting, motion, and conversation out into the bright light of public scrutiny until no one can hide their slimy little deals under the phoney need for secrecy. So, they broke my old man for trying to do the same thing as a newspaperman; well, they'll play hell breaking me because I've learned my politics from a master teacher."

At the table things reached a point of order, again, and a quick motion, supported by the superintendent and abstained to by Edna Keefer, left the questionable slide in its place rusting out on the playfield. Should anyone be injured on it, or any further outcry over it occur, fingers would point only at one person, Dr. Imberlay.

"It seems we have a delegation of students with a petition to present concerning our cafeteria," Chairman Dobson read from the sheet in front of him. "The board recognizes Billy Lane, High School A.S.B. President."

237

"Thank you, Mr. Dobson," said young Lane, rising and moving along the aisle then finally heading down the incline until he stood, facing the audience, behind where Bill Murchim faced the table.

"What you think you're doin?" questioned Cosgrove, gruffly, turning his head back to glare at the young interloper.

"Getting on an even basis with you, Mr. Cosgrove," said Billy, lightly. "We're all speaking from equal power positions, now that I'm here at the stage center with the rest of you."

The audience murmured loudly about that one. "Damn kid's smartern' a whip," admired Tom Coleman, sitting up in his seat and nodding his head to Baily who, apparently felt like thoughts. "That's what I, by God, ought to do when my turn comes tonight. Everytime I get into a shouting contest with that bastard Cosgrove I always feel like he's the teacher and I'm the damn student who's going to be sent to the principal's office, or something. Give him hell, Lane, but save a little skin for me to peel."

"May I present the board this petition signed by over three hundred high school students and by over one hundred and eighty five Timbertop parents," Billy began, handing the stapled sheets first to the board chairman.

"And that's the way the kids get things started," Brian Mc Quade told me the next day, during our lunch break.

Mc Quade's been around here maybe five or six years working on the mill yard crew the same as me. He and his old lady went to their first board meeting because she was one of the seven women who complained about the North Elementary playslide.

"Yep," Brian goes on, "the whole thing seems crazy as hell when I look back on it, now. All them growed folks setting there at the table spitting, shoutin' and sometimes sulking like angry little kids. And through it all this high school boy, this Billy Lane who I don't know, but who I'd by God vote for for anything, puts them through a rigamarole about food and the way the cafeteria's run telling them how it should be done just as cool as a drink of spring water. Polite as all get out, he was, and he made old Cosgrove, Murchim and Imberlay look like fools while the others quick learned to keep their mouths shut."

"Ray's sister-in-law runs that there kitchen," I interrupted, to point a fact out to Brian.

"Whatever," he said, laughing like his thoughts still bent back to the meeting," only thing I know is my kids won't get no more arguments about eatin' school lunch—the banker made it clear about his kids not eating there, too. I told the Lane kid, when he passed me on his way back to his seat, should he want to get up another petition he, by God, could count on me and my old lady to sign it."

"He got his way, then," I said, glad for the kid 'cause I think he's great, too.

"Hell, no," laughed Brian, "but he took that all cool and calm, too. 'Thank you, ladies and gentlemen,' he says, as right as you please. 'Our committee gives notice to you that from here we plan to be heard at the Intermediate District Office and from that office we plan to carry the matter on to Olympia. Let's hope, for the sake of the District and further expense to our taxpayers, we don't have to take this matter into the courts.' "

"Well, what in hell did they do about it?" I asked, growing exasperated with Brian's theatricals.

"Old Steve Dobson says what he usually says, I imagine: 'Get me a motion to table this matter so's we can examine the whole thing further,' " laughed Brian.

When Billy Lane left his place at the director's table and returned to his seat, he got a general round of applause from the audience and a wink of praise from Mr. Huntington. Elaine, and a few of his other classmates, physically pressed their compliments upon him, and he got some verbal accolades from Mr. Mc Quade and a few other adults who sat near his group of student participators. His passing and getting seated caused audience noise to hold up the meeting for a few minutes, so Steve Dobson finally pounded heavily on the table as he shouted "meeting come to order!"

"We have a request from Mr. and Mrs. Nelson that their boy, Tim, be returned to school," said Dobson, when the room quieted. "The request reads here that Tim Nelson, expelled officially from school on December 17, be readmitted to school until the matter of his expulsion can be re-heard. What's it all about, Ivor?"

"We got Mr. Huntington here to speak for us," said Mr. Nelson, his voice uncommonly high from nervousness that dried his mouth and tightened his throat. (A murmur ran around the audience, louder in the student section than other parts of the room.)

"Okay, Mr. Huntington," said Dobson, giving the surname its proper due respect in this county.

"Dr. Imberlay, Clerk Sebastian, and Timbertop school directors," David Huntington began (he seemed to tower where he stood arms folded across his chest—the poor auditorium lights made his cream clothing and bright blonde hair seem monumental). "Despite the thinking of your august group, and despite the alleged expertise of our high school principal, Mr. Wellington ('The son of a bitch!' thought Roger), it pains me to inform you that a gross miscarriage of justice took place in the expulsion of Tim Nelson from classes at Timbertop High School. Tonight, I stand here to give you a very simple warning—if he's not re-instated, as per requested, by next Monday morning, at the latest, those of you at the table, except Mrs. Sebastian, shall, in-dividually and collectively find yourselves sued in an amount that will make your Purcell case seem like a penny bank."

He stopped, let the bits of applause from students and surprised exclamations from the adult audience subside around him. His eyes, fixed squarely on Imberlay, challenged the superintendent to make any response at this moment in the proceedings. Imberlay, no complete novice, held his silence hoping Cosgrove would take the defense or better yet, Wellington, who now sat red faced with angry eyes on David.

"According to student rights procedure, no student can be removed, permanently, from his studies without, first—just cause; secondly, a properly followed hearing program, and finally, the opportunity to appeal the matter to a civil court, if necessary. During his time of trial, he experiences the same as any other American citizen his status of 'innocent until proven guilty.' As an innocent, he cannot be deprived of his constitutional right to an education," intoned Huntington, and his hard, clearly enunciated words registered on every mind present.

"Tim Nelson, we contend," he continued, in the now totally silent room, "should not be out of school for smoking in the first place, as the violation in no way disturbs the educational process at Timbertop. We can show, secondly, that he received only a cursory hearing in the principal's office about the matter, that he was not invited to defend himself at the board meeting of his expulsion, nor was he properly notified that such an action would take place, and, finally, he should be in school now while awaiting an answer to a civil court petition currently being filed by his attorney. In that petition we show that Tim Nelson faced accusers, prosecutor and judge in the person of Mr. Wellington (not one wooden seat creaked in the room); we show the only evidence, or arguments, introduced in the board's action came from the same Mr. Wellington, and, as a result of that action damages to the educational loss and mental health of Tim Nelson now stand in access of one million dollars."

The room exploded into a cacaphony of sound. Students, all standing, whistled, cheered, and applauded. Adults, some of them also standing, applauded and stamped approval with their feet. Wellington, standing and waving his arms at Dobson, demanded loudly that the chair recognize him to speak. Cosgrove, on his feet, too, roared undecipherable words in David Huntington's direction. Red faced and perspiring, also standing and recognizing no one to speak, Steve Dobson battered the table beneath the block of his gavel until a corner split and flew away.

"Tomorrow I resign from this shit," he told himself, this time meaning it. "I ain't got no reason to put up with this kind of crap for no pay."

"The meeting will recess for ten minutes!" he screamed, at last. "We meet back here at twelve o'clock."

"You really told 'em, Mr. Huntington," said Billy Lane, as the worshipping students gathered around their favorite teacher out in the hall.

"It's easy to play the white knight when you've got the full force of law and order on your side, Billy," laughed David.

241

"What do you think they'll do?" asked Ivor Nelson, shyly, from a place by David's left elbow where the big logger stood sheltering his tiny wife under one arm.

"They'll promise to give us a decision on the matter by the weekend," David advised him. "Tomorrow Imberlay will huddle with the district's lawyer. I'll tell you, frankly, Mr. Nelson, if Tim didn't have the good marks and the fairly good school record he had up to this expulsion, my little performance tonight would have been a pretty shallow bluff. Oh, don't get me wrong, we got all the legal right on our side, but they got tradition and a sympathetic circuit court judge on their side. They could stall this thing off until Tim would probably give up and you wouldn't care anymore. The district lawyer, however, will see the good grades and the good attendance record Tim shows, and he will advise Dr. Imberlay that there's a good possibility that a persistent, clever attorney could convince a jury that the board expulsion action did cause financial loss to Tim, even a great deal of mental pain, and the ruling could favor Tim with a big chunk of cash. All this the attorney will tell to Dr. Imberlay along with his advice that the board back off, schedule another hearing for some nebulous time in the future—then postpone that again until after Tim's graduation. Dr. Imberlay will then advise Tim to return to school on Monday. Now, you take this advice to Tim for me. Tell him not to strut about this thing when he comes back. He plays their silly little game of get along with the establishment, and he particularly stays clear of Mr. Wellington. Understand?"

When they returned to the auditorium it went pretty much as David promised, so most of the people (who had sleepily hung around to see more fireworks) drifted out of the meeting room in ones, twos and threes until only Tom Coleman, four of his original seven teachers, David Huntington, Billy Lane, Mrs. Overholt, Mr. Wellington, and the people at the board table remained.

After Ray Cosgrove addressed several remarks to the board on how "on this night's work the last discipline left at the high school went to hell," Mrs. Overholt waved her hand and was again recognized by Mr. Dobson.

"In my earlier report," she said, her voice fluted as if trying to still troubled waters, "I forgot to give credit to the Booster's Club who plan a 'get out the vote' drive in which they will provide rides to the polls and baby sitters for mothers who need one to get out."

"That's wonderful, Mrs. Overholt," Imberlay managed to intone, grandly, though tiredness ate the marrow out of his bones. "I'm sure with people like you behind us our success at the polls is assured."

"God!" he thought, wearily. "I hope Willy finds something for me in a big central office, someplace. They need lion tamers here in the boondocks, not men of knowledge and vision."

"May I suggest, Mr. Chairman," said David Huntington, uninvited, from his place nine rows up from the table (all at the front, except Mrs. Sebastian, grimly readied themselves for his next onslaught), "you entertain a motion commending Mrs. Overholt for her great service to our district."

"So move," breathed Edna, with a sigh of relief.

"Passed," said Dobson, quickly, and he indicated that Mrs. Sebastian enter the motion into her minutes.

"Who had the second?" asked the meticulous old lady.

"Second," said Mick, quickly.

"Passed," reiterated the mentally staggering board chairman.

"Mr. Chairman," called Tom Coleman.

"Mr. Coleman," answered the chair, slowly pulling himself together for another outburst.

"May I please claim the floor for a report on our negotiations?" asked Coleman.

"I thought we agreed to lay off that business until after levytime," interrupted the still bull voiced Cosgrove.

"Our report still needs to be made an official part of a board meeting," argued Coleman.

"Mr. Coleman's correct," arbited the superintendent.

"Directors will hear report from teacher's negotiations," said Dobson.

Covering her mouth, daintily, to stifle a yawn, Mrs. Overholt rose slowly, waved a fluttery bye bye to Edna Keefer and Dr.

Imberlay, then, her legs partially paralyzed again from the pinch of the wooden seat, she plodded slowly up the aisle toward the door as the old linseed oil soaked floor creaked under each of her steps.

"Members of our teacher's negotiating team met with Mr. Cosgrove, Mr. Dobson, and Dr. Imberlay last Thursday night in Dr. Imberlay's office," Coleman began to read from a paper held in his hand, as the creaks from Mrs. Overholt faded in the distance behind him. "On point one, an increase payment by the director toward our medical program, Mr. Cosgrove and Dr. Imberlay said no, and Mr. Dobson passed on his vote. On the second point, a district dental plan shared equally by the teachers and the district—Cosgrove voted no while Imberlay and Dobson both passed. The right for teachers to negotiate and determine curriculum got a no vote from all three district representatives, as did the right for teachers to negotiate the calendar. A proposed change that would pay coaches according to a percentile of their contract instead of on a fixed per sport figure got a yes from Cosgrove, a no from Imberlay, and an undecided from Dobson. Teacher request for ending official work week at 3:30 on Friday also got three no votes. Finally, and here I feel we face our biggest problem—teacher's salaries—we are the length of a football field apart. As you know, we settled for a cost of living increase last year so the levy amount could be reduced for its third attempt. This left us still very much behind, paywise, compared to other areas of work in our county. We ask this year, in return, that we get a cost of living plus ten per cent which will bring us up fairly close to the others. In our good faith, then, we promise to accept in the future a cost of living index raise regardless of what other unions get from their bargaining. I thought our request a great concession on the part of our membership, but the district representatives vetoed it and, in fact, Mr. Cosgrove suggested a 3% raise instead of the 6% cost of living. (At this point Tom raised his eyes from the paper and fixed them balefully on Ray Cosgrove's apparently dozing head.)

For perhaps ten seconds a hush settled over the room as if the eye of a hurricane had just settled in.

244

"Three per cent's too damn much for you part-time workers," Cosgrove snorted suddenly rearing his head up from his pretended napping.

In an angry babble of voices all members of the teacher's negotiating team clambered to their feet and started shouting at the directors. Tom pushed one back down into his seat, got the three angry women members finally soothed and seated again. He turned, still on his feet, back toward the table under an obvious personal struggle to control his emotions.

"You directors not privileged to that meeting can appreciate the lack of good faith shown by those directors present," Tom continued, his voice shaky.

"The roll call vote would read a bit differently had I been there," interjected Mick Randolph, his voice edged with anger and disgust for Cosgrove and Dobson.

"We appreciate that, Mick," said Tom, real camaraderie in his voice. "It was that thought that prompted us to agree with the suggested layback in negotiations until after levytime. We wanted this negotiations report, however, as an official part of Mrs. Sebastian's board minutes so, should we need fact finders or arbitration, we can present evidence of the kind of faith some of our school directors showed in negotiations."

"I've put your report into my minutes," promised Mrs. Sebastian, who seemed the only unweary person at the table.

"Thank you," concluded Tom. "Anyone on my team like to add a word?"

Getting no response, Tom, still on his feet, jerked his head toward the door in the back, and his four teammates, legs also suffering partial paralysis, rose to follow him out of the assembly.

Cosgrove made an aside remark to Murchim who laughed in snide appreciation. For a moment Tom hesitated, then moved on.

"That concludes our agenda," said the chairman. "The board now welcomes new business from the floor."

Roger craned his neck and saw only Huntington and the Lane boy besides himself in the audience. He wanted to talk to the board, officially, about the Nelson case; wanted to introduce to them a motion to censor Huntington for his night's effort (as a part of the minutes); wanted to share with them some ideas he had that might muzzle the growing number of students coming to board meetings. David Huntington surmised these things, and he surmised, also, that both Imberlay and Cosgrove had things on their minds they would like to make official parts of the meeting without their being overheard by an outsider.

"We stay as long as Mrs. Sebastian stays," he whispered to Billy Lane. "Once she leaves there's no way they can get any crap past her and into the official minutes."

He could not, however, hear Mr. Cosgrove whisper to Mr. Murchim:

"What do you suppose would happen, Bill, if one of us came out in the paper in opposition to this here levy?"

# CHAPTER NINE

As an explosion of voices dinned the area around him, A.T. shook his head and felt a painful moment of empathy for Mr. W. At the same time, however, he found himself pulled into Nelson's camp by Huntington's rhetoric. Relieved when Steve Dobson pounded through the shouting and established a recess, Cromwell decided to split and get home for a few hours sleep.

Outside he found a flurry of snowflakes swirling down out of a black, starless sky. For moments he stood near the first street light he reached and found a deep aesthetic enjoyment from the sparkling pink and white lace of wetness that drifted onto his upturned face. With an amused smile at his own childishness he knelt, crunched up a snowball, and lofted it toward the light. Then he set off down the street toward home, his heavy rubber overshoes crunching a deepening track at every stride. Outside of Timbertop, he thought in a form of religious wonderment, beyond our county and state lines, millions of people suffer the kinds of belly ripping agony I saw in Korea. Instead of squabbling like a bunch of chickens pickin shit in the barnyard, them folks back there ought to pray to God, their good fortune fairy, or whatever great force put them in this special place on the universe. He had twice seen war up close, and he prayed it never came to this land he loved.

Snow whirled around him and dropped like wet Leghorn feathers onto his parka and face, and the sheer wonder and beauty of it recalled past winter fun shared with his two boys when they yet lived at home. For the moment he compared his sons to what he knew of Tim Nelson—compared himself to Tim's father, Ivor, whom he had known for many years.

"You do your thing, if you must," A.T. had told his boys, the first time their clothing brought home the telltale odor of marijuana. "Pot won't hurt you, of that I'm pretty sure. Remember this though, do you get caught by John Law it can damn well cripple you for life. And do you get caught don't look to me for help or sympathy. Be you man enought to break a law or rule, then you be man enough to pay the penalty it asks when you're caught."

His warning, he knew then as he knew now, failed to stop them from further pot, cigarette experiments, or participation in the famous "keggers" that happened from time to time. Both boys, however, apparently acted most discreet, for neither, to his knowledge, ever got tagged by police officials, school authorities, or the ire of other adults.

"We respect you, Pa," his eldest son told him, long after the boys' graduation from high school. "Those damn pea brained characters who sneak around looking to bust some kid made us—still makes us—mad, not respectful toward them. Face it, dad, our generation learned early that the law doesn't mess around with the big boys, they just fill their trophy cages with little guys who can't afford the bread to pay for their trip."

"Well, maybe the young ones had it figured right," he thought, now, as he swung out into the street (the next half mile to his home lacked both sidewalks and street lights). "Still you got to have rules and somebody's got to try an make them rules work. For all my big talk to my boys, though, would I not have been just like Ivor Nelson had one of them been expelled from school? Now, Barbara she does as I say, not as I do, so I know she'd have cried her hurt away in some private place sure that what old A.T. said was the right thing to do. I'm not sure I really believe it myself, all that much. Thank the good Lord I never had it put to the test, yet. Just glad I'm not Mr. W. trying to look in a dozen different directions and pick the right way to go. By God! This damn snow's really startin' to pile. Better call Coxy when I get in the house."

His early morning call (it was now 12:28 a.m.) woke Mildred Cox (husband Fred holds title of Bus Superintendent). When she, at age sixteen, was Mildred Adams, she often rode the country backroads in A.T.'s '36 Ford.

"It's A.T., Milly," he said, in response to her sleepy "who is it?"

"You know what time it is?" she asked, incredulously, breaking her question off into a nervous squeak as was her habit.

248

"Better set a four thirty alarm for Fred," said A.T. "Looks like we could have snow trouble this morning."

Though A.T. found little to respect about Dr. Imberlay, he much admired an innovation in school bus transportation instigated by the new superintendent. Under previous administrations the appearance of more than three or four inches of snow entailed an immediate school closure. Imberlay, on the other hand, produced alternate plans for bussing the hazardous road conditions faced in many of the outlying school bus runs. Plans A, B, and C were mimeo'd and sent to each home, each school personnel, each law enforcement agency, and the local and two Castleview radio stations. To instigate one of these plans, the Bus Superintendent made an early morning check of road conditions then called his recommendation into the superintendent. Dr. Imberlay, in turn, called the information to the radio stations, law enforcement centers, and his three principals. Each principal, in turn, called his assistant and his secretary, and the three people of each team called designated teachers on their respective lists. Already December had tested a two day application of the plan, and it worked with an efficiency that pleased most of the parties concerned.

This morning Fred Cox called a Code C in to Dr. Imberlay, and the concentric waves of communication rolled into action. Code C meant that outlying county roads carried dangerously high drifts of snow with their narrow shoulders hidden traps for the bus driver who made a slightest miscalculation. In Code C action buses would make pickups only along major roadways, and those pickups would be one hour later than the usual bus run schedule. Teachers, too, were advised that they enjoyed an extra half hour to arrive at their respective buildings. All were informed, too, that school closure for students would be one half hour earlier.

At his home, Mr. Wellington, awakened by Imberlay's call, spoke crisply and efficiently into his telephone. To further complicate his morning he got sick calls from Audrey Settlemeir (who lived in Castleview), Bill Goss (who lived way back in the hills), and Steve Hutchinson (who suffered frequently from

249

bronchitis). He called eleven substitute teachers on his list before he located three who could replace his missing soldiers.

As Emily lay, half awake, listening to her husband's patient, firm, efficient phone delivery, she experienced some nostalgia for those good, vibrant, togetherness days of their early marriage. Then she re-captured the reality of today, and she remembered that on this day she planned to invest her $5,000.00 Christmas bonus in Bud's new real estate project. Her decision in this matter weighed heavily on her conscience, for she saw it as the first step away from her husband. "Well," she told herself to destroy any mental malingering, "he took his first step away from me when he started fucking Madeline Forbes."

"Poor Roger," her thought line continued. "You're really so damn naive and little boyish. How could you ever possibly think the word of your playing around wouldn't get back to me in this tight little island we live in. Well, bunky boy, I guess you'll just have to do your thing, and I'll start in to do mine. Who knows, maybe step number two will be a crawl into bed with some stud who turns me on like you used to do. Sure hasn't been any exciting sex with Mr. Principal for a mighty long time. Wonder if you really get it up for old Madeline?"

She heard him hang up the phone and make his way into the bathroom. Last night she had just finished the late show when he came shambling in from his school director's meeting. Once he would have shared his triumphs and frustrations with her; maybe they might have ended up in a crazy snowball fight on the front lawn. Last night they barely grunted goodnight—this morning they might not even grunt a hello.

"The school world's a phony world," she tried to explain to her brother-in-law (who couldn't believe she wanted to leave a job that paid her nearly twelve thousand dollars for 180 days work for a job with him that took at least 45 hours out of every week and started at a flat four fifty a month). "School concerns itself primarily with school; not with children, not even with people, certainly not with life as we really live it. Success or failure in school bears no relationship to success or failure in the outside world. Do you know we don't teach one course on how to be

250

happy? We hardly teach health at all. What more important thing could a person learn than her own physical and mental well being?

They sat eating a lunch in one of Castleview's darker, more intimate restaurants where they had come to discuss Emily's wish to come to work for her brother-in-law. Because of the dim light in which they sat, she failed to catch the boredom and non-understanding that lay dull in his eyes.

"When I first started to teach," she continued, "I felt appalled by the many teachers who just slid through their days playing a role of professional baby sitter. Soon I discovered new categories: the entertainer, the slave overseer, the mental sadist, and the simpering masochist. Don't get me wrong, Bud, I found some darn good ones, too, but they seemed such a minority I felt myself lost in among the others. During that first year, one of the older teachers I got to know pretty well told me candidly: "If you can get over the first six years, the next twenty four are easy. By that time you realize what a hopeless sham the whole thing is, and you smile when you cash a paycheck right along with the rest of them." Well, that's my problem, Bud, this is my sixth year and I've vomited almost every morning before I headed to work. I can't face year number seven. I've got to do something real, for a change."

"Come on, Em, things can't be all that bad," chuckled Rotarian Bud (and she realized her words had just bounced off his hide).

"Let me hit you with it this way, brother-in-law," she said, with an intensity that stifled his chuckle. "One very wrong thing about teachers is that they go right from school to teaching and never find what that great old outside of school world is all about. Outside of a few minor summer jobs, and a barmaid spot one year in college, I've never had a chance to find out what goes on in your big old business world. I want that chance! Can you help me get it?"

"What do you want to do?" he asked, a bit amazed by her vehemence.

"I want that receptionist job, Mr. Wellington, Jr.," she said, brusquely. "I want to find out what it's like to have to produce in order to get my pay check. I want to compete in a produce or perish environment where I stand or fall by my own efforts. I want out of this welfare state I'm in and its welfare treatment of the clients It's supposed to be servicing."

"That many welfare kids in school now?" asked Bud, amazed.

"I'm sorry, Bud," she laughed, "I'm just trying to be semantically cute. We forget that people outside of school have little idea what really goes on inside."

"You're right," laughed Bud, happy things had grown less heavy. "I always just thought schools were for kids; same as it was for me."

"It's the same," laughed Emily, merrily and honestly, "really the same, old buddy. Same old teaching ducks how to climb trees, squirrels how to swim, and ground hogs how to fly."

"What in hell are you talking about, Em?"

"Nothing," guffawed Emily. "Do I get the damn job?"

"Sure," he said. "What the hell, maybe you, at least, won't leave me to work for the God damn Huntingtons."

Davey Huntington got his call about the Plan C for snowfall from Sarah Metzger, but he already knew the information from an early KCVW news bulletin. He, like A.T. Cromwell, anticipated a snow slowdown when he left the board meeting around one a.m. accompanied by Billy Lane. By the time he got the student president home, his Porsche did some fancy sliding on its way back to the condominium.

Unlike the bulk of his colleagues, David took little interest in the extra half hour reprieve Plan C allotted him, so he arrived in the teacher's parking lot near his general time of 8 a.m. Parking the Porsche he found Wellington's car, Anderson's and Findlay's pickups, Heidi's Honda and Bettermen's old homemade flatbed rig. Barely settled in his room with a grade book and some report cards he intended to work upon, he soon found himself joined by a noisy growing group of juniors and seniors who, having driven or ridden in cars to school, congregated in his room in one of their inumerable teen-age discussions.

"I say they're both stupid and vindictive," argued a thin faced girl bulked out in blue wool ski pants and a heavy, jagged orange

252

lighting design blue wool sweater. "Dog in the manger kind of stuff. They can't enjoy school so they want to wreck it for the rest of us."

"Why don't they enjoy school, though?" persisted a bearded boy (who appeared to be her chief antagonist in their argument). "That's the question that needs answering before we really start leaning on these people."

"We got it right here in Mr. Huntington's class with the I'm okay—you're okay bit of action," offered a plump but pretty faced senior girl.

"Except we—let's at least say, they—don't really believe that stuff even though they want to in the worst way," argued blackbeard.

"What more to do, then?" cried the thin faced girl. "Do we just go on doing for them—making excuses for them—losing privileges because of them?"

"Snuff 'em out," laughed a small sized junior boy (his laughter, high and splintery, triggered others into giggling).

"Funny," snapped thin face girl, her disgust at the clown attempt very evident.

"What do you think, Mr. Huntington?" asked the bearded boy (he saw Davey's eyes come up briefly from his grade book study at the sound of the girl's cutting tones).

"What can I say that hasn't been fruitlessly said a thousand times before?" asked David, shrugging his shoulders and sharing his glance with the now some two dozen students huddled toward the center of his room. "Jesus of Nazareth offered a simple, foolproof solution to all social problems—love one another. In his name our bloodiest wars have been fought, our very best people have been persecuted, and a hundred wonderful cultures have been destroyed. One of you mentioned I'm okay, you're okay, and I say wonderful to that, but as Sylvia pointed out it's after the fact. Frankly I find a strain of madness in people. Don't look so shocked, Beverly. I find a strain of genius, too—a strain of godliness, of animality, and of childlike simplicity. All these I sense are mixed up in mankind's genes so that each of us carries from the miniscule to the maxuscule of each of these characteristics.

We boast that we've come a long way since our cave man ancestry, but I rather think our ancestors killed only to eat—not for sport, greed, or personal glory. Viewed one way we progressed a long way from Torquemuada's Inquisition, yet only forty years ago we let six million Jews be slaughtered by the German war machine. Right today, in our own country as well as others around the world, people band together to fight for 'the right to life', and those same people let millions of others already living starve to death, nor will they claim any responsibility toward the new lives they make possible. Insanity? It seems to be unless you look across the total spectrum. Then you begin to get the feeling of something—the idea of variety and the wonderful spice of differences. Crazy, too, isn't it? We fear differences in others with a near paranoic intensity, yet we find our greatest enjoyment in life when we open ourselves to a new experience. Well, I've got away from the question, as usual. . ."

"No! NO!" pleaded a cacaphony of voices.

"Yes, yes," laughed David, "because whether you believe it, or not, I've got other things to do besides bulling with you guys. Back to the original on the vandals, bad heads, and others you laid out for disection—we got two groups here like any other society: the ins and the outs. Most of you sitting here this morning are ins, or you'd be darn well taking advantage of the late school start to stay out. Let me, then, play the devil's advocate to you. When was the last time one of you ins tried to cultivate an out? Cultivate, I said, remember, not convert. By cultivate I mean you tried to know and understand not criticize and seek to change? Despite what we 'ins' like to hold out as the holy grail, men are in no way created equal. We each emerge with differing degrees of the genetic strains I mentioned, and I can't be you and you can't be me."

Silence mobilized the room for perhaps ten seconds, then bodies shuffled in seats, feet rustled against the floor, and voices murmured, whispered and began to grow in volume.

"You got a little too heavy for us, Mr. Huntington," said blackbeard, at last.

"Sometimes I get too far out for myself," laughed David.

"Do you believe there's such a thing as a generation gap, then?" asked one priss senior girl whose social life, for the most part, consisted of reading books and practicing two hours each day on her piano.

"Generation gap, Tana?" asked David. "You mean a physical age gap?"

"Well, sort of," she answered, lamely.

"In that way, no," said David. "Thinking gaps exist both in and between varying age groups, however, so amongst yourself, right here, thinking gaps exist that make it difficult, sometimes impossible, for one of you to relate to another."

"How do you fit with your generation?" quipped the small junior boy with his nervous laugh.

"I try to keep an open mind—a current mind," said David, matter-of-factly as possible (the clown knew he had been put down gently). "I try to respect other people's thinking, and I hope that, perhaps, they may in return respect mine."

"What do you think about junk?" giggled clown boy, unable to back away.

Several voices protested this smart ass action, but Davey waved them to quiet.

"It takes a very mature person to handle junk—any kind of junk—whether it comes in a bottle marked beer, a stick marked marijuana or tobacco, a powder marked cocaine or heroin, or an oral secretion known as words," said David, slowly. "The trouble with junk in society occurs when the immature use it because they live under a false impression that under its influence they do, in fact, become mature. This results in a sad situation, for the deluded become more immature than they were prior to using. Now, if we could just find a way to give those immature people faith in themselves without the use of junk, then they could use the stuff in a pleasurable way as its creator intended it to be used."

Had Mr. Wellington had the intercom open to Mr. Huntington's room (as he often did when he wanted to secretly monitor a teacher) this risque dissertation on narcotics would have been transcribed into the file folder about Mr. Huntington that daily grew more fat with personal information. This morning, however, the intercom sat unused while Mr. Longfellow enjoyed a rare cup of instant coffee with his principal in Mr. Wellington's office.

"Of course I know nothing for sure," said the principal, setting his shiny brown mug down on the desk blotter, "but after last night's board meeting I suspect we may find some real opposition to our levy. Should it fail three times, you know, we'll have to lay off at least forty teachers in the district."

"How about administrators?" asked Longfellow, trying to appear casual.

"My guess is we'll be back in the classroom in one capacity or another," said Mr. W., offering some surcrease to his underling, but not letting him slip entirely off the hook.

"So you feel we need to review and update all teacher files between now and June 1?" said Longfellow.

"Right. Let's really get tough on evaluation reports, too," said Wellington. "Each of us will write a narrative evaluation of a teacher's out of classroom performance. I'll split the list with you, and we'll re-evaluate all educational background credits so we can produce an overlay of who's qualified to teach where. Let's see if a restructuring of our room assignments allows for some double sized classes in math, English or social studies. I want to see what happens to daily student flow if we cut out metal shop, woodshop, art, home ec, band, driver's ed, and ag."

"How about coaching assignments?" asked Longfellow.

"I'll handle that when and if the time comes," said Mr. W.

A bell sound buzzed dimly outside the room—8:35.

"Well, looks like the honeymoon's over," said Longfellow, draining off the last of his coffee.

"Make a quick check and see who's in and who comes late, okay?" asked Mr. W.

"Sure, chief," said Longfellow rising for a quick look out the front window. "I just saw Mooney's car turn the corner."

"That means Overstreet's late getting in, too," said Roger, with a harsh chuckle that drew a like response from his companion.

When Wellington's phoning voice first informed Pat there would be a half hour delay in the school day's beginning, her immediate reaction was: "Thank God for small favors." When, however, he followed up that message with a request that she pick up Lisa Overstreet on her way to work she thought to herself: "Why does shit always fall on me?"

She experienced even further frustration when she found her car needed chains to negotiate its way out of the apartment parking lot. Fortunately a small, water soaked boy she recognized as the freshman, Schwarz, happened along scraping snowballs from the parked vehicles and, for fifty cents (and with painful slowness) he affixed the chains for her in a haphazard manner. He declined her offer of a ride to school as he "wanted to fool around until the bus came his way."

Puffing and grunting, Lisa plowed her way through front yard snowdrifts, and with a great maneuvering effort she managed to squeeze her broad rear into Pat's small bucket passenger seat.

"Too bad dear old Miles Pettigrew left us," said Lisa, as her door finally scrunched closed. "If he were still here we'd have had no school this morning."

"Yes, but we'd have felt badly making it up in the Spring with the sun nice and warm," said Pat, as pleasantly as possible (she tried to ignore Lisa's body odor but the small confines of the front seat made it impossible).

"I should have taken sick leave this morning," groaned Lisa. "I would have if it hadn't been for semester exams."

"Suppose we'll be on the shortened period schedule today," said Pat. "That bad for your semesters?"

"Oh, I scheduled all mine for tomorrow, 'cept sixth because of that darn pep assembly," snapped Lisa.

"Everybody's so excited about our team," Pat offered, conversationally.

"Poppycock and rubbish," snorted Lisa. "Sometimes I think schools put more stock in the games they play than the work they do."

Pat left it at that—lowered the window a crack to let in some fresh air.

257

"My defroster doesn't work too good," she said lamely, when Lisa protested a draft on her fat neck.

She glanced at her wrist watch and saw they'd be about ten minutes late.

"More shit for Patricia," she thought. "I suppose we'll have a blizzard so I can't make it to Portland this weekend."

A dim ray of sunlight dusting through her lace curtains brought Heidi to her home ec window just in time to see Lisa and Pat disembark from the counselor's car onto the snow choked teacher's parking lot.

"My goodness! that woman would break down the springs on my little Honda," she thought, wickedly, then chided herself on another thought that she'd probably have to confess to Father Mueller on Sunday.

As she watched her two teaching companions gingerly pick their way toward the main building, their entrance door opened and two of her three naughty senior boys came charging out heading her way kicking up clouds of snow in front of them.

At first, being alone, she experienced a moment of panic. On impulse she moved to lock her door, then she laughed at herself, nervously, scolding herself that she, an adult, should command respect from these high school boys. Composing herself, as best she could, she seated herself behind her desk and pretended to be busy with work in her plan book. A gust of cold air told her the outside door had been opened, and she slowly, somewhat dramatically, raised her small gold hair framed face and fixed bright, big blue eyes on the advancing duo.

"Good morning, Miss Vandercamp," said one boy, as the two stood at attention in front of her desk.

"Good morning, Rollo. Good morning, Steven," she answered, her voice brisk and businesslike. "What can I do for you boys this morning?"

"We come to apologize, Miss Vandercamp," said the boy, Rollo, and Heidi, looking at him more closely, found a bruise on his left forehead and a band aid stripped along the corner of his left eye. "Jake, he'll be in later on the bus to do his. Me'n Steve drove this morning."

"What is it you need to apologize for?" asked Heidi, innocently—enjoying, for the first time in her life, a sudden sense of power.

"We said some dumb things to you," said Rollo, and he started to fidget. "Honest, we didn't mean no harm by them."

"It's not what you said to me," said Heidi, primly (even a bit forcefully, she told herself with some exhultation), "it's the interruptions during my class period that make it hard for me to teach."

"That, too," said Steve, hurriedly. "It won't happen no more."

"Then I accept your apologies," said Heidi.

"And would you mind letting Mr. Huntington know?" pleaded Rollo.

"Mr. Huntington? Why, whatever for?" asked Heidi, fighting back a huge smile that threatened her whole professional composure.

"He just might like to know," said Rollo, lamely.

"Of course, if that's what you want," said Heidi. "Anything else?"

"No, thank you, ma'am," the two chorused, then both heaved noticeable sighs as they exchanged goodbyes with her.

When the door clicked closed behind them Heidi began to shake with controlled spasms of merriment. Wait until she got home to Olympia tomorrow night and told Daddy about the apologies. Wait until she had a chance to tell David Huntington thanks. She might, perhaps, even pass the good word on to Pat Mooney.

Elaine Perry, however, proved to be her first confidant. Nodding and smiling, Elaine (already appraised by cousin Billy that 'the guys from the wrestling team took care of Miss Vandercamp's problem last night') heard the little teacher out then, after giving warm congratulations to that matter, she launched into an account of last night's director's meeting.

"And you should have seen and heard Mr. Huntington," she said, with reverence, after first accounting the asinine adult board response to Billy Lane's cafeteria challenge. "He put them all down. Directors, superintendent, even Mr. W."

"Even Mr. W.?" asked Heidi, awe voiced.

"Mr. W.," echoed Elaine.

"What did they fight about?" asked Heidi. "Would you like some coffee, Elaine?"

"You bet! I missed mine this morning," said Elaine. "Donut Shoppe was closed. 'Guess Doug didn't think he'd have any business with all this snow."

"About Mr. Huntington," continued Heidi, when the two young ladies sat facing each other over steaming mugs of instant coffee.

"I don't think you know Tim Nelson (a negative Heidi headshake), but he's about as sweet a guy as you'd like to know," said Elaine. "Big guy—much more'n six feet and must weigh far past two hundred pounds. Well, ever since we got into the ninth grade Mr. Wellington, Mr. Findlay, Mr. Patterson, and a few other coaches been working on Tim to get him to turn out for football. Tim's not interested—just won't do the thing for any of them, so they all started bad mouthing Tim last year—looking for things to give him a bad time or a lower grade."

"That's hard to believe," said Heidi, incredulously.

"Maybe so, but it's as true as what Mr. Wellington did to Tim when he kicked him out of school for smoking a cigarette," said Elaine, firmly.

"Smoking? In a classroom?" asked Heidi, shaking her head in bewilderment.

"Heavens, no," exclaimed Elaine. "Tim just lit up on his way walking home from school. He was way out at the far end of the football practice field."

"And he got expelled from school for that?" asked Heidi, believing but not believing.

"You should know some of the funny things Mr. W., Mr. Patterson, and the other coaches pull on boys who won't go out for sports," said Elaine, ominously.

"But Mr. Patterson's supposed to be a counselor," argued Heidi.

"Why does everybody call him 'coach', then?" asked Elaine. "I think that he's the worst of them all."

Bert Terwilliger did not listen to radio in the morning nor did he ride a school bus—neither fact, however, did he make available to Mr. Patterson when the counselor ordered him into his office for an interrogation.

"Okay," said Patterson, voice cold and belligerent, "you won't tell me why you happen to be in school an hour early, so tell me what you were doing by the wire around the steelyard supplies."

"Nothin," said Bert (his answer to all Patterson's questions to this point.)

"You're quite the hood, aren't you, Terwilliger? Just like your old man," snarled Patterson. "We're all a bunch of squares around here because we're serious about what we do. You ever serious 'bout anything, *boy*?"

"Dunno," monosyllabled Bert.

"What do you mean—you don't know?" sneered Patterson. "I hear you're always 'in the know'."

"Not me," said Bert.

"Okay, bright boy," Patterson's voice dropped back to its earlier colder mechanical tones, "we're going around this tree until you get ready to climb. Now, why are you on the school grounds one hour early?"

"Don't want to get any more tardies," said Bert, bored now, with baiting the counselor.

"But an hour early?" already Bert could read mollification in Patterson's voice.

"I walk," he said. "Couldn't be sure how long it might take me in the snow."

"Okay," said Patterson, unctuous now, "I can buy that. With your record I sure as heck wouldn't want any more tardies, either. Now, why were you out by the steel shed?"

"School doors were locked," said Bert, improvising as he went along. "Lots of time Mr. Betterman comes in early, so I went out to the metals shop."

"But you were in the back of the shop," persisted Patterson.

"Knocked on his front door and nobody answered," lied Bert. "I heard noises inside so I thought maybe I could raise somebody from the back."

"First time you were ever back there?" asked Patterson.

"First time," lied Bert.

261

"Well, Terwilliger, I'll let it go, this time, though you know I should refer the matter to Mr. Longfellow," said the counselor (big buddy voice, now). "You could make something of yourself here, Terwilliger, if you got in with the others and tried to work to your potential. Ever think about turning out for track or cross country? You look pretty wiry."

"Giving track some serious thought for this spring, sir," lied Bert.

"Good—good thinking, Bert," said Patterson, effusively. "Okay, fellow, buzz off now and see you fly right. Don't want to see you back here again except for some small talk or friendly advice."

"Thanks a lot, coach," said Bert, trying desperately not to gag.

"Anytime," offered Patterson, warmly, trying to remember what warnings Wellington and Longfellow had both given him about this pretty cooperative boy.

Wellington's morning at school, like his early moments at home, consisted primarily in acting as an extension of the telephone. He answered half a hundred phone queries on emergency bus stop times and assured another half hundred callers that "yes there would be school today—one hour later than usual."

When the buses started to arrive, he turned his answering service over to Mrs. Metzger while he took his constable position in the upper hall. Near the library door he ran into Billy Lane, and with last night's nightmare director's meeting fresh in his mind, he decided to spread a little grease.

"I felt very proud of you young people last night," he offered, having cornered Billy in the alcove which held the library door. "Made me feel our work in student council's been worthwhile."

"Thank you, Mr. Wellington," said Billy, guard up but face open and amenable, as per Hutchinsonian instructions. "I felt the board, as a whole, treated us pretty well."

"Tolerance, like you displayed last night, is a wonderful asset in a young person," said Wellington, this time with honest admiration. "I'm afraid, at your age, my fuse was a bit short."

"Three years of student council taught me to look at things from a number of viewpoints before I decide how to act," said

Billy ('I really mean three years of David Huntington has given me savvy and poise you'll never have,' he thought).

"Well, you're probably anxious to get on into the library," said Wellington, fatuously (accepting Billy's statement as a testimonial to his own guidance work in student council). "Drop into my office, anytime, Billy. We should have a good informal chat about school things every now and then."

"Thank you, sir," said Billy, as the principal moved on down the locker row like a police dog on patrol.

"What a creep," he told himself. "Is there anything more destructive than a man who goes all out doing the wrong things because he believes completely that he's doing the right things? Okay, Billy boy, you stole that from Mr. Huntington's assessment of the White House plumbers. By God! though—it sure do fit our fine Mr. Wellington."

David Huntington, too, gave some unflattering thought to Mr. Wellington this morning, as well as Dr. Imberlay, Ray Cosgrove, and a few other hackneyed Timbertop educational leaders. His confrontation by students on matters of drug usage and the generation gap hyped his thinking and it created the spaced out feeling that his classroom grew to be more of a cage as the morning progressed. Before any further students could corner him for the lunch period, he took the last five minutes of his planning period in the home ec room where he borrowed a pan to heat some mushroom soup brought from home this morning.

"Sunshine's beautiful outside, now," said Heidi, joining his table with her own salad from the frig as the last of her students went out into the snow with a high girlish scream of excitement.

"That stuff outside'll turn to slush if it gets a few degrees warmer," he said, for conversation.

"Can I join you two?" asked George Anderson, appearing with his lunch bag.

"Like some tea?" asked Heidi.

"Great," said George.

"Me, too," said Davey.

Laughing and shouting like children, Willy and Sylvia burst into the room still carrying snow in their hair and on their clothing from their romp to Heidi's building.

"Don't mess my floor," called the little home ec teacher.

"Right!" shouted the love birds, and they retreated to the porch to brush each other clean of their snow crusts.

Quietly Dave Gorman slipped into the room with a smile and answering nods to three "Hello, Daves" that greeted him.

"Wonder if Pat's coming out, too?" Heidi asked, framing the question all four of them felt.

Again Willy and Sylvia entered, followed this time by Betterman and O'Malley with their black oblong lunch boxes.

"Bill Goss called in sick," said Mike O'Malley, as if someone had asked. The others nodded and continued on with their lunches.

"Hope the highway gets clean of this stuff before we leave for Camas tomorrow," said George.

"You'll be okay going down," said Huntington, the old timer in these parts, "it's coming back around midnight that gets you caught in the ice."

"Rooter buses going?" asked Dave Gorman.

"Understand they've got two nearly full, so far," said George. "Cheerleaders plan to hit first period class tomorrow."

"You going?" Gorman asked Heidi.

"No," she said, apologetically to George. "Going home to Olympia right after school tomorrow. My mother has some things planned."

"How about you?" George asked Gorman.

"Headed out for a ski thing at White Pass," said Gorman, also in a voice tinged with apology.

"And everyone knows I never go to games," offered Huntington, with a laugh. "Though I secretly admit watching tennis is starting to turn me on."

"Think there's too much emphasis on sports in school?" asked George.

"Too much emphasis on winning in sports," said Davey Huntington. "Too much seeking after glory—too much 'thrill of

264

victory and agony of defeat.' I applaud the exercise (which I hate) the teamwork (of which I'm a poor example), and the competition (which I get mostly in challenging myself). The glory, however, tends to create a society of sports neurotics both as participants and fans."

"I agree," said David Gorman.

"You're supposed to be a coach," said George Anderson, his voice showing his surprise.

"I coach because it took that extra ingredient to get my teaching job here," admitted Gorman. "Don't get me wrong—I love sports. I'd love them a lot more, however, without the glory factor. I like to challenge myself, or work with someone else to overcome a serious challenge. I guess I actually resent it when some spectator tries to vicariously share in my output effort. Their presence cheapens me—like I'm sort of a performing circus animal. That's why I quit baseball after I got out of high school."

"How about you, George?" asked Huntington. "You got that big spotlight in the sky fastened on you all the time. How does it feel to be a celebrity?"

"Sometimes I feel like it's stifling me—burning me into a crippled cinder getting more brittle by the moment," said George, moodily. "Sometimes that spotlight's the sun—my source of energy—my strength—my power. You can't believe the times I've tried to visualize what my life would have been like had there been no spectator sports for me. Yet, how can I discover what I've never seen—never known. Basketball's as much a part of me as the heart that pumps blood into my body. I go to sleep with it; I wake up with it. Even when I want to be something else with somebody else, I can't get the monkey off my back."

"Know something, pardner," said Huntington, who had pushed aside his soup bowl and tea cup to lean his elbows as a chin brace on the table, "you need a retreat from all this jazz. When was the last time you spent a quiet week with your family or twenty four hours alone by yourself?"

A long silence in which all at the table seemed to apply that question to their own situation.

"Can't remember," George sighed, at last.

"Tell you what," said Huntington, "if you're not put uptight by it, I'd like to introduce you to transcendental meditation."

"Heard of it," said George.

"I never have," said Heidi.

"Why don't I hold a session at my place for all of you one night next week," suggested David. "You could bring a wife or friend, if you wanted to."

"Sounds good to me," said George.

"Me, too," said Heidi, with fond memories of that apartment.

"Count me in," said David Gorman (excited by a chance to see Heidi away from confines of the school grounds).

Despite widespread snow melting, the school bell rang a half hour early this Thursday. While released students whooped it up with slushy snowballs, the faculty gathered in their usual bitching places to speculate on tomorrow's weather and to complain about this day's inconveniences.

"Gonna catch any of Billy's games?" asked Tom Coleman (whose wrestlers had no practice tonight as did Eph's and George's basketeers).

"Don't think so," answered Dave Weydermeir. "What's the latest on your wrestling match here with Centralia tonight?"

"Confirmed cancellation," said Tom. "They closed school today. Think I'll take my old lady out and give her a treat, for a change."

Generally teacher morale remained pretty good for a Thursday, as in various places around the building each prepared to wait out an hour instead of the usual half hour past final bell time. Not so, however, for Marsha Kemper who found, when she arrived at the North Elementary gym, that two of her starting five girls had failed to show for their game against Camas.

By halftime her outer veneer of civilization had cracked and peeled away exposing root nerves of emotion more tender than the bared nerve of a tooth. Twice already referees had penalized her with technical fouls, and the general apathy of her girls toward her own show of temper as well as their own slovenly style of play made her scream at them in the locker room. The locker room, itself, provided reasons enough to grate salt into the wounds opened by her team's poor play, for it lay cold, smelling of ancient sweat and years of lysol; its scarred old green benches, battered lockers, and three open dripping shower heads reminded her that Anderson and Findlay had the high school plush outlay for "practice" while in the ancient old gym with no seats for spectators her girls played a "league game" against the number one team in their conference.

"Time to go up, Mrs. Kemper," one of her managers called from the doorway.

"My God!" she thought, gritting her teeth. "What do I do to get them to call me coach?"

"All right, girls," she said, harshly, fighting back tears of frustration that threatened to explode from her ducts, "want you to get back up there and show a little spirit this second half. Remember, some of your mothers are here watching you play. We don't want to be known as quitters, do we?"

"It won't be as though I were quitting something because I couldn't handle it," Billy De Haven mused to himself, as he absently watched his ninth grade team drive to another score against Camas. "I'll just be looking out for Myrna and old number one. A degree in education sure doesn't mean you have to spend your life grubbing along as a school teacher if there's a better way to make a buck."

His thoughts concerned a letter he began mentally to compose during the past Christmas holiday. This letter, directed to Mr. Wellington and Dr. Imberlay, would inform them that William De Haven would not be available for a teaching contract in the ensuing year.

"Go ahead, baby," Myrna had encouraged him. "I don't like these little schoolteacher cliques and the pitiful pay any better than you do. Besides, I can get a job in Portland that pays almost as much as you're getting here, anyway."

"It's more than just money, Myrna," he tried to rationalize. "I went into teaching because I wanted to do things for kids. Now that I'm in it, I find that kids are the lowest thing on the totem pole. School directors first—administrators second—teachers third and kids and animals left to last."

"Hey, lover, you don't have to sell me," laughed Myrna. "I've already started to pack."

For sometime now he and a tennis teammate from college had toyed with a concept they called "Short Court Tennis." Designed, first, by Billy as a class project for wheelchair people, its playing area confined itself to just the tennis forecourt with the baseline at the backline of the forecourt and the net lowered to a respective height. Billy had pretty well forgotten the project (which got a lot of praise from his instructor) when he entertained his college friend during last year's spring vacation. The friend, who had gone from college to sell "Greensward" (a competitor of Tartan Turf) painted a sad picture of his father's franchised business, and more as a joke, than anything, Billy had recalled his "Short Court Tennis" program.

"Hell," he said, "why limit it to wheelchair people? At most it takes maybe sixty to seventy feet of space as compared to 130 for regular tennis. Think of all those people who could have a tennis court right in their backyard if they could get it under seventy five feet."

"And what could make a nicer green backyard than 'Greensward'," shouted his friend in laughter, raising high the stubby of beer he held.

Then a few more smart remarks and it wasn't quite so funny, anymore. By the end of the day they were engaged in serious cost accounting, and by the end of last summer they had made more money selling and installing short courts in Portland than either had made in a full year before that time. Articles of Incorporation were already filed for Weydermeir and Goetz, Tennis Court Installations, Inc. By June Billy would be full time into the business.

"Good work! Good work!" he called, now, clapping his hands as the team came floorside to him for a between quarter rest. A small electric scoreboard at one end of the gym informed him his boys led 41-33 at the end of the third quarter. Across from him a small group of ninth grade students cheered from their folding chairs led by three hard working ninth grade cheerleaders. Near the end of the court he saw a small group of adults—recognized Wellington, Patterson, and the South Elementary principal. Their animation told him they felt pleased with his boys. For one brief second he thought of Marsha and her girls in the old North Elementary gym. What the hell, God looks after those who look after themselves.

"Okay, guys," he said to the five sweaty young faces around him, "just keep it cool and fundamental. Just eight minutes and we can be tied for the league lead."

# CHAPTER TEN

Roger Wellington left the South Elementary gym a few minutes after five p.m. Despite the late afternoon chill, he felt warm and flushed with victory. They were all part of the same team, the ninth as well as the varsity and junior varsity. In fact, the attachment extended on down into the grades where his own son, Bobby, played a forward for the South Elementary Sixth Grade Team. (Watching her shivering girls fight the cold showers at North Elementary, Marsha Kemper would have enjoyed a head to head debate on the "team" concept with her boss.)

"How come we always gotta give up our practice for these ninth graders?" Bobby had asked his dad, as the two Wellingtons stood watching the game together.

"All part of the old pull together thing," Roger soothed, seeking to placate his son. "Everybody gives a little someplace along the line for the good of the whole group."

"Yeah? Well, whyn't the varsity give a little once in awhile so we can have our own practice time?" asked the boy.

"Priorities," mumbled Roger. "You'll understand when you're older."

"Like all them other things," said the boy, just a shade off smart alec.

"Easy, guy," said Roger, low voiced, sidling a glance to see if Patterson or any of the others nearby had noticed the tone of disrespect.

"Sorry, dad," said Bobby, who usually played the game very well. "Alright with you if I go sledding with the guys?"

"Be in by dark," his father warned.

"Catch you later, dad," breezed the boy, and he moved to join a group of his friends who had been hanging by the door.

"Good looking kid," Patterson appraised to the smiling father, as sturdy Bobby swaggered to join the other displaced members of the sixth grade team.

"Got the stuff to be a quarterback," said Roger, voice thick with pride.

"Good hands; good bone structure," Patterson agreed.

"And a damn good head on him," Roger concluded.

The two men had then gone on to review other great football talents both local and national. Now, as his car engine caught its first spark and belched forth black carbonated smoke, Roger eased it into gear and guided the wheels along slushed streets just starting to crust again. Slowly, as he progressed the blocks toward his home, a digressive thought from his usual game review pattern filtered into his mind. An entire evening lay ahead of him free from any school responsibility. The wrestling match cancellation left him with an opportunity to follow his own bent. Maybe he could take the time to sit down with Em and take a look at some of their growing problems. From the car radio a voice advised him that highways north to Chehalis and Centralia lay snow clogged and dangerous. A state patrol bulletin, however, further advised that roads south to Castleview and Portland were "clear with patches of black ice."

Emily Wellington, flushed with the heady excitement of her first big real estate investment, sat at a table in the Holiday Lounge with Dick Rooney, a salesman from her office, and Will Travert who managed a title and trust office in Castleview. Into their third drink, each tried to add to the others enthusiastic appraisal of Wellington Realty's latest development undertaking.

"It's going to outdo anything Bud's put together before," said Rooney. "I made better'n sixty thousand on the last one."

"Hear you're studying for your license, Em," said Travert.

"Don't wanna stay poor forever," she laughed.

"Well, this old boy'd better get it in gear," said Rooney. "After six, now, and I need some dinner before I start seeing double dollars."

"Go ahead, Dick," said Em. "I'll stay here a while longer. The great Mr. Principal's got a wrestling match tonight, so I got no great reason to go home."

"I planned to eat here, Em," said Travert. "Want to have some dinner with me?"

"Long's you don' make me lose this glow too soon," laughed Emily.

When Willy Norburt came to play music at nine, it surprised him to find Mrs. Wellington at a table near the dance floor with a tall, tanned, slender young man dressed like a Johnny Carson clothing ad. Mrs. Wellington, who appeared to sway a bit when she got up for a walk to the powder room, looked right past him with glasslike eyes, so he decided it best not to say "hello" to her.

Snug in her own little apartment, Heidi sat surrounded by garments she carefully studied before giving each its grade mark. The student completed projects served as her categorization of a semester examination, and she applied a very rigid marking measurement as the pieces represented a fourth of a student's semester grade. In all her classes she credited twenty five per cent for a semester project, fifty per cent for the accumulation of quiz marks and smaller projects undertaken, and twenty five per cent for classroom attitude. It pleased her, much, this evening, so far no one rated less than a C on their report cards. Her own struggle for grades in school remained still vivid in her mind. It would be nearly three a.m. before she finally completed her grading project.

At his pad, Davey Huntington, too, worked on report cards. In the block for "Remarks" on each card he penned some observations, advice, criticism or acclamation. For the most part his class members rated B's (for good work) or C's (for average, expected efforts). A few of his more dynamic people garnered A's (for superior production or innovative thinking), and five received D's (a poor effort on the student's part in which, under remarks, David apologized for not being able to interest the student into making an average effort). David, too, worked until an early morning hour before his cards were ready for the day.

Thursday night meant town team basketball, again, for George Anderson, and his group traveled to Castleview where they took on a strong five representing Huntington Enterprises. Once again the combination of Findlay and Anderson proved too powerful for their opponents. Because he rode over from Timbertop with Eph, George spent some bartime at The Magic Lantern Tavern with "the boys." Pleading a need to work on report cards, however, he managed to get a reluctant Eph to leave after only one pitcher. Home by eleven thirty, he tumbled, exhausted, into bed, and he fell sound asleep before Madge could switch out their bedlamp.

For Pat Mooney the night proved again to be a long and frustrating one. She tried to sedate herself with grass and music, but the depressing problems unloaded onto her all day by first one girl and then another floated back into her consciousness where, ghostlike, they haunted any and all of her reaches toward serenity. One thing, however, she promised herself, firmly. Never again (as long as the group in the home ec room lay available to her) would she let students trap her away from her lunchbreak. Like a lifeline in a storm, the short half hour she experienced on Wednesday provided her some hold on her own reality. She finished her third, and final, stick, but she felt none of her usual euphoria. Even her favorite Chopin Etudes failed to give the usual soar to her spirits. Shaking her head at her own inadequacy, she walked stiffly into her cramped bathroom, got a bottle of Sominex from the cabinet, and swallowed three pills. Her head would ache and be thick in the morning, and her mouth would taste of shit, but at least she knew those three pills would eventually, help her shut out the pain of loneliness she felt here in the night.

For Lisa Overstreet, on the other hand. Thursday night provided a weekly treat. Her guild met in the library on these nights, and on this evening the girls sat discussing Taylor Caldwell's "Glory and The Lightening". When Lisa spoke to the group on the heroine's role in the making of history, her listeners sat enthralled for it were as if Lisa, herself, experienced the perversity of male dominance. "Had I been forced into a harem," Lisa thought, as the splatter of applause made her evening even more complete, "some man would have paid for it by losing his balls."

"Where in hell can that woman be?" thought Roger Wellington, as the eleven twenty TV weather report assured him there would be no more snow on next day.

He had shared a tuna-noodle casserole with his son and daughter—joined them in a game of Monopoly, then shared an old Western movie on TV that Betty left around ten for the radio in her room, and Billy left a little after ten when he could no longer stay awake. After the kids moved into their own rooms, Roger mixed himself a triple scotch and soda that helped him through fifteen commercials and the final reels in which the hero avenged himself of all past wrongs done to him and the other little people in the valley. Two or three times during his shared bemusement and boredom, Roger fought off the desire to call his brother and ask about Emily. By eleven twenty he felt an agonizing need to call the State Patrol, the Sheriff's Office, his brother's home, or someone. Just as he decided to start first with Bud's phone number, his own phone rang beneath his outstretched hand.

"Hello!" he almost shouted, jerking the instrument up to his mouth and ear.

"Roger?" came Em's voice (did it sound a little thick?)

"Where in hell are you?" he did shout.

"Look I've had a few celebration drinks, and I think I'll stay all night here at the Holiday rather than drive home," said Em.

"You will like hell," he gritted. "I'm coming after you."

"Don't be silly, Roger," she said. "That's a sixty mile round trip and it's freezing out. 'Sides, I'll just have to turn around and slide my way back here again in the morning."

"What in hell you celebrating," he half-roared, helpless before her logic.

"Tell you what, old buddy, I'll give you the whole scoop during dinner tomorrow night," said Em (yes, her voice was definitely thick as if she'd been drinking). "You got a principal's meeting over here, right? I'll take you out to dinner. My treat. Okay?"

"I still think I should come after you," he said, cooled almost to a chill, now.

"You're an old sweetheart," she said, "but I'll be asleep five minutes after I hang up this phone."

"Okay, Em," he relinquished the argument. "You sure everything's all right?"

"Good night, dear," she said. "I'll call you from work tomorrow."

Silence clicked to his ear as she hung up at her end. He placed the pale blue instrument carefully back into its cradle as if it were made of crystal or some highly brittle substance. How many times had he called Em from a motel himself with one excuse or another? Times he spent with Madeline or some other one night stand? Still, he knew Em well enough to know she would never fool around with another man. After all, she was a mother, and, besides, she knew her responsibilities as the principal's wife. He slowly moved through the rooms shutting off lights on his way to bed. Under the sheet and electric blanket he felt very small, very alone, and sleep eluded him as he tumbled first one thought then another through his head. Among those thoughts he included Madeline who would need to be told some kind of a story tomorrow now that he had a date with his wife.

Fridays, for A.T. Cromwell, promised no special pleasures or rewards. He followed his regular work-a-day routine and felt no great excitements about the coming weekend. School closure for snow, in fact, changed his work pattern very little, so though he heard periodic morning radio broadcasts that schools would operate on a normal schedule, those announcements made little impression on him.

They did, however, invoke moans and groans from many teachers and students who had hoped that a new snowfall might come bringing them a three day holiday (none were conditioned, yet, to believe Dr. Imberlay's edict that schools would operate regardless of snow conditions).

"At least it's Friday," Lisa Overstreet grumbled, as she worked her way painfully through her morning ablutions. "By God! I'm gonna sleep in tomorrow."

"You kids take hot lunch today," Roger Wellington ordered his two still disheveled, just out of bed youngsters. "Your mother stayed in Castleview last night, so you get yourself some cereal or something for breakfast."

"Will you get a chance to come home and eat before the bus leaves for Camas?" Madge Anderson asked her sleepy-eyed husband.

275

"Just put an extra sandwich in my lunch," he answered, mournfully. "You know, I think I'll just stay in bed all day tomorrow."

"Hope the hiway clears off by this afternoon," Heidi said to herself as her little Honda fishtailed on a patch of ice near the school. "Oh, I can hardly wait to tell the folks all the exciting things that have happened to me this week."

"If I had to face kids on Saturday, I'd just poison myself," mumbled Pat Mooney to her morning mirror image. "Yes, you stupid bitch, you're gonna be late again this morning."

David, in his Porsche, thought ahead with some pleasure to a weekend jaunt to Portland planned with several young friends from Castleview. Then he remembered, with a grimace of false agony, a dinner party date with his father and family friends promised for this evening at the Huntington home.

"Win some, lose some," he said, to the purring car. "Let's get through the day, first."

Despite constant radio broadcasts about the regular school conditions, Wellington's office phone rang continually again this morning as hopefuls called about school closures or later bus runs. Patient, and polite to each caller, he gave them a: "Yes, school as usual," or a: "Yes, bus runs at regular time." Regardless of what efforts the district put forth, Roger knew (and the morning rolls proved his correctness) that absenteeism would be high today despite announced semester examinations. Monday morning the absentors would arrive with carefully penned notes from mother proving that the bearer was ill on Friday. This morning, however, only one teacher failed to show and he got a substitute with his first call on that order of business.

School buses disgorged shrieking snowballers, and soon the downstairs hall lay streaked with mud and water that would add an extra chore to A.T.'s work day. Twice Longfellow charged outside to break up fights, and upstairs Wellington caught the Schwartz boy stuffing snowballs into his locker, so he sent the freshman down to the waiter's bench where he joined a growing group in Mrs. Metzger's office.

Fridays always produce the highest noise level of the week in all our school buildings, and the added excitement of snowballing, the night's game with Camas, and a special release feeling that another semester's effort was concluding made this day one of the year's noisiest. Shut away in her room, Lisa Overstreet paid little attention to the growing din, but Pat Mooney felt new pains lance into the occipital portion of her brain as decibels piled on decibels like waves pounding onto a storm tossed ocean promontory. Like cowboys barely holding back a stampede ready to break at the first provocation, both Wellington and Longfellow moved from group to group warning against pushing, shouting, and scuffling. David Huntington, Eph Findlay, and several other teachers welcomed students into their classrooms as they sought to siphon off the crowd swelling the inside halls.

"I'd love to meet your folks some weekend," Elaine Perry was saying to Miss Vandercamp, as the two girls sat together over mugs of coffee in the relatively quiet confines of the home ec room. "Can't go this weekend, though, I promised to help Billy with some school levy stuff. 'Sides—I can't miss that big game down in Camas."

"You riding the rooter bus?" asked Heidi.

"No. Going down with my dad and my kid brother," said Elaine.

"Would you believe, I've never ridden on a rooter bus?" said Heidi.

"You ought to do it—can be lots of fun," said Elaine. "Maybe we can take the next one together."

"Say, that sounds peachy," said Heidi, and both young ladies laughed with delight drawing attention from the five other girls working in the room.

In the privacy of his office bathroom, George Anderson knelt before the john where he had vomited his breakfast. All that good hot oatmeal and toast Madge put into his stomach this morning had lain like a brick until five minutes ago when his guts started to burn as if caught by a blowtorch. Fortunately this morning he had avoided his usual stint in the faculty lounge. Had it happened there it might have given him some real moments of embarrassment.

Drained, at last, he lunged back to his feet and washed his face and hands in a wall basin. Above the shiny metal taps a steel mirror reflected his very grey, bloodshot eyed image.

"Guess I'd better quit kidding myself and go see a doctor," he thought. "That's got to be ulcers. My nerves aren't all that shaky this morning."

"You going to the ball game tonight?" David Huntington asked Billy Lane, just before the first bell rang to officially start the day.

"On the rooter bus, as per your advice," said Lane, making a wry face.

"Play the role all the way," laughed Davey. "Too bad there aren't any babies around here for you to kiss."

"There's a few babes I wouldn't mind bussing," suggested Lane.

"Keep it cool, man," said Davey. "Remember, you're a man for all the people."

Shortly after the tardy bell first one room and then another experienced an invasion of cheerleaders who, backed by authority from Mr. Wellington, came breezing into the learning areas wearing big smiles and short ballerina skirts.

"Our boys need all our support," they commanded the troops (while at her desk Lisa Overstreet fumed and swore under her breath).

"If you can't pay right now we'll take your pledge to pay when you board the bus," came the hard sell pitch to the home ec class.

"How much does it cost?" asked Heidi, as the cheer girls waited for a show of hands.

"One dollar for the bus and fifty cents for admission ticket," one of the yell leaders told her. "'Course teachers ride free and get chaperone passes to the game if you'd like to go Miss Vandercamp."

"Not this time," said Heidi, a merry ring to her voice. "I could loan anybody, though, who wants to go and who doesn't have her money this morning."

"Bus leaves at five thirty from the school parking lot," they announced to the combined first period Freshmen gym classes.

(Freshmen provide the largest single segment of school population to ride the rooter buses—Reuben Schwartz signed his name to the pledge list, as always, but he failed to show for the bus having no dollar and a half for the venture).

By nine fifteen, with all rooms negotiated, the girls returned to Mrs. Metzger's office carrying lists of names, promises to pay, and about sixty dollars in cash. Carefully Mrs. Metzger went over the lists with them, recounted the money and issued them a receipt. Excused for the entire period, the girls took a leisure eight minutes in the girl's rest room as they waited for a bell to end their first period class.

"Looks like about a hundred and fifty going," Mrs. Metzger told her boss. "They only list four chaperones, though, and I don't see one teacher's name on the list."

"I'll get Weydermeir or De Haven to go," promised Wellington. "Got a principal's meeting or I'd go myself."

"Shall I order three buses, then?" asked his secretary.

"Yes. Tell Cox to send one big pusher and two sixty passenger jobs," said the principal. "There's always a dozen or so who show up at the last minute and want to go even if they're not on the list."

"What time you leaving for Castleview?" asked Mrs. Metzger.

"About noon. Right now I'd better have a little talk with Mr. Longfellow," said the principal.

In the vice principal's cubby hole office, Roger laid out business he felt needed airing at the afternoon's district administrator's meeting Longfellow would attend in his absence. They carefully covered various options on all items, and Roger asked that Longfellow be particularly insistent about the plumbing problem.

"I'll tell Pat to handle things when you leave," he told Longfellow, finally, (Coach Patterson acted as unofficial third man on the Timbertop High School Administrative Pecking Order). "You got anything I need to take to the league meeting?"

"Nothing I can think of," said Longfellow, dutifully (Wellington rarely involved his V.P. in any league activities).

"Okay, then. I'm going to try and clear out of here by eleven forty five," said Roger. "Got some business with the A.D.'s I want to clean up before the meeting, if I can."

"Wrestling?" guessed Longfellow, shrewdly.

"Could be," laughed Wellington, in his flat, metallic administative way.

His car, in fact, cleared the school parking lot at eleven thirty a.m., and he sipped his first martini in the Holiday bar at exactly twelve fifteen. In the motel lobby a tote board advertised the Columbia River League Luncheon at one p.m. in the Conifer Room.

Back at Timbertop, with the chief warden away, classes grew more restless and the noise level swelled to a new intensity. At lunch time food got thrown in the cafeteria and several fights started from snowballing out on the school grounds. One of the more bloody ones (fights usually stopped after pushing and a little name calling with one scared and the other one damn glad of it) involved Reuben Schwartz and a sophomore boy about twice his size. This one, in full view of the home ec window, brought George Anderson and Davey Huntington away from a very enjoyable lunch conversation. They pulled the two boys apart from where they rolled in the slush on the ground, while Dave Gorman, who had followed his luncheon partners out, quickly dispersed the crowd with terse orders that sent them in separate ways.

"Little animals," snorted Lisa Overstreet, who had witnessed the melee from her own classroom window.

"You guys better split to the locker room with me and get cleaned up before Longfellow gets into this," Coach Anderson suggested.

"You cool now?" Huntington asked the sophomore boy held tightly in his grip.

"Hey, Mr. Huntington," protested the boy. "It ain't me that's hot—it's this Reuben."

In Mr. Anderson's huge hands Reuben felt like an Olympic winner who had just received his first gold medal. The pain in his side where Toby's fist had caught him, the throb on his forehead

280

where a knot started to swell, and the blood that seeped slowly from his nostrils to his mouth (inside) each carried its own badge of bravery. Coach Anderson could appreciate a guy who stood his ground no matter how big the odds. Toby wouldn't be about to call him a dumb Kraut Shithead, again.

"How about it, Reuben?" asked George, softly.

"Whatever's fair, Coach," said Reuben, and blood bubbled from his lips.

"Come on, you two, then," suggested Anderson. "Shake hands and let's get in and get cleaned up."

"Anybody get hurt?" asked Heidi, when the two Davids returned to the table.

"Nothing that won't heal by dinnertime," laughed Huntington.

"It's amazing how many boys want to wrestle each other in street clothing, but they won't turn out for a wrestling team," said Dave Gorman.

"One act requires a commitment, the other happens on impulse," said Pat Mooney. "Very few people feel comfortable making formal commitments. Lots of kids would like to wrestle, play ball, be in plays, and all kinds of things, but they don't want to commit themselves to it for fear of public embarrassment. Hell of a thing, isn't it? Part of the legacy we adults provide for modern children. I suppose that without divorce we'd have far less commitments to marriage."

If Emily Wellington had ever entertained any secret thoughts about divorce from Roger, those thoughts disintegrated in the aftermath of her last night's abortive affair with Will Travert. In the flush of booze and music supplied by the Holiday bar, a bedroom scene with the handsome Mr. Travert gathered to it an aura of romantic illusion that never achieved a reality. After calling her husband, Em slipped her naked body into bed where Will lay hard and waiting. Her mind had demanded that this be a thrill long to be remembered, but her body—her gut feelings—rejected the whole affair as the organs within her body would have rejected a transplant. What passion she managed to pretend lasted only as long as his short, panting series of sexual lunges. Then he hurried home to his wife while she took a long, hot soapy bath, masturbated, and daydreamed about her fat old balding husband.

"I've really got to cut calories," Roger Wellington thought, as he studied his lumpy reflection in the dark polished Holiday backbar mirror (then he ordered his second martini to help mitigate the pain of that resolution).

By one he managed to get aside, individually for conversation, each of the seven athletic directors attending their league meeting. Three agreed readily to wrestling cancellations feeling sympathetic toward the smaller school's problem. Three other agreed, reluctantly, after he pointed out that most of the matches would likely be forfeited, anyway, if Timbertop wrestlers continued to abort the team at their present rate. Only Cy Gobles, from Lakeview, offered any real static, (Lakeview's only league victory to date had been against Timbertop), and the two men compromised by leaving the match scheduled at Lakeview but considering it a non-league contest.

When most of the participants finally gathered at the bar, on signal from the league president the men moved on into the Conifir Room. Roger carried with him his third martini, a warm feeling of accomplishment *re:* the wrestling team, and a bouyant sense of comradeship with the other seventeen men present (statistically it is significant to note that though this assembled group represented over 3,000 girls—some 400 of whom took part in league organized sports—not one member of the representative group was a female). Seven of the men were high school principals; one was a high school vice principal; seven were athletic directors, and two represented insurance companies who underwrote athletic insurance.

"Did you hear that Martin resigned?" asked the young vice principal (next to Roger) from Woodcenter.

"I knew he felt pretty grim about these past couple of years," said Roger.

"Well, he's 55," said the VP. "With his thirty years plus he takes home almost as much from pension as he does from working. Why not, I say. He started to grow a new set of ulcers this fall, you know."

"No, I didn't," said Roger. "I knew he got part of his intestines cut out last Spring. Fact is, I haven't seen much of Martin since he quit drinking."

"Anyway, he told me to pass the word on to you," said the VP.

"You moving up to his chair?" asked Roger.

"Not sure I want it if it's offered," said the young man. "My wife nags hell out of me to get out of this business."

"Mine, too," said Roger.

"Likewise," said Tracy Underwood, Lakeridge principal (he sat on Roger's other side).

Tracy, Roger and the absent Martin formed a usual principal three musketeer conclave as the senior trio in the Columbia League group. Each had served in all capacities as League officers and representatives to other groups. Roger, alone, remained more than an at-meeting-advisor as he served on the State Football Championship Council.

"So, what did you tell her?" asked Roger, who always considered Tracy's wife, Mary Ann, the perfect principal's consort.

"Same thing Martin told Winnie these past five years," said Tracy, grimly. "Hang on, baby, we ride this thing out to retirement."

"That's better'n ten years for me," said Roger.

"And that's why I'm looking for something better right now," said the young vice principal.

"Ed's moving into an Intermediate District spot and Cal's going with Athletic Suppliers," said Tracy Underwood.

"God! We really turn them over, don't we," exclaimed Roger, leaning forward to look along the table to where the other two mentioned principals (both about his age) sat busy in their own conversations.

"Then, why not," he thought, to himself, leaning back in his chair, heavily, to sip the martini fire slowly into his throat. "They got us sandwiched like a piece of shit in a squeezing vice—board on one side and teachers on the other. We're supposed to be a walking boss and we got less authority than our custodian has. We're supposed to be educational leaders, but some clown with an eighth grade education sits on a school board and tells us what learning is all about. Teachers say okay to our face and fuck you behind our backs as they go on doing whatever it is they want to do. Kids get a lawyer everytime we look at them crosseyed, and with their parents we're damned if we do and damned if we don't. We spend most of our time planning tomorrows with no real thought of what tomorrow is all about. Why do I stay in it? Because something's always happening, and I can't stand to be bored, that's why. Hey, old Roger, maybe you're only kidding yourself. Other things out there might be fun to work at, too, you know. After all, what have you ever done besides work for a school?"

"Roger?" he heard his name called from the head end of the table.

"Yeah, Ben? Sorry, I got myself far out in space," said Wellington.

"Any changes to report for next year's playoffs?" asked the league president, Ben Iverson.

"Our committee took some suggestions under advisement," mouthed Roger (who got only as far as the hotel when his committee met in Seattle two weeks previously). "We plan to place some of these with recommendations at Spring Parliament."

"Thank you," said Ben. "Now, Bert will pass out next year's football schedules. Some of us need some help on pre-league games, so get ready to do some head banging and let's come up with some good suggestions."

"Some of us could use some help on filling up the holes in our lives," thought Roger.

Well, hell, it wasn't the end of the world, and it was Friday with a couple of fun days lying ahead. Madeline made no fuss when he cancelled their date for the night, and he felt a bit excited about being out nightclubbing with his own wife for a change. He realized, in his musing, that his glass had gone dry. The salad hadn't appeared, yet, so he had time for one final shot. He signalled a waitress who had brought in several drinks for others at the party. "Kind of a cute little trick," he thought, as she gave

him a great warm 'how are you' smile. Then he recognized her—
Susan Montford, or at least she had been five years ago when he
handed her a diploma at Timbertop graduation.

When George Anderson got Reuben into the locker room, he
told the scrawny kid to strip and get himself into a hot shower.
He wondered what kind of courage well this kid went to for the
spirit to tangle with someone older and twice his size and weight.

"I'll get you some track warm-ups to wear to class," said
George, unlocking his equipment room. "Come in when the bell
rings for pep assembly this afternoon and I'll have your clothes
washed and dried for you."

"Got Mr. Royce for fourth," warned Reuben, as, head still wet
from his shower, he bent over tying the old tennis shoes George
managed to scrounge for him.

"I'll write you an excuse in case you are late," George assured
him.

"Gee, coach," said the skinny kid, looking up at him with eyes
that glowed like twin neon signs, "you are the greatest, you
know? I'm gonna be a coach, too, when I grow up."

"Oh, yeah," chuckled George, more amazed than amused by
this nearly perfect flunk boy's reasoning.

"You bet! All the guys here think you're the greatest ever. More
even than Coach Findlay," rambled Reuben, cinching up the final
shoe.

"Got a college picked out yet?" asked George, carrying along
the illusion.

"Figured to go where you did," said Reuben, stoutly, slithering
into a twice too large Timbertop Track Team sweatshirt.

"You don't seem to work very hard at getting there, Reuben,"
George admonished him lightly.

"Guess maybe I'm too little and skinny for basketball this
year," Reuben said, in a tone of agreement. "I figure this summer,
though, I'll grow up a lot."

"Tell you what, Reuben," said George, improvising on an
impulse he would later be unable to explain to himself or to his
wife, "I'm starting a special before school group on basketball fun-
damentals next week. Can you get to the gym by eight a.m.?"

"Can I? Boy, can I!" shouted Reuben, and his further protestations got lost in the roar of voices that accompanied Anderson's fourth period gym class into the locker room from their lunch break.

"Hey, Bellyfat," George heard Reuben (on his way out) yell at one of the boys. "Guess what? I get to work special with coach next week."

George shook his head in bemusement as he moved to get out of the traffic stream. "Guess that's what it's all about," he thought, watching Reuben elbow his way through the incoming crowd as if he were suddenly a full foot taller. "Well, I might as well work with some kids like Reuben in the morning instead of firing up my ulcer in the faculty lounge. Still and all, I'm still going to have that talk with Madge tomorrow. Well, if we lose this game tonight, I might put it off until Sunday."

When the pep assembly broke sixth period, one of the supplicants to Miss Vandercamp's room was Debbie Fairweather. Eleven other girls beside Debbie came to work on their home ec projects, and Heidi moved slowly from one to the other sharing a bit of help, a bit of encouragement, a few moments of idle conversation. Occasionally all would stop in their efforts with heads at alert when a muffled roar floated toward them from the gym direction.

"Don't know how anyone gets all that excited 'bout a dumb old basketball game," Debbie confided to Heidi, as the little home ec teacher showed her how to rip out a seam and sew it correctly.

"Aren't you going to Camas tonight?" asked Heidi, as she released the project back to her student.

"Heck no, I hate that dumb rooter bus. 'Sides, Mom thinks I ought to stay home and rest tonight; tomorrow I got my abortion," said Debbie, matter-of-factly.

Momentary catatonia clutched Heidi as if a bomb exploded right beside her head. Despite her offhand discussion of birth control with David Huntington, she held some pretty strong Catholic feelings about abortions, and she held some pretty old fashioned ideas about a fifteen year old girl involved in sex.

286

"What does the father think about this?" asked Heidi, in stunned surpise.

"Oh, he don't even know," responded Debbie, who thought that Heidi (who had automatically thought of a priest) meant her boy friend.

"Don't you think you'd better discuss the matter with him?" persisted Heidi.

"Nope. Both my mother and Mrs. Mooney think it's best this way," said Debbie, laconically. "I got to agree with them."

"Mrs. Mooney advised you to get an abortion?" whispered Heidi, and the sound of her near strangulation pulled Debbie's attention from the sewing to her teacher's face.

"What's the matter, Miss Vandercamp," she asked, "you sick, or somethin?"

"No, it's nothing," said Heidi, forcefully, pulling herself together. "What else did Mrs. Mooney advise?"

"Oh, she told me real women have a number of affairs with men," said Debbie, half-interestedly in the subject as she returned to her work. "I guess she's had lots of abortions. I'm gettin' on the pill, myself."

"You're fifteen years old, Debbie," remonstrated Vandercamp.

"Well, that's old enough to get pregnant," said Debbie, with a short hard laugh. "Don't I know that! 'Sides, there's one certain teacher in this school I got my eye on."

"Come on, now, Debbie," said Heidi, painfully realizing she'd let this thing with a student go again too far. "Teachers don't go out with students."

"Come on, yourself, Miss Vandercamp; everybody knows about one certain coach and one certain cheerleader in this school," said Debbie, knowingly.

"Well, I don't," said Heidi, crisply, and with that she closed out the conversation and moved on to help another one of her girls.

She couldn't close out her thoughts, however, and they crowded in on her until she wanted to run someplace and hide. Repeats on her naughty boy's innuendoes ran back and forth in her mind as if in an echo chamber. Snatches of chatter from her Castleview girl friend about David Huntington's parties slipped back into her consciousness and soon the word party changed to orgies. Unbidden the horrible mental image of Pat Mooney in her housecoat with the mirror, razor blade and cocaine bottle in her hand leaped like a lantern slide that flooded out the vision of reality that lay around her. With a mumbled excuse she hurried to the sanctuary of the classroom toilet. Here she reached with agonized mental antennas for a contact with her priest or her parents. Her mother had long discussed sex knowledge with Heidi, carefully answering her little girl questions as they came one after another. She knew the sex act was something wonderful that happened between her mother and father—other married people—sometimes even special lovers. She needed now, however, to find out what her mother knew about people who had sex as casually as an animal out in the streets. "Maybe I should really think seriously about working with younger children," she silently said to her distraught image in the bathroom mirror. "I'll talk it over, carefully, with the folks and with Father Mueller this weekend. I wonder if Elaine knows what coach is fooling around with what high school cheerleader?"

As the troops stormed out of the gym after the week's final bell, David Huntington took refuge under one corner of the senior bleachers where Billy Lane quickly joined him.

"Good talk Mr. Anderson made," said Billy. "He's no dummy, is he?"

"Far from it," agreed Huntington. "Fact is, he's too damn intelligent for the kind of load he's trying to carry."

"How do you put up with all this bullshit?" asked Billy, feeling eavesdrop secure because of the din above and around them.

"You know me," laughed Davey, "I get my kicks people watching. Can you fictionalize a better comedy team than Lisa Overstreet and Roger Wellington? Cast Coach Patterson in the role of Moses and see if you can keep away from hysterics when you start laughing. Christ, this place features more freaks than P.T. Barnum ever dreamed about. What do you mean, how do I put up with it?"

"Come off it, David," said young Lane. "How many boring hours do you spend each day with people who can't relate to you intellectually anymore than a pet poodle could? How do you stand the paucity of thought, that's what I'm asking about."

"Billy Boy," said Davey, and they found themselves in sudden quiet as last eddies of the noise storm washed on out the four double gym front doors. "I've told you many times there's no special place to find intellectual companionship. I found one when I went to college in Hawaii, a couple in a Giesha house in backstreet Yokahoma. There was this taxi driver I met in Greece, my grandfather, of course, and a little old nun I've only recently remembered. Pat Mooney comes close, and you've a bent that way, yourself, old friend. I hope you find more solid things to pursue than philosophy and its mental high jinks, but a taste for it can add a lot of your life where a belly full only gives you a belly ache."

"How about Anderson, you didn't mention him?" asked Billy. "Think he might get a belly full—flip out, or something?"

"Not as long as he's got sports to compensate for his self confusion," said Huntington, as the two young men moved on out into the snow laden yard. "I've invited him, and a few other teachers, to join with me in a little transcendental meditation group."

"Good," said Lane. "I hope it does as much for him as it has for me, Elaine, and the others in our student group you work with; to say nothing of my old man who wants to canonize you before the world."

"Still off the sauce?" asked David.

"Not a drop in over a year," said Billy Lane.

"Well, I guess that's what real education's all about," said David.

"How's that?"

"Having disciples like you," said Huntington, unconsciously placing a hand on Billy's shoulder as they plowed along.

"There's that fruit playing with his little boy again," thought Eph Findlay, who saw Huntington's shoulder pat from his station near the gym side door where the team bus sat taking on its load for Camas. "Guess I'd better make a memo of that little love pat for Wellington. Few outside comments won't hurt in the Huntington personnel file."

Pat Mooney, entering the south hall outside door with Elaine Perry, saw Mr. Huntington out on the parking lot, too, and she waved, cheerily, got his wave back in return.

"Nice man, Mr. Huntington," said Elaine, as she preceded the counselor into the hall where the two women moved along to the counselor's office.

"He sure is," Pat agreed, wholeheartedly. "Wish I were about half as old and twice as beautiful."

"Come on, Mrs. Mooney," chided Elaine. "You, too, are one very nice person, and not a bit old."

"Flattery will get you anywhere, Elaine," laughed Pat. "Now, let's get on to those college catalogues."

"I won't keep you too long," promised Elaine. "I know you're anxious to get started on your weekend."

"You know the old rule," said Pat, her flat leather heeled shoes spatting a rim shot tattoo on the oiled maple hall floor, "nobody leaves until four p.m."

"With Mr. W. away and Mr. Longfellow gone," Elaine laughed, softly. "Everybody knows Coach Patterson splits as soon as the first bus run is gone."

"Youth! Youth! Where went thy naivety?" chortled Pat.

"With Vietnam, Kent State, Watergate, and a hundred other political perversions," said Elaine.

"Heavy!" kidded Mrs. Mooney. "Honestly, Elaine, sometimes you talk like one of my old college professors."

"I very much hope to be just that, someday," said Elaine, as they paused while Pat unlocked her office door. "Somewhere out there a Phd waits for me in Political Science, and I'm eager to get started earning it."

"Don't be so eager you forget the important things in life, little girl," thought Pat, as she opened the door and ushered Elaine on inside in front of her. "Loving somebody more than yourself, and having their love returned in the same manner—now there's something much to be desired. You won't find the key to that kind of real happiness in a textbook or in someone else's intellectual charms. Oh, God, what I'd give to be you with all that wonderful secure love your parents passed on to you. You've got to share with someone else, but don't ever go public and try to share it with the world."

"Did you say something, Mrs. Mooney?" asked Elaine.

"No, dear," sighed Pat. "Dreaming. I was just daydreaming. Now, let's first take a look at this catalogue from my old alma mater, University of Oregon. It may not be as exciting as Reed College or some of the other places you've asked about, but you do meet some good sound young men when you go there."

"You'll be a fine teacher someday," Lisa Overstreet confided to Pricilla Martin, as the girl moved around the English room straightening desk arm chairs into rows and adjusting shades to prescribed uniform levels.

"It's always been my dream, Miss Overstreet," gushed Pricilla. "Of course sometimes, just sometimes, I dream about a musical career."

"Concert, perhaps," agreed Lisa. "Concert could be a wonderful compliment to your teaching. No show biz, though. Flaunting your body—prostituting your talent making a public display of yourself like Mr. Norburton does."

"Mr. Norburton?" questioned Priceilla, her usual honey syrup tones suddenly sharp with suspicion.

"Everyone knows he plays at Holiday Inn," said Lisa, her attention more fixed on the report cards stacked in readiness for Pricilla to carry them to the counselor's office.

"So, is that so bad?" asked Pricilla, voice flat enough, now, to raise Lisa's eyes in the form of an inquiry.

"But, my dear, you must know," simpered Lisa. "They serve liquor there—loose women frequent the place—and it's common knowledge how entertainers carry on with women that hang around the bars."

"Mr. Norburton's a musical genius," said Pricilla, lead voiced. "He's also too much of a gentleman for those kind of women."

"Oh, come now, Priss," chortled Lisa. "You and I are too much friends for this kind of hokum. You know, as everyone knows, what goes on between Mr. Norburton and Ms. Scanner. What do

291

you suppose happens on the nights Ms. Scanner doesn't follow him over to Castleview?"

"I don't know anything about Mr. Norburton's private life," said Pricilla, a note of desperation forcing her voice to rise in pitch and intensity.

"Pricilla Martin, I do believe you have a school girl crush on Mr. Norburton," cooed Lisa, merrily.

"That's not true!" Pricilla spit out—nearly a shriek—then she suddenly dashed from the room leaving an openmouthed Overstreet behind.

"What do you know about that?" asked Lisa, as if tasting strawberries and cream. "Wait until I tell Cece and the others that Norburton's been fooling around with one of our high school girls. Wow! This one's loaded with dynamite; the Martins are really somebody in this town. Now, how'm I gonna punish that little twit for running off without permission leaving me to carry these damn cards all the way down to Mooney. An A minus for young miss as my Teacher's Aide. Let me find that card. Yeah, here, I'll just add the minus and she'll find out next week what it means to crap on Lisa Overstreet. I dont care if her dad is a big shot lawyer."

"Your old man made one bad mistake, boy," said A.T. Cromwell, as he and Bert Terilliger crouched side by side in the boy's lower hall john. "Sometimes that's all it takes to mess up a lot of lives; other guys screw up a whole damn lifetime and never cause themselves or anybody else any pain. Ain't no use of you asking what's fair in life—they ain't no such thing as fair. Life's life, it seems to me, so you ought to live every day like it were your last one."

"Who knows, it could be," agreed Bert.

"I suppose," said A.T. in a tone that made it clear it made little difference to him one way or another.

"How does a guy know whether he's living or not?" persisted Bert, cranking away on the handle that turned the long steel snake which disappeared into an opened sewer pipe in front of them.

From hooded side-eyes Cromwell studied the intent, hawk faced youngster who kept his own eyes on the twisting snake. His own credo for living he shared, to this date, only with his sons. 'Each man lives his own life,' was his general answer to criticism of others. 'I say let him live it according to what he thinks he wants most out of it.' That answer here, he realized, would sound pompous and as phony as it was to this very bright boy suddenly struck with a deep case of the seriousness.

"Want me to spell it out for you?" asked A.T. laconically.

"I'm here to listen," came the cryptic answer.

"Well, for me I got a six part program," said A.T. "My boys, they sorta copy it from me, but I ain't saying it'll work for you nor anyone else."

Bert stayed silent. Continued to crank. Had he come up with some remark at this juncture, A.T. would have sheered off from what now came as a follow.

"I figure my life, day by day, on a hundred point count," he said, slowly. "Thirty count do I like myself on this day; twenty count, each, do I like what I'm doing and who I'm doing it with. I give myself ten points if I like what I been doing in the immediate past, and I get another ten if I like what I plan to do with the close tomorrows. The last ten points gets splintered up 'cause it rates how do I feel in my physical. Like, today, I got me a seven cause my bones kind of aches a bit from the cold. I don't often get tens anymore, but I ain't never had a one, neither. Anyway, I put them figures together anytime a day I got the feeling for them, and if they come up better than fifty points—well, fifty one I figure's barely being alive."

A.T. clammed up, again, and Bert thought on that one for awhile. He also thought about his own efforts to pull himself out of the shadow life he felt had almost engulfed him. For the first time, ever, he had attended a pep assembly today, and his first apprehension turned to one of pique, for no one seemed to notice the unusual fact that he had come. Afterwards he sought out A.T. with a powerful, awakening need to talk to someone besides his mother. Someone who wouldn't try to con him as the counselor did; someone unafraid of him as he sensed in the few boys who fraternized him; somebody besides his mother whose judgement he felt too much clouded by her ever constant love.

293

He found the custodian cranking the snake into a drain, and he took over the cranking effort without a word. After five minutes of silence, he asked A.T. point blank what he thought of Bert's old man. The ensuing information and the disgorgement of A.T.'s credo seemed over simplified to him, yet he found no direction inside him that offered concrete argumentation. He just felt there needed to be more. Perhaps Huntington, not Cromwell, could provide him with answers.

"You alive, today?" he asked, lamely, to renew the conversation.

"Woke up with a ninety seven," said A.T. (take it or leave it, boy, his tone of voice seemed to say).

Bert began to experience the same frustration he suffered during the pep rally. He felt like a man talking to people who had no ears; signalling to people who had no eyes, pinching people who had no feelings. The fault could not be Cromwell's; he, Bert, had to be talking a foreign language.

"Do you really think I'm killing ma?" he blurted out, suddenly, and he changed, Jekyllike, from a hard mouthed young hood to a concerned teen age boy.

The change caught Cromwell by surprise. He recalled his statement to Bert out in the schoolyard.

"Looks that way to me," he said, after a pause.

"Well, I'm changing that," (Bert started to say 'Crommie', but somehow the name didn't fit with the circumstances). "I wanted you to know I'm straightening things out a bit."

"Why tell me, Bert?" asked A.T., not unkindly. "Whyn't you tell your mother."

"She knows," said Bert, quietly. "She guessed it right off when I started the change."

"Sounds good," said A.T., unemphatically.

"I wanted to tell you, Mr. Cromwell," said Bert, after taking a deep starting breath, "because I think you care about me—sure about my ma. You know something, Mr. Cromwell, ain't nobody else in this school cares a damn if I live or I don't."

For a few seconds the old and the young eyes looked deeply into each other, found a kinship way beyond genes and bloodlines and family names. Then, with a chuckle, A.T. started the crank, again, which Terwilliger had relinquished.

"You could be right about that, Bert," said the custodian, his dry laugh continuing in his speech like a series of punctuation marks. "That's pretty much the way things were for me when I went to school here over forty years ago. Folks really don't change much, I guess, when you get down to the basics."

Postscript

From one of Davey Huntington's "Note Cards":

Definitions:

A good student is one who causes the teacher no problems.

A good teacher is one who causes the principal no problems.

A good principal is one who causes the superintendent no problems.

A good superintendent is one who causes the school board no problems.

A good school board member is one who causes the parents no problems.

# ROBERT LEE GARDNER

"With malice toward none and with charity to most," says Robert Gardner of his character portrayals in *Thank God It's Friday*. Robert uses satire, tongue in cheek, light humor and straight presentation to share with you his twenty years of school experiences and observations. The end product produces a candid slice of American culture known as "the small school district."

A graduate of the University of Portland (Oregon), Gardner received his advanced degrees from the University of Washington in Seattle. He played the roles of high school and college teacher; coached high school football and basketball, and served twelve years as a school administrator. "I didn't retire from public education," Gardner laughs, "I escaped from it."

Today the author works for Belmont School in Portland (a private daycare center that features pre-school, kindergarten, and primary education). Teacher-pupil ratios are rarely greater than six or eight to one, and the adults employed there must, above all else, find great pleasure in working with little children.

"Children at this age are excited about learning. Their experiences, in fact, will help establish a basis for their continuing feeling about education," says Robert. "We don't promise their parents or the public that miracles will be performed, but we do insure that children will learn in a positive oriented atmosphere."

"An old boy I used to principal with," says Gardner (in keeping with the general feeling of *Thank God It's Friday*), "used to express amazement at how much children learned in spite of their teachers. He figured that it took maybe three teachers to turn a kid off to learning, but I think he was maybe a bit too harsh. Four seems like a better number."